Imogen Parker was born in Hertfordshire in 1958. She has worked as a literary agent and in television development and is the author of two crime novels. She lives in London with her husband and son.

MORE INNOCENT TIMES

Imogen Parker

CORGI BOOKS

MORE INNOCENT TIMES
A CORGI BOOK : 0 552 14498 3

First publication in Great Britain

PRINTING HISTORY
Corgi edition published 1997
Corgi edition reprinted 1997

Set in 10½/11½pt Linotron Plantin by
Deltatype Ltd, Birkenhead, Merseyside

Corgi Books are published by Transworld Publishers Ltd,
61–63 Uxbridge Road, London W5 5SA,
in Australia by Transworld Publishers (Australia) Pty Ltd,
15–25 Helles Avenue, Moorebank, NSW 2170,
and in New Zealand by Transworld Publishers (NZ) Ltd,
3 William Pickering Drive, Albany, Auckland.

Reproduced, printed and bound in Great Britain by
Cox & Wyman Ltd, Reading, Berkshire.

ACKNOWLEDGEMENTS

Many thanks to Jo Goldsworthy, Linda Evans, Mark Lucas, Colm Tóibín, Becky Parker, Nicholas Duggan, Connor Duggan, and especially to my marvellous mum, Kath Parker, to whom I dedicate this book.

For Kath

Part One

CHAPTER 1

The city that never sleeps had fallen into a fitful doze. Though never perfectly quiet, at this time in the morning sounds were muffled, less urgent, almost still. Gemma was wide awake, as she had been most of the night, lying in bed, paralysed by a heady draught of fear and excitement. She had not felt as nervous since the day she started her first real job.

Finally, she threw back the duvet and went to the window. Above the tenth floor, the high buildings disappeared into cloud, not individual cotton wool clouds, but a general kind of smog. Her face fell. She had been so certain that on her last day the skies would clear and New York would sparkle for her, its angles picking up sharp rays of spring sunlight, glistening.

It was going to be one of those days when it felt as if a nuclear bomb had been detonated in the night and the sun would never shine again.

She was shivering. She had already packed her robe, so she draped her new trenchcoat around her shoulders. The black shiny PVC looked almost fetishistic against the white lace of her nightdress.

In the kitchen there was one bowl, one spoon and just enough cereal and milk for one person's breakfast. She made herself a cafetière of strong coffee and poured it into an oversize Portuguese ceramic mug. When she had eaten, she washed and dried everything carefully and wrapped the crockery in the sheets of tissue paper she had saved. She placed it all on the top of the open packing case and, after a moment's hesitation, sealed the lid with tape. She had always loved those mugs, their bright primary colours and primitive design. She had considered shipping them back, but had decided not to. It was going to be a fresh start with new things. She entertained a brief image of herself opening up a trunk of crockery and finding it smashed in transit. That was too much of an emotional risk.

The only thing she still couldn't make up her mind about was the duvet. It was goosedown, gossamer light, warm in winter and almost cool enough for the hottest New York summer night. She was certain that she would not be able to purchase something of the same quality in London, her thoughts about shopping in England still based on her experiences of living on a slightly enhanced student grant. She decided to pack it, but when she stepped out of the building she changed her mind, turned back, ran up the five flights of stairs and tugged it from its box. She brought it downstairs, bundled under one arm as she locked the front door behind her, then presented it to the bag lady who was walking up the street. The woman examined it suspiciously, as she did all handouts, checking for quality as if she were buying a carpet in a Turkish bazaar. Then she folded it, tied it to her shopping trolley with knotted string and went on her way without a word.

'Guess where I am?' said Gemma.

'It's too early in the morning for me,' said a sleepy voice at the other end of the phone. Meryl didn't start to function until she had drunk at least two cups of coffee.

'The top of the Empire State Building!'

It was just after nine-thirty. She was the only person there, the first visitor of the day, probably the only one if the cloud cover continued. The lift-attendant had thought her crazy.

'Oh really? Trying to catch a plane?' Meryl asked.

Gemma laughed.

'Trying to have the ultimate New York experience. D'you know, I've never been here before?'

'How's the view?'

'Can't see a thing,' said Gemma. 'I thought I might get above the cloud. Crazy idea, but I couldn't leave without coming up here, could I? Where are we meeting?'

Meryl named their favourite restaurant.

'What are you going to do for the rest of the morning?' she asked.

'All my favourite things,' Gemma said.

What she most liked about Elizabeth Arden was the ritual. Once your clothing was exchanged for a pink robe and paper slippers, the demands of the real world disappeared and the imperatives of the beauty parlour took over. Which pristine copy of *Vogue* or *Vanity Fair* would you flick through absently while waiting for your personal masseuse? Would you opt for aromatherapy or lymph-drainage massage? Would you choose the same shade of polish for your finger and toe-nails?

Cocooned on the eighth floor above Fifth Avenue, the only clue that another world existed was the faint drone of traffic, an almost undetectable background rhythm to the soothing words of the attendants. Gemma had booked a massage followed by a Scotch shower, a manicure, a pedicure and a facial. Normally, she would have chosen only one or two options, but on her last day in New York, she would be extravagant. It hadn't occurred to her that there might be an Elizabeth Arden in London, or some equivalent, because when she had last been in England, beauty parlours were not part of her milieu or her price range. When she mentioned to the beautician that she had a transatlantic flight that afternoon she was presented with a complimentary mineral water atomizer. She stepped back into the mêlée of mid-morning Manhattan feeling gloriously pampered.

Brooklyn – a nice place to visit, a great place to live! The sign with its faded message, the peeling paint making it look as half-hearted as it sounded, always made her smile. There were places in Brooklyn where most New Yorkers would not dare walk. When she had first lived there she had been braver and poorer, or maybe more foolish, and she had ridden the subway all over. She hadn't come to any harm, but as soon as she had moved to Manhattan, Brooklyn had seemed a long way away, an alien urban desert only safely traversed by cab. For a nostalgic second, she regretted not having the time to trundle over the Manhattan Bridge on the subway train for her last visit.

The diner was the first place she had ever eaten dinner with Boy. It was a small, ordinary diner with a counter and a few Formica tables, situated in a grubby neighbourhood near Atlantic Avenue. There was nothing distinctive about it except for its name – *El Palacio de Batidos Y la Casa del Famoso Biftek* – which seemed inordinately grandiose for a place that probably seated a total of sixteen people.

The Palace of the Milkshakes AND the House of the Famous Beefsteak. It was the AND that had so amused Boy.

'It's like the title of a novel by Gabriel Garcia Marquez,' he had said. 'I picture two Cuban brothers, one an expert milkshake-maker, the other a consummate barbecue chef. They both set up their restaurants, but poverty, or marriage maybe, force them to merge, but neither brother is willing to give up his restaurant's name . . .'

She remembered him waving his arms about, giggling, wildly elaborating on his theme. They had

14

trekked for at least an hour in a subway carriage with no air conditioning to get there. The food was adequate, no different from any other neighbourhood diner, but Boy had made it seem an enchanted place. She remembered thinking the *batido de mango* one of the most delicious ambrosial drinks she had ever sipped. Now, it tasted very sweet, as if the mango had come in syrup from a tin. She drained her glass quickly and paid, slipping the check into her pocket as a souvenir.

The cab driver, whom she had told to wait, looked at her in his mirror and shook his head. He didn't say a word all the way back to the Village. I gave a ride to a crazy English lady, he would tell his friends over a hot dog later, forty bucks to drink a milkshake!

Meryl was already sitting at the table. She was dressed for work in a black and white houndstooth jacket and red silk shirt.

'Look at you!' she said, kissing Gemma on the cheek, '. . . all smooth and radiant. I expected Mrs Mop, a sweaty brow, maybe a headscarf, smudges of dust and dirt.'

'I packed most things up at the weekend,' Gemma replied.

'You're so organized! How can you be so organized? I always leave everything to the last minute . . . I bet you even made a list!'

Gemma opened her small quilted purse, extracted a slim leather-bound notepad and slid it across the table, laughing at herself. There was a list labelled 'Work', where everything had been ticked off neatly, a list labelled 'Home', where there were still a couple of outstanding entries, and a list headed 'Last Day'. She had ticked off the morning's activities in the cab back from Brooklyn.

'Hey!' said Meryl, 'what about my gift? It says here "Meryl's gift", but you haven't ticked it!'

Gemma's hand went into her purse again. She took

out a small gift-wrapped box and pushed it across the table.

'Oh, I didn't mean . . . you shouldn't have . . .' Meryl's protestations vied with her eagerness to tear off the wrapping. 'Oh my God, they're gorgeous!'

Meryl had always said that her greatest wish was to find a man who would buy her diamond earrings. Sometimes, in her more desperate moments, she said she would settle for rubies, or even semi-precious stones.

'I thought that maybe, if you had the earrings already, it wouldn't be so difficult to find the man . . .' Gemma suggested.

She was delighted by her friend's reaction. They were only tiny diamonds in simple white gold settings.

'Oh my God, you're too generous,' Meryl was wailing. 'I'm going to miss you so much. Are you really sure about going?'

Sitting in her favourite restaurant with her best friend, the aura of Elizabeth Arden around her, and the happy feeling of having chosen the perfect gift, Gemma found it difficult to believe that she was about to leave all this, abandon a life that was so comfortable and familiar. She felt a momentary judder of panic.

'Let's order,' she said, fighting back the urge to cry with abandon as Meryl was doing, and admit just how nervous and ambivalent she actually felt.

'I hate the fact that you're doing all these really final-sounding things today . . . I mean, the Empire State Building is always going to be there. You *are* coming back, aren't you?' Meryl sniffed, 'I mean, I know you need a break, a change of scene, who wouldn't? I know it sounds selfish, but I can't bear to lose you for ever . . .'

'I'm sure I'll be back,' Gemma said, but really she didn't know. She had no idea what would happen, but she was certain that she would miss her friendship with Meryl.

* * *

They had met about five years before, at the American Book Fair. An agent who liked to score points had introduced them as each other's greatest rival at a cocktail party. They were both up-and-coming editors, he said, young, sharp and ambitious.

'This should be a fascinating encounter,' he teased.

As soon as he had left them, Meryl pulled a face at his back and said, quite loudly, 'What a jerk!'

And that was the beginning of a great friendship.

For an American, Meryl's sense of humour was unusually sardonic. Gemma found that she was sharing jokes with her in a way she hadn't since she left Oxford. There was also an immediate trust between them and an unspoken agreement not to talk about work. If one of them was having a bad time personally, she didn't feel afraid to admit it to the other, as she might to her boss, or one of her valued writers, in case they thought that her work would be adversely affected. It was a friendship that Gemma particularly needed at a time when she might otherwise have gone to pieces.

After months of minor illnesses, culminating in an attack of shingles, Boy had just been diagnosed HIV-positive. Gemma had anticipated the result of the test for some time. It almost came as a relief to know, but she didn't know what to do, or how they would cope. Understandably, Boy was panicking. Even though she was desperate to get away, to find some space to think, she had been loath to leave him even for the couple of days of the Book Fair, which that year was being held in Seattle.

At dinner with Meryl, then a stranger, she had found herself pouring out her worries, surprising herself by taking the uncharacteristic risk of mixing her personal and professional life. Meryl had been terrific: supportive, non-judgemental and tremendously practical. Most of Gemma's other New York acquaintances had been friends of Boy's first. She got on well with them, but sometimes she couldn't help feeling that to them she was a curious foreign accessory. Meryl was really the only person in New York with whom she had built a close rapport all her own. She treasured her friendship, and was quite possessive about it, never letting Boy get close enough to take over, in that mad, charming way he had.

When Gemma announced that she was quitting her job and returning to London, Meryl hadn't been able to believe it.

'You're doing so well here,' she said, referring to work, 'England is such a small market. Won't you be bored?'

'Maybe,' Gemma had replied, 'but there are some things in my past I need to sort out . . .'

That was the kind of language New Yorkers, with their attachment to analysis, understood.

Finally, Meryl had accepted that Gemma was making a brave decision. 'So you're going to become an expert on romance,' she had remarked, referring to the job Gemma had taken at a company famous for the sentimental fiction it published.

'Yes, and what a bloody irony that is,' said Gemma.

Men, or the lack of them, was the other thing Meryl and Gemma had in common. There just didn't seem to be any available men in New York. All they wanted, Meryl would say, were a couple of nice guys. Was that too much to ask? They'd have to be intelligent of course (Meryl would add) and solvent (Gemma would chip in), and reasonably good-looking, and single (Meryl would remind herself), because they never leave their wives (they would chorus together), and that was all really. Except that they'd have to be tall (Meryl would say – she was over six feet with a model's figure, and she liked to wear high heels), and witty (Gemma would insist) and good in bed (in fact, Meryl would say, they could be quite ugly or even sports enthusiasts in exchange for that). There were minor differences in taste. Gemma had never met a bald man she fancied, but Meryl could tolerate that as long as he didn't have hair on his back. Once, after several Martinis and much discussion, Meryl got into a terrific panic.

'What if we meet this guy, but there's only one of him?' she cried.

'What do you mean?'

'Well, what are *you* going to do?' Meryl asked.

'Oh, I see, it's age before beauty, is it?' Gemma teased back. Meryl was several years her senior.

'Well, it's my country. I feel I should get first go.'

'God, that's so American, so imperialist. You know what's more likely to happen?' said Gemma.

'No . . .'

'We meet this perfect guy, and guess what, he falls in love with Boy.'

Gemma and Boy's relationship had all the trappings of a perfect romance – he had picked her up in MOMA in her first week in the city. They had both been gazing at the same Matisse. They had gone for coffee. Delighted by her English accent and her resemblance to a young Grace Kelly, he had insisted they meet again. He had shown her all the best places in New York, from dingy jazz clubs on the Lower East Side, to Carnegie Hall. He was rich. He treated her to dinners in deepest Brooklyn and lunches in the Windows on the World. They got on incredibly well together. He became her best friend. After a year, he proposed. She accepted.

The only trouble was, he was gay. Not that she had ever been under any misapprehension. With Boy that would have been difficult. She had known from the first moment she talked to him: his clothes, his baby blond, rather feminine, beauty, the way that he walked, keys jangling from his belt loop, but, most of all, the unmistakeable camp drawl he spoke in.

It was a marriage of convenience. The irony was that the whole point of the convenience was to make it possible for her to stay in the States. And when Boy died, she didn't want to stay anyway.

One large tear plopped into Gemma's fettucine. Funny how grief had the ability to sneak up on you and shake you by the shoulders just when you thought you had dealt with it. Gemma looked up to see if Meryl had noticed.

'It's only been three months,' Meryl said, understanding immediately, 'It's bound to take some time.'

'I'll be better when I get back to work,' Gemma said. 'It'll take my mind off it.'

'It's important to grieve too, you know,' Meryl replied, uncharacteristically solemn, 'it's not a character defect.'

'I didn't want to be unhappy on my last day,' Gemma protested, annoyed with herself for giving into emotion.

'Honey, sometimes you don't have any control on these things. Even you. Anyway, I'm going to cry buckets when you go, I have no shame.'

Yes, she was going to miss Meryl tremendously.

Gemma stood in the street waving all the way as Meryl's cab inched up 6th Avenue. After about a hundred yards, the traffic started to move away faster and the cab disappeared out of sight. Suddenly she felt as if everything were happening too quickly. This morning, eight o'clock, when her plane was to leave, had seemed ages away. Now it was almost three o'clock. There wasn't enough time. She had been intending to walk round SoHo, taking mental pictures of all the places she liked best, but it was too late. She hailed a cab.

Even though the furniture was still there waiting to be collected by Boy's father, the apartment already felt empty. She had packed away into boxes all the little things that made the place look inhabited. The vases and photos, the pinboard in the kitchen with her lists and Boy's doodles. Boy's mother hadn't wanted any of his clothes, so Gemma had given them to a thrift shop. A couple of days later, when she was taking down the curtains, she looked out of the window and saw one of the lanky black kids who hung out on roller skates at the corner of their street wearing one of the hand-made rose-coloured silk shirts Boy favoured. It was a weird *déjà vu*-like sensation followed by a deep feeling of satisfaction. She thought Boy would have approved.

She had taken down all the paintings and wrapped them in corrugated cardboard and brown packing tape. They left bright white rectangles on the walls which were an irritation to Gemma's natural sense of order, but it was too late to start re-painting now. She felt curiously stranded. Ten minutes before, standing on the street, she had thought that she had no time left. Now the two hours before she had to take a cab to the airport stretched out in front of her. Her two suitcases stood by the door, padlocked and neatly labelled, her powder-blue vanity case next to them. Everything was neat and clean and accounted for.

She slumped into the leather Chesterfield, trying to conjure up happy memories of the apartment, trying to see Boy's face as it was when she had first met him.

'What's your name?' she had asked him.

'Everyone calls me Boy,' he had said, 'Boy Bench.'

'But what's your real name?' she said in what he came to call her earnest English way.

'Park,' he said. She had never known whether he was joking until their wedding day, but Boy suited him perfectly. Then.

At the end, he had looked like an old man.

Perhaps it had been seriously weird to marry him.

She could see shock and disbelief on the most liberal-minded faces on the rare occasions she told anyone the truth about her marriage. At the time, she hadn't been in the best state to judge. Boy had been one of the only normal things in her life.

He proposed about a year after she arrived in the city. She had received a letter from immigration that week. She had been unlucky. Most illegal aliens, her official status, got away with staying a little longer before the bureaucracy caught up with them.

She had gone round to Boy's apartment to watch a video. They were eating Ben and Jerry's Cherry Garcia straight from the tub. She had picked up two pints at the grocery store on the corner of the street.

'What can you say about a boy who loves ice cream, the Beatles and . . . men?' he had asked her, as the credits rolled over the last tear-jerking moments of *Love Story*.

Boy was so sentimental. If allowed to choose the video, it was always a piece of Seventies' melodrama – *The Way We Were* being his absolute favourite – or a Bette Davis movie.

'I really identify with that movie,' he continued. 'Ryan O'Neal's father and mine have a lot in common. Except that I doubt mine would soften at the end.'

When she thought about it now the ironies were heartbreaking. Mr Bench Senior had cried at the funeral, but she had thought they were tears of relief. At least his son was safely out of the way now so that he could cause no further embarrassment to his father. If that was the way he had chosen to live his life, she had heard him say at the hospital, when Boy's mother had broken down, then he knew the risks. It was as if Boy had deliberately chosen a dangerous career against his father's advice, like sky-diving or stunt driving, and had met with the sort of accident that anyone sensible could have predicted.

'I've got a proposition for you;' Boy had said, 'you're going to be thrown out of this country in a month or so if you don't do something fast. Do you want to go back to England?'

'No, I don't, but I'll never get a Green Card.'

'Unless you marry.'

'Except that I haven't really had a serious date since I arrived, so it would be a bit of a miracle . . .'

'Unless you married me.'

'Oh Boy, I never knew you cared!' she laughed. 'Look, I know you love that movie, but . . .'

'No, I'm serious, for once in my life. It's not purely altruistic . . .'

'You surprise me,' she said with sarcasm. Boy was terribly spoilt and selfish, but at least he knew that he was, and that was a redeeming feature.

'I think my old man is beginning to suspect my orientation, you know, and much as I hate the old bastard, I wouldn't want to lose the fortune that is my due for putting up with him all my life.'

'And you're looking for a new lodger for this apartment.' She tried to follow his thought pattern.

'Hey, that's an idea . . .'

'Wouldn't your father be just as appalled at the idea of you marrying a penniless English girl?'

'Except you're not penniless.'

'Oh Boy, you're not trying to marry me for my inheritance . . .'

'Of course not, we'd have a pre-nuptial agreement. That would please my father, and it would safeguard you too.'

'Real people don't have pre-nuptial agreements, do they? I thought that was movie stars and the Trumps. Boy, are you serious?'

'Never been more serious. D'you want me to go down on one knee?'

She had said yes. Because she wanted to stay in New

York. Because she could. Most people had parents who would be worried by the idea of their twenty-three-year-old daughter entering into a loveless marriage. It was one of the benefits, she had thought, perhaps the only one, of being an orphan. She didn't have to explain herself to anyone.

Boy had worn a white linen jacket over his usual black T-shirt and jeans. She wore a cotton 1950s dress that she found in a shop called Reminiscence at the bottom of Fifth Avenue. It had blue and yellow roses printed on it, a boat neck and huge gathered skirt. She borrowed white low-heeled slingbacks from a girl at work. They were a bit too big and she kept losing them as they ran to City Hall where the ceremony was taking place.

That evening Boy presented her with the vanity case: a slope-sided rectangular box, covered in powder-blue leather, lined with cream watered silk and topped with a pearlized handle. It was straight out of a Doris Day film. It was the best present she had ever been given.

'A little something, in lieu of a honeymoon,' he said and kissed her on the cheek, before going out for the night cruising.

However odd their arrangement appeared to the outside world, Gemma had always felt safe with Boy, and cherished by him. She never really knew why he liked her, what it was about her, or the Matisse, that had made him strike up conversation that first day. Perhaps he had seen how frightened she was then, or how lonely. He had never asked about her background or why she was in New York. She assumed he knew that she was running away from something, just as he was, in his own fashion. In that sense they were kindred spirits.

She loved not having to explain herself. For some reason, he had decided to like her, and it could have

24

nothing to do with her father or her mother or her sister because he knew nothing about any of them. It was a wonderfully releasing feeling. She had hoped that in New York she could reinvent herself, sketch herself on a large white sheet of paper and paint herself in with the colours that were in fashion. But after only a few weeks it occurred to her that she had forgotten to change the way she was, but people still seemed to think she was OK.

Marriage was a strange institution. Even though it wasn't a real marriage, she was sure that she felt a greater bond of loyalty towards him because she was his wife. Perhaps she had just imagined it, or perhaps because they had to practise so hard at the beginning not to give themselves away to the immigration authorities or his parents, she managed to convince even herself. Perhaps because there had never been any spark of sexual chemistry between them, she felt she could give her love to him unguardedly.

She was glad, for his sake and theirs, that he had eventually told his parents the truth, even though by then he had only days to live. It was a terrible shock for them to learn, at the same time, that he was gay and terminally ill. She didn't know which truth troubled his father more. It had made it very difficult for her because when he finally died she did feel like a real widow, not just a widow of convenience, or a person who had lost a close friend, but Boy's parents had felt duped by her and turned their unresolved anger against her, accusing her of fraudulence, and, most hurtfully, of exploitation. It was that venom, where she had expected and needed sympathy, as much as anything else, that had shocked her into the frame of mind in which she began to consider returning to England.

Gemma pushed her suitcases out onto the landing and rang for the lift. Then she came back into the flat and picked up the vanity case.

'Bye Boy!' she shouted, as she had every morning as she left for work.

Then she shut the door behind her, closing a chapter of her life.

CHAPTER 2

Had Gemma imagined her homecoming on the day that she left London, she would not have pictured herself eating breakfast alone in a Piccadilly hotel. On the day she left, she hadn't imagined that she would ever return.

Early morning London was blue and crisp. In contrast to the sticky leatherette sweatiness of the cab to JFK, crawling through the Queens' Midtown tunnel the evening before, the taxi ride from Heathrow to the centre of town had been fast, refreshing, unexpected. She felt it was a good omen.

She had chosen an international hotel, craving the anonymity, the pastel vacuum to compose herself in. She wanted a shower that worked, remote controlled television and no old-fashioned cosiness or familiarity with the staff. She wanted to start the future fresh and blank.

She gazed around the dining-room, its pale turquoise walls, the buffet table – individual packets of cereal in neat rows, a bowl of fresh fruit that no-one ever touched – it could have been anywhere in the world. There were a couple of businessmen breakfasting, one reaching into his new-looking briefcase to answer his mobile phone. A call from his wife, Gemma suspected, or his secretary, pre-arranged to impress his companion. She looked down at her newspaper, pretending not to listen. Her mind was racing and blurry with jet lag. She felt herself struggling with unnerving snatches of thought without really knowing what they were. She decided to make small decisions first – avoid cooked breakfast, choose Earl Grey tea, then a shower and sleep, even though it would put her internal clock out of sync. When she woke, things would be more manageable.

On clear days in New York when the sky was pure blue it seemed such a long way away, but here in London it felt as if you could reach up and touch it. She was struck by how low and uniform the buildings were as she wandered up Regent Street. It was very different from how she remembered. She only knew Regent Street as the place her family came to once every winter to see the Christmas lights. It always seemed to be raining when they got there, so they would drive slowly up the street, she and Daisy craning their necks to look out of the back window of the car. Somehow the lights were always a disappointment.

'Not as good as they used to be,' Estella would say, and Gemma would wonder why they bothered year after year. She supposed it was just one of those traditional things you did as a family, like going to the circus, even though the smell of the animals made you sneeze, and they always ran out of the ice-cream you wanted in the interval.

She had not expected to see cafés with tables on the pavement serving cappuccino, or American clothes stores like Gap. The prices were slightly higher, she calculated, but the merchandise was exactly the same. In fact, if she kept her eyes down to shop-front level, she could almost have been on Fifth Avenue. London smelt fresher. In New York there was always the distinctive lingering human scent of frying donuts and pee. Here it was just diesel fumes. She looked at her map. It was still sunny. She decided to turn back and find her way to Green Park.

She had just crossed the road when a display in the window of a china shop caught her eye. Perched on a pyramid of hessian-covered cubes was a complete set of nursery crockery: bowls, plates, mugs and tea cups. The porcelain was white, and the designs were painted in clear bright colours. A label gave the name of the manufacturer and the title

ANIMALPHABET RANGE by BERTRAND RUSH

Seeing her father's name and work without warning brought stinging tears to her eyes. She stood in front of the plate glass window, bewildered. Some vague memory of signing a contract for merchandising rights floated into her mind. She had thought it inconsequential at the time. She hadn't begun to imagine that it meant her father's work was about to become the stuff of Christening present lists.

Her childhood bedroom at Whitton House had been decorated with the original drawings. She had always felt that they were hers. Seeing them now displayed next to Beatrix Potter china in an expensive shop gave her a mixture of feelings. She was proud that they looked so attractive but, at the same time, she felt invaded. It was as if a photograph of herself as a child was now the image on a popular greetings card. Without knowing quite why, she found herself inside the shop enquiring about the price of the china. It was expensive.

'They're lovely, aren't they?' the shop assistant said. 'Quite exclusive too. An interesting and tasteful gift. What initial are you looking for?'

'Initial?'

'There's a mug for every letter of the alphabet. It makes it more personal, you see,' the assistant explained.

G was for giraffe, its friendly face munching on the topmost leaves of an acacia tree. She didn't need to see it.

'I . . . I don't want to buy anything,' Gemma stammered.

She wondered why she found it impossible to say that it was her father's work. Feeling foolish, she turned and walked smartly out of the shop.

It was all happening too quickly. She had thought she could stave off the painful memories until she was ready to deal with them. Then, she had planned, she would go back to Whitton House, visit her parents' grave, even possibly see Daisy. She would come to terms with the past once she was settled. Not now. Not on her first day back.

She was due at Kathy's at eight. She bought some flowers for her from a stall in Bond Street and chocolates from Charbonnel et Walker for the children. Then she took a long hot shower.

On her own, time seemed to be passing incredibly slowly. Although it was less than twenty-four hours, it seemed an age since she had actually spoken to anyone apart from stating requests to air hostesses, receptionists and shop assistants. She had wanted to have hours to herself, spaces of peace in which to think calmly about the future and the past, but the trouble was that whenever she stopped and tried to relax, her head flooded with confused memories. Thoughts and grudges she thought she had left behind ten years before suddenly seemed as sharp and painful as they ever had. She had thought she would enjoy a few days' solitude, but she found she was craving company to distract herself from herself.

It was a wide street a couple of blocks away from Kentish Town tube station; on each side stood large plane trees, their roots easing up the paving stones around them. Even though the clocks had gone forward at the weekend and spring had officially begun, their leaves were still tightly furled in hard brown buds. One side of the road was already in shade. There was no warmth in the early evening sunlight.

Gemma put her hands in her pockets, regretting her optimistic choice of linen jacket. It was still winter coat weather. She could see Kathy's house right from the bottom of the road. The one with the magnolia tree, Kathy had said. It was on the still-sunny side of the street and the tulip cup flowers shone, radiating the last feeble rays of evening sun like white wax candles. It was an early Victorian terraced house. Three storeys, a small front garden entirely filled by a beautiful tree. She pushed the door bell, noticing, as she looked up at the frontage, a small inquisitive face disappear from one of the tall first-floor windows.

'What have you done to your hair?' Kathy opened the door holding a year-old child in one arm.

Gemma's hand went instinctively to her head.

'I mean, it looks fantastic!' Kathy leaned forward as far as she could, and kissed Gemma's cheek. 'Whatever you do, don't let this child ruin that jacket. He's got a bit of a cold and he'll snot all over it if you hold him.'

'It's washable,' said Gemma.

It seemed an odd greeting for the best friend she hadn't seen in years but, as soon as Kathy had opened the door, it was as if they had only been parted for days.

In their last year at Oxford, they often found themselves sharing an alcove in the Radcliffe Camera, and afterwards they used to wheel their bikes along together, chatting and laughing, until they reached the roundabout where they had to pedal away in different directions. Kathy to Roger, Gemma to Oliver. The next time they met, they would pick up the conversation almost mid-sentence where they had left it, as if the space in between hadn't existed. It felt the same now.

Gemma followed Kathy through the hallway to the

kitchen at the back of the house. It felt narrower than it was because of a pile of coats that seemed to be heaped sideways onto the wall, defying gravity. The floor was littered with shoes and Wellington boots of various sizes.

'I know what you're thinking,' Kathy was saying, 'not like the old days, when I couldn't bear to have a cushion unplumped and out of place. Children change things. It's not just that you can't be bothered any more, it's that they've got personalities too. Even though you've no idea where they inherited the messy gene. Now, sit down, there . . . oh sorry, I told Zoe to take her paints away . . .'

'Where is Zoe?' asked Gemma.

'She's upstairs. A bit shy. I think she's probably making you something. She ought to be, given the beautiful wardrobe you've sent her over the years. Did you know she was the first in her class to have Gap clothes? They totally superseded the hugely expensive bike we had bought her. It's awful to see them becoming so vain, so young.'

'Sorry.'

'No. Not your fault. I'm sorry to say I think that might be genetic too. So much for all the train sets we bought her . . . still, you'll like them, won't you?' She kissed the little boy on his cheek and set him down on the floor. He crawled over to Gemma's legs.

'Hello Alexander,' she said. She picked him up and sat him on her lap.

'Honestly Gem, be careful. You'll ruin those beautiful clothes.'

'They're only jeans, Kathy.' She started bouncing the little boy up and down gently. He giggled. She leant forward and kissed the top of his head, inhaling the clean baby smell of his curls.

'Don't babies smell wonderful?'

'Hmm. That way up, maybe,' said Kathy.

'And how does Zoe like her little brother?'

'She's very good normally. It was a bit of a blow to her after nine years being an only child, but she's so much older, she feels she's more like another mummy to him. She'll be down anytime. Tea, or a drink?'

'Drink, please.'

'Only wine, I'm afraid. White Australian something or other. It's all Australian these days. OK?'

She uncorked a half-full bottle and poured big glasses.

'Welcome home!'

'Thanks.'

Both women's eyes were suddenly sparkling with tears.

'You know, you look fantastic,' Kathy said, hastily filling what was in danger of becoming a sentimental silence. 'I mean you were always pretty,' she went on hastily, 'but the difference is that you're now groomed. I used to be the groomed one!' she added with a wail.

'What do you mean?' Gemma said, 'You're making me sound like a horse.'

'It's your mane . . . I mean your hair,' Kathy joked. 'I suppose it's the same colour, but it used to be kind of fuzzy and light brown and now it's all shiny and pale gold. We're talking Shetland pony turns into Palomino. What do you use on it?'

'Hundreds of dollars,' said Gemma with a laugh.

'Tell me all about this new job,' Kathy said.

Did she ask that because women above a certain age could only be defined by job or children, Gemma wondered. She didn't want to talk about work, she wanted to talk about how strange it felt to be sitting in Kathy's very grown-up kitchen. She took a gulp of the wine. It was cold and smoky and good.

'Well, I'm going to be an editor at Red Rose. You know the sort of books they do?'

Kathy nodded. Red Rose was a household name

33

synonymous with women's romantic fiction. The image was so firmly fixed in the popular imagination that any clichéd romantic scenario was referred to as 'a kind of Red Rose situation'.

'Well,' Gemma continued, 'they're chugging along, but sales are falling a bit and their market research says that they're considered old-fashioned, so they've hired me to spice them up a bit.'

'How exciting . . . do you have lots of ideas?'

'One or two. I've had a look in the bookshops today. The market research seems to be about right to me. Their covers look very unsophisticated, and there are areas which they're not doing at all.'

'Like?'

'Well, there seems to be a bit of a vogue for erotic fiction for women over here . . .'

'Gemma! You can't be sitting here telling me that you're planning to publish soft-porn?'

'Why ever not?' Gemma grinned. 'Anyway, it's only an idea.'

She wondered why people in England always expected an interest in books to be serious and intellectual. Kathy had just employed exactly the same tone of voice as her tutor at Oxford had many years ago when Gemma was tentatively discussing a career in publishing. The tutor claimed never to have heard of Judith Krantz and her face folded into a grimace of distaste when Gemma had pulled the bright pink paperback of Krantz's latest out of her bicycle basket in order to demonstrate the state of the romantic tradition in the early 1980s.

There was a seriously frivolous side to Gemma that almost everyone, from her mother and father onwards, had found difficult to understand.

Gemma thought she knew where her fondness for glossy magazines and romance had originated. She remembered the thrill of reading *Woman* magazine for

34

the first time lying on the sofa in her Auntie Shirley's front room when she was convalescing from chicken pox at the age of ten.

Downstairs in the shop, the fryers were heating and Shirley was peeling pound after pound of potatoes. Uncle Ken was slapping wet pieces of fish into batter and dropping them with a sizzle into the hot fat. It was growing dark outside and the chain of lights strung all the way along the seafront had just been switched on. Upstairs, Gemma was discovering romantic stories and problem pages for the first time. She read furtively, holding the magazine right under the eiderdown so that she could hide it quickly if she heard anyone approaching. But when Shirley came up with a glass of fizzy orange and saw the magazine peeping out as Gemma sat up to drink, she seemed quite unperturbed, and said that they would try the knitting pattern together when she got a moment.

From then on, Gemma was an addict. Like any addiction, it was all the more attractive because it was forbidden at home. She only had to look at her mother's face when she asked to be bought *Jackie* magazine rather than a bar of chocolate at the village newsagent to know that she had transgressed. She was the first girl in her class to buy *Cosmopolitan*, which she hid in her shoe bag, not daring to take it home, and she had been docked marks when she listed Colleen McCullough as well as Eliot and the Brontës among her favourite authors.

'Anyway,' Gemma said, 'let's not talk about work. How are you? It suits you, being a mother . . . do you enjoy it?' There she was, falling into the same trap, she thought.

'Oh, does it?' Kathy looked slightly distracted. 'I don't know. I've stopped thinking about whether I enjoy life much. Was it difficult to leave New York?' she asked.

Gemma thought about it. She was in a kind of limbo. It didn't feel as if she had quite left yet.

'I couldn't stay in the apartment. It was too sad,' she began, 'Boy was so bloody pervasively lively, every corner had an association, a memory of him when he was well. He kind of filled a room. He filled the whole bloody flat. Even *my* room. Even if I had the door closed, for heaven's sake, I could hear him laughing, on the phone, bringing me tea . . . even if I had a guy there, I'd know that Boy was tiptoeing around outside, exaggeratedly quiet . . . you know how he was . . .'

Kathy nodded. She had met him only once, before he became ill. She and Roger had spent their fifth wedding anniversary in New York. They had all gone out for a meal together at the Odeon. Gemma knew that Kathy had liked Boy, although Roger had clearly felt uncomfortable.

Roger hadn't really been able to cope with all the bizarreness of New York, particularly not with Gemma's domestic arrangements. 'Why does she always go for impossible men?' Gemma had overheard him asking Kathy. 'Well, she didn't exactly go for Boy, did she?' Kathy had replied sharply, to Gemma's relief. 'If it's convenient for them and they're both happy with it, why shouldn't you be?' Roger had pursed up after that, as if taking his wife's defence of Gemma as admiration, envy even, for her idiosyncratic life. It hadn't been the most successful evening.

'Boy could be infuriating, of course . . . No, it's important to remember that too,' Gemma was saying. Then, catching Kathy's look of surprise, she added, 'People seem to think it's not on to say anything mildly critical about someone who's dead. That's ridiculous, almost insulting to their memory. Let's face it, Boy could be a petulant, arrogant, pain in the butt, he could. He would admit it, if he were here . . . well, perhaps not the arrogant bit . . .' she laughed, then sighed.

'Anyway, I just couldn't seem to be bothered to find another apartment. His parents were pressing for it back. Legally, I could have contested that, but I couldn't be bothered. I was in a kind of daze. Working eighteen hours a day, coming home to sleep. Then the head of Red Rose happened to be in New York. We had a drink together and he offered me a job. A new challenge, a new life. It appealed. New York when you're thirty-two is different from when you're twenty-two. Sure, you now have the money to enjoy it, but somehow you don't find yourself going out at two o'clock in the morning to catch some jazz, or have an ice-cream. Most people I knew were moving out of town, having kids. I thought maybe I should give London a try. A change of scene to help me forget. It worked before . . .' Gemma's voice trailed off.

'When you went to New York? I often think about that, Gem, how strong you were. I don't think I was much use. I'm sorry, I just had no idea how to help you get over it,' Kathy said.

'I don't think you do ever get over it,' Gemma said, 'You just get used to it, somehow. Anyway, you were great. You've always kept in touch, even when I was in my Greta Garbo phase. I don't think I was much good at grief then. I've learnt a lot this time. When my father died, and Estella, I suppose, I just tried to pretend that it hadn't happened. I never talked about it. Now I know that you have to let other people share it with you, because you can't keep it under control. You don't just lose your friends that way, you lose yourself.'

Kathy nodded sympathetically, not really understanding. Until you experienced it, Gemma thought, you couldn't begin to imagine what it would be like when someone you loved died.

'The odd thing is', Gemma continued, 'that when

37

you're with someone who is dying over a long period of time, you think it will be a relief when they go. But it's not. It's still a shock. Almost more of a shock, because there have been so many days when you've woken up wondering whether this will be the day, and when it hasn't happened, you almost begin to believe it never will . . .'

It was growing dark in the kitchen. The clock marked out seconds of silence. Alexander had fallen asleep in Gemma's arms, lulled by her soft voice.

'I'll just take him upstairs,' Kathy whispered.

Gemma sat for a few moments before getting up to put on the light. Zoe was standing in the hallway watching her.

'Hello, do you know who I am?' Gemma asked, brightening her face with a smile.

'You're my American godmother,' Zoe replied.

'Oh?' Gemma said, surprised.

'Well, that's what I call you,' Zoe continued, 'although Mummy said that you weren't really American and you didn't believe in God. But that doesn't matter because Leonie has three godmothers who don't believe in God, and one godfather. The other one's a vicar, so he must do.'

'Is that so?' Gemma asked, 'And how does Leonie know that her godmothers don't believe in God?'

'She heard them talking to her mum in the kitchen. She wanted a glass of water. They were drunk,' Zoe added contemptuously.

'Oh, I see.'

'I've made you a card,' Zoe said, coming nearer.

'Oh, that's beautiful!' Gemma said, examining it carefully. There were tissue paper flowers stuck on with glue that hadn't yet dried.

'I got fourteen cards for my ninth birthday,' Zoe added proudly.

'Lucky you,' said Gemma, 'is that a record?'

'I think so,' Zoe replied with a solemnness that made Gemma want to laugh.

Gemma had an astonishingly clear memory of her own childhood years. Each birthday was pinpointed in her mind exactly because she remembered every card that her father had painted for her. They were stuck up round her childhood room beneath the animal alphabet he had also created.

Nine, Zoe's age, had been a family of rabbits in a field of poppies. That year, she remembered, she had been given a doll's house. Such a beautiful doll's house too, a Georgian town house, with a front door painted shiny red and a real brass knocker. Inside there were real curtains that pulled across at night, and a proper staircase with banisters, unlike some doll's houses she had played with where the dolls had to jump floors when they wanted to go to bed.

She asked Zoe if she had a doll's house.

'Yes, but I am a little too old for that now,' Zoe explained.

'Are you?' Gemma exchanged glances with Kathy who had just come down from putting Alexander to bed, 'I think if I still had my doll's house I would still enjoy playing with it.'

Zoe laughed. 'That's silly,' she said.

'I suppose it is,' said Gemma, adding to Kathy in a whisper, 'probably true, though!'

'Come on, Missy,' said Kathy, 'time for bed.'

'You're not going to get drunk, are you?' asked Zoe, looking pointedly at the empty bottle of wine.

'Most probably,' said Kathy. 'God, they're so moralistic, kids. Were we like that? I don't think I knew what drunk was until I was about sixteen . . .'

'It's very dangerous,' said Zoe, 'and rather un-pleasant.'

'Bed!' said Gemma and Kathy in unison.

Kathy took the heap of purple Calabrese broccoli that was lying on the draining board and plunged it into a large panful of boiling water.

'Are you hungry?' she asked.

'Mmm. Yes. I haven't been, really, since I got off the plane, but your kitchen smells so wonderful.'

It looked rather wonderful too, all antique pine and willow-pattern china. It was the sort of kitchen rich New Yorkers would pay a fortune to have designed for their weekend places in the Hamptons. But what was nice about this was that it was lived in. Sure, some thought had gone into the specially made units, painted the exact Delft blue of the patterns on the china, and the big farmer's table at which she was sitting, which had probably been made to fit the conservatory alcove exactly, but the nice jugs and glasses on the dresser sat happily next to less successful papier mâché objects created by Zoe. Discarded dolls and drawing materials littered the floor, and Alexander's play-pen with its poster colour plastic accessories contrasted gaudily with the terracotta quarry-tiled floor. There was a large green bowl at the centre of the table containing plastic hairslides and a pair of broken sunglasses, as well as some apples and a couple of brown-spotted bananas. The room felt warm and slightly steamy. A real family kitchen.

'When does Roger get home?' Gemma asked.

'Depends. He's working on a big case at the moment. Sometimes he's quite late. We won't wait for him to start. It's nicer just being on our own, isn't it?' she added, girlishly.

'Things are OK with you two, though?'

'Oh yes. I suppose so. Did I tell you I'm training to be a Relate counsellor? Quite honestly, listening to other people's problems puts your own into perspective. I think we both feel a bit stale, but every relationship gets that way after ten years. Must do, mustn't it?'

Gemma didn't feel qualified to comment. She'd never had a relationship that had lasted. Not really lasted, or ever looked as if it would go on for ever.

Privately, she'd always thought Roger a bit dull. On paper, he was perfect for Kathy. They came from the same kind of nice middle-class background. Kathy had been head girl of a direct grant school, Roger had been to an independent boys' day school, so he wasn't a drug-taking neurotic, like most of the more interesting public schoolboys they had encountered at Oxford. Kathy wanted to go into market research, Roger wanted to be a barrister. They were good, sensible, compatible professions. He was nice looking, quite clever, and capable; so was she. But the thing about Kathy was that although she appeared to be a conventional, extrovert type, she possessed enormous humanity, sympathy and humour, qualities Gemma had never detected in Roger.

Kathy had rowed for their college, Roger was captain of his college's second eight. They met at a party in the Teddy Hall boathouse.

'Do you think', Gemma could remember Kathy asking when she arrived home, looking slightly pinker than usual, 'you could ever fall in love with someone called Roger?'

'No,' Gemma's answer was unequivocal.

'It is a terrible name, isn't it?' Kathy had persisted. 'Do you think you could ever get used to it, or think of a decent shortening, or nickname?'

'Not really.'

'Oh dear,' said Kathy.

After that she called him 'this bloke I met' for a few weeks. Then he became 'the dreaded R', then one night he came over to dinner and introduced himself to Gemma as Rog which, Gemma supposed, was the compromise Kathy had been able to accept.

After that, he stayed a lot, which began to irritate Gemma because they had always said that they wanted to avoid sharing with a third person. Luckily, she had never had to say anything, because either through Kathy's intuition, or Rog's meanness, they announced at the beginning of the Trinity term that they were planning to live together at Roger's, and that Kathy would move out just as soon as Gemma had found a new housemate.

She didn't know whether it was a touch of jealousy, or whether she had seen him as taking her best friend away from her, but Gemma had never really felt comfortable with Roger since then, and it was quite a relief that he only arrived home as she was leaving the house, rather drunkenly, around midnight. They exchanged air kisses, and she hurried into the waiting mini-cab.

She thought she would sleep well, helped by jet lag and the bottle and a half of Chardonnay they had shared. But as she lay in the huge hotel bed trying to decide whether the hum of the air-conditioning was worse than the noise of traffic when she opened the window, her mind was speeding through the images that the evening had awakened. She hadn't really thought about Oxford for years, or her childhood, or that doll's house.

When she finally fell asleep she dreamt that she was small, very small, and she was walking across a Persian carpet towards a red shiny front door with a big brass knocker.

CHAPTER 3

She thought she would like a house. Apartments were quintessentially New York. They were *Barefoot in the Park*, *Breakfast at Tiffany's*, and her life with Boy. She couldn't imagine living in a flat in London.

The time she had been happiest in England was in her final two years at Oxford when she had lived in the little house in Boulter Street, not just after Oliver moved in, but before, when she and Kathy had first rented the place together, and made it their own.

It was in an unprepossessing little cul-de-sac off St Clements, and it smelt bad. An old lady had recently died there. Her nephew had shown them around. There was a horrible brown feeling to the whole house. Walls that had not been decorated for decades were brown with grime. It was impossible to tell the original colour of the paper. The kitchen cupboards were brown with years of cooking fat splatter, and the bathroom, which had obviously been modernized in the early Seventies, had a brown plastic suite and brown and orange swirly patterned tiles.

Kathy, who had been brought up in a nice part of Croydon, turned her nose up and signalled with frantic hand movements and facial contortions behind the nephew's back that she wanted nothing to do with it. But Gemma had seen possibilities. The rent was very reasonable. It was two up and two down, so they could have a bedroom and another room each without worrying about sharing the expense with a third person, something they were both reluctant to do.

'We'll think about it,' Gemma had said, and the nephew had looked downcast, as if he had heard those words before and then nothing further.

She had marched Kathy, protesting mildly, up the street and into the nearest pub.

'Gem, it's impossible.'

'It's not, really, it's purely cosmetic. Give me a couple of weekends with some Ajax and a pot of white paint, and it'll look fine.'

'But the furniture . . .' said Kathy, taking a despairing slug of lager.

'I agree the furniture's got to go. But I think we could persuade him to buy us some basics, if we say we'll do the place up. He's obviously desperate to get some income out of it. Come on, I promise to do the really dirty stuff, and painting's fun. You'll like it.'

Kathy had looked doubtful, but she'd agreed to take the risk, even bought herself a boiler suit so as not to spoil her clothes, and it had been worth it.

Estella had proved an unexpected ally, finding bits of interesting furniture in the local auction room and driving them up to Oxford in a rented van. She brought palms in terracotta pots from her veranda, and even suggested a way of disguising the vile bathroom by draping fishing nets down the walls and dotting shells and plastic starfish all over. She made a curtain out of dark green plastic, cutting it into a fringe that looked uncannily like wet seaweed.

'A touch of the tropical theme cocktail bars,' she remarked, stepping back to look at her handiwork, 'but better, don't you think?'

Kathy took a while to get used to it, but Gemma felt really proud of her mother. The bathroom looked like something out of an interior design magazine. She invited people round especially to see it.

*　　*　　*

The estate agent advised that north London or west London was where her 'type of person' lived. Gemma longed to ask him what type that was, but refrained. He seemed to take his job very seriously.

North London had some advantages. It was where Kathy now lived and it was nearer the office. It also had Daisy. She wasn't sure she wanted to live close to Daisy. The question of Daisy was going to be unavoidable, but she wasn't yet ready to address it. A flood of acid, a cocktail of anger, bitterness and loss still washed through her whenever she thought about her sister.

She had seen Daisy's byline blazoned across the front cover of a woman's glossy on the newspaper stall at the airport. It was as if her sister was waiting to greet her. *What happens when your best friend steals your man?* screamed the neon yellow letters. *Daisy Rush finds out.* Had she really found out? Did she have any idea? or, Gemma had thought, did she just siphon off the most intimate experiences of the people around her and make them her own, as she had always done.

Journalism seemed a strange occupation for Daisy to have chosen, especially that woman's magazine sexual/ emotional type of journalism. When it came to conveying her own emotions, or sympathizing with other people, Daisy had always been hopeless.

Dear Biscuit,

I was ever so sorry to hear about Boy. I know you really liked him a lot. I don't suppose there's anything I can do, but if there is . . . Lol sends his love.

Lots of love,
Donut

It was a child's letter, using the childhood language they had spoken when they were little girls. Daisy was twenty-eight years old, for heaven's sake.

*   *   *

She met the estate agent at Holland Park tube station and they walked up Ladbroke Grove together. It was another sunny spring evening. The cherry trees were just about to blossom. Seeing the elegant white stucco frontages of the crescents leading off the main drag, Gemma wondered whether she hadn't been too hasty dismissing the idea of a flat, but when she saw the little mews house, just behind Portobello Road, she knew it was perfect.

The owner was away for a year's sabbatical in Florence. He was a professor of archaeology and the walls were lined with bookshelves and framed prints of Roman wall-paintings. Downstairs was one large airy room with a couple of sofas and a roll-top desk at one end, and a kitchen area at the other with a table that could comfortably seat six, eight at a push. The back door led out into a tiny unused yard. Upstairs was one fairly comfortable bedroom with a wall of fitted cupboards with louvred doors and a double bed, a bathroom and one other room which was locked.

'It's his study. All his stuff is in there. We're really talking about a one-bedroom flat here,' said the agent. 'It's very expensive. The owner's idea was that anyone who would appreciate it would pay.' It was obvious the agent had advised against this idea. 'It's not been let so far. I could only offer you six months.' He obviously thought she would be mad to accept. 'For the same price there's a beautiful two bedroom first floor on Lansdowne Road.'

'There's only one of me, though,' said Gemma. 'Have you a key to the locked room? I'd just like to see what's in there before signing anything.'

The agent obliged by opening the door. There were piles and piles of books and papers.

'No skeletons,' said the agent, closing the door when she had had a thorough look.

'I'll take it,' said Gemma.

*   *   *

She moved in straightaway, glad to be out of the hotel. It had seemed like a good idea when she arrived, but the silver grey walls and the candy pink linings of the swagged curtains in her bedroom were beginning to give her claustrophobia. The foolish leap of joy at finding another little bottle of shampoo and another disposable shower cap in the bathroom each evening, as well as a single boxed chocolate with a printed message 'Good Night!' on the corner of her turned-down bed, had worn off after the first day.

She had brought very little back from New York. Most of the stuff in the apartment had been Boy's anyway. A trunk of clothes was following by sea but, apart from that, her luggage consisted of two large suitcases, and her vanity bag.

She bought pillows, a new duvet and white Egyptian cotton sheets and covers from Heals, almost fainting at the price. In the end, she calculated, it would have been less expensive to ship her linen from New York. But it was good to smell the newness of the cotton, to lie in a virginal white bed.

She woke early the next morning, jolted from a dream-filled sleep by unfamiliar sounds. The street market was setting up. She could hear the metal frames of stalls being dragged along the road, and the revving of lorries delivering goods. She threw on a long white T-shirt and went downstairs to make herself coffee, feeling excited, like a child beginning a new adventure.

She shopped all day. At her end of Portobello Road there were fruit and vegetable stalls. She came back to the house at lunchtime laden with bunches of asparagus and fresh herbs, heavy nets of root vegetables, a brown paper bag stuffed with different sorts of mushroom. Then she went out again.

Further up the long narrow market street were

47

antique stalls and clothes stalls selling the sort of clothes her mother had worn. Had they always been there, she wondered, or were they only now coming back into fashion? She imagined her mother, on one of her many solo trips to London, walking down through the market, picking out embroidered smocks and brightly coloured dresses made from crinkly material and bits of mirror. Those dresses that used to hang on the line at Whitton House, their skirts tied in knots to stop them sagging, dripping their indigo or cochineal dye onto the lawn.

She spotted a pair of silver candlesticks she liked very much and persuaded the stall holder to drop the price by ten pounds.

'You Americans,' he said, 'you're great ones for a bargain.'

'I'm not American,' she said, handing over her money, and noticed that he looked rather shamefaced.

'Here,' he said, picking up a handful of beeswax candles, 'have these on the house.'

By late afternoon, she was exhausted and hungry. She rang Kathy. 'Come to supper.'

'Oh love, I'd adore it, but I couldn't get a babysitter this late. Come to lunch, tomorrow.'

'But I want you to come here!'

'I will, as soon as I can. Is it lovely?'

'It's perfect,' said Gemma. She wanted someone to share it with right that moment.

She looked up a few phone numbers, but most of the people she knew in London were business contacts, not real friends. Anyway, who would be free at such short notice? She found herself ringing her half-brother, Jonathan.

'I wondered if you would like to have a trustees' meeting?' she asked on the phone, 'I'm back. Are you free for supper?'

He sounded a little cautious and began to make an

excuse about training on Wednesday evenings, but then he stopped, admitting that he had run a marathon the week before in under four hours, so he could allow himself a break.

She was surprised at how conventional and middle-aged he sounded, as if he were suspicious of spontaneity, but, she reasoned, it was ten years since they had seen each other, and their contact in between had been limited to a couple of letters each year, mostly about their father's estate, with the odd line or two of news. Very infrequently, she had rung him from her office and they had chatted for a few minutes before deciding whether to accept or reject a deal.

She observed him walking down the mews towards her front door and was filled instantly with a mixture of love and protectiveness. He walked just like Bertie. He looked just like her father too, she thought. Perhaps it was the way his fair hair was cut – long at the front, so that he kept having to smooth back the bit that flopped over his eyes. It was a gesture so reminiscent of Bertie, but one that she had forgotten until she saw it again.

A sharp pang of *déjà vu* caught in her throat. Sometimes she panicked when she felt she could no longer conjure up what her father looked like, but seeing his mannerisms repeated in his son was hugely comforting.

She threw open the door and went to hug him, kissing him enthusiastically on the cheek. As she stepped back to allow him to pass into the living-room, she was touched to see that he was blushing.

She offered him a glass of wine, feeling suddenly very grown-up as mistress of her own home. Apart from Bertie's funeral, when she hadn't really spoken to anyone, she couldn't remember seeing Jonathan since she was quite a young girl. He was eleven years her senior and she had hero-worshipped him when she was growing up. It was a strange, almost embarrassing, sensation, to confront him now as an adult.

He used to stay one weekend every month at Whitton House. He was a moody boy, who would lock himself in his room for hours reading, but he had always been extremely kind to Gemma, even though, she now thought, her arrival in the world had been the direct cause of the break-up of his own family. She remembered how he allowed her to sit with him as long as she was silent, and sometimes he would reward her patience by reading her a chapter from *Swallows and Amazons*.

Now he was sitting on her sofa, sipping his wine as he tried to remember out loud the last time they had met before Bertie's funeral.

'Did you ever visit me in Oxford?' she asked.

'You invited me, I know that. You were having your twenty-first in some cricket pavilion. I felt too old to come. I remembered those parties – Brown Sugar at ear-splitting volume, people throwing up in the grass, snogging bodies on the porch!'

She laughed.

'Yes, it was a bit like that,' she admitted. 'I remember coming up to see you when you were at Oriel . . .'

'With Bertie?'

'Yes, it was just before your finals. We went to tea in Browns. I think it was the banana malted shake more than anything else that made me want to go to Oxford myself!'

'Oh yes. I remember now. You were a terrifically solemn little girl, until it came to sucking the last bit of milkshake out of your glass, then you slurped it really loudly . . .'

'Thanks for reminding me!' she laughed.

She didn't know whether she really remembered the conversation they had had that day in the mock colonial setting of Browns, surrounded by large mirrors with moulded frames and palms, or whether she had heard her father telling his friends about it so often that it had become a kind of family folklore memory, something she remembered in the third person, one of a set of stories about herself that made up her childhood.

She had apparently announced that she was going to come up to Oxford too.

'To read what?' Jonathan had asked.

'Books and things,' she had replied.

'No, silly, what subject? We all read books.'

'Well, what do you read?' she had asked, cottoning on to her mistake immediately.

'PPE. Politics, Philosophy and Economics,' he had replied.

'Oh, that sounds interesting, I think I'll do that too,' she had said, and Bertie had apparently kicked Jonathan hard under the table to stop him laughing out loud.

She filled his glass and they began to swap stories about what they had been up to in more recent times.

'God, what an unfortunate pair!' said Jonathan. 'My marriage breaks up. You lose your husband. What is it about our family, do you think?'

'It happens in every family. It's just that in most families the blows are spread out a bit,' said Gemma cheerfully. 'I comfort myself with the thought that I'm just getting all the nasty bits over while I'm young. At least I should have a relatively happy old age.'

'My mother's still going strong,' Jonathan said.

Gemma had met Bertie's first wife on only a couple of occasions. She couldn't even remember whether she had come to Bertie's funeral, but then Gemma couldn't remember very much about that day, except for the wails she had heard emanating from some deep place inside her when everyone had gone home, the animal howls of pain as she rolled about the floor of her childhood bedroom privately mourning her father.

'Did your mother hate Bertie when he left her?' she asked.

'Well, we both did, I suppose, although the funny thing is that I wasn't really aware of it until David was born. Then I got really angry with him, rest in peace and all that,' he added quickly. 'You see, when you're a parent yourself, it's even more difficult to understand. I mean, you love this little thing you've created in indescribable ways. It's a love you never thought yourself capable of. So, of course you think, how could anyone give this up?'

The strange thing was, she thought, he talked just like Bertie too.

'How old's David now?' Gemma asked gently.

'He's seven. Sarah is five.' He drew some pictures out of his wallet to show her. They were dressed up for a fancy dress party and their faces had been painted.

'The owl and the pussycat,' Jonathan explained.

'They look sweet,' said Gemma, 'beneath the feathers and whiskers.'

'Oh they are. Not all the time, of course,' he added, with a smile. 'I have them every other weekend. You might like to meet them?'

'I'd love to,' said Gemma, feeling a rush of pleasure. For the first time since she had been back she felt really at home. There was something special about family. Even Kathy, who was a very good friend, didn't approach it. There were things Jonathan knew, even though they would probably never discuss them, that she could never explain to anyone else. Jonathan understood, simply because he had known her since she was born.

'Do you see a lot of Daisy?' he said.

How typical, thought Gemma, that her name should come up just when she was feeling so comfortable.

'No,' she said simply. 'Do you?'

'No. I send her cheques of course, but she never bothers to acknowledge them. I haven't seen her since I last saw you. I never really liked Daisy,' he admitted. 'I suppose that the age difference was so vast, there wasn't much point.'

'But she's only four years younger than me,' said Gemma.

'I know, but you were always grown up for your age, and she was always the baby. Anyway, I think I thought she had enough admirers . . .'

Gemma laughed, but there was a strange sensation in her gut. One half of her loved to hear criticism of her estranged sister, the other was still fiercely protective. She was allowed to be as nasty as she liked about Daisy, but when other people joined in, she still felt the urge to defend her. She didn't want to talk about her sister. She couldn't stand the pain of it, and the vacuum of comfort that no-one, however much they wanted to sympathize and support, could fill.

'I never liked Estella either,' Jonathan continued, the wine making him more garrulous.

'Oh, I think you made that pretty clear,' Gemma said, as an image of him – a sulky teenager sitting in hostile silence at the dinner table – flashed through her mind.

'I thought she was a witch, with her long black hair and that stuff she put round her eyes,' he continued.

'Kohl?'

'Yes, that's it. It was only when I started dating women and getting intimate enough to watch them putting on make-up in the morning, that I learned what kohl was. I always thought Estella was blackening her eye-sockets with the stuff people make fires from!'

Gemma got up from the sofa and went to check the temperature of the soup. She had made a vichysoisse scented with lemon grass. It was almost cold enough.

53

She took the tureen out of the fridge and ladled out two bowls, then she dropped a couple of ice cubes into each, followed by slices of lemon and a generous snip of fresh coriander. She put the bowls on the table, indicating that Jonathan should join her.

'Actually,' Jonathan said, pulling up a chair, 'I think I was probably a bit unfair to poor Estella.'

Gemma raised her eyebrows, but said nothing.

'I suppose I was too influenced by my mother and her sisters. Their favourite pastime was sitting around playing bridge and bitching about her. They called her all the names under the sun and not one of them ever imagined that she might actually *love* my father. His money, yes. It was only when she died, the way she died, you know . . . I felt a bit guilty. I thought perhaps we had all underestimated her . . .'

'It was easy to underestimate Estella,' Gemma said in a clipped voice. 'She was capable of such ridiculously exaggerated behaviour.'

She started sawing through a loaf of brown soda bread, 'Butter?' she asked, with a finality that created a cold space between them.

'I suppose that we had better talk a little about the estate,' Jonathan said, after a few moments' silence.

Bertie had made Jonathan and Gemma co-executors of his literary estate. At the time it had seemed an odd thing to do, since he could not have known that Estella would survive him for such a short time. Perhaps it had been his way of reconciling the two halves of his life. If it had been, then it had been successful, because Gemma and Jonathan found that they worked well together, although Jonathan, being older and living in England, had taken on the bulk of the work.

'I've done this brief summary.' He took a folded piece of paper from his pocket.

Most of Betrand Rush's famous work consisted of illustrations for the writer Ronald Diamond's children's stories. Diamond, who was still alive, had never forgiven Bertie for dying, because however many new illustrators he tried to work with, his sales continued to drop on each new book. The books he had made with Bertie, however, continued to sell, and recently, due to the forthcoming animated film of *Tusker's Garden*, the shops were filled with Tusker merchandise – from envelopes and notelets to keyrings, baseball caps (with Tusker's ears and trunk sewn on in grey felt), to soft toys. Gemma had even seen a Tusker water pistol in the window of Hamleys that afternoon. She was getting used to her father's work popping up in front of her when she least expected it, but she wasn't sure she approved of the elephant she had spent her childhood with being used for aggressive purposes.

'The animators are very keen to do more Rush stuff,' said Jonathan. 'They won an Oscar, you know, for an animated short they did.'

'Oh, was that them?' Gemma exchanged their empty bowls for plates and put a large green salad and a selection of pungent European cheeses on the table. 'Supper's very simple, I'm afraid,' she said.

'It's utterly delicious,' Jonathan said, 'I never cook for myself. This is a real treat.' He cut himself a wedge of ripe Vignotte. 'They want options on all the other Diamond books, and also,' he added, his mouth full, '*Biscuit and Donut*.'

'No.' Her reaction was immediate. 'No, not those.'

Bertie had published two pieces of work entirely on his own. The first was the *Animalphabet*, all the letters of the alphabet illustrated with animals, the originals of which had lined Gemma's childhood bedroom. The second was the cycle of books about two dolls, Biscuit, a floppy rag doll, and Donut, a robust roly-poly doll, who lived together in a house with a shiny red door.

Over the years, the estate had received numerous offers for the books, but apart from the licences that were in place with British and American publishers when Bertie died, Gemma had vetoed any request for further exploitation of the *Biscuit and Donut* books. She knew Jonathan found her attitude frustrating, although he was too reasonable ever to challenge it. She had sometimes been surprised that Daisy hadn't kicked up more of a fuss when there were large amounts of money on the table, but perhaps it was one thing that she and Daisy still had in common, that they didn't want those curiously personal tales about their growing up disseminated all over the world.

Gemma began to clear away the plates. She handed Jonathan another bottle of wine and a corkscrew.

'So how are you finding London after all these years?' he asked. Clearly Gemma didn't want to talk any further about the estate.

'It's a bit of an adventure . . . I never really knew London anyway. We only came up once or twice a year, you know. A little more when I was fanatical about ballet. Do you remember?'

There was a phase, when Gemma had been having ballet lessons, when Bertie used to take her to Covent Garden for Saturday matinées. It was only an hour or so's drive from Whitton House, but it was a different world, so noisy after the peace of their country lane. Gemma remembered the traffic and the buses and the gorgeous red and gold spectacle of the Opera House. Most of all she remembered the ice cream cones they bought on the way home from an Italian ice-cream parlour in Camden, which they licked surreptitiously as they drove through the suburbs, Gemma taking her father's cone in her right hand whenever he had to change lanes or negotiate a difficult corner. The ice-cream was their unspoken secret. If Daisy had known, she would have made an awful fuss, so it was best she did not find out.

'He used to take me there too,' Jonathan said, 'on our

days in London together. He loved ice-cream, didn't he?'

'Yes. I seem to have inherited that,' Gemma said, going to the fridge again and taking out a tub of Haagen Dazs' Pralines and Cream with a flourish.

'Me too,' Jonathan said, helping himself to a good-sized portion.

'I wonder if that place is still open?' Gemma mused.

'Marine Ices? Yes, still going strong. I take David and Sarah there every other weekend. You'll have to join us.'

Gemma felt tears welling in her eyes. It made her indescribably happy to think that Bertie's grand-children were being initiated into the family tradition of ice-cream on Saturday afternoon, but sad too that he was not there with them. He loved children. He had always claimed that he wanted to be surrounded by grandchildren in his dotage.

'I think you must be going prematurely senile already,' Estella would respond jokingly, but with a telling edge to her voice. 'God, I've spent most of my life trying to find interesting adults to talk to, and I end up with a grown man who's happiest on his knees communicating with toddlers!'

'It's all research,' Bertie would counter gently, which would shut Estella up, because even she had the grace to acknowledge that without his phenomenal skill as a children's book illustrator, she would not be able to live the lazy life she so enjoyed.

CHAPTER 4

'Gemma Rush,' said a voice that sounded familiar, 'it is you, isn't it?'

It was only when she spun round that she recognized the speaker.

'Patrick!'

Of all the people in all the world she did not want to bump into as she trawled the women's erotica section of a bookshop. She lowered the paperback she had been speed-reading, hoping that he hadn't seen the soft focus picture of a man's hand fingering the lacy top of a woman's stocking on the cover.

'*Intimate Secrets*,' Patrick said, pushing up the book with a fastidious forefinger and reading the title, 'well, well, well . . .'

'I'm just doing a little research . . .' Gemma said, flushing to the roots of her hair.

'Oh, I'm sure you don't need to,' Patrick winked at her.

'I didn't mean . . .'

'You are a naughty girl,' he said, adding as she was about to interrupt, 'for not letting me know that you're in town. How long do we have the pleasure of your company?'

'I'm not sure,' she replied awkwardly. 'I've come back to see what life in London's like, but I'm finding some unpleasant surprises . . .' she added, looking at him directly. 'What brings you into a bookshop?' she asked, as if it were the last place she would expect to find him. The last time she had seen him he was writing an article for the *Sunday Times'* Style Section about Brits in New York.

'I'm just checking the positioning of my magazine,' he said. 'Did you know that I'm the editor of *Sixpack* these days, the British side, that is?'

'I didn't . . . congratulations . . . sounds the perfect job for you,' she said tartly, taking a pile of books she wanted to the cash desk.

There on the counter was a stack of the new issue of *Sixpack*, a decidedly lads-only magazine, aimed at men who liked football and called women birds. Patrick hovered, waiting for her. 'So what are you up to?' he said, as they started ambling down Charing Cross Road together. 'On holiday?'

'No, I'm back. I've got a job at Red Rose.'

She didn't particularly want to start a conversation with him about the reasons for her return.

'How lovely for you, an English Rose working for Red Rose,' he said, smiling his twinkly Irish smile.

Touché, thought Gemma.

'And what are you up to this very minute? Could I tempt you to a drink at the Atlantic . . . for old times' sake?'

Gemma thought that he must practise twinkling in front of the mirror each morning.

'Old times as in we make out, and you sneak off leaving your card by my bed . . . I don't think so,' she said, smiling disarmingly. 'That doesn't happen in New York, you know. You call the next day to say what a great time you had. That's what happens. You pissed me off.'

Patrick looked shocked. There wasn't really any excuse for his behaviour that night, but most women he knew would have pretended that it hadn't happened. It was hardly polite to bring up a one-night-stand so blatantly two years later. But, he supposed, sneaking out of her Chelsea apartment while she was still asleep, leaving his card beside her bed, had hardly been polite either. He rather admired her guts for mentioning it. There was something steely about her, something he had found very attractive then, and not a little daunting.

'Perhaps I can make up for it,' he suggested, trying to keep the lightness in the conversation.

'That I doubt,' said Gemma, enjoying their banter. 'You see, there is something fundamental that you lack.'

He wanted to ask, but he wasn't absolutely confident that he wanted to know the answer.

'Manners,' she said, after a perfectly timed pause. 'If you want casual sex with someone these days you have to have two things. Condoms and manners.'

'Which way are you going?' Patrick asked, after a suitably contrite moment. They had come to a crossroads.

'I thought I'd take a cab,' she said, making him work a bit.

The choice was going back to her house and spending the evening reading, or going for a drink with an attractive man, which, even though he was a rogue, wasn't too difficult a dilemma.

'Oh do come for a drink,' he insisted. 'You'll love the Atlantic. It's your kind of place – elegant, chic, very, very expensive . . .'

He was so outrageously charming and good-humoured that she smiled. 'Why not then?'

The walls of the circular room were painted in broad horizontal stripes of cream and brown. The surface was shiny, as if still wet. It made Gemma feel as if they had walked into a giant glass of white and dark chocolate mousse.

A friend of Patrick's was drinking at the bar. Patrick introduced him and ordered a bottle of champagne. Ralph was doing some book reviews for *Sixpack*, he explained. Ralph was American and she immediately felt comfortable with him.

The three of them bantered their way down the bottle, then Patrick ordered another. He explained who Gemma was, although not what their previous relationship had been, and referred, mockingly, to her new job. She carelessly rose to the bait.

'Oh, you're surely not going to lecture me about literature! At least what I publish is honest escapism. I'm absolutely sick of tortured male confessions about masturbation and confused sexual identity passing as literary fiction. There's nothing worse, in my view, except perhaps earnest young men reading their poetry . . .' she rattled on archly.

At times, she thought, I sound just like Boy.

She noticed that the twinkle had disappeared from Patrick's eyes.

'What? What have I said?'

'Ralph's a poet and he's just published his first novel,' said Patrick.

'And if I may just quote my blurb,' Ralph interrupted, totally dead-pan, ' "this searingly moving exploration of masturbation and confused sexual identity goes even further into exploring the male psyche than his award-winning epic poem, *Ejaculation* . . ." '

'You're kidding?'

He held his serious look for several seconds, then cracked.

'You *are* kidding!' She burst out laughing.

Ralph was laughing too.

Patrick didn't seem to think it was *that* funny.

'I've got to run now,' he said, 'dinner. It's lovely to have you back, Gemma,' he continued, as if they were old friends, adding, as he kissed her warmly, 'we must meet *properly* soon.'

'Have you eaten?' Ralph asked, as they deliberated about sharing another bottle.

'No, but I'm starving!'

'Let's see if they have a table,' he said.

He asked her how she came to work in publishing, and she wasn't quite sure whether he was interested, or just teasing her again. But she told him how she had started in the business.

Her father's publisher had always had a soft spot for Gemma, and when she wrote to him in her last year at Oxford, asking how she might begin a career in publishing, he said he would give her some names. When she saw him just a couple of months later at her father's funeral, he asked her kindly whether she had made any progress. She told him that she was no longer interested. She just wanted to leave the country and get as far away as possible. Later, she had regretted her rudeness, but was too worn out with grief to do anything about it.

But a couple of weeks later he wrote to her. He hoped she wouldn't mind his mentioning it, but his oldest friend, Larry Marx, a semi-retired publisher in New York, was looking for someone to take care of his correspondence, and do some reading for him. Would she be interested? There was even a small room in the basement of Larry's Brooklyn home where Gemma could stay until she found somewhere she liked.

It had been like the magical granting of a wish. Within six weeks, she was living in New York with a job that she loved. She had quickly moved on to a secretarial position for the editor-in-chief at Marx's publishing house and a rented apartment of her own in Manhattan. A couple of years later, she had become an editor herself.

'That was really delicious,' she said, as their main courses were swept away, anxious in case he thought she was talking too much.

'Great food, but very bad for dental hygiene,' Ralph replied, leaning across the table conspiratorially. 'Before the moment passes, I have to tell you that you have a fleck of spinach on your left incisor. Do I have any on mine?'

He grinned at her, baring all his teeth. They were nice regular teeth. All white, no green bits visible. They kind of went with his above-average, boy-next-door face. He had freckles and curly red hair that was longish and parted at the side.

'So, Gemma,' he said, when she returned, having cleaned her teeth with her finger and taken a squirt of Chanel No. 19 from the array of perfume bottles in the powder room, 'tell me more about yourself.'

'So that you can write it in a novel?' she joked.

'Oh no, I only write about masturbation and confused sexuality, you know,' he said with a smile.

'Well, I've just told you everything,' she said.

'No, you've told me about your job,' he said, 'but you've told me very little about yourself. Where is your husband tonight, for example?'

It was the casualness of the enquiry that threw her off balance. Her eyes immediately filled with tears.

'Hey, I'm sorry,' Ralph looked mortified. 'I had no idea it was a sensitive subject. It's just that Patrick said . . .'

'Patrick said what?' she said icily, composing herself. 'And when?'

'When you first arrived,' he faltered, 'when you were checking in your coat, Patrick mentioned that you had a cool arrangement with your husband . . .'

'Oh, I can just imagine what Patrick said. Was that the reason for the invitation to dinner?'

'No,' he replied slowly, 'I don't think so.'

The equivocation was honest at least.

'I expect', she said, with less hostility, 'that Patrick told you that I had some weird open relationship thing.'

She remembered Patrick that evening. It had been his first visit to New York. To him, everything was buzzy and different and cool. She understood his excitement. It was what she had felt when she had arrived in the city. It was re-living that puppy-dog enthusiasm and naïvety that had attracted her to him.

When he called her office, telling her that everyone was saying he must talk to her for his article, she hadn't known who he was. But she was flattered by his very engaging phone manner. They met for drinks at the Royalton, where he asked her serious and irrelevant questions about New York publishing, and kept looking past her to the next table where Robert de Niro was drinking with a woman Patrick thought might be a supermodel.

They ate sushi in a sushi bar in the East Village where they made an agreement to go off the record. Then she took him downtown to her favourite bar in Tribeca, where they drank White Russians and played pool to Motown on the jukebox.

At some point, one of them, she couldn't remember whether she had been the initiator or Patrick, grabbed the other, and they smooched around the pool table for a couple of tracks of Marvin Gaye. Then she took Patrick home with her, whispering and giggling in the lift to the fifth floor, trying not to make any noise, because she hadn't warned Boy that she would have company. Not that he would have minded, she thought, but he was always rather competitive when she brought a good-looking man home.

'Actually,' she said, deciding to tell Ralph everything – it would seem coy not to – 'the truth is very much more pedestrian than Patrick's feverish imaginings. I was married to a gay man. It was a marriage of convenience. He died of AIDS just before Christmas. Period.'

Ralph nodded.

'. . . Except that the *whole* truth is much more complicated than that,' she went on, encouraged to talk by his calm reaction, 'because he was my best friend, the person closest to me in the world. He was also the kindest man I've ever known, apart from my father. I really loved him and my life with him. And I miss him.' She looked into Ralph's eyes.

'. . . And before you ask, I'm not some kind of fag hag who thinks that gay men are only gay until they meet her,' she said, defensively.

Ralph held his hands up in a silent gesture of protest.

'. . . But I did love him,' she said. 'You can love someone and not have sex with them, you know.'

'Of course,' he said.

Sometimes, at the beginning, she and Boy had shared a bed just to be companionable. The first summer had been so hot that they dragged Boy's futon onto the roof and slept up there, until Boy realized with horror that the tar surface was melting and ruining the blue and white ticking cover.

She smiled at the memory.

Ralph reached across the table and very gently brushed a tear from her cheek with the tip of his forefinger. It was such an intimate action that she started and sat back.

He was looking at her with great concern. She felt that he had been moved by what she said. She averted her eyes, not wanting to meet his and cry again. They were silent for several minutes.

'Coffee?' he offered eventually.

She was relieved that he didn't have any comments to make or condolences to offer.

'Yes, please.'

'So,' he said, trying to turn to a happier subject, 'what about the rest of your family? Are they in the States, or over here?'

'I don't really have any,' she said.

'Oh, I thought . . .' he stopped.

'What?' she pressed.

'Well, there's a journalist who does a column for *Sixpack* called Daisy Rush. Patrick thought she might be related . . .'

'Goodness me,' she said, in a clipped voice, 'Patrick does seem to take an enormous interest in my life, doesn't he?'

Suddenly the companionable rapport between them had vanished, and Gemma felt very separate from him, and slightly vulnerable, having revealed so much about herself.

Ralph laughed, embarrassed.

'She's my sister, but we really don't get on. What does she write about?' Gemma asked, trying to keep her voice even.

'It's called "A Bird's Eye View". It's kind of the woman's perspective on issues . . .'

'Issues?'

'You know the sort of thing – is it the quality or the quantity?' he explained, slightly sheepishly.

She wished she hadn't asked.

'I think I'd better go now,' she said.

It came out sounding awfully British and prudish, but she couldn't help that. Suddenly, in the beautifully decorated, elegant, high-ceilinged room she felt unable to breathe.

'Oh?' He looked disappointed. He called for the check and handed over a gold American Express card.

'What do I owe you?' she asked him, taking out her wallet.

'It's on me,' Ralph replied. 'No, really. You buy next time.'

'Well, thanks. It's been nice,' she said, trying to sound polite.

'Come back to the bar and have a drink,' Ralph suggested, keen to re-establish the intimacy.

'No. I'd better go, I think. I've got lots of reading to do before I start my job,' she explained.

He hailed a taxi. They looked at each other for a few significant seconds. In the end, she held out her hand.

'It's been very nice meeting you,' she said.

'I'm sorry if what I said, about Patrick, was clumsy,' he ventured.

'No, not at all,' she said, closing the door.

She realized as the taxi pulled away that they had not exchanged phone numbers.

She found she was unable to sleep. She felt cross with herself. Why had she behaved so peculiarly? She seemed to have lost the ability to flirt with men. She must be out of practice.

It had been ages since she had slept with anyone. There had been the brief holiday romance with the German in Las Vegas, but that had been as unreal as the rest of that city, and, before that, Patrick was probably the last.

She hated the idea that Patrick had talked about her. One night stands without repercussions were like free lunches, she thought. They didn't exist. She got up and made herself a camomile tea, but it made her feel even more awake.

She sat down on the sofa, opened the shopping bag and took out the books she had bought. The experience of being caught red-handed by Patrick had made her decide already that if she were to create a new list, the covers would be extremely tasteful and low-key.

She read fast, taking notes:

What do women want?
Mind v Body

Bondage
Lingerie?

A quick flip showed a depressing preponderance of what Gemma had always imagined were male fantasies. There was a lot of black lace and leather, quite a bit of gang-banging. Many of the stories seemed to be centred round health farms or luxury gyms.

There had been a time in New York when Gemma had caught the fitness bug. In the first gym she had visited the machines smelt of old sweat, and the showers were flooded, swirls of hair blocking the plug hole. The sensation of showering standing ankle-deep in a luke-warm soup of other people's shampoo scum was about the least sensual experience Gemma could imagine.

Meryl had introduced her to another gym on the Upper East Side, which was spotlessly clean, but the almost puritanical fanaticism of the regulars, their fashion-victim designer leotards, as well as the cross-town bus journey, had put Gemma off joining. She was sure she had never associated either place with a sexual fantasy.

If she were honest, she asked herself, was she really the best person to judge what women wanted? What sort of fantasies did other women actually have, she wondered. Maybe it *was* all group sex, crotchless panties, being strapped to a Nautilus machine and masturbating in the jacuzzi.

She had never really talked to anyone about theirs. She and Meryl had the occasional chat about sex, which normally ended with Meryl saying despairingly, 'On the whole I have more fun eating a mango.'

Gemma had never told anyone her own fantasy because she suspected, almost superstitiously, that if she did, it might disappear.

She slumped back in the sofa and closed her eyes.

Oliver. Whenever she closed her eyes at night, he

was there. Whenever she had closed her eyes while making love with a man, he would be there. She always tried to keep her eyes open. It seemed impolite, especially if she was having a good time, to invite Oliver into bed too. It had often tainted perfectly delicious sexual experiences with guilt.

Oliver. She knew every contour of every part of his body. The delicate patch of smooth skin at the small of his back that made him twitch with pleasure when she tickled it, the curve of his shoulder blades, the weight of his body. The silken hairs around each nipple, the boyish chest, the long sweep of muscle from buttock to knee. The smell of him, clean, unperfumed, male. The dry, light touch of his fingers as they stroked the back of her knees, her thighs, that baby soft skin between her legs. His floppy brown curls, silken, resting on her belly. When they made love it was always with the hunger of passion denied, the flooding relief, the exhilaration of finally finding each other again, and coming, yes, yes, yes, together. And afterwards they would lie entwined, and he would stroke her hair from her face and kiss away her tears.

And she would wake up, sobbing, her pillow wet, her body wet, spent and exhausted, strangely satisfied by his phantom presence.

There would never be anyone like Oliver.

CHAPTER 5

There were four huge terracotta pots, a couple of hanging baskets, and eighty litres of multi-purpose compost on her trolley before she considered the question of getting it all home. The garden centre that she had stumbled across in her Sunday morning stroll around South Kensington was a revelation. She was sure that such places hadn't existed when she left England. There certainly hadn't been one in Oxford. She piled on trays of pansies, petunias, lobelia and red geraniums, and individual pots of chives, parsley and rocket, a trowel, a pair of tough garden gloves. She hoped that a kind London taxi driver would take pity on her.

She stood on the Gloucester Road beside her laden trolley for about ten minutes trying to flag down a black cab, then she decided to ring Jonathan. He had his children with him and was delighted with the suggestion of a new kind of outing to amuse them. He didn't think he could stand another museum, even if the kids could, he said, offering to drive over straightaway.

David and Sarah found the garden centre almost as thrilling as Gemma, and Jonathan ended up purchasing some smaller flower pots and some brightly coloured packets of nasturtium seeds as well as a set of children's gardening tools each for them to experiment with.

When they had unloaded Gemma at her little house, she invited them in for tea, but the children were eager to play with their new acquisitions and insisted on staying in the car so that their Daddy could take them back to his garden straightaway.

'I don't think I've ever seen them so happy to spend time with me,' Jonathan said to Gemma, as he carried the purchases through to her back yard. 'I'll ring you when I'm next short of ideas for them!'

She decided to plant the pots first. In the mornings the yard was shady, but towards the late afternoon, Gemma had noticed, some sunlight found its way onto the cobbles. There was just enough room for the pots and a couple of chairs. Gemma planned to eat and work out there in the summer evenings.

In New York she had never had a yard, only a fire escape outside her window in the tiny flat in Minetta Street where she first lived on her own, and nothing, not even a window box, in the Chelsea apartment she shared with Boy.

She put the polystyrene trays of bedding plants into a plastic washing-up bowl and ran some water over them to loosen the soil, then she lined the bottom of the pots with some pieces of broken tile and filled them almost to the brim with compost. In three pots she planted a geranium at the centre, surrounded by petunias. The fourth she kept for the herbs.

The weak sunlight on her face, the slightly acrid odour of geraniums and the feel of the compost under her fingers as she bedded the plants firmly in brought back a memory so clear she could almost smell it.

That too had been an unseasonally warm spring day. On her way back from the pool in Summertown where she swam each Saturday, Gemma had spotted a flower shop with rows of marigolds outside. The golden yellow was so vivid in the sunlight that she had stopped to look at it, and, without really thinking, bought a

71

dozen marigold plants and a couple of taller garden daisies. She put them in her bike basket and cycled back to Boulter Street, feeling rather pleased with herself.

Roger and Kathy were just leaving the house, taking a picnic to the Parks.

'What are you going to plant them in?' Kathy asked sensibly.

Gemma hadn't really thought about that.

'If you make up window boxes, they're bound to get stolen in this area,' Roger had added. 'Seems a bit of a waste of money to me.'

'Well, I'm not asking for a contribution,' Gemma had snapped.

His comments, and the fact that she was so obviously not invited to share their picnic, made her determined to prove him wrong. She had cycled back into town and bought a bag of compost and three green plastic boxes from Woolworths.

She was standing on the bare patch of concrete out front where the dustbins were, totally absorbed in her planting, when she became aware that a passer-by hadn't passed by, but had stopped and was watching her from the other side of the little brick wall on top of which she was working. She could feel, even before she saw his face, that he was smiling.

She looked up and thought, with the clarity of a vision, 'This is the man I am going to marry.'

It was such a strong sensation that she almost felt that she had said the sentence out loud. The way he looked back at her was as if he had heard it. He kept smiling, but his eyes, eyes that were dark brown, but clear, almost translucent, like polished semi-precious stones, flickered with startled curiosity as if his soul had been touched for a second. Some deep undercurrent of recognition had passed between them. It felt like fate.

Why that sentence? Those words rushing through her mind? Marriage wasn't something she had considered, or even speculated childishly about as Daisy had. She couldn't imagine where the thought had come from. Perhaps, she thought, trembling, this is how love at first sight feels.

She realized that she had dropped a marigold plant and was gripping the wall that separated them, as if desperate to cling on to reality and not be swept away in this uncanny, unbalancing sensation.

'I'm Oliver,' he said, 'I hear that you have a room to let?'

She remembered taking him into the hall, catching a glimpse of herself in the mirror, her hair scraped back in an elastic band, not even brushed after her swim, her face streaked with peat. No wonder he's looking at me strangely, she thought. Her hands were covered in compost. It was lodged under her fingernails. She rinsed them under the tap in the kitchen and offered him a coffee.

'I haven't got much time,' he said, 'so shall we just skip the niceties and get on with it?'

It was his brusqueness and confidence rather than his looks that made her realize initially that he was considerably older than she was. She showed him Kathy's bedroom, then hers, then the unusual fish-net bathroom that made him smile again. The front room with its sagging sofa.

'The television is Kathy's, I'm afraid.'

'The one who's moving out?'

'Yes.' She squeezed past him as he stood in the doorway, embarrassed by the closeness.

'And this is the back room,' she said, thinking immediately how silly she sounded.

It was obviously the back room. It was behind the front room, any fool could see that. It was rather dark,

73

as the sun was round the front of the building. Oliver walked in.

'Ever thought of putting a French door in there?' he said, pointing at the window.

'No. Well, I mean, it's not my house, so . . .'

'It would be a great improvement. What do you think? Then we could step right out into the garden.'

'Yes.'

We!

'Can I take you up on your offer of coffee?' he asked, taking a packet of Marlboro from his shirt pocket and offering her a cigarette.

She was trying to work out his accent. It was soft, part-American, part Beatle.

'No, thanks. I don't. I don't mind, of course. My father smokes . . .' She turned away from him and filled a kettle. What was it that kept making her say silly things?

They discussed the rent and the bills.

'Any questions you want to ask?' he finally said.

She didn't know what she was supposed to say. She had never interviewed anyone before. She had only put up the notice about the house on her college notice-board the day before.

'How did you know about the house?'

'I saw your notice,' he said. 'I have a friend at your college. I left a note in your pigeon hole, but then, I was passing, and I saw you outside, so . . .'

'Oh.' Hers was the only all-female college. She felt instantly jealous that some other woman there knew him.

'What are you reading?' she asked him, not even certain that he was a student; his looks and poise made him more the age of a lecturer. But a lecturer would surely have the money for accommodation in a better part of town, she thought.

He understood the question, and began to explain.

He was doing his first degree in law. He had decided to live a little before university, he said, and the look in his eyes invested that simple sentence with sparkle and mystery. He had travelled quite a bit, he said, taking odd jobs around the world, which was why he was the only middle-aged undergraduate.

'Oh, but you don't look middle-aged . . .' she began, realizing only halfway through the sentence that he was teasing her.

'How old are you, actually?' she said, recovering her composure.

'Thirty-two. Does that rule me out? I do like your little house. You've made it very attractive.'

Thirty-two. Her age now, Gemma thought. He had seemed so mature and charming. She wondered if she appeared as grown up now as Oliver had that day.

'No, of course it doesn't rule you out,' she had said, swelling with pride at his compliment. 'I'll get back to you,' she said, feeling she ought not to agree on the spot. 'And,' she hesitated before daring to say it, 'there is one rule. I don't mind people staying the night, but I don't want to live with two people, if you know what I mean?'

Afterwards, she couldn't think why she had said such a silly thing. She almost ran after him up the street. What if he found another place he liked better? What if he changed his mind overnight? What if he thought about it and decided what a bore it would be to live with someone so young? What if he hadn't been real at all?

She hadn't mentioned him to Kathy then. There never seemed a moment to talk to her when Roger wasn't around, and she didn't want to share Oliver with anyone. For the moment, he was her delicious secret. She almost felt that if she talked about him the spell would be broken, and he would disappear into the

75

ether, just as he had materialized from it. She went round to his college later that evening and left a message in his pigeon hole saying that he could move in as soon as the summer vacation started. Then she agonized for a week, not hearing from him, until one day, when she was trying to work in the Upper Reading Room of the Bodleian, she looked up and he was there.

'I thought you might be here,' he said, dragging her away from her books and down to the quad so that he could have a cigarette. 'I've brought you a deposit.'

She had been intending to spend most of the summer at home. Her father had been ill with flu that wouldn't seem to go away, and she knew that he was looking forward to her return. When she made her weekly call from the telephone box outside the Sheldonian, he had suggested that they might work together in his big attic study.

He had another Tusker book to finish urgently. He was months behind deadline and if he didn't finish by July he risked the wrath of Ronald, who desperately wanted the book out by Christmas.

'*Tusker at the Circus*. I'll be quiet, I promise, we will help each other concentrate,' her father said.

'Didn't Tusker go to the circus years ago?' Gemma asked.

'He did, yes, and he enjoyed himself, but these days that's considered ideologically unsound, so he's going again and setting all the other animals free . . . can you believe it? Here's your mother . . .' He passed over the phone.

Estella and Daisy were going on a grand tour of Italy, a trip Estella had planned as a reward for Daisy's A-level results.

'But you don't even know what they are yet!' Gemma pointed out.

'Oh darling, don't be mean. If they're wonderful

76

then she deserves it, and if they're bad, then she'll need a holiday even more . . .' It was the kind of logic Estella had always used where Daisy was concerned.

'And I need a holiday too. It hasn't been very nice for me, you know, with your father always being ill. Do you want to come along, darling?' she added half-heartedly, somehow managing to make Gemma feel guilty on two counts, as if she had been neglecting her father, leaving her mother with all the responsibility, and now she was trying to shirk her duty and spoil her mother's holiday as well.

'No,' Gemma said crossly, wondering how it was that her mother always managed to achieve this effect.

She knew Estella had been planning the trip for months. She couldn't help feeling that she had got the idea from seeing the Merchant Ivory film, *A Room with a View*. Daisy bore an uncanny resemblance to Helena Bonham Carter. It would be her mother's last chance to spoil Daisy before she left home for her year off learning French in Paris, and then university. Gemma knew that her own presence would be seen by Estella as an intrusion, although Daisy begged her to come when she picked up the other receiver.

'Oh, please come, Bisc. Honestly, what am I going to do in the evenings when Mum goes to bed? At least we could go out to discos or something and have some fun.'

'I can't, Dodo,' Gemma had replied, stifling a giggle. She knew that Estella would still be listening in. Daisy must know too. How did she always manage to get away with it? 'I've got a lot of work. It's finals next year.'

'Oh, you are a bore!' said Daisy. It was one of her new words, and much overused at the time. 'Can I come and stay before we go, when term's finished?'

'I think I'll be coming home more or less straightaway,' Gemma had lied immediately.

She had already decided to stay in Oxford for the vacation, and she had found a job working in a pizza restaurant six evenings a week. She wanted to be on her own when Oliver moved in. She didn't know why she couldn't tell them, or why she hadn't mentioned then that she had a new lodger.

Until she met Oliver, Gemma's experience of love had been much the same as that of many other middle-class girls of her age. She had attended an all girls' state school in the small town nearest to Whitton. It had once been a grammar school, and the headmistress was struggling to keep up appearances. Uniform was compulsory, but the way girls rolled up their navy-blue skirts and loosened their red and blue striped ties on their way home probably made them look more provocative than if they had been allowed to wear their own clothes.

School blazers worn too small were *de rigueur* even at weekends in the era of punk rock. All the girls wore badges and safety pins. The most coveted was a set of five brightly coloured buttons from the Ian Dury tour with tiny white writing that read 'sex' 'and' 'drugs' 'and' 'rock and roll'. Gemma had a selection of red and gold enamel pins depicting Lenin, which Bertie had brought back from a British Council trip to Moscow, pinned to her lapel. They had been confiscated by the head-mistress several times, but they were always returned, partly because Gemma wasn't a particularly rebellious girl, and partly because the headmistress had a rather pathetic desire to remain on good terms with Bertie, or indeed anyone she considered remotely famous.

The boys' school was situated at the other side of town. Consequently, joint activities such as drama group, choir and orchestra were massively over-subscribed. The headmistress was proud of her girls' achievements in music, although she seemed to have little idea as to why their results should be so much better than those in the mixed schools in neighbouring towns.

Because she had always idolized her London half-brother, Jonathan, Gemma seemed to miss out on the schoolgirl crush stage of love. Daisy later made up for it. From the age of about eight Daisy's bedroom walls were covered with pictures of horses, but at eleven there was a sudden transformation. The ponies were torn down and discarded, up went footballers, pop stars, film actors. Even Estella was moved to remark, with a critical tone that scarcely masked her pride, that Daisy's walls exhibited extraordinary infidelity in one so young.

Throughout her teens Gemma's room remained as it had always been, decorated with Bertie's illustrations. But underneath her bed lay a clandestine stash of magazines from which Gemma prepared herself for 'relationships'. All the quizzes – Are you a Flirt? Are you the Jealous Type? Are you a Sex Kitten or a Cat? – she filled in meticulously, adding up her marks and soberly noting the results. Gemma spent her pocket money on mud pack facials, hot oil hair conditioners and deodorizing body sprays, all of which seemed to be essential items in the pursuit of love. She practised kissing on her mirror, keeping her eyes open to see what she looked like mid-snog, although when she had her first kiss (Christopher O'Toole at the bus stop after a drama-movement class) she found that the cold glass had not prepared her at all for the warm, slightly slippery sensation of his lips on hers.

After that, she felt qualified to discuss with her classmates whether wet or dry kisses were better, and, in particular, to decide how *far she would go* with a boy. The magazines were little help on this matter. The problem pages issued dire warnings about contraception, and the articles gave plenty of advice about how to attract a man, but there was little guidance on the bit in between.

She was reasonably popular and, at the age of fifteen,

she had been out with six different boys and, she estimated in her diary, had been about seven-eighths of *the way there*. (This figure was rubbed out and changed to five-eighths a year later when Gemma lost her virginity.)

In the sixth form, Gemma went steady with Mick Lancaster, who was generally judged to be the best-looking boy in the drama group. Mick had slept with a girl when he was fifteen on a French exchange trip, and reckoned himself pretty *au fait* with sex and Jean-Paul Sartre. Mick liked to discuss existentialism and listen to Joy Division. Gemma went to bed with him under the black sheets of his single bed one Sunday afternoon when his parents were at Mass. It seemed very wicked and felt rather painful. They tried again a few times, once in the trees that fringed his father's golf course, but Gemma began to find the experience, which seemed to be more about rebellion than tenderness, increasingly depressing. She left him for the Head Boy, Mark Walton, who was good at sport and had read about foreplay. They made half-hearted promises to write to each other when she went to Oxford, and he to Loughborough, but neither of them ever got round to it.

At Oxford, Gemma had quite a passionate relationship in her first term with a guy she met at a Freshers' party, but it turned out that he was in love with a girl who was still in the sixth form of his public school, and he was only passing the time with Gemma, until Miranda joined him the next year at Oxford. After that, there were a couple of one night stands and a number of dinner dates that Gemma decided not to pursue any further (men from Merton, which was well-known to serve the best food, seemed to think that dinner in hall should earn them sexual desserts).

So when Kathy and Roger became a nauseatingly lovey-dovey couple in the second term of the second year, Gemma didn't feel jealous *per se* (Do you fancy your friend's bloke? YES/NO. Definitely NO. Score 1 point), but on occasion, watching Kathy's television, when they were sitting on the sofa together and she was in the armchair, she did feel it might be nice to feel that way about *someone*.

Then Oliver walked into her life and he made all the boyfriends she had ever had seem hopelessly immature.

Oliver knew a lot. He had lived. He taught her how to cook, what films were good, what writers she should read, what art she should admire, what was bourgeois.

When she finally went home at Christmas, her family found that few of Gemma's sentences were not preceded by the words 'Oliver says . . .'

'Who is bloody Oliver?' Daisy asked over dinner one night, rudely posing a question neither Bertie nor Estella had yet dared to ask.

'He's this amazing guy that lives with me,' Gemma had replied triumphantly.

'Kathy's moved out, has she?' Bertie asked, gently.

'Yes.'

'Darling, how lovely!' said Estella. 'Why haven't you told us you're living with someone?'

'Because it's not like that,' Gemma snapped. She hated Estella automatically jumping to conclusions.

'Oh.' Estella looked histrionically disappointed, which annoyed Gemma even more.

'It's not like *that*, either,' Gemma said. 'God, why do you have to be so bloody conventional?'

Estella looked, for once in her life, genuinely surprised. It was probably the first time that she had ever been called conventional. It stung.

Gemma looked around the kitchen table, at her father in his corduroy trousers and checked Viyella shirt, at her mother in a shapeless camel jersey dress, her strings of ethnic beads and the cloud of heavy perfume that hung around her, and thought how very *bourgeois* they were. Particularly her mother, who loved to spend huge quantities of money on herself, but pronounced herself a socialist. She had been reasonably proud of her parents when she was at school, even though they did embarrassing things like going off on Ban the Bomb marches, when that sort of protest had been long overtaken by a kind of stylish anarchy. But now that she knew Oliver, they suddenly seemed hopelessly middle class, rather like anyone else's parents.

Oliver didn't like to talk much about his background, but she gathered from little bits of information he dropped into the conversation, and which she fell on like a bird on a crumb, that he had grown up in Liverpool poverty and had run away to sea when he was eighteen. A gypsy life to go with his gypsy looks. He had seen the world. He was highly intelligent and, because he was completely self-taught, his views on all sorts of things seemed to Gemma to be more relevant than other people's. He had got through life on his natural wit. Everything he had done was touched by a kind of glamour. Everything she had ever done in her life seemed, by contrast, utterly ordinary. After she met Oliver, Gemma's life became an unending challenge to win his approval.

Sometimes, she felt she had pleased him. He would look at her fondly, or stroke her hair roughly, leaving the skin at the back of her neck tingling for hours afterwards. He had worker's hands, square and hard, not soft boy's hands. Once, he came back late from a party and found her asleep on the sofa. (She wasn't actually asleep, but pretending, in case he should suspect, rightly, that she was waiting up for him.) He bent down and kissed her gently on the mouth. As he stood up, she felt that he was watching her with love, as one might watch a sleeping child. She had yearned for him to go on kissing her and for her to wake up drowsily, pretending only to half-know what was happening, and for them to make love there on the floor of the front room.

When it finally happened, she thought, it would be like that, both of them falling into sex, overtaken by mutual attraction. It had to be. Ever since he had first looked at her, she knew it must happen.

She couldn't talk about her attraction to him. She had no vocabulary. Sometimes she felt inadequate, like one of the middle-class girls in those black and white films from the Sixties that Oliver so admired, the girl whom the working-class hero shouted at constantly, punishing her for her privilege and shallow sensibilities. Not that Oliver ever shouted at her, but his temper lurked darkly around him, and sometimes there were outbursts, perfectly understandable ones. If she tried to please him too much, it irritated him. Once he had expressed a liking for Marmite soldiers when she asked him what he wanted for tea.

'I could live on Marmite melting into hot toast,' he said, making it sound the most mouth-watering dish.

For days after that she made him Marmite toast to go with his tea in the morning, and offered him Marmite toast when he came back from the library, until he smiled his peculiar angry smile at her and said, 'For God's sake, Gemma, you really know how to spoil a good thing, don't you?'

That sentence stayed with her for days, and she invested it with wider significance and tortured herself with it, not knowing how to make amends.

Her love for Oliver was physically painful. There was a kind of tension in her stomach whenever he was around. If she sat next to him on the sofa, she ached for him, her thighs twitching to be spread, a hollowness, a void at the top of her legs craving to be filled.

He never brought any other women home. He never

talked about a girlfriend, although his reminiscences about the faraway islands and territories he had visited were peppered with exotic women. He talked with particular relish about a female doctor who had removed his appendix in Bermuda and proposed to him as the anaesthetic was wearing off. Gemma knew that she couldn't compete with such women, but, she consoled herself, he had chosen to live with her, and they generally got along very well.

And there had been that first look. She was sure he had felt it too.

She was good to him, she kept the house clean, and tidied up the Sunday papers that he threw around the front room. He appreciated these things. She knew by the way he smiled at her and patted her head sometimes.

When she finally decided to discuss her dilemma with Kathy, they agreed that he must have a problem about commitment. Kathy also thought that he might not want anything to interfere with the harmonious relationship they enjoyed in the last term before finals. Perhaps it was too precious to jeopardize, she suggested. Sex, especially the kind of explosive passionate sex they were bound to have, might be a distraction, and Oliver had often stated his intention of getting a First. They resolved that Gemma should be patient. After finals, if nothing had happened, then she might pounce.

In the Bodleian, she sometimes caught herself staring into space, imagining herself and Oliver making love. He would come in while she was selecting a book from a high shelf. She would suddenly feel her legs being stroked as she stood on a library ladder, she would slide down the ladder into his arms, and he would carry her out past the rows of students, their heads down, pretending not to see. As soon as they reached the stone staircase of this ancient building they would not be able to hold themselves back any longer. The cold stone steps would press into her back, her head snapping back as he kissed her, the smell of hundreds of years of dust mixed with his sweat.

She must have been glowing with a kind of sexual anticipation, because she started receiving single red roses and notes on her desk whenever she popped out of the library for lunch or tea. The first time it happened, her heart leapt for a second, allowing herself to think . . . but, she reasoned, it just wasn't the sort of thing that Oliver would do. Finally, a perfectly nice looking boy from Trinity revealed himself as her admirer. She thanked him, said she was a bit too busy for a drink, or even coffee, in his college, and tried to fight back the tears of utter dejection that it really wasn't Oliver after all.

In New York, it had been easier to forget. She had only once heard a Liverpool accent in New York, and it was a woman's voice. Here on the tube she picked out those strange vowel sounds every day.

When she decided to come home, she was certain that she had forgotten the pain of losing Oliver. It had been replaced by another, more profound, pain.

It wasn't true, she thought, pressing soil round the roots of the last geranium. The wound that had been plastered over with years of dressing was still open and raw underneath. Nothing she had ever felt for a man came close to what she had felt, still did feel, for Oliver.

CHAPTER 6

The phone was ringing as Gemma opened the door, reminding her that she must get an answering machine. It had been a long day. All she wanted to do was take a cool bath, drink a lot of ice cold water, cook the fresh pasta she had managed to buy just as the local delicatessen was closing, and eat it, before dropping into her cool white cotton bed. She had been on the phone so much that afternoon, she felt she had the imprint of a handset on the right side of her face.

She put the brown paper bag of provisions on the kitchen table, and dumped her manuscript bag on the sofa. Still the phone rang. She stared at it, willing it to be quiet, then gave up the fight, pulled the large pearl clip from her right ear and picked up the receiver.

'Gemma?'

'Hi Kathy. Sorry, I just got in from work.' Gemma slunk down on the sofa next to her manuscript bag, and began toying with a stray piece of cotton from the stitching in the canvas.

'It's nearly ten o'clock. Is that normal?'

'Well, it was my first day . . . I was in meetings all morning, and I didn't get a chance to look at the paperwork until after six.'

'You sound worn out. I'll talk to you some other time. Really. It can wait.'

'No. It's lovely to hear you.' If it had been anyone other than Kathy this would have been a lie. 'What's up?'

'Nothing. Nothing really. Listen, you get an early night. Are you in tomorrow? I'll talk to you then.'

Beneath Kathy's soothing tone, Gemma knew that there was an urgency in her voice. Kathy wanted to talk.

'Kathy . . . you've got me intrigued now. What is it?'

She heard a sigh at the other end of the phone.

'I don't even know whether I should be calling, Gem. It's just . . . it's just I ran into Daisy today in Camden Sainsburys . . .'

'Oh.'

'Gem. She didn't even know you were back. I'm sorry if I put my foot in it, but she was really upset . . . I thought you ought to know . . .'

There was a long, cold, silence.

'Yeah, well thanks, Kathy. Listen, I think I will ring you tomorrow, if that's OK.'

Gemma's business voice, calm, chill, unreachable.

'Why don't you come round here for supper, Gem. Roger's out 'til late,' Kathy persisted.

'OK, then.' Gemma was too tired to put up any resistance.

She put down the phone feeling slightly nauseous. Her stomach turned a flip of pleasure on top of the persistent acid of guilt. Uncomfortably, the pleasure came at imagining Daisy upset. Gemma had a fleeting vision of her sister standing with a wire shopping basket next to a wall-freezer stuffed with bags of oven-bake chips, in tears. She felt a sting of triumph that she possessed the power to hurt her. The guilt was always there. It was a kind of background noise in everything she did.

Daisy seemed to be closing in on her. She had only to open a glossy women's magazine to find her byline. Patrick employed her, now Kathy . . .

Gemma put the pasta in the fridge. Her appetite had disappeared. She pulled a manuscript out of her bag and started reading.

At four o'clock in the morning she woke up shivering with cold, her neck stiff from its unaccustomed angle on the sofa. She heaved herself upstairs and flopped on her bed, but sleep wouldn't come again. She spent the rest of the night trying to find a comfortable position, trying to think of boring subjects to outwit her racing, headachy mind. Eventually, at about six o'clock, she gave up the fight, took a brisk shower and set off walking to work.

The air was crisp and blue, the avenues bright white with flowering cherries, their leaves lime green in the morning sunshine. She arrived at work before the security guard and had a cappuccino in the sandwich bar on the corner of the street. The caffeine shot through her like a jolt of electricity. She managed to go through all the letters in her tray and dictate a thirty-minute tape before her secretary, Sally, arrived.

Her first lunch with the sales reps seemed to go on for ever. Gemma slunk wearily back to her office in the late afternoon, the lack of sleep beginning to catch up with her.

On her desk was a pile of manuscripts and an enormous hand-tied bouquet of lilies.

'What on earth?' Gemma said out loud as she smelt the exotic perfume.

'There's a card attached.' Sally was obviously as curious to know who the sender was.

'Yes, OK, thank you, Sally,' Gemma dismissed her, wanting to open the little white envelope in private.

The message was simple.

'Good luck with the new job, Ralph.'

She was about to pick up the phone to ring *Sixpack* and find out his number when it rang.

'So how's it going and why haven't you called?' asked Meryl, direct as ever.

'Fine,' Gemma replied, surprising herself by adding, 'well, actually, it's more difficult than I thought it would be.'

'Work?'

'No, I don't know. It's too early to say,' Gemma replied. 'No, work actually seems normal. It's the rest. I feel kind of isolated . . .'

'It's only been a couple of weeks.'

'I know, I know, it's just . . . I kind of find I don't know how to talk to people here . . .'

'Men?'

Gemma looked at the lilies on her desk. Sweet smelling gouts of pollen had fallen in little amber avalanches onto her papers, staining them orange. Before she had a chance to answer, Meryl found she had a call from the president of the company waiting.

'Listen, I've got to run,' she said. 'Talk to you soon.'

Gemma glanced at her watch. It was five-thirty. She suddenly remembered that she was meant to be going to Kathy's for an inquisition about Daisy. She had meant to cancel, but the prospect didn't seem so bad now. Even a brief conversation with Meryl had lifted her mood.

'Zoe is demanding you read her a story in lieu of hush money.' Kathy opened the oven door and took out an earthenware pot. She lifted the lid and the fragrance of herbs and red wine wafted over to Gemma.

Gemma looked at her quizzically.

'I told her that we wanted a bit of peace and quiet,' Kathy explained. 'I should have known better. You know, I'm not sure whether I believe in all this negotiating with kids.'

'But doesn't she read herself?' Gemma asked.

'Of course she does, but I made the mistake of explaining what you do – she's very interested in women's careers at the moment, they're doing a project at school, and they didn't have a publisher – and then I happened to mention your father . . . I'm afraid she went and got out all her *Biscuit and Donut* books. She always loved them . . .'

Gemma sighed. 'Well, since dinner smells so delicious and I'm ravenous, I'll do it. But only one book. How do I negotiate that, do you think?'

'I thought you were good at doing deals,' Kathy said, replacing the lid on the casserole and putting it back in the oven.

The front of the doll's house was open and Zoe was crouched behind it.

'Hi there,' Gemma greeted her, looking over the top of the roof.

'Last time you were here, you said that you wanted to play with it.'

'So I did. Well-remembered. But I thought, missy, that you were supposed to be in bed?'

'I'm all ready,' Zoe stood up. She was wearing sea-green pyjamas with fish on.

'Teeth brushed?'

'Of course. What happened to your doll's house?' Zoe asked as she jumped into bed.

Gemma was kneeling on the floor. She began to pick up the dolls, smoothing down their clothes and kissing each one good night before she put them into bed in the upstairs rooms of the house.

It was a nice doll's house, Arts and Crafts-style architecture with a gable. Inside, it was not too tastefully furnished. There was a mixture of expensive miniature period furniture as well as some garish plastic modern pieces, a bit like the style of Kathy's kitchen. Some of the dolls were slightly too big, out of proportion. Gemma would never have tolerated them in her doll's house.

'Well, let me see,' said Gemma, 'I think it must have been given away to another little girl . . .'

In fact, she could remember the event precisely.

She had come home one afternoon from school to find an empty corner in her bedroom. Estella had unilaterally decided to give away the doll's house and all its contents to a charity auction one of her artist friends was running in London. Everything was gone, even the dresser with the plates that Gemma had spent days making out of bottle tops, bashing her fingers as she flattened them out with a hammer, then painting them with white enamel and tiny blue flowers.

'But you're far too old for it, and so is Daisy,' Estella had said, as Gemma wailed her protests. 'And don't you want to help the starving children in Africa?'

'That's not the point,' Gemma could remember herself screaming, 'it was mine. If I wanted to give it away it should have been my decision.' She resented the way that Estella was trying to turn the issue into one of her selfishness.

'How did I ever manage to produce such materialistic children?' Estella had said, swanning out of the room, leaving in her wake a waft of Shalimar.

Gemma closed the front of the house. 'Goodnight, all of you!' she said softly to the dolls.

Zoe giggled.

'Now where's this story you want me to read?' Gemma asked.

'Here. I can't decide which one,' Zoe replied. She was holding several worn copies of the *Biscuit and Donut* books like a fan in her hands.

'Well, you must choose one, otherwise I won't read any,' said Gemma, beginning to understand how Zoe's mind operated.

'OK then. *Biscuit and Donut in the Snow*.' Zoe handed it to her.

How ironic, thought Gemma, that she should choose that book. She began reading the familiar words.

The picture on the first page showed the two dolls, one tall and floppy rag doll with pale gold hair ('the colour of a rich tea biscuit' Estella had remarked when Gemma was little, and the name had stuck), one small roly poly doll with round red cheeks and dark brown curls ('Daisy's as round as a donut'). In the background was a Georgian-style doll's house with a shiny red door.

Donut was the naughty younger doll who got into scrapes. Biscuit was the older, more sensible, doll who sorted things out.

The story that Zoe had chosen for her to read, even though it was apparent that she knew it off by heart, was about a freak snow-storm that came to the nursery where the dolls lived.

. . . While Biscuit was in bed resting she heard a strange sound, and when she got up to look out of the window she saw that a great white cloud had descended on the garden. She thought that winter must have come, so she put on her warmest clothes and went out to investigate.

Donut was nowhere to be seen.

The roof of the house had turned white and all around the house the garden which normally had flowers and birds in it (and looked rather like an intricately woven Persian carpet, thought Gemma) *had disappeared under a thick blanket of whiteness.*

It was quite eerie.

'Why are you crying?' Zoe interrupted.

'I'm not,' said Gemma.

'Well, your eyes are all watery. They're blinking with tears,' Zoe said knowingly.

'Well, I suppose that this has brought back some memories,' Gemma explained, 'nice memories . . . you see when I was little, I was very like Biscuit, and my sister was very like Donut. She was naughty, but nobody really minded because she was so funny and pretty, and she laughed such a lot . . .'

Zoe lay back in bed, obviously enjoying this story much more.

'I told you I had a doll's house? Well, it was a beautiful doll's house and I made lots of furniture for it and looked after it very well. I was a careful child, you see. Well, one day, Daisy . . .'

'Is Daisy the same as Donut?'

'Well, sort of, yes . . . Daisy was learning about the seasons at school, and she thought that the dolls ought to know about the seasons too. So she took a great big can of talcum powder from the bathroom . . . like baby powder, you know? . . . and she poured it all over the doll's house. Everything was white . . .'

'Just like in the book?'

'Yes, and it smelt of perfume.'

'Just like the snow in the book?'

'Yes.'

'And it wouldn't melt and it took ages and ages for Biscuit to clean up?' Zoe continued eagerly.

'I'm afraid it did,' said Gemma.

She had been furious. The doll's house had been her birthday present and Daisy had ruined it within a couple of days. Time and time again, her father had assured his distraught older daughter that she hadn't done it deliberately. Daisy was only five. She was only playing, he had said. Estella couldn't understand what all the fuss was about. She hoovered up the floor and wiped down the roof, but she didn't seem to see that the doll's house was never quite the same afterwards,

93

however much Gemma spring-cleaned it and tried to get the dust out of the corners using cotton wool buds. From then on it always exuded a slightly sickly smell of cheap scent. Daisy said it made her feel sick, which at least meant that she stayed away from it.

'Did you put her up to that, Kathy?' Gemma asked, only half-jokingly, as she came downstairs.

'What?'

'Getting me to talk about Daisy. I hope you're not going to be trying your counselling techniques on me. They don't work. I tried once in New York . . .'

'You had therapy in New York?'

'Yeah. One session. Everyone seemed to be having it – a bit like everyone seemed to be worrying about sodium in their mineral water – so I thought I'd try it too.'

'What happened?' Kathy handed her a glass of wine.

'I sat in silence for an hour, then handed over eighty bucks. I felt that spending the money on a manicure would be better value and probably more therapeutic. So that's what I did after that.'

Kathy looked instinctively at Gemma's nails. They were perfectly clean but unvarnished.

'Yeah, well, I haven't had time to check out Elizabeth Arden since I've been here,' Gemma admitted.

Kathy laughed.

'I'm not trying to counsel you,' she said. 'I wouldn't dare. I just thought you might want to talk about Daisy. I mean, you're bound to bump into her one of these days. You can't go on pretending that she doesn't exist.'

'I know. I know. What is this?' Gemma asked, as Kathy ladled out the casserole onto the heap of mashed potato. 'It looks delicious.'

'It's beef stewed in red wine with juniper berries,' Kathy said.

'When did you become such a good cook?' Gemma asked admiringly.

'I did a course when Zoe was little. It seemed about the only recreational activity Rog was prepared to fork out for, since he would be benefiting too.'

Gemma noted that there was a degree of bitterness in her voice.

'Are you and Rog OK?' she asked.

'Yes. Well . . . look, don't start me, Gemma, it's you that we're meant to be talking about.'

Kathy began to describe her chance encounter with Daisy. It wasn't the first time she had bumped into her in Sainsburys. Since the Camden branch had opened it had become a kind of social Mecca for housewives, she said, the place where one saw one's friends most often.

'Not that Daisy's a friend, really,' Kathy added.

'Or a housewife. I can't imagine Daisy slaving over a hot stove.'

'You might be surprised. When did you last see her? Before you left? She was only eighteen then, Gem. Late twenties is a lot different from late teens.'

'What's she like now?'

'Oh, I don't know. Still very beautiful. Not as round and curvy as I remember. Not as open, maybe. But I never really knew her.'

Daisy had stayed a couple of weekends in their second year when they had the house in Boulter Street. Although she was four years younger than Gemma, she looked just as old, if not older. Whereas Gemma had gone through all the stages of adolescence and puberty quite gradually, Daisy, at the age of thirteen had made the change from roly poly little girl to mature woman in a matter of months. Her face had always been beautiful, and old for its years, and her hair had always been dark and abundant like her mother's. Daisy was very much Estella's little girl. Beside them, Gemma, with the more fragile fair looks that she inherited from her father, looked washed out, insubstantial.

Daisy was spoilt and naughty, but she had always had a bouncy open character, and her dimply smile was irresistible. Given the attention and praise Daisy enjoyed from the moment of her birth, it was surprising that Gemma didn't feel perpetually jealous. But Gemma was as enchanted by Daisy as everyone else, and until she was much older, it never occurred to her to do anything other than try to please her little sister. And just as Daisy was her mother's obvious favourite, so Gemma was her father's. Gemma's serious and measured approach to life suited his quieter temperament. Her interest in his work delighted him. Daisy never seemed to have the patience to concentrate on his stories for more than a minute.

Gemma remembered going to a party in New College with Kathy one weekend when Daisy was staying with them. She and Daisy had been very close then. Daisy hung on her every word, taking hip phrases from Gemma's vocabulary and using them repeatedly. Gemma was often exasperated by Daisy's ability to manipulate a situation to her own advantage, but she loved her fervently and always rose to her defence like a protective she-wolf if anyone dared to criticize Daisy's antics.

It must have been before Kathy met Roger, Gemma thought. Because they were both on the look-out for attractive men. She and Kathy always attracted a fair amount of interest, but, with Daisy alongside, they had both felt totally eclipsed. Men swarmed around Daisy like bees around honey.

Gemma had been slightly shocked and protective,

whispering to Kathy, 'She's only sixteen. I don't think she's had a boyfriend.'

She could remember Kathy's look of disbelief. It was clear to everyone, she said, that Daisy knew exactly where she was with men. Touching it may be, but she was sure that Gemma's concern was misplaced.

'I never really knew what went wrong between you two,' Kathy was saying.

The question seemed casual, but Gemma knew that it was unresolved business that had hung between them for some time. Ever since that evening in New York, when Kathy had casually asked how Daisy was and Gemma had replied that she had no idea.

A silence had fallen on the table, then Boy had said, 'Who's Daisy?' and Kathy had known that something was terribly wrong. She had looked across the table at Gemma, her eyes seeking an explanation, but Gemma had looked down at the menu and made some joke about life being too short to bone a quail. It had seemed too intimate a subject to explain there in the restaurant, and, after that, Gemma remembered, there never seemed to be a moment when she was on her own with Kathy. Perhaps she had engineered it that way, she thought now.

'We fell out. After finals,' Gemma began, in a clipped voice. 'I was really pissed off with the way she behaved towards my father. She knew he was dying, but she's so selfish, she hardly went to see him. And then afterwards, Estella was going off the rails, she needed Daisy there, but no, she was so tied up in her new relationship, she didn't help at all. I had to do everything. And then I realized that I had always done everything. Daisy had always got her own way. She was just unforgivably selfish. When Estella died, I

97

decided I didn't want to have anything to do with her anymore.'

She had made this little speech on several occasions. It was what she had told Boy when he pressed her about her sister, and Meryl. It sounded good enough, plausible. It had the advantage of being true, as far as it went, and, well, that was as far as anyone else needed to know.

But Kathy knew her too well to be taken in by this well-rehearsed version. 'It seems such a shame,' she said, disingenuously, 'you were so close. It must have been an awful shock for both of you to suddenly lose both parents . . . I mean, it seems so sad that you couldn't comfort each other . . .'

'We didn't *lose* both,' Gemma said, trying to divert the subject, 'Bertie died of cancer. Estella killed herself. It was her decision. Anyway, don't you see? Daisy wasn't capable of comforting me. Why should I always be the one?' she asked, her voice rising, her eyes giving up the fight against tears.

'Have you ever really grieved, Gem?' Kathy asked gently.

'I cried when Bertie died,' Gemma said. 'It was so sudden. The day before finals, he came up to Oxford with a bunch of roses he had picked from the garden for me. He seemed tired, but fine. The day after finals, I spoke to him and he told me he wasn't very well. I went home straightaway. I arrived at the same time as the ambulance. He had known for three weeks. The doctor had given him six months at the most. The thing I most regret, I think, is those weeks when he knew and he didn't tell me. He didn't want to upset me before my exams, you see.'

A tear had escaped Gemma's left eye and was rolling slowly down her cheek. Kathy watched it, its lonely rivulet, and she reached across the table and put her hand on Gemma's clenched fist.

'How long did he live after that?' she asked.

'Just ten days. He had secondary tumours everywhere. They didn't even begin chemotherapy. It was straight on to morphine. I saw him every day. Estella and I were with him when he died.'

'And Daisy?'

'She came to see him once. She brought him a bunch of daisies, probably filched from my window box.' Gemma let out a wry chuckle. 'I remember her telling him that when he looked at them he could think of her. He tried to explain that he was really very ill, but she wouldn't have it. I tried to tell her too, but she said we were being defeatist, upsetting Estella. With that kind of attitude, she said, he'd never get better.' Gemma shook her shoulders, as if trying to shrug off the bad feelings.

'Perhaps she didn't understand, or perhaps she was denying it . . . not wanting to admit it,' Kathy suggested.

'Well, maybe . . . but I was sick of making excuses for her, Kathy. I'd had enough.'

'And then Estella committed suicide . . .' Kathy led her on.

'Yes. That's where Daisy gets her selfishness from, of course. Estella was so selfish. God, she couldn't even bear to be the one who hadn't died. Suddenly Bertie was the centre of attention and she couldn't stand it.'

'Oh come on, Gem. That's too hard, isn't it?' Kathy said, shocked.

Gemma shrugged again and looked at the ceiling, as if by holding her face at an angle the tears would cease to fall.

'I know you'll hate me saying it,' Kathy continued tentatively, 'but I've studied bereavement a bit at my Relate training, because sometimes the stages people go through are similar when a marriage breaks up. I

99

think that you're still very angry with Estella. Anger is one of the first stages you have to get through, and you obviously haven't gone through it . . .'

Gemma bristled.

'And maybe you're transferring that anger on to Daisy, Gem,' she suggested. 'You need to express it to her, you know, before you can start to forgive her . . .'

'I'm not sure I want to forgive her,' Gemma said.

'What? For your mother's death? You can't honestly blame Daisy for that, can you?' Kathy took a deep breath. 'Or are we talking about something else?' she continued resolutely. 'Are we really talking about what happened on the day you finished finals?'

CHAPTER 7

The night before her final exam, Oliver cooked dinner. He didn't prepare food very often, but when he did it was always a complicated dish involving very precise ingredients that the manager of the local Spar had never even heard of. Grumbling, Oliver would borrow Gemma's bike and pedal off towards North Oxford where there was a delicatessen, and she would wait anxiously in case he returned empty-handed to spend the evening complaining about the provincial quality of English cuisine.

That evening, Oliver had decided to introduce her to *vitello tonnato*. It had taken him the entire day. She had been upstairs revising, but each time she came down to their tiny kitchen to replenish her mug of coffee, or take a can of Coke from the fridge, he was occupied with a different element of the dish.

A perfectly lean piece of veal was roasted and left to cool. A box of eggs and a bottle of thick, dark, olive oil became a great yellow drift of mayonnaise in their glass salad bowl. A tin of tuna and a tin of anchovies were drained and mashed. Oliver sharpened a carving knife and cut thin pieces from the meat and began to layer it in a pie dish with the other ingredients.

'Oh Christ!' he shouted suddenly, making Gemma jump back from the sink and drop the coffee mug she had been rinsing.

'What is it?' she asked, terrified that he had cut himself with the knife.

'Capers,' he said, 'I've forgotten the bloody capers!'

'I'm sure it will be lovely without them,' she said, uncertainly.

'It'll be a disaster without them,' he corrected her, sullenly. 'Can I borrow your bike?'

Gemma went back upstairs. She was nervous about the last exam. The rest had gone almost too well. This was the one she had prepared for least. All the caffeine she had taken in was making her feel light-headed and a little sick. She wondered apprehensively whether she would actually be able to stomach the meal Oliver had taken so much trouble over. She found it impossible to imagine what the strange combination of foods would taste like.

It was delicious, of course. Oliver's cooking always was. He insisted she have just a little glass of red wine, and that seemed to cut through the richness. He had put the kitchen table out into the back yard and they sat there eating and chatting, until long after the sun had gone in. Oliver went up to his room and brought down a couple of candles stuck into old wine bottles, but it was too breezy and they wouldn't keep alight.

'Nothing beats eating *al fresco*,' Oliver said.

He raised his glass, 'Good luck tomorrow, Gemma.'

'I shall need it.'

'It's a pity I never got around to making that French door,' Oliver said, nodding at the window of the back room.

'Well, the weather hasn't really been nice enough to eat out until this week,' Gemma replied.

She thought she could detect a grin flitting across his face in the gloom. Why, she asked herself, did she always manage to make obvious comments in response to his imaginative ones.

'The end of an era,' she said, wistfully, trying to put as much depth and mystery into her voice as possible. 'Tomorrow all this will be over,' she added, trying to elicit a response.

'Why do you say that?' Oliver asked, never able to let a platitude go untested.

'Well, exams . . . I mean . . . it's the end of Oxford, the dreaming spires, all that . . .' Gemma stammered.

'Artifice, all of it,' Oliver pronounced. 'It's the people you meet who matter . . . they go on . . .'

The words hung in the warm, dark air.

After a while, Gemma said, standing up, 'Well, I'll just do the washing up.'

She went into their little kitchen and sighed. Oliver's characteristic mess. He seemed to have used every kitchen implement they possessed. The sink was full of oily pans and bowls. She turned on the hot water tap, feeling suddenly impossibly sad. This would probably be the last time she cleared up after Oliver. Oxford had made it possible for them to meet and live together, because that was the sort of place it was. In the great big world outside they would drift apart and he would forget all about her.

Gemma wiped her eyes with the tea towel.

'What's the problem?' he asked, standing very close behind her.

She turned round and said, 'I don't want it to end, Oliver . . .'

He put his arms round her, gently. 'Hey!' he whispered, 'hey, love, don't cry.' He put his forefinger under her chin and tilted it upwards.

'Hey,' he said softly, as if talking to a child, 'you'll spoil your pretty face.'

She laughed a little through her tears.

'That's better,' he said, then drew her towards him, pushing her face against his shoulder, and patting her on her back. 'There, there,' he said soothingly.

She wanted to stay for ever with her face resting against his warm cotton T-shirt, smelling the light clean trace of washing powder. She could feel his slow measured breathing against her cheek.

I love you, I love you, I love you, she wanted to tell him. It was like a mantra in her head, becoming more and more insistent.

What had she got to lose, she asked herself, suddenly feeling reckless.

She raised her head from his shoulder to look into his face at the same instant he looked down at her.

'I . . . I . . .' she started to say.

Then he kissed her.

It was just a delicate kiss. A light brushing of lips.

He drew back and looked at her again. A quizzical look. She didn't know what it meant.

Please . . . she wanted to say.

Her nipples had become hard under the loose T-shirt dress she was wearing.

He bent and kissed her again. This time for a fraction longer. She responded with her whole self, throwing her arms around his neck, pulling him towards her.

She could feel a wet line across the small of her back where her dress was dipping in the washing-up water. The mixer tap was jammed between her shoulder blades. She held her breath as Oliver's hand felt between her legs, and he smiled, discovering how wet she was. Without saying anything, he lifted her so that she was sitting on the edge of the sink, unzipped his jeans and thrust himself into her.

She gasped. Oh my God, it was happening! Oliver was inside her and it was gorgeous. She locked her ankles underneath his buttocks and pulled him into her, deeper, harder, her hands gripping the draining board, the veins in her arms standing out with the effort. She wanted to be good at it. She wanted him to think she was the best he had ever had.

His chin was wedged over her shoulder. She couldn't see his face but she could hear him beginning to moan right next to her ear. He was going to come. He was going to come inside her.

'Yes . . .' he said, 'yes, yes, yes . . .'

She began to move with his rhythm, bucking with each thrust, delighting in giving him pleasure. Then at the last moment, she threw her head back and looked into his face. His eyes rolled back.

He's in ecstasy, she thought triumphantly, and I have taken him there.

And then she felt him shudder inside her, and she imagined his essence seeping into every vessel of her body, as if she were soaking him up like a sponge.

'Mmmm,' he said, withdrawing after a few seconds, and kissing her nose, 'you *are* lovely.'

Oddly, she felt too embarrassed to watch him pull up his jeans, and zip up his flies. She turned round and squirted washing-up liquid into the sink.

I love you, she wanted to say.

'I'm on the Pill,' she told the kitchen window.

'Good girl,' Oliver said distractedly, then he picked up the local newspaper and took it into the front room.

When she had tidied up the kitchen, Gemma followed him. He had fallen asleep on the sofa. He looked happy and peaceful. She gently took the paper from his hands in case the rustle of it should wake him, then she adjusted the cushion under his head, turned off the television and switched out the light.

Even though she wanted more than anything to spend the whole night making love, it was almost a relief that he had fallen asleep before she could join him. It would be easy enough to be patient for a few hours. She still had revision to do, and she felt energized. She was even more determined now not to make a mess of the last exam.

There was no urgency anymore, she assured herself, checking the stickiness between her legs, the evidence that she hadn't imagined it. After the next day, they could spend as much time as they wanted to in bed together.

Tomorrow, she thought excitedly, it will all be over, and it will all be beginning.

Ever since Daisy had heard that Oxford tradition demanded finalists should be greeted after their last exam with champagne outside Schools, she had always planned to meet Gemma when she finished. Because of this, she returned a little early from her year in France where she had been working as an assistant. She hadn't seen her sister in all that time. It was the longest they had been separated, ever. Daisy thought it would be lovely to surprise Gemma, and it also might be fun to join in the celebrations afterwards. Gemma had told Bertie when she last called that the exams were going better than expected. She and some friends planned to hire a punt afterwards.

'Don't drink too much and fall in the Cherwell,' her father had said, adding that he had just put a cheque in the post to cover refreshments.

It was a beautiful summer morning when Daisy prepared to set out from Whitton. She was wearing a floppy straw sun hat and a simple white cotton dress with white embroidery on it. She went to kiss her father goodbye. He looked up from a drowsy sleep and smiled delightedly when he saw her. 'You look like a beautiful summer nymph,' he said.

When he heard that she was intending to hitchhike, he insisted that she take enough money from his desk drawer for the train fair, plus a taxi ride to the station.

Daisy helped herself to the cash, and a little more, fully intending to hitchhike anyway.

She got a lift to Aylesbury almost immediately. A woman driver with a daughter the same age as Daisy worried what would become of such a beautiful girl hitchhiking across country. Daisy assured her that she would get a bus from Aylesbury onwards, but as she was standing at the bus-stop, a guy in an open-top red sports car drew up alongside her, and, well, she couldn't resist. The driver was late for a meeting in Oxford, so he drove deliciously fast and didn't bother her too much when he let her out. He seemed quite happy with the false telephone number she had given him, and said he would call very soon.

Seeing that the front room window of the house in Boulter Street was slightly open, Daisy climbed over the window boxes, accidentally knocking one to the ground where its display of yellow and white flowers burst out onto the concrete in an explosion of earth. Once inside, she went into the hall, opened the front door to collect the canvas bag she had left outside, and came face-to-face with a man holding a pint of milk in one hand and a key in the other.

'Who are you?' she asked him.

'I'm Oliver,' he replied, stifling his amusement. 'I live here. And who are you?'

'Oh, *merde!*' Daisy pulled a face, 'I'm Daisy. Won't you come in?'

When Gemma emerged with a skip from the forbidding grey portals of the Schools building into the sunny High Street that afternoon, she searched the crowd for one beautiful, dark-eyed face surrounded by long floppy curls. She was greeted by two.

'Over here, Gem!' Daisy screamed, shaking the magnum of champagne she had purchased with the money Bertie had given her and spraying it over the people around her like a champion motor racing driver. Oliver was soaked and clearly enjoying himself. The two of them seemed so at ease with each other, it was a second before Gemma remembered that they had never met before.

Amid much kissing and hugging and congratulation, she asked Daisy how she and Oliver had arrived together.

'I was just leaving my stuff at Boulter Street, when, luckily, Lol arrived back from the shops.'

'Lol?'

'Don't you think it suits him? He's so tall, and kind of droopy. We've been sitting in the back yard. Have some of this.' She held out the magnum. 'I've had quite a lot already. Lol bought a bottle for you, but we drank it!' she laughed.

'But when did you get back?'

The relief that the exams were over, the sun, Daisy's unexpected presence – Gemma was finding everything confusing.

'Last night. I came home a week early so that I could see you today; aren't you impressed?'

'Have you been home?'

'Of course, briefly.'

'How's Dad?'

'Seems fine,' Daisy replied blithely. 'Oh, look, here's Kathy!'

Kathy was flustered. She pushed her bike through the crowds, pink with exertion.

'I'm sorry I'm late,' she panted. 'Oh, hello, Daisy, you look well. How was France? . . . It's just that Roger's got this punt at five and he's gone to the boathouse so they don't give it to anyone else. We'll have to hurry. Roger's got the food.'

Gemma's heart sank slightly. She wished that she hadn't let Roger take over the organization of her celebrations. Now they would all have to do as he said for the rest of the day. Oliver didn't really have anything in common with Roger anyway, and now Daisy was here, she was bound to offend someone.

From Magdalen Bridge they punted downstream towards the river. After the crush of the High Street, the cool shade of big trees, their tops rustling slightly in the scant breeze and the slop of the punt pole falling through water were soporific. They found a deserted creek where they ate pork pies and strawberries and drank plastic mugs of champagne. Roger and Oliver, both lawyers, had finished finals the week before. Kathy's would begin in a few days.

Everyone seemed mellow, as if the sun and wine had smoothed down their edges. Gemma lay back and looked up through the leaves to the oscillating pattern of blue sky above and thought, just before dozing off, that she had never been happier.

When she awoke, Kathy was packing up the remains of the food. 'I've got to get back and work. Roger's going to punt me back now. Will you be all right walking?'

'Where are the other two?' Gemma asked, sitting up and rubbing sleep from her eyes.

'They went for a walk,' Kathy said briskly. She was so matter-of-fact, Gemma wondered if something had happened that had offended her.

Just then, they heard Daisy's distinctive laugh, echoing through the trees. 'I told you it was this way. Come on. I'll race you.'

She emerged running through some bushes, Oliver in close pursuit. Daisy's dress was covered with bits of sticky weed and several of the tiny mother of pearl buttons down the front were open. She leapt at the tartan blanket Kathy had been about to fold, and collapsed on to it, laughing and gasping for breath.

Gemma, who had seen her sister like this many times before, couldn't help laughing too, although she was surprised and delighted to see Oliver behaving so childishly.

'I fell over and cut my knee,' Daisy said, showing the wound to Gemma.

'It's just a graze,' Gemma reassured her, handing her a tissue.

'Well, we'll be off,' Kathy said, picking up the hamper. 'Roger?'

'Aye Aye, Captain!' he said, good-humouredly.

When they had disappeared round the bend in the river, Daisy, who had been waving them goodbye said, 'What next?'

Instinctively Gemma looked towards Oliver for inspiration.

'Oh, I think the only sensible thing to do', said Oliver severely, 'is have a good deal more to drink.' He looked at Gemma and winked.

Daisy squealed with laughter.

On the path back through Magdalen Fields, Daisy linked arms with Gemma, and it seemed quite natural that Oliver should link arms with her.

'A Daisy chain,' he said.

Later when they were all sitting in the garden of the Turf Tavern and Daisy playfully punched Oliver on the arm to stop him teasing her, he responded with a slap in return, followed by a kiss on the nose to show her he didn't mean it. Even then Gemma hadn't picked up the signals. She just felt gloriously, drunkenly euphoric that exams were over, and she was with the two people she loved most in the world.

Much later, she left them talking in the front room, drinking some dark rum Oliver had stashed in his room. Gemma's eyes just wouldn't stay open.

The house seemed very quiet when she woke up the next morning. She peeled off the sub-fusc clothes she had been too exhausted to take off the night before, put on a towelling robe and ran herself a hot bath. Then she went downstairs, creeping silently past the door of the back room so as not to wake her sister. Daisy usually slept like a log until about noon, which would give her several hours alone with Oliver. She made a pot of tea and poured out a mug for him, then she checked her face in the hall mirror and tiptoed back upstairs, trembling with excitement and nervousness, and knocked on his door.

She heard his customary cross mumbling and smiled, then she took a deep breath for courage and gently pushed open his door.

Her first thought was that he was sleeping with his arm around a pillow, but then the pillow moved and Daisy sat up, pulling the sheet up to cover her full bare breasts.

'Hello, Biscuit!' she said, reaching out to take the steaming mug. 'Isn't it wonderful? Lol and I are in love!'

Part Two

CHAPTER 8

'LOVE OPTIONS . . .' Daisy typed, 'Five women talk to Daisy Rush about life and love at thirty . . .'

It was a pretty banal article, thought Daisy, even by her own standards. She had actually gone to the trouble of finding five women in different situations who had been prepared to talk to her, but when she looked at her notes she found she needn't really have bothered, since they all said exactly what she thought they would: the mistress started off by declaring that she had the best of both worlds, her independence and great sex. She didn't have to wash his dirty sports socks, she said. In fact, she said it so often that by the end of the interview Daisy thought that either he had the most appallingly smelly feet, or that really the mistress would have liked nothing better than to peel off the offending items at the end of the day and give them a thorough going-over in the whites cycle of the Zanussi machine that had pride of place in her spotless kitchen.

The lesbian said she was completely fulfilled, thank you very much, and asked chippily why Daisy looked surprised. Daisy resisted the urge to say that she had seen the woman's partner leaving for work just as she arrived, and she found it difficult to believe you could have a fulfilling relationship with a traffic warden.

The married woman with one small child whined that having children was much more tiring than you'd think, but it was worth it. She talked like a martyr, as if her suffering was not only to be sympathized with, but somehow admired.

The woman who had been living with her boyfriend for some years seemed to have swapped romance for a passion for DIY. Daisy wondered how they managed to have sex on the platform bed they had built, which demonstrably left loads of room for shelving units and a workstation beneath, but seemed perilously close to the ceiling.

The single career woman said she was too busy to establish relationships with men, but her biological clock was ticking.

Why, thought Daisy, do I never find someone single without a biological clock? Or a woman who has lived with her boyfriend for years and is prepared to admit that she is bored, but too bloody lazy, or frightened, to get out? Or a woman who plays around? There again, why would anyone want to tell a journalist the truth? If one of her colleagues had asked Daisy about her own love life, she wouldn't have been exactly honest herself.

She looked at the pictures the photographer had taken of the interviewees. They were all grinning falsely but, maybe it was her imagination, the ones with partners did seem to be smiling wider than those without.

'Monogamy in its various forms, it seems, is still the preferred option for most modern women. ENDS.' she typed. Well, the editor, a woman who called herself a post-feminist as if it were something to be proud of, would certainly approve.

There were, of course, plenty of other love options. The elderly couple in the basement flat, whom Oliver referred to as Hansel and Gretel, were brother and sister who had lived most of their lives in the huge Victorian house in Hampstead. When their parents died, they had sensibly moved into the lower floor and had the rest of the house converted into three large flats.

Oliver had always longed to know what their sleeping arrangements were, but had never quite had the courage to snoop. He had suggested pruriently that Daisy interview them for this article, but they were in their eighties, far too old for the magazine.

Daisy had thought of doing a divorced woman, but the editor said that it would be too depressing. Daisy had briefly wondered whether she could track down a marriage of convenience, a lavender marriage, she thought they were called, but after her sister's recent experience, that seemed too sad. Now that Gemma was apparently back in London, she was extremely relieved she hadn't pursued the idea. If Gemma were to read it, she might think that Daisy was plundering her experiences, using them for cheap gain, a phrase she had used once before.

Daisy got up and wandered into the kitchen to make a cup of coffee. It was strange to think that Gemma was back, had been back for some time, had probably passed within a mile of Daisy's flat, and that she hadn't known. She felt it was almost a failing that she hadn't been able to sense her sister's presence in London.

They used to be so close. Why weren't they close anymore? Daisy stirred boiling water onto the instant coffee so vigorously that when she looked down there were splashes all over the draining board. Floods of spontaneous tears began to pour down Daisy's face, as they had that morning when she had run into Kathy in Sainsburys.

Kathy had been surprised, she could tell, that Gemma had not been in contact with her. She had hugged her and told her where Gemma worked, but made up some story about Gemma not yet having a phone connected at home. Daisy had known she was lying. She didn't blame Kathy, but it was so hurtful to think that Gemma was still trying to avoid her. Why?

You could easily ring her at work, Kathy suggested,

but Daisy didn't dare. The last time they had spoken was on Gemma's birthday. Despite years of silence from Gemma, Daisy always rang on her birthday. This time it had been more difficult than ever, like having a conversation with a wrong number. Then, a few days after that, she had bumped into Kathy in Inverness Street market (forget the Internet, Daisy had thought, I'm getting information from New York as I shop). Kathy had told her that Gemma's husband had died. Daisy wrote to her, not knowing what to say, but wanting to say something. She hadn't received a reply.

Kathy was another love option, thought Daisy, wandering back to her typewriter. Married to college sweetheart, two kids, nice house, husband having an affair. Daisy wondered whether Kathy knew about the affair, but she didn't know her well enough to ask. As Kathy had hugged her beside the pyramid of red peppers in the produce department, Daisy had felt a fleeting urge to tell her about Roger's reputation, partly so that she would have something to cry about too, and partly to punish her for being the bearer of Daisy's tears. Thankfully, she had stopped herself.

Daisy wiped her face with a tissue, blew her nose and started to read through her article. How much longer, she wondered, can I go on writing this stuff? Each week she had to turn down more offers of commissions than she could handle. Her name, she thought, must be in some Editorial Yellow Pages under general section HACK, subsection, SEX. The money was great, even if she sometimes had to get Oliver's outdoor clerk to chase it up, and it was easy enough work. But she was bored. Bored, but also amazed that she could still find the words to write marginally different articles on the same subject, week after week, month after month, year after year. If she didn't find something different to do soon, thought Daisy, she would be able to say decade after decade.

She had thought that she would have more freedom by going freelance, but, it seemed once you had a reputation for a certain sort of expertise, that was the only thing people wanted you to write about. Sometimes she received a letter from an agent wanting to talk to her about writing books, but she knew, because she had met with a couple of agents, that what they had in mind were either self-help books for the single girl, or frothy sexy romps, preferably featuring horses, and Daisy knew that she didn't want to write either of these. The problem for Daisy was that she was absolutely certain about what she didn't want to do, but equally uncertain about what she did.

Even in the beginning she had never consciously decided to be a journalist. In 1985, she had returned from France with no plans other than to take up her place at Durham University, and become a student reading French for three years. Then over a period of just a couple of months she had met Oliver, her parents had both died tragically, and Gemma moved away. She had been abandoned by everyone except Oliver.

She went up to Durham for a term, but found she couldn't settle or work. One of her tutors, who was sympathetic, had suggested counselling. At her first session, Alice, the counsellor, had asked Daisy to write an account of what it felt like to lose both parents. It had proved the best therapy. Oliver read it and said she should get it published. Having no idea how to go about this, she sent it in to a Young Journalist of the Year competition, and, just before Christmas, she found out, to her amazement, that she had won. She was inundated with offers from magazines, which were attractive mainly because they were in London, and Oliver was in London too, articled to a firm of left-wing solicitors.

She decided to put university on hold for the time being and move in with him. He was renting one room in a damp house in Brixton. His salary just about covered his rent, food and fares. Daisy's was used up buying suitable clothes for work and paying for meals out when it was her turn to cook. They were poor and blissfully happy. Their lovemaking seemed stimulated and enhanced by the lumpiness of the bed. It was like a drug that got them through difficult times. Most mornings they would make sleepy love before leaping out of bed, defying the cold, and running down to the local swimming pool where Oliver swam vigorously and Daisy decorously for a few minutes before they both took hot showers (there was never any hot water in the bedsit). Then, clean and smelling of chlorine, they would walk home and often be unable to resist making love again before catching the tube to work. Sometimes now, in their beautiful flat in Hampstead, Daisy longed for that dingy Brixton room, how they were then, at the height of their passion for one another.

When Bertie and Estella's estates were settled, and the house at Whitton sold, Daisy found that she had inherited quite a substantial sum of money as well as the income she would receive from her third share in Bertie's literary estate. Now, while Oliver supported her emotionally, she could support them both financially, beyond their wildest dreams. Daisy bought herself a sports car the day the money went into her account. Oliver was furious when he saw it.

'It won't last a night on this street,' he said.

'We'll have to move then,' Daisy replied, and checked them into a hotel in Swiss Cottage with a swimming pool while they were house-hunting. She remembered hearing Estella saying that if she were very rich, she would live in a hotel permanently, like Salvador Dali did. She felt her mother would approve of her spending the money this way. It was a kind of emotional justification for wanton extravagance that even Oliver, with his new found love of litigation, couldn't find an argument against. At the beginning, he seemed to enjoy it too.

They found an elegant flat with three bedrooms and an enormous living-room with ceiling cornices, a fireplace and a balcony looking out on to the tree-lined street. It was more money than they had intended to spend and would use up all of Daisy's capital, but once they had seen it, all the other flats they saw looked poky in comparison. Oliver worried that there would come a time when they would never be able to keep up with the bills. Daisy thought he was being ridiculously pessimistic and handed over the asking price.

Perhaps, Daisy thought now, it had been a silly purchase. They only ever used two rooms – the huge living-room, where they ate, read, watched television and worked, and the enormous bedroom at the back with its long windows looking out on to the gardens behind. Few people came to stay, and when Daisy was in the flat on her own, she sometimes felt overwhelmed by it. It was terribly difficult to keep warm, and in winter the bills were a constant reminder of Oliver's warnings. But the most regrettable thing was the subtle shift in the dynamic of their relationship. Even though they had moved in together, the fact that Daisy had blithely overridden any caution about the flat and that she had put up all the money, meant that it never quite felt as if they were equal sharing partners as they had been in Brixton. Having lots of money at the age of nineteen was so much fun, it really hadn't occurred to Daisy to consider this. After the gloom of bereavement, winter in Durham and Brixton, suddenly it was spring in Hampstead and Daisy's life had seemed filled with light and happiness.

Daisy sipped her coffee. She ought to begin reading through the cuttings that *Sixpack* had sent over, but she couldn't concentrate. She began to unpack the plastic carrier bags she had brought back from Sainsburys and dumped on the sofa.

She had forgotten about the ice-cream. There was a pool of sticky beige liquid in the bottom of one bag that dripped through a tear as she took the shopping through to the kitchen. Daisy swore loudly, then grabbed some kitchen paper and started to dab at the spots on the carpet.

She heard Oliver's key in the lock.

'You're not cleaning, are you?' he said, his voice faintly amused at seeing her kneeling on the floor.

'I forgot I'd bought ice-cream,' she said, in explanation.

'Daisy,' he said affectionately, stooping to kiss her, 'you are amazing. God, it was Haagen Dazs too. They cost about five pounds a carton.'

'Surely not,' she said. She had no idea what things cost. She just fancied the idea of ice-cream with Bailey's liqueur in it.

'Here,' he said, 'I'll do it. You're only making it worse. You need a damp sponge.'

'Thanks,' Daisy said.

She decided to leave him to unpack the groceries too. She had heard the litany of complaints before. The way she packed the bags, throwing everything in together, squashing the delicate things; the fact that she bought bags of ready-washed salad instead of lettuces; the list was endless. Yes, Daisy was prepared to admit, I am an absolutely useless housewife, but I don't really care. And, she would think in her more confident moments, you're not supposed to care either.

She went back to her typewriter. Downstairs in the ground floor flat, their neighbour with the steel guitar had just begun his evening practice. She braced herself for Oliver's usual outburst.

'For God's sake, SHUT UP!' he shouted, banging

their floor with a broom handle he kept in the hall especially for the purpose.

Daisy didn't really mind the noise. She liked to know there were other people in the house, and it was a gentle, soothing sound. Oliver was determined not to get used to it, but equally resolved not to confront their neighbour face to face. In fact, whenever they met him in the communal hall, Oliver was always rather charming. It was one of the many things that Daisy would never understand about him. Like the way he could moan for hours about a dinner party they were going to, then be the most engaging and witty companion when they arrived. If Daisy had ever told anyone that Oliver could be capricious, irrational and downright difficult at home, they would have looked at her in total disbelief. Perhaps, she often thought to herself, it's me. Perhaps I make him like that.

'LOVE POTIONS,' Oliver read over her shoulder. 'Oh come on, Daisy, isn't that a bit downmarket, even for you?'

'Oh bugger,' said Daisy, unscrewing the Tipp-Ex. 'I always get those letters muddled up.'

'You ought to get yourself a computer,' Oliver said.

'You always say that. I'm quite happy with this. I don't know how to use a computer anyway.'

'Well, learn.'

She knew he was right, but she didn't like being told. She never told him how to run a defence. It wasn't as if he knew how to use a computer himself. She felt her temper rising, her body clenched up trying to contain it. She didn't want a row, not tonight.

'Gemma's back,' she said.

She didn't look up.

'What?'

'Gemma's back, here, London. Living. It seems.' It had been difficult enough to say it the first time.

'Did she ring?'

'Of course she didn't ring,' said Daisy, hotly. 'I ran into Kathy at Sainsburys.'

'Kathy as in Roger the . . .'

'Yes,' Daisy said impatiently.

He knew exactly who Roger was. Roger was having an affair with Oliver's outdoor clerk, Emily. Daisy was slightly suspicious that Oliver fancied her too, because he was always saying, disparagingly, that he couldn't understand what she saw in Roger.

'Oh,' said Oliver.

'What's that supposed to mean?' Daisy asked.

'It doesn't mean anything,' Oliver countered.

She never knew what Oliver thought about Gemma. A couple of years after all her attempts at communication with Gemma had been rebuffed, Daisy had read an article about post-traumatic stress disorder, and decided that Gemma must be suffering from it. She had tried to discuss it with Oliver, wanting his confirmation of her thoughts, but he had just looked at her, bemused by her attempts at rationalization.

'She's a stupid little bitch,' he had said eventually, as if that settled the matter.

'No she's not!' Daisy had found herself sticking up for her sister. Oliver had simply walked out of the room, and after that she had to bear the pain of her desertion alone.

Now, she couldn't look at him.

'Come on,' he said, after a few moments' silence, 'we're going out.'

'Where to?' Daisy asked dispiritedly.

'A surprise,' he said.

Daisy's face brightened. She loved surprises.

'A big surprise or a little one?' she asked.

'Oh, big, definitely big,' Oliver replied, thinking on his feet. He picked up his mobile phone, and asked Daisy where she had left the car.

'I think it's just down the road, near that skip,' Daisy said. It was always a nightmare parking in their street and Daisy never remembered where she had left the car.

'Well, give me the keys and I'll find it and pick you up in a minute. Wear something nice,' he added.

Oliver loved to sing. Most mornings he would attempt an aria or two from *Il Trovatore* in the shower, but his voice, pitched slightly unsurely between a tenor and baritone, was in truth more suited to mawkish ballads from the Fifties and Sixties. It was a cause of wonder to Daisy that he knew all the words. In one of his many youthful incarnations, Oliver claimed to have been lead singer in a Liverpool band.

Capitol Gold was having an Everly Brothers evening and the car radio was on at top volume.

'*Dr..ee..ee..ee.eam, dream, dream, dream* . . . Come on Daisy, sing the harmony!' he shouted.

She knew the chorus, but it always gave her fits of giggles that Oliver took the singing so seriously. He would have made an excellent conductor, she thought. He was so bossy.

At times like this, speeding down the M40 into the sunset, on a beautiful spring evening, with Oliver singing at the top of his voice, she could feel totally, passionately happy with him. His company made her shiver with pleasure, her face beam with laughter.

Why, she wondered, were such evenings becoming so rare? Oliver had always suffered (and made other people suffer) from mood swings. His brooding, existential despairs had even been attractive in the first couple of years. Especially when sometimes she had been able to tease him back from the abyss with a well-timed joke or a kiss. It had given her a great sense of her own value and strength. But usually, then, she was the one who had been depressed, or sad, and Oliver always managed to cheer her up with some spontaneous act, some mad gesture, like taking her bowling at two in the morning or going for breakfast in Boulogne, mid-winter, when they were the only people on the night ferry.

In fact, she thought, Oliver was always much nicer to her when she was down. She had begun to realize recently that he found her generally happy and equable states irritating and that he seemed to like to punish her for her good moods by making her feel utterly trivial or useless.

She tried to sympathize with him. She knew that he felt traumatized by his background, although, she sometimes thought meanly, he hates his parents, at least they're still alive. Whenever she tried to draw him out of his dark silences, he would sigh and look at her disbelievingly, and say, 'Daisy, you have no idea.'

It was a phrase that annoyed her beyond all others. The way it dismissed her intellect and her powers of understanding echoed the way she always felt her father had written her off as silly, and it made her think bitterly of Gemma, her father's favourite, who had now written her off as well.

Sometimes she found the strength to retaliate. 'Oh, for God's sake, grow up!' she had recently said to Oliver, adding unnecessarily, 'You're over forty! Get over it!'

But mostly she took his criticism silently, absorbing it into her system like poison.

'Charms,' said Oliver, as the song finished, 'isn't it a great word? Have I ever told you about your charms, Daisy? It's a word we never use these days, isn't it? Shame. Daisy, I want you with all your charms!' He turned from the wheel and grinned at her lasciviously.

She smiled at him.

'It's only in all those songs because it rhymes with arms,' she said.

'God, woman, you're so pedantic!' he said, with

unusual good humour, and then began singing along with the next song.

It was almost dark when they pulled into the gravel driveway. It was only when she saw the sign that Daisy guessed their glamorous destination. She leapt out of the car delighted. She couldn't begin to imagine how it was that Oliver had managed to book a table at the Manoir aux Quat' Saisons at such short notice, and he refused to tell her. Oliver liked mysteries. It would have spoilt it to press him.

The wine made her light-headed and she began to giggle at every funny remark Oliver made. He was brilliant at lightning-sharp descriptions of their fellow diners, cruel impersonations of the somewhat pompous waiter. She loved him when he was like this. It was as if, tonight, he had tuned into her misery and had decided to put on an entertainment especially for her. In the end he had to stop, when she laughed so much that she sprayed the pink tablecloth with a mouthful of Burgundy.

The food was perfect, delicate and delicious. Sitting in the conservatory, with its pretty curtains and parlour palms, she felt as if they were on holiday.

'I'll have to have lots of strong coffee,' she said, suddenly realizing that she was not sober.

'Why?' Oliver asked.

'Well, I can't drive back like this,' she said.

'Why would you want to do that?' he asked. 'I've booked a room.'

'God, Oliver, you're making me feel like a mistress!' she said rather too loudly. A couple of the very well-dressed women in the room shifted uncomfortably in their seats. He smiled as if at a private joke.

'Come on,' he said, 'I have to be up early.'

*　　*　　*

She looked out over the garden. It was bathed in moonlight. The lawns had been mown that day. The fragrance of cut grass wafted up through the open window. It was so quiet. He stood behind her and started to massage her shoulders, expertly, kneading the tops of her arms and finding pressure points down the rim of her shoulder blades. She felt tension draining from her.

Sometimes he knew so perfectly what she needed, she felt he was inside her, part of her. Feeling her feelings, thinking her thoughts.

Sex between them had always been like that. Ever since the first time they kissed in the woods by the Cherwell, the day Gemma finished her exams. Then, it had been overwhelming, exhilarating, and Daisy had known that this was what people meant by falling in love. It did feel like falling – she was giddy, almost nauseous with pleasure and fear. And later, when they made love for the first time on the floor of the living-room at Boulter Street, every bit of her body felt delighted, suffused with sensation. The waves of pleasure were so high that she felt that if she were lifted any higher she would cross the boundary into pain. It was unbelievable, joyous, almost frightening.

She tipped back her head, letting it roll from side to side against his chest. He swung her round so that her face was pushed against his shirt. She closed her eyes and inhaled. He always smelt so wonderful. It was a combination of the starch that he used to iron his white shirts, the soap he washed with, and him. Even when he sweated, his skin smelt fresh, just slightly musky, like the peculiarly pleasant smell of skin that has a light tan from a day in the sun. Almost automatically, she began to unfasten the sharp-edged mother-of-pearl buttons on his shirt.

*   *   *

Afterwards, she lay naked on the floor looking up through the open window at the black tops of the trees and the stars beyond. She hadn't the energy to get up and close the curtains. Oliver came back into the room wrapped in a towel. His tummy that had always been flat and boyish, was getting slightly rounded. He was finally beginning to look his age. He crouched down beside her, kissed her and handed her a glass of red wine. She sipped a little, scarcely bothering to sit up and a drip rolled down her chin. He caught it on his finger and rubbed the purple liquid like lipstick round her perfect plum-plump lips.

'I love you,' he said.

He never used to say it, not regularly, and now he seemed to say it whenever they made love. She wondered why it was beginning to irritate her. She looked at him. There was almost a hint of pleading in his eyes, those peculiar eyes that were dark and somehow light at the same time.

Why, she thought, even after such an enchanted evening, do I not feel completely happy with you anymore?

'I love you too,' she said, turning away from him to pick up her dress. She could no longer look at him when she said it, because she wasn't sure it was true anymore. And she knew that he would *know*.

CHAPTER 9

In Shepperton Studios they had built a street that was
supposed to look like a city of the future. In fact,
thought Daisy, it looked pretty much like any street in
any town in 1995, with its burger bars and video games'
lounges. There were gangs of extras standing around.
They were wearing knee-high bovver boots and slashed
bits of rubber and leather, and sporting odd Mohican
hairstyles dyed fluorescent shades of blue, yellow and
pink. Daisy couldn't work out whether they were in
costume, or whether they had been hand-picked off the
streets. She had arrived between takes and there were a
lot of technicians standing around eating bacon
sandwiches.

The film they were shooting was called *Star-Crossed*,
and, as far as she could gather from the press release, it
was an inter-planetary *Romeo and Juliet*. *Aliens* meets
West Side Story fifty years on without the music, Daisy
wrote on her notepad. She also noted that the artificial
street she was standing in was called Montague Street,
and one of the burger bars was called Capulet's.

She asked one of the bunch of grungey kids where
she could find the press officer, and was surprised when
he replied in a perfect public school accent. He led the
way to the green room down a side street that stopped
abruptly as soon as it extended out of the line of the
cameras.

She explained that she was here to interview Cal

Costelloe, the star of the movie, for *Sixpack*. The young actor raised his eyebrows. In its first few months on the newspaper stands, *Sixpack* had already managed to acquire exactly the reputation it was seeking. It was a boys only magazine, but one that stopped short (just) of being pornography. Just as it had been perfectly normal in the late 1980s for any man, even a be-suited city executive, to carry a copy of the vulgar comic *Viz* in his briefcase, so *Sixpack*, in the 1990s, was the acceptable face of the unacceptable. With its high production values and star journalists it managed to churn out unreconstructed male values in sophisticated, stylish packaging. Daisy, in her lilac linen shift and oversized Levi's jacket, didn't look like the sort of person who would be working for it.

It was Daisy's outrage at a couple of the interviews *Sixpack* had run with women in its early issues that had led to her commission for the Costelloe profile. She had been in the *Sixpack* offices one day when they were laying out an interview with a female Hollywood sex symbol, and she had read some of the copy over the designer's shoulder.

When Patrick, the editor, had appeared for their monthly meeting, Daisy said to him, 'Can you really get away with this sort of overt sexism? I mean, this interview is more about the journalist's fantasies about her bum than it is about her.'

'He's very good, isn't he?' Patrick had responded. 'We had a great response to the one he did in February about the thinking man's crumpet.'

'Where does the thinking bit come in?' Daisy asked, 'I mean, how would you feel if I did an article about Daniel Day Lewis's bum or wrote about how damp my knickers got when he was talking . . . ?'

'Would you?' Patrick replied. 'That'd be fantastic. Who would you like to do?'

'Don't be ridiculous . . .'

'Tell you what, we've got Cal Costelloe on the cover for June. I was going to get a fashion shoot with him, but let's have an interview too.'

'Well . . .' It had been a long time since Daisy had done an interview, and she didn't think she would have any scruples about trashing Costelloe. He had made some remark, she seemed to remember, about women having no sense of humour about sexual harassment, and, in the photos, he always looked so damn pleased with himself.

'All right then,' she had agreed, rising to the challenge.

Cal Costelloe was a good deal slighter than she had imagined. He was only a little taller than she was. He had the kind of Irish good looks – blue eyes, light brown hair, broad sexy smile – that, she had to admit, she did find extremely attractive. As he shook her hand, and looked very intimately into her eyes, she sensed to her horror that she was blushing. He smiled his trademark smile, which was pure sex mixed with arrogance, and she knew that he was used to having this effect on women, and probably spent hours practising it. His hair was longish for this film, and had highlights the colour of hay. She conjured up a vision of him sitting in a hairdresser's chair with a hedgehog comb of tin foil wrappers on his head, and felt she had regained control of herself.

The PR man was saying that there wasn't a lot of time, and she would have to do her thing between takes.

'What, on the set? Standing up?' Daisy said. The PR man exchanged a look with Cal and they both smiled knowingly.

'I meant standing up, as opposed to sitting down,' Daisy said, only making them smile more. 'Fine,' she added, trying to compose herself.

She realized that they were waiting for her to begin.

'Do you really need your minder with you for this?' She looked directly at Costelloe.

Slightly embarrassed, he waved the PR man away.

'Right,' said Daisy, 'let's start at the beginning. It's a long way from home to here, isn't it?' She gestured around the set.

'Well, actually I was brought up in Kilburn,' said Cal. 'I should say it's not more than ten miles.'

'That's a very smartass reply,' Daisy responded. 'Were you born with such a sense of humour, or is it the result of media training?'

She sounded as deeply unamused as she could, and she noticed that he shifted his weight from one foot to the other rather uncomfortably. One all, she thought.

She had managed to ask him about his leap from a minor role as teenage idol in a television soap to movies in Hollywood before the director came over and ordered her off the set. She sat down on a canvas chair in the wings of the set and watched them talking over the scene. Costelloe's back was to her so she had a chance to make notes about his bum.

'Smaller than expected, like everything about him,' she wrote, 'nice muscles, well-defined in silver star suit.' Costelloe was dressed in a kind of medieval costume with a short doublet and tights and knee-high boots with floppy cuffs. What distinguished his outfit from a traditional pantomime Robin Hood was the fabric it was made from: very fine silver grey leather, or something that looked like that. She thought he looked more like a ballet dancer than a space-age hero.

The set suddenly filled with people and when the director shouted 'Action!' they all started running and screaming and fighting. For a second Costelloe disappeared in the crowd, then as the riot dispersed he looked up at the second storey of the building that contained the burger bar. There stood Antoinette Da Souza, the female lead.

'Cut!' the director shouted.

They repeated the whole scene. Then the director shouted 'Ten minutes' and Daisy noticed the PR man waving her forward to resume her interview. There were drips of sweat on Costelloe's temple.

'Don't tell me', said Daisy, 'that's about to be the balcony scene.'

'How did you guess?' Costelloe replied, wiping his forehead with his sleeve and smiling at her. The weariness in his voice betrayed for the first time how silly he thought the whole thing was too.

'What attracted you to this role?' she asked, hoping to capitalize on his slight discomfort.

'Well now,' Costelloe replied, 'I could tell you what a great part it is, or I could say that I needed a romantic lead after playing the villain in my first two movies, or I could say, I suppose, that the money was fucking irresistible.'

Daisy laughed and dutifully wrote it down. It was a good quote, but one that had the practised nonchalance of a soundbite trotted out many times before.

The director was approaching again. Daisy slunk back to her chair. This was not going well. She was not getting anything that he wouldn't give any other journalist. She could certainly belt out 800 words from what she had already, but an in-depth 2,000-word piece was going to need something more.

They were running through the fight scene. Daisy realized that she had come on a day when they were just shooting crowd scenes. How disorientating it must be, she thought, to jump from one bit to another. She would have liked to see him tackle the balcony scene. When he returned again, she asked him if he had done it.

'Oh yeah. A couple of weeks back. Maybe you could see the rushes?' he volunteered. Daisy said that she would like that.

She looked at her notes. She needed to ask him about his love life, but she didn't feel she could, with so many people milling around. He had had a much-publicized affair with a much older American actress, which had recently broken up. Her mind was whirring with ways to pose questions about it, when she realized that he was speaking to her.

'Listen. I'm all through for the day,' he was saying. 'How about I change, and we go and find a coffee somewhere?'

'Great,' she said.

When he returned, he was wearing black jeans and a leather biker's jacket. He looked much more terrestrial, and very attractive.

The cab dropped them outside the Coliseum and Daisy hurried with him off the main street and up a little alleyway called Brydges Place.

'Where on earth are you taking me?' Costelloe joked, stepping over a pool of urine. 'On a tour of Dickensian London?'

'You'll see,' Daisy stopped in front of an unmarked door and rang the unmarked bell.

'Hello?' said a voice.

'Hello,' said Daisy. The door was buzzed open.

Costelloe followed her up a rickety staircase to the first floor and into what looked like someone's sitting-room. There were several tatty, comfy sofas.

'Welcome to my club,' said Daisy.

'I thought it was someone's home!' said Costelloe. 'Very nice.'

'What would you like?' said Daisy, pleased that he was impressed. She indicated that he should sit down on the sofa.

'Oh, some champagne, I think. Call me working class if you like, but I'll never get used to the stuff.' He had put on a very camp voice.

For a second Daisy thought, 'Oh God, he's gay,' and she felt a tremendous rush of disappointment. *Sixpack* Man was not gay. *Sixpack* Man was a red-blooded het. However was she going to make this article work?

'Do you mind if I use this?' she asked, producing a tape recorder from her handbag and putting it on the low table in front of them.

'Oh! Are we still doing the interview?' he whined. 'And I was just beginning to enjoy myself.'

He wasn't gay. She could tell by the way he was looking at her. She had taken off her denim jacket. The lilac linen shift wasn't an ideal garment for sitting on a low couch. It was short and it creased dreadfully, making it seem even shorter when she sat down.

Although Daisy had lost some weight in recent months, her body still had the curvy woman's shape it had had since she was twelve years old. She longed for a flat chest and bottom, but she knew she would never have them without radical surgery. Sometimes she made the mistake of buying clothes designed for less voluptuous women, like this lilac shift, which she hadn't been able to resist because of its colour, but she knew that towards the end of the day, when she had sat down in it a good few times, it was crumpled and made her look a bit of a slut.

'Well, why don't you tell me a few things you haven't told any other journalists, and then we'll see,' she joined in the flirtation. Perhaps, she thought, rationalizing her behaviour, the way she should do the article was by pretending to be on a date.

'Your eyes are violet,' he said. 'Now, I haven't told any other journalist that. I'm sorry,' he retracted as he saw a steely look of disapproval pass over her face, just when she had been getting relaxed.

'So what happened with Eliza Beth Jacobs?' she asked.

'We had a ball. And then . . .'

'You changed into a pumpkin?'

'That kind of thing.'

'Or a white mouse?'

'Possibly.'

Come on, thought Daisy, think date. What sort of questions would I ask him if I were on a date.

'What do you think about marriage?' About the last question she would ask.

'I approve,' Costelloe replied. 'My parents are very happily married and I have a brother and three sisters. I'd like to do that myself, with the right person. I haven't told any other journalist that, by the way,' he said, leaning towards her.

'You'd like to have five children?' Daisy asked.

'Yeah. Well, several, anyway.'

What was this thing men had about children these days, Daisy wondered. Lol was always trying to persuade her that they should start having them, and now a sex symbol in his early twenties was saying he wanted half a dozen. Had they all been watching too many shaving cream adverts, with square-jawed men nestling their bottom-smooth chins against baby's cheek? Or was it just the latest form of subjugating women, dressed up for the caring, sharing Nineties?

Daisy wished that she were writing her article for a tabloid.

'MY GREATEST WISH, HOLLYWOOD ROMEO CONFESSES: FIVE CHILDREN!'

She wasn't sure how well it would go down with Patrick. *Sixpack* Man liked sex with no ties. Condoms were tolerated for self-protection, but *Sixpack* Man would generally be happier with his bird on the Pill.

'So you had a happy childhood, you're successful and rich, and the one thing your life lacks is a wife and children?'

'That's more than one thing,' he countered.

'True, but it doesn't make good copy.'

'Anyway, I'm in no hurry,' he added.

'Oh God, you're not waiting for Miss Right as well? You're so bloody well-adjusted,' Daisy exclaimed. Perhaps she should have included him in 'Love Options', but she had already faxed it in that morning.

'Maybe I'm not like this with every journalist . . . maybe, it's just with you.'

She was belatedly rather suspicious. Was this just a way of flattering her, she wondered, trying to leaf back in her mind through the cuttings she had read the evening before.

The only personal details she could remember were the pictures of Costelloe accompanied by Jacobs at premières, and little pieces of copy about their romance. Well, if it was just an elaborate chat-up line, he had chosen the wrong woman, Daisy thought. She was one of the growing number of women she knew who positively did not want to have children, ever.

They were coming to the bottom of the bottle of champagne.

Her tape recorder clicked, then whined, indicating that it was full.

'Well, I suppose that's a wrap,' Daisy said. She put the tape recorder back into her handbag and slipped the jacket over her shoulders.

'I'll just get the bill,' she added.

'Would you like to have supper?' he asked suddenly. 'Off the record, I mean?'

'Do you mean, off the record, would I like to have supper, or would I like to have supper off the record?' said Daisy, playing for time. She was surprised at the question.

'I mean I'd like to have dinner with you, but I don't want you recording everything I say. I don't know which that is.'

'OK, then.' I can't believe this is happening, thought Daisy. I'm being asked out by a major sex symbol and

I'm treating it as if I'm having a drink with a colleague after work.

'We'll go to the Groucho. Is that OK?'

'Fine.'

Daisy hated the Groucho, but it seemed churlish to argue, and she rather relished the thought of walking in with him. That would give the chattering classes something to chatter about. She hoped that Patrick would be standing at the bar. He was one of the regulars. She would ignore him, of course, and he could come to his own conclusions about whether her interview got a little deeper than just fantasizing about Costelloe's bum.

'We'll get a cab,' said Costelloe.

'But it's only five minutes walk,' said Daisy.

'The trouble is that it might take a bit longer with me,' Costelloe said. 'I keep getting stopped, you see.'

She found she was beginning to like him. He really was a normal, rather uncomplicated guy, unphased by his fame, and touchingly realistic about it. There was no false modesty, and the arrogance she had detected earlier was something she had read into his looks. He was very handsome and very young, and that made you automatically assume that he was arrogant. In fact, it was just the way he looked naturally. She wasn't about to start feeling sorry for him because of his good looks, but she didn't want to hold them against him either.

He seemed to love talking about his siblings. He was the oldest child in the family and he was proud of the younger ones, like a parent would be. Daisy heard about his younger brother's football team, the twins' GCSE results and Nuala's admission to RADA. He was delighted and thrilled that his own fame was making it easier for the ones who followed. He laughed a lot when he talked. It was an unguarded, young laugh, and between bursts of it, he spoke quietly so that Daisy found she was having to lean into his conversation. If anyone were watching, she thought, it would look as if they were having a very intimate chat. If anyone were watching, she reminded herself, one bottle of deliciously crisp Australian Riesling already stood empty on the table and Cal was ordering another.

It was still quite early and the dining-room was not too crowded. Daisy's eyes focused for a second on a writer she had met briefly at the *Sixpack* offices. He was sitting on his own with the *Evening Standard*, occasionally stirring a Bloody Mary with a celery stalk. She waved at him. He smiled cautiously back. She felt momentarily disappointed that there was no-one she knew to be impressed by her dinner companion. A waiter handed them menus and started going through the day's specials. It was a good performance, but when he had finished, Daisy realized that she hadn't registered a word of what he was saying. The menu seemed to swim with possibilities. It felt too early to start eating and yet she had got past the point of feeling hungry. She ordered scrambled eggs with smoked salmon, hoping they would bring a lot of bread to mop up the alcohol she had already consumed.

Cal poured her another glass of wine. It was so light, and she was so thirsty, it was gone before she sensed that she should have ordered some mineral water. She smiled at Cal, holding his gaze for several seconds. He had nice eyes. He had asked the question twice before she realized he was waiting for an answer.

'What about your family?' he repeated.

'What?'

'What sort of family do you come from?'

'Guess,' she said, flirtatiously.

'Well, your mother must be very beautiful . . .'

She felt tears coming to her eyes. Why on earth had she allowed him, encouraged him even, to pursue this subject. She had to stop him now.

'I don't really have a family, actually,' she interrupted. 'Both parents are dead and my sister and I are estranged. There is an Aunt Shirley in sheltered accommodation near Brighton, but I never knew her very well and we're only on Christmas card terms.'

'I'm sorry,' he said, now obviously embarrassed to have asked. He looked so genuinely upset that she felt she had to offer some more explanation.

'My dad died of cancer, you see, about ten years ago, and my mother committed suicide a month later.'

There was a long silence, then he broke it, saying, 'Did she love him so much?'

'. . . That she couldn't bear to live without him? Like Juliet and Romeo? I suppose so,' Daisy replied.

Well, it sounded crazily romantic, and Estella would have liked that. In life, she had always created melodramas around herself, as if life weren't worth living unless it were seething with passion and intrigue.

It had been wonderful growing up with such an exotic mother. When Daisy thought about her, Estella was always wearing the crimson crushed-velvet dress she had worn to the school sports day once, when all the other mothers were dressed in pastel frocks with matching hats.

Estella never just arrived somewhere, she always made an entrance. That sports day, when every other parent had parked their car outside the school gates and walked over the playing field, the black limousine (how did Estella always manage to get the only black limousine when anyone else ringing the taxi rank got a shabby old Cortina?) had slid up the drive and Estella had waited inside until the Head of Science had run across to open the door for her. Only then had she climbed out, shimmering with beads and a rainbow of silky scarves, her glossy black hair like a heavy curtain that reached almost to her waist. Daisy was sure the whole school had gasped. She looked so beautiful.

*   *   *

Tears began to spill down her face. She knew she shouldn't have drunk so much. Too much alcohol invariably made her flirtatious and naughty, or maudlin and tearful.

'I'm sorry,' Cal was saying, 'I shouldn't have . . .'

'It's OK. I've just had too much to drink.' Daisy managed a smile. 'You see, people think you get over it, but you don't, ever . . . the thing is that you never really understand why . . .'

'I'm so sorry.' Cal put his hand over hers.

She stared at his hand resting on hers, as if it were an interesting object on the table, somehow detached from her. She was just beginning to panic, wondering how it would be removed without either embarrassment or disappointment, when the waiter arrived and Cal sat back in his chair to allow space for the food.

They ate in silence. They had come to an impasse. Somehow there wasn't anything much to say anymore. To go back to trivia would feel somehow disrespectful, to crank up the emotional intensity would be too scary. This is what a one night stand must be like, Daisy thought. A climax of intimacy but nothing to back it up, so it just becomes mildly embarrassing the next morning when there's nothing to say.

It was only nine-thirty when Daisy hailed a taxi home. She sat in a jam on the Tottenham Court Road, wondering how much she would tell Oliver about her encounter, and she realized, with a pang of guilt, that she hadn't mentioned him to Costelloe once, not even when she was detailing the members of her family.

'I'm so sorry I'm late,' said Gemma, taking off her jacket and plonking a heavy bag of books down on the chair beside him.

'That's OK. You just missed your sister,' said Ralph.

'What?'

'Daisy Rush. She was just having dinner with some guy over there.' Ralph pointed at an empty table.

'What kind of guy?' said Gemma, abruptly.

'Youngish, long hair, kind of good looking. I don't know, I only saw him for a moment. Most of the time I was looking at his back.'

'Long dark curly hair?' Gemma was shaking slightly.

'No, fairish.'

'Was he very tall?'

'No. Short. Not much bigger than her. Hey, what's with the inquisition?'

Gemma laughed. 'I'm sorry. It's just I haven't seen my sister for so long. I was just wondering what kind of guy she hangs out with these days.' Gemma recovered herself. 'Hey, this looks delicious,' she said, picking up the menu the waiter had left when he showed her to the table.

CHAPTER 10

'I wanted to let you know that I'm about to pick up the phone to Daisy,' said Gemma. 'Apparently I almost collided with her at the Groucho Club last night, and I thought, this is getting ridiculous!'

'Gem, that's great!'

'And Kathy, thanks for the other night.'

'That's OK. Good luck.'

'And Kathy, are you OK?'

'I'm fine. Big kiss.'

Gemma replaced the receiver and took a deep breath. She rehearsed again what she was going to say. She didn't intend to be over-friendly, just civil. They would have to take this step by step. She was determined not to be rushed into anything. It was easy to be bounced by Daisy's infectious enthusiasm. She wanted to be in control this time. She would just inform Daisy that she was back and suggest they have lunch. Lunch was a brainwave, it could be on neutral territory, it had a definite beginning and end, unlike a drink, or supper. That would be enough for the first call. Since she was at work, and there could be a clear background noise of computers beeping and phones ringing, she would have lots of excuses to get off the phone. She lifted the receiver and punched out the number quickly. The connection was immediate. The phone rang twice and on the third ring it was answered. Gemma held her breath.

'Hello,' said a familiar voice, 'we can't come to the

phone right now, but please leave a message after the beep.'

Gemma put the receiver down quickly.

She had thought of a million things that Daisy might say, but she hadn't predicted a machine. She looked at her hands and found she was shaking. Hearing Oliver's voice after so long was a profound shock. Suddenly she didn't know whether she was strong enough yet to confront the past.

DREAMBOAT: what's it like to meet the guy you've dreamed about?

Slight exaggeration, thought Daisy, still, here goes. *In my dreams, he had always been tall, with sinewy strength. I'd have to stand on tiptoes to kiss him. My head would fit snugly into his shoulder when we walked along beside one another. I'd seen him arresting people on television, torturing people on film, I was sure that my fantasies were a long way from politically correct, but they still made me wake up tingling.*

In reality, my date with Cal Costelloe was more like snuggling up under a warm blanket than slithering wantonly over satin sheets. He's handsome, he's gorgeous, and he is – and his publicist won't like me saying this – a really sweet guy . . .

'It's great copy, Daisy,' said Patrick, reading through the fax in one hand, his phone clasped between his chin and neck, 'but it's not *Sixpack*. I mean, you make the guy seem like a puppy dog.'

'Well, that's what he is like, really,' Daisy replied.

'I thought you were going to talk about his bum, that kind of thing?'

'I did. Paragraph 4.'

'Smaller than I imagined, like everything else about him . . .' Patrick read. 'What's that supposed to mean?'

'It's the quality not the quantity,' said Daisy.

'That's not what you said in "The Ten Lies Women Tell Men" last month.'

'Oh, bugger.'

'I hear you were in the Groucho with him.'

News travelled fast in literary London. That was less than twenty-four hours ago, thought Daisy.

'So?'

'And you were seen leaving the restaurant with him quite early,' Patrick continued.

'So?'

'So, did you bonk him? Is that why you're being so coy?'

'No!' said Daisy. 'I went home. I don't see that it's relevant anyway,' she added.

It was odd, Daisy thought, that Patrick who prided himself on knowing about everyone obviously didn't know that she lived with a man. He was always flirting with her himself, imagining her to be the rather raunchy, promiscuous girl-about-town that was the persona she adopted for her *Sixpack* column.

'Well, there's a fucking great bouquet of flowers for you here from him, if you want them, but I can't run this, Daisy, you know I can't.'

'You don't mind if I try it elsewhere?'

'As long as it's not *Esquire* or one of our rivals.'

'Well, you'd better pay me for it anyway, then.'

One of the benefits of her bantering relationship with Patrick was that she didn't feel embarrassed about being cheeky about money.

'All right,' he agreed, somewhat reluctantly.

You had to hand it to Daisy Rush. She wasn't nearly as fluffy and frothy as she sometimes appeared to be.

Daisy read through the interview again. Not bad, for someone who had started the day with a major hangover, she thought, and decided to try *Cosmopolitan*. It was a long time since she had done a piece for them.

She had just left a message for the features editor when the doorbell rang. At the same time her phone started ringing. She decided to let the answerphone pick it up.

An enormous bouquet of blue flowers stood in front of her. The colour ranged from frilly lavender irises to deep royal blue delphiniums. They were surrounded by the palest lemon tissue paper, and the polythene was sealed with a gold label from a most expensive florist.

'Wow!' she said, making the delivery boy smile.

She signed for them and opened the envelope.

'Sorry. Opened in error. Thought I'd save you a taxi ride,' Patrick had scrawled on *Sixpack* notepaper.

Attached to the bouquet with a narrow gold ribbon was a smaller envelope with her name written on it which had clearly been torn open. Inside the card read, *Thank you for last night. I'm sorry if I said anything to hurt you. Let's do it again sometime. Cal.*

No wonder Patrick had got the wrong idea. He shouldn't really have opened her mail, but she felt more amused than annoyed.

She was dumping the bouquet in a bucket of cold water when she heard Oliver arriving back.

'Who are the flowers from?' he asked.

'The guy I interviewed yesterday.'

Daisy pocketed the card she was still holding, wondering why she felt so guilty all of a sudden.

'Have you had a good day?' she asked, her high spirits faltering.

'As a matter of fact, we got an acquittal. If you ever took any notice of what's going on in the real world, you'd have seen it on the news.'

'What, the strangler?' Daisy had long since given up asking Oliver too much about his work. It gave her nightmares.

'Not guilty,' said Oliver with a wicked smile.

'And do you think he was innocent?' asked Daisy, trying to show an interest.

Oliver sighed wearily. 'God, woman, how many times do I have to tell you that it's entirely irrelevant what I think. I'm not paid to have opinions. The jury decided that they couldn't convict. The police didn't do themselves any favours . . .'

Oliver spent his working life defending people who were alleged to have committed the most horrendous crimes. He had a record of acquittals that ensured that his name got passed from one prisoner on remand to another. Daisy supposed it was his very disregard for the emotions a case aroused that made him so success-ful. She thought it was a shame that such intelligence was put to use defending such horrible people. After all, you didn't get charged with murder unless there was something in it, did you? She had once made the mistake of saying that and Oliver had reminded her of the Guildford Four and the Birmingham Six and a long list of miscarriages of justice. She had felt very ashamed of herself.

He was so persuasive about the morality of his work, but just sometimes Daisy felt that he was secretly disillusioned with it too. He loved the thrill of victory, the sense that he had outwitted the Establishment, but when he looked around the Inns of Court, with their Oxbridge college buildings, he must surely see that what he belonged to was just a different kind of Establishment. He had chosen to be a solicitor, not a barrister, so at least he didn't have to wear the silly clothes, but he drank and socialized with barristers, and the ones that Daisy had met seemed very amoral people.

Sometimes she wished that Oliver's clients *were* the sort of people who had been accused of politically motivated crime rather than the murderers and rapists he seemed always to defend. She knew better than to say this to him, though, because Oliver would counter that all crime was rooted in the class system, and could run a very good argument to the effect that hence it was all politically motivated. Daisy had long given up trying to argue with his practised polemic. She couldn't believe that he really believed it himself, so what was the point?

She contented herself that she, unlike most of his peers, knew the truth about Oliver's own background. She knew that his politics and his anger were the central props in defining his identity and she was too loyal to want to undermine that.

He went into the bedroom to change from his suit into jeans.

'We're going out to dinner to celebrate.'

'What, with the strangler?' Daisy teased.

'No, with the barristers. I take it you don't want to come.'

'Not really,' said Daisy. She had been to one or two celebration dinners. They were very male affairs, with lots of claret, cigars and self-congratulation.

'I'll see you later then,' he said, kissing her on the forehead as he left.

She knew he would be very late, and probably very drunk, if only to punish her for doing the same the night before.

From the front window, she watched him walking down the road. His step looked laboured, tired, and he was stooping more than usual. She thought, 'I'm making him miserable.'

The flat seemed suddenly empty and cold. She wished she had just made the effort and gone with him. She knew it would have made him happy. Lawyers always seemed to fancy her and she knew that secretly Oliver quite liked to show her off. What was wrong with playing the trophy for one evening? She deliberated whether to run down the road after him. If there were no taxis around, he would still be standing on the corner waiting for one if she hurried. She checked her white T-shirt. It wasn't the sexiest garment she owned, but it was clean. She grabbed her handbag. She could put some lipstick on in the cab. She was just about to slam the front door, when the phone started ringing.

'Hello?' she said breathlessly.

There was a long silence, then a tiny choked voice said, 'Daisy?'

'Gemma!'

'Daisy, I'm back in London.'

The voice was gaining more confidence.

'Really?' said Daisy, feigning surprise, wanting to encourage her.

'Yes. Er . . . I wondered if you would like to have lunch.'

'I'd love to!' The thousand times she had told herself that if Gemma ever rang she would be cold and formal flew out the window. 'When?'

'When are you free?'

'Tomorrow?'

There was a pause.

'OK. Tomorrow,' said Gemma.

'Orso's? Do you know where that is?'

'I'll find it.'

'I'll see you there,' Daisy said, unwilling to risk talking too long in case she said something wrong and Gemma changed her mind.

She put down the phone, flushed with joy. Then opened the door and ran all the way down the street.

She could see Oliver getting into the cab. She shouted and waved, but he didn't hear her. He slammed the door and the cab drew away.

She kept on running, waving her arms, hoping to catch up with the cab at the lights. But they turned green as Oliver's cab approached and the driver put his foot down.

Another cab drew up behind her. For a moment Daisy was tempted to jump in and shout 'Follow that cab!' but she had a momentary loss of confidence. What if Oliver didn't want her to go to the dinner? He hadn't put up much of a protest when she refused. What if she arrived after him and he gave her one of his completely cold, angry looks? In her jeans and white T-shirt, she didn't feel strong enough to deal with that.

'You all right, love?' asked the cab driver.

'Fine, thanks, a bit out of breath,' said Daisy. 'Actually, I think I'll just go home.'

CHAPTER 11

Daisy was watching him sleep. In repose, his face lost all its anger. It was calm and beautiful. She saw a frown flicker across his brow. She wondered what he was dreaming about. Then he smiled, grunted, opened one eye and looked at her, smiled again and turned over. She turned over too.

It was only later, when she heard the door bang, that she realized she hadn't told Oliver about her meeting with Gemma. He had come home in the early hours, she thought, and, although she had been sleeping, the acrid smell of beer and smoke had woken her for a few seconds when his weight collapsed onto the bed beside her. He was soon snoring.

It always amazed Daisy that however late Oliver went to bed, he was always up, showered and spruced up for work by eight o'clock. One of the most difficult things Daisy had found about going freelance was actually getting out of bed when there was no timetable imposed on her.

She rolled over to his side of the bed where his smell still lingered and hugged his pillow to her face. Sunlight streamed into the room through the yellow and white striped curtains. She closed her eyes tightly, but sleep wouldn't come again. She was as nervous as if she had an exam that morning. She got up and showered, then put on her white towelling dressing-gown and threw open all the cupboard doors, hoping that an outfit, the perfectly suitable outfit for the day, would catch her eye. The weather couldn't seem to make up its mind whether to be winter or summer. It was sunny, but there was still a bite in the air.

Daisy tried on a couple of suits. No. This wasn't an interview, however much it felt like one. Baggy blue jeans wouldn't do either. She wanted Gemma to think that she was grown up now, not sloppy like she used to be. In her red jersey dress even she could see that she looked too much like her mother for comfort. In the end, she opted for clean, newish black jeans and a white shirt, which she pressed diligently. It had been waiting to be ironed for so long she had forgotten she owned it. She belted the jeans with a black leather belt with a silver and turquoise Mexican buckle and fastened a rope of unpolished turquoise beads round her neck. By the time she had finished dressing, her thick shoulder-length hair had dried into its natural springy ringlets and she knew there was nothing she could do to smooth it, short of washing it all again. It was twelve o'clock. She made herself a cup of coffee and tucked a tea towel into the neck of her shirt so that she wouldn't spill drops down her front.

When the phone rang she hardly dared to answer it in case it was Gemma cancelling. Daisy looked at her watch. Surely she wouldn't do that only an hour before their meeting? She decided to pick it up the second it switched to the answerphone and had to speak to the editor of *Cosmopolitan* over the top of Oliver's curt message.

'Thank you so much for your fax,' she was saying, not realizing that Daisy was listening. 'We love it.'

She named a sum of money that exceeded what Daisy was already being paid by *Sixpack*.

'Oh, that'll be fine,' Daisy interrupted her.

'You're there!'

'Yes.'

'Daisy, I'd love to have lunch sometime. I wondered if we could interest you in becoming a contributing editor . . .'

'Mmm.' It had taken Daisy years of biting her tongue, but she had finally learnt not always to show her natural enthusiasm. 'I'd love to, let me get my diary,' she added.

She put down the receiver while she pretended to search for her diary. It was on the desk in front of her, looking decidedly blank. After a lot of toing and froing, they agreed a date. Daisy put down the phone and punched the air. She liked the editor of *Cosmo*, but, even more, she liked the idea of a cheque appearing in her bank account every month just for the privilege of allowing her name to appear on the masthead.

Gemma leaned over her desk and lifted the pile of paper out of her in-tray. She began to stack it in order of priority. Then she decided to make two piles, one for really urgent and one for thinking about. She divided the really urgent pile into those that needed to be responded to by phone, and those that required letters dictated, then asked Sally to bring her in a coffee, her third that morning. She went to the washroom, re-applied her lipstick, brushed her hair and came back to her desk. She looked at her watch. That whole manoeuvre had taken just ten minutes. She took a deep breath and picked up the first letter on the urgent phone pile. It was querying a clause in a contract. When she looked at it more carefully, Gemma realized that she needed to do a bit more research and talk to the contracts manager. She put the piece of paper on the thinking pile and turned to the next. It was an invitation to the launch of a book by a controversial American feminist. She decided to get Sally to respond. She picked up her dictaphone and pressed the record button.

'Sally, please accept this invitation, and in future just accept any invitation for me and put it in my diary. Unless I'm on holiday. OK?'

She turned the machine off and looked at her watch again. She didn't think she could drink any more coffee. Her stomach was full of butterflies, and the caffeine had made her feel light-headed in a hot, rather unpleasant way.

'Sally. Where is Orso's? I'm lunching there,' she called through her open door to the work station outside where Sally sat.

'It's in Covent Garden,' Sally replied. 'Have you booked a table?'

'Will I need to?'

Booking a table was not something she could imagine Daisy thinking of.

'Friday lunchtime? Yes, I should think so,' Sally replied.

'Just ring and ask if they have a booking for Rush at one.'

'OK,' Sally sounded mystified.

A few moments later she walked into Gemma's office.

'They didn't, so I booked one for two people. They'd just had a cancellation for one-fifteen. Is that OK?'

'Wonderful,' said Gemma. 'When's my meeting with the boss?'

'Four o'clock.'

'Well, I should be back in plenty of time.'

Daisy hurried through the crowds milling around the piazza. There were a couple of young women singing arias to the accompaniment of an orchestral backing track blaring out from a tinny tape recorder. Daisy stopped to watch as one of them threw herself into the role of Carmen. She was good at all the gestures and sexy glances, but her voice sounded more suited to an amateur production of Gilbert and Sullivan. Still, thought Daisy, it must be difficult to compete with a carousel with its musical box repetition of tunes from *The Sound of Music*. Next to the Punch and Judy show, two men dressed as clowns were juggling with batons, and beside them an earnest-looking Pierrot enacted the clichéd mime of being in a glass box. It was Daisy's opinion that all mime artists should be forcibly locked away in boxes, since that is where they seemed happiest, preferably ones with opaque sides so no-one would have to watch them. What on earth did all these people do before city councils decided to tart up their warehouse areas and turn them into bijoux shopping malls, Daisy wondered? People were always talking about the Laura Ashley-fication of town centres, but who ever complained about the proliferation of street theatre? Even though it was generally incompetent and downright boring, it was almost a sacred cow of the liberal classes. Daisy wondered if she could get an article out of it.

Gemma walked up Long Acre, wondering why all the restaurants and most of the shops had red, white and blue bunting in their windows, then it dawned on her that England was about to descend into a frenzy of flag-waving because in a couple of weeks it would be the anniversary of fifty years since victory in Europe. Unlike most of the people she had spoken to, she was feeling quite excited about the re-enactment of the celebrations. VE day itself had been a special day in her family's history. It was the day that her Uncle Ken had proposed to her Aunt Shirley. Gemma didn't know how many times she had made Shirley tell her the story when she was little, but she remembered every word of her account.

They had all danced in Piccadilly Circus. Estella had been with them, for some reason, although she must have still been a child. She had once asked her mother about it.

'Yes, we danced,' Estella had said, looking out onto the fields that surrounded Whitton House. 'I thought that people danced all the time in London. When I finally arrived there, I found out it wasn't true. But it was still fun,' she added wistfully.

Sometimes Estella tried to recreate the fun of London in her home, inviting people she knew down for weekends, making huge bowls of punch on hot summer afternoons. The party would start very loudly with lots of glamorous women screeching at each other, and men in crumpled white jackets attempting to play croquet on their bumpy lawn, but, by the end of the afternoon, they would all be sleeping in various combinations in the bedrooms and sofas round the house, and Gemma would sneak downstairs to steal leftover cocktail sausages, and bits of melting Brie. Once, she remembered, a very drunken actress had casually flicked a long grey column of ash from her cigarette onto Gemma's hair, setting it smouldering. Gemma ran screaming to her mother, who was sitting on a garden seat, in the shade of the horse chestnut, talking in hushed tones to a man with a striped jacket and oily hair. She had unceremoniously poured her glass of sticky liquid over Gemma's head to douse it and instructed her to go upstairs if she couldn't behave like an adult. One of Gemma's recurring nightmares ever since had been that her hair was falling out in sticky clumps filled with pieces of cocktail fruit.

She found the restaurant easily enough, pushed open its heavy wooden door and walked down the stairs, her right hand instinctively smoothing down her silky hair. It was exactly one o'clock. There was no sign of Daisy. She ordered a mineral water and waited at the bar, surveying the scene. The restaurant was obviously popular and very noisy. It seemed an odd place to have chosen for their first meeting, but perhaps, Gemma thought, it was as private as a quieter restaurant, since here everyone was practically shouting to make themselves heard, and there was no hope of eavesdropping on the nearest table if you wanted to keep up any kind of conversation at all.

The woman in charge of reservations came over to tell her that her table was ready, and Gemma was deciding whether to go and sit at it or have another drink at the bar, when she heard a noise that was almost as distinctive as a voice behind her. Daisy had never been able to walk quietly downstairs, she always clattered down, making a sound that their father had likened to a herd of elephants. Gemma turned round to greet her sister, unable to stop herself smiling. In one leap from the bottom step, Daisy was in her arms, hugging her with child-like abandon and apologizing breathlessly for being late.

Gemma managed to catch some long-winded excuse that seemed to involve *Cosmopolitan*, Carmen and the fact that Daisy would be paying for lunch. She disentangled herself from the embrace and took a step back from Daisy to look at her properly. She was as beautiful as ever, perhaps slimmer, especially in her face. She looked a little older and there was something different about her expression. At first Gemma couldn't think what it was. Her clothes, a kind of designer cowboy outfit, suited her figure well, although the blue and white checked scarf round her neck looked dirty, as if it had coffee rings on it.

Daisy saw that Gemma's gaze had settled on her neck. Her hand went nervously to her throat and in horror she pulled out the tea towel and stuffed it in her shoulder bag.

'Oh God!' she wailed, half laughing, 'and I was trying to look so smart.'

'What was it?' Gemma enquired.

'It's just I didn't want to spill anything down my shirt. You know how that always happens if you're wearing something white? And then the phone rang and then I had to rush . . .' Daisy began to laugh.

Gemma couldn't stop herself laughing too. 'Actually, I thought it looked fine. If it had been a bit cleaner, you could be on to something . . .'

'Designer dishcloth. Hmm. Is our table ready?'

'I'll have a Negroni. I don't know why, but I always have a Negroni when I come here. Why don't you have one?' Daisy suggested.

'Remind me what's in Negroni,' said Gemma.

'I've no idea, but it's absolutely delicious.'

'And strong?'

'Oh, I don't think so.'

'OK, then, why not?'

Daisy beckoned the waiter over and ordered their drinks.

'I love it here. I used to come here the whole time when I was lunching people for *Panache* . . .' Daisy chattered away.

She's as nervous as I am, thought Gemma.

'When did you leave *Panache*?' she asked, sounding like an interviewer.

'Oh, it must be a couple of years at least – 1990, I think. Oops, that's five years. You see, I got head-hunted to be deputy on a new weekend magazine thing, but I wasn't any good at it, really, so after a miz couple of years I gave that up and decided to go freelance. You see, I'm only any good at writing my own stuff. I hated trying to have ideas for other people. Shall we have a look at the menu? I'm starving . . .'

Why do I always have to fill a silence, thought Daisy, why can't I just shut up and let Gem take over? Why, when asked a simple question, do I go off into paragraphs of unsolicited explanation? Just shut up, she told herself.

She looked at her sister who was perusing the menu intensely. Gemma looked like a proper career woman now, she thought. Her strawberry-blond hair, that hung in an expensive bob with a side parting, was all shiny, her skin was smooth too. It was the skin of someone who had regular facials and kept up a skincare regime in between. She was slim as a wisp. The black Capri pants and the close-fitting powder-blue cashmere twinset emphasized her perfect figure. If Daisy had worn the outfit, the bottom of the cardigan and the top of the trousers that met so perfectly at Gemma's slim waist, would have gaped just slightly, showing a little midriff and making it look tarty rather than elegant, and, Daisy thought, she never would be able to carry a white Kelly bag without it getting scuffed.

'The rocket salad with Parma Ham and shaved Parmesan is very good . . .' she suggested. 'Then I'm going to have the risotto', she said to the waiter, 'and some red wine. Is red OK, Gem?'

'I don't normally drink at lunchtime . . .' said Gemma.

'But it's such a special occasion,' said Daisy.

Gemma felt unable to refuse. She had forgotten how easy it was to get swept along in Daisy's enthusiasms. And, she had to admit, she had rather enjoyed the hit she had got from the Negroni which, as far as she could taste, contained a combination of vermouth and gin and no mixer. She felt as if all the tension that had built up during the morning was slipping away from her.

'So, are you happy being freelance?' Gemma asked, as the waiter put two hand-painted ceramic bowls of salad down in front of them.

'Oh yes, I love it. It's so much nicer being in control . . .' Daisy began on the answer she usually gave then stopped suddenly.

'Not really,' she said, surprising herself with her candour, 'I mean, I'm not unhappy or anything, but . . . I mean, are you happy, do you think, or do you ever think that there must be something more? . . . I don't know, I just feel so valueless somehow . . . Also . . .' she found herself trying to articulate something that disturbed her more and more these days, 'I don't think that really I'm any good at anything. No, I'm not trying to be falsely modest . . .' she said, seeing Gemma's eyebrows rise. 'I mean, for example, the editor of *Cosmopolitan* asked me to become a contributing editor this morning. In my field, that's pretty near the top, and on the one hand I'm thrilled, but if I let myself think for even a second that it's no more than I deserve, I suddenly get swamped with these feelings that I'm no good really and people will find me out, and I don't know anything, and everything I think is completely banal and stupid . . . Am I making any sense?'

'In the States it's called the Impostor Syndrome,' Gemma said. 'Everyone feels it, I think. Particularly women. Don't you think?'

'Do *you* ever feel like that?' asked Daisy incredulously.

Gemma suddenly realized that the quality in Daisy's face that she hadn't been able to place was a kind of solitariness, loneliness almost. Whereas Daisy had always looked out towards the world, now part of her was looking inwards, critically.

'Of course I do. Perhaps not so much recently, perhaps it gets better as you get older, although I feel I have a lot to prove in my new job,' said Gemma reassuringly. She pushed the salad round her plate, wishing she had chosen something that was easier to eat.

'The trouble is', said Daisy, 'that with you it probably is just a kind of nervousness, whereas with me it's more fundamental.'

She dipped a piece of Italian country bread into the saucer of basil-scented olive oil in the middle of the table and brought it to her lips. Since Daisy had drawn attention to it, Gemma couldn't help watching the front of her shirt. So far Daisy had managed to avoid spilling anything but a few crumbs.

'But doesn't that go with the territory?' Gemma responded, falling into her natural role of the older, wiser sister with perfect ease even after ten years of separation. 'You feel that your feelings of unworthiness are more genuine than anyone else's. When you think about it that's really an inverted form of competitiveness . . .'

'But in my case, it's *true*!' Daisy insisted, half-giggling, realizing that she had just proved Gemma's point. 'I mean, I never went to university, I've always winged it, haven't I?'

If she had been having this conversation with her imagination Gemma would have said yes. Yes, Daisy, as a matter of fact you have always got away with murder. But now, with her sister sitting in front of her, obviously distressed, she couldn't bring herself to say that. If she had been coldly analyzing their conversation, as she had analyzed so many of their past conversations in the last ten years, she would have concluded that Daisy was being as manipulative as ever, forestalling any kind of criticism that might be coming her way by criticizing herself first and making you feel sorry for her. The trouble was, Gemma thought now, that manipulative behaviour implied some kind of premeditation, and what she had forgotten about Daisy, in her re-creation of her as a hate figure, was her totally spontaneous approach to life, the quality of unconscious innocence that she possessed. It was what made her so very endearing.

'The thing is, Gem,' Daisy was saying, 'I write these articles the whole time about sex and relationships and I've only ever had two lovers,' she giggled.

Gemma looked at the wine bottle and realized it was nearly empty.

'Who was the other one?' She wanted to steer the conversation away from Oliver for as long as possible. Gemma thought that Daisy must have lost her virginity in France when she was away for that year, but, for obvious reasons, they had never had a chance to discuss it.

'Didn't you know?' Daisy looked astonished. 'I thought you must have guessed!'

'Who?'

'Vincenzo, of course.'

Daisy put down her fork and let the waiter remove the rest of her salad. She took a slurp of wine. She was unable to meet Gemma's eyes.

Gemma drained her own glass. Daisy poured them both some more, finishing the bottle.

Vincenzo was one of their mother's friends from London. Gemma hadn't given him a thought for years. If she had been asked to name all the people she knew in the world, she doubted whether his name would have come up, and, if it had, she would have described him as one of her mother's many homosexual admirers.

'I always thought he was gay!' she said, shocked.

'Oh no!' said Daisy.

'But he was so old. You poor thing! When did it happen?'

Daisy paused with uncharacteristic discretion as the waiter placed a shallow bowl of steaming risotto in front of her and a hunk of roasted cod with strips of yellow and red pepper in front of Gemma. 'It wasn't just once. We were lovers for quite a long time.'

'I don't believe it. How long?'

'About a year, before I went to France. It was one of the reasons I was so desperate to go. I mean, he was sweet, but he was getting to be a bit of a pain, really . . .'

'But why didn't you tell me?'

'You were up at Oxford. I didn't think you'd approve. I mean, listen to what you just said. No-one knew, really. Only Mum. She kind of set it up, I think.'

'She what?' Gemma was horrified.

'She always said she wanted me to learn about sex from someone who knew,' Daisy replied.

'Oh God, and she no doubt offered you her bed to be deflowered in?' Gemma banged down her fork, huffily, 'Don't you think there was something horrible about that kind of Sixties liberalism? I'd have preferred a mother who fainted at the thought of marijuana rather than one who was constantly passing you a joint.' Gemma paused.

Daisy obviously wasn't going to join in the tirade against Estella. She had always been much closer to their mother and more sympathetic to her excesses.

'Anyway,' Gemma continued, 'how did she know he knew about . . . oh no, they hadn't been lovers too?'

'Well, I think they must have been,' said Daisy. 'I kind of knew that he wanted me just because I looked so much like her. At first, anyway. He adored her.'

'They all adored her, that Chelsea Arts Club lot. They all painted pictures of her and probably screwed her afterwards. I don't know how Bertie put up with it,' said Gemma.

'Oh Gem! Don't be so hard on her. Bertie understood what she was like.'

Gemma stiffened. 'Do you think so?'

'Of course he did. He introduced her to that lot, after all.'

'I suppose he did.'

Gemma had never thought of her father as one of the bohemian crowd whose company Estella so enjoyed. He was so much quieter, more modest about his work, a gentler, more thoughtful person.

Estella had been one of his students, as she never

stopped telling people, as if to make their age difference quite clear. She couldn't have borne it for a second if someone had made the mistake of thinking that she was his age, but wearing well. Not, thought Gemma, that she was quite as young as she would have it understood she was.

A couple of years before, when she herself was twenty-nine and suffering from an attack of pre-thirty blues, it had occurred to Gemma that this was the age Estella must have been when she first gave birth. At first the thought made her even more depressed – there was absolutely no-one in her life right then, nor had she ever had a relationship that looked capable of lasting six months, let alone a lifetime of sharing and children. She felt an uncontrollable sadness that time was slipping away from her, and for several days she had wandered round in a mildly catatonic state of panic, until Meryl took her out for a lot of martinis and told her about all the women she knew who had had darling babies at the age of forty.

It was only when the cloud of depression lifted and Gemma was trying to talk her self-confidence back that she realized how much she had achieved in the last ten years, and how little, by contrast, she knew about those years in her mother's life before she married Bertie. Twenty-nine, or twenty-eight as she must have been when she met him, was quite an age for a *student*. Had her mother, she wondered, also suffered from a pre-thirty panic attack? Had she really wanted a child? They were questions that she had never thought of asking Estella when she was alive, and now she would never know the answers.

'Well, did you?' she asked Daisy.

'Did I what?'

'Did you and Vincenzo take Estella up on the offer of her bed?'

'Ugh, no! Actually, we did it in a field first of all.

Aesthetically pleasing to be surrounded by golden corn and poppies, but bloody uncomfortable, I can tell you. He did bring a lovely picnic, though,' she remembered.

Gemma couldn't suppress a laugh.

'He took a lot of photographs of me afterwards,' Daisy went on, 'I had a great big blood stain on my dress that matched perfectly with the poppies. I thought it was terribly cool then, as you can imagine, far better than losing it in the back of your boyfriend's dad's Escort like most of the girls at school. Now, I sometimes wonder whether he wasn't a bit of a Humbert Humbert. Do you know something?' She leant forward confidentially, 'I'm sure he dyed his hair. His pubes were completely grey!'

'Daisy!'

'Well, men are always smirking to one another about natural blondes aren't they? I don't think Vincenzo was a natural brunette!'

The waiter removed their empty plates and offered them pudding menus.

'I'm going to have some of those lovely nutty biscuits with Vin Santo. I'm so drunk now I might as well,' said Daisy.

Gemma looked at her watch. It was after three. She couldn't imagine being sober enough in one hour's time to have a meeting with her boss, but there was no way she could cancel it now. 'I'll have coffee. Double espresso. I need to use the washroom,' she added, standing up, checking her balance.

'Shall I get you some of those biscuits, Biscuit?'

'If you wouldn't mind, Donut,' Gemma replied without thinking.

'What about your love life, then,' Daisy said as soon as Gemma returned to the table. 'Here I am prattling on. I don't know anything about what you've been up to in

New York. Except about Boy, of course. I was so sorry about that, Gem, I really was.'

For a moment, Gemma felt a rush of vitriol returning. Why, she wanted to ask, why is it, do you think, Daisy, that we've been out of touch? Could it really be that Daisy hadn't worked it out? Surely not. And, for heaven's sake, even if she didn't know, she should have. Wasn't there a phrase in law, culpable negligence or something?

But, she thought, how much more difficult it is to hate someone when they're sitting across a table, two feet away from you. Nothing seemed to matter half so much now. Anyway, there wasn't time to start explaining. There would only be tears. She breathed her anger down. What was it Daisy had been saying?

'In the last couple of years he was almost a fulltime occupation. What with work as well I didn't get a chance to have much of a life of my own. Somehow it doesn't seem to matter when there's someone dying right next to you.'

'I don't know how you stood it,' Daisy said. 'Two years of constant illness. I'm hopeless when Lol gets a cold. Mind you, he is a terrible hypochondriac. He never has a cold, always a chest infection, or he suspects his lung has collapsed. He never throws up because he's had too much rich food, it's always gastric flu, or an incipient stomach ulcer, d'you know what I mean?'

A brief memory of Oliver lying groaning on their sofa in the front room when he had a hangover and her rushing in and out with Alka Seltzer and cold compresses made Gemma smile. Yes, she supposed, he was inclined to exaggerate a bit, but she would never have dared to think that then, let alone say it.

'It wasn't like that, though,' she tried to explain, blotting out the image of Oliver. 'There was so much that Boy wanted to do. Half the time I was either trying to keep up with him, or trying to get him to conserve his energy. Like one day last winter, it was really freezing outside, you know? Boy's eyesight had virtually packed up, but he wanted to see the skaters in Central Park. I was saying to him, you can't go out in this weather, and he said, "Oh are you worried I'll catch my death of cold?" We did a lot, though. Once he said he felt it was a kind of liberation to know that you were going to die, so that you had to do what you always wanted to do now. We went to every concert and every play and every exhibition. And Boy seemed to think that the rules of polite behaviour didn't apply to him anymore, so if we were at a private view and he thought the paintings were bad, he'd say so.'

'Did he have a boyfriend?' Daisy asked.

'Not in the last few years. He had loads of friends, but he didn't have a steady partner. And you need someone there, you know, for those existential sweats in the middle of the night. Boy had plenty of people to laugh with, but when he wanted to cry, there was only me.'

Gemma felt tears coming to her eyes. 'When we found out, you know, my first instinct was to run away. But I didn't. I'm really glad I didn't. Yes, sometimes it felt like too much responsibility, but we had a lot of fun too.'

'Fun?' Daisy asked.

'We went to Las Vegas last year,' Gemma said. 'You know how most people, if they found out they were going to die would have one ambition – to see the Taj Mahal, or Botticelli's Venus, or something worthy like that?'

'Yes, well, I can imagine . . .'

'Boy wanted to see Caesar's Palace. He wanted to sit in the Forum, which has wonderful air-conditioning, where the sun sets every ten minutes. He worked out that he could fit a whole year's sunsets into five days that way, and, he said, it didn't smell bad like real Rome!'

'He sounds nice,' Daisy said quietly. Then, after a moment's thought, she asked, 'When he died, did you feel that you'd said everything to him that you wanted?' There was a catch in her voice as if she were talking about an unresolved quandary of her own.

Gemma was silent for a few minutes, then she looked at her sister and said, 'I think his death taught me that you never do get that last half hour with someone, however much you're prepared. And it's no good feeling guilty all your life that you didn't say the things you wanted to say.'

As she spoke the words, she realized that she wasn't really talking about Boy anymore, but that maybe his death had enabled her to come to terms with the guilty sadness she had buried deep inside. A sadness that united her with Daisy.

They sat in silence for a few moments.

Then Daisy said, very quietly, 'Why do you think Estella killed herself?'

Gemma looked at her watch.

'I've got to run,' she said.

'No. You can't go now,' Daisy said desperately, 'not now, for God's sake.'

'Daisy, I'm meeting the chairman of the company in five minutes' time. I can't just put my life on hold because it suits you.'

'I didn't mean . . .' Daisy faltered.

She had thought that the barriers were coming down, that Gemma was warming to her a little. Now she seemed as cool and distant as someone whose foot she had accidentally stepped on in the tube.

'When will I see you again?' Daisy asked, admitting almost under her breath, 'I'm frightened to let you go now.' She clung to Gemma's arm.

Gemma looked at Daisy's hand. Her hands hadn't

changed, they were small and round and the nails were all bitten. She felt herself softening slightly. 'I'll call you over the weekend,' she said. 'Really, I will.'

She bent forward and kissed her sister's cheek. Daisy's skin was peachy, and there was an underlying scent of baby soap, only partially drowned out by the rotting smell of red wine.

Daisy put her arms out and hugged her tightly, burying her nose in Gemma's shoulder and starting to cry.

'Come on, Dodo, it's OK,' Gemma said, giving her an embarrassed half pat on the back. She looked round the restaurant anxiously. Nobody seemed to be taking any interest in Daisy's scene-making. 'It's OK, it's OK,' she said more gently. 'Ugh, Daisy, don't blow your nose on my jumper!' she added as Daisy sniffed loudly.

CHAPTER 12

'OK, so you've got a Lamborghini in your garage at home, but that doesn't stop you going for a spin in a friend's Alfa, does it?' Nigel was saying.

The other men chuckled. Although Oliver was at the same table he seemed to be sitting a slight distance away from them. He was listening to the conversation but not participating in it. He acknowledged Daisy's approach to the table with the briefest look.

'What about you, Oliver,' Nigel continued, 'you've got a luxury ride at home but d'you ever feel tempted to have a day round the track at Silverstone?'

'I think this conversation is being driven by a bit too much Ferrari Testarossa,' Oliver replied.

The others laughed.

'Hi, everyone!' said Daisy.

They turned round. It was only when she saw their slightly shifty looks that she realized that they had not really been talking about cars.

'What can I get you?' Nigel leapt up, offering her his seat.

'Oh, I don't know. I've been drinking all afternoon. A glass of red wine, maybe.'

'Are you sure? It's rough.'

'I don't think I could tell the difference,' Daisy said, sitting down.

'Watch yourselves, lads,' Nigel whispered, as he muzzed up her hair affectionately, 'or you might find yourselves being quoted in next month's *Sixpack*.'

Daisy sat patiently like a dog being patted, hating every second of Nigel's attentions. He was the sort of man she absolutely loathed. Early forties, getting fat through unhealthy living, slightly sweaty. He looked as if he smelled even if he didn't. He had no sense of physical boundaries, or, she sometimes thought, perhaps he did, and his pats and touches were a challenge, a test of power. Daisy pitied all the women who worked in the office. It was difficult to believe that Nigel, whose pub and after-dinner conversation had the maturity of an insensitive eleven-year-old, was the head of the firm of solicitors in which Oliver was a minority partner. Nigel had been to a good public school, but he insisted on talking in a fake working-class accent as if it gave him street credibility. Daisy looked around the table and noticed that all the partners were present and not one of them was a woman, not one of them was from an ethnic minority. It made you wonder about British justice.

Conversation seemed to have stopped since Daisy's arrival. She began to wish she hadn't come. As she left Orso's, blinking as she stepped out into the sunlight, she had noticed that the wine bars and cafés of the Covent Garden piazza were filling up with office workers having a drink at the end of the week. It had seemed like a good idea to meet Oliver out of work. The firm always went for a Friday night booze-up in the pub opposite the office.

'We were just debating the merits of fidelity,' Nigel said, putting down her drink and drawing up a stool rather too close to her. 'What's a beautiful woman's view of that? I expect you get dozens of offers.'

She felt that he was trying to provoke Oliver.

'Oh,' she said, 'I rather adopt Paul Newman's maxim.'

'Which is?'

'Why go out for a hamburger when you can have steak at home?'

Instantly, she thought of the steak that Oliver had left her the other night when she came back from the Groucho. It was still sitting in its marinade in the fridge. She stifled a giggle.

'And I suppose', said Oliver, 'that you think comparing a man to a piece of meat is perfectly acceptable?' He made it sound like a joke, but there was an edge to his voice.

'Not really,' she admitted, giving him an exasperated glance. 'I was only trying to come down to a level that Nigel would understand.'

Oliver laughed and clapped.

'Although I don't get as worked up about reification as a lot of women,' she continued, expanding on her theme. 'That's making women into objects, for those of you who didn't know,' she bantered. 'I mean there are compliments that are strangely acceptable to most women and there are some that aren't ever.'

'Do tell,' said one of the other solicitors.

'Well, it's always nice to be told that you have great legs, but most women wouldn't like to hear that they "go like a train". That's one I've heard you using, Nigel. I would caution against . . .'

'I'd never say that *to* someone, only *about* them . . .' protested Nigel.

'I'll take your word for that. But would it stand up in court?' Daisy asked with particular emphasis on the words stand and up.

'Does she always give you so much verbal?' Nigel continued, trying to bring Oliver in on his side.

Oliver merely smiled enigmatically.

The conversation turned to the FA Cup.

Daisy often found that the Friday night drinking sessions were useful research for her *Sixpack* column. Excluded from the talk – she knew next to nothing about football, and thought the only women who did take an interest were those who found it difficult to get boyfriends – she began to think out a piece about compliments that women like (sometimes despite themselves) and compliments that never work. Most women, she thought, would like to be called intelligent or intuitive, but would hate being referred to as brainy. She began to picture a chart with columns of Hits and Misses. It was exactly the sort of mindless article with graphics that Patrick was crazy for.

She realized that she was daydreaming and her eyes were resting on a couple who were canoodling at a table at the other end of the pub. She saw his fingers take the hand that was resting on the seat between them and begin caressing her wrist. Just as she took in who it was and started to look away, the man looked up and recognized her. It was Kathy's husband Roger, with Emily, Oliver's outdoor clerk. Daisy didn't know whether to wave or look away. In the end, she contrived to wave and look disapproving at the same time. Roger drained his glass. The next time she looked they had gone.

'I wonder', she said, leaning across the table to Oliver and whispering, 'whether I should tell Gemma about Roger and your clerk, you know, so that she could warn Kathy?'

'It wouldn't be the first thing I'd share with the estranged sister after ten years' silence,' Oliver responded.

Daisy looked at him quizzically and then remembered that he didn't know they had met.

'I've just spent the afternoon with her.'

'Really?'

'Lol, we had the *best* time . . .'

Her eyes were shining with love. It was a look that he hadn't seen for some time. He knew it was irrational, but for a second he felt almost blinded by jealousy.

*   *   *

So many memories, so many images. Gemma lay flat on her back and closed her eyes. Her bedroom was cool and the mews was insulated from the sounds of the street except for the muted non-specific hum of traffic. In the distance a police siren wailed. Compared to any of the places she had lived in New York, it was an oasis of tranquillity.

She had been back in England for less than a month, but the ten years she had spent in New York seemed each day to get more and more distant, like the sound of the police siren as it passed down Ladbroke Grove and away up the Harrow Road, fading until there was a moment when she didn't know whether it had quite gone, or whether she was imagining it.

Time seemed to have collapsed, so that the ten years could just as easily have been ten months, or even ten weeks.

She thought that she had changed, and she had, in superficial ways. Her past, the years and people that had created her, had not changed. Even though she had blocked them out from her consciousness, they had continued, and she had been part of them, just as they had always been part of her, because if you shared a past, she was beginning to realize, you shared a present and a future too.

With no touchstone to remind her, no Boy to talk to on the phone, no Meryl to have a coffee with after work, the memory of her life in the States had become like a series of postcards, or photos in an album: two-dimensional and objective. Some events, like the trip to Las Vegas, seemed as unreal as that city itself, with its virtual Sphinx and its ten-minute sunsets, and yet at the time she had thought she was really living.

They had taken 5000 dollars in cash which, Boy insisted (and it was his money), was all to be lost gambling – 1000 dollars a day. The first night, playing roulette for the first time, she had won 10,000 dollars. Boy had been furiously disappointed.

'The one extravagant gesture I make in my life, and you ruin it!' he said sulkily, and wheeled himself off to bed, refusing Gemma's offers of assistance.

The lift doors closed behind his chair and Gemma was left holding a large marbled plastic chip in her hand. She decided to cash it in, putting half the money back in her purse and getting low denomination chips for the rest. Then, turning away from the cashier, she noticed that a man who had been at their table was watching her. He started to walk towards her.

This was becoming a little too much like a Mario Puzo novel for comfort. Gemma turned back to the cashier, but another customer had slipped in front of her.

'May I introduce myself?' The man bowed slightly, 'My name is Herman.' He had a slight European accent. 'I, too, find myself alone in this strange city,' he continued. 'Would you care to join me for a drink?'

'Well . . .' Gemma hesitated and looked at her watch. It was nearly midnight. Officially, there was no time in Las Vegas, because there were no clocks, and no daylight once you were inside. It had succeeded in disorientating her. It felt earlier. She was lively, exhilarated by her winnings. 'OK,' she said, telling herself she couldn't come to any harm as long as they stayed in the hotel.

Herman was Swiss. He said he was a student at Harvard, but he was neither as poor nor as young as any student Gemma had known. He was driving a Cadillac from the east to the west coast, and had stopped for a day or two in Las Vegas. She didn't know whether any of it was true, nor did she particularly care. She wondered briefly whether he was really a male prostitute, but he talked so much about himself that she decided it was unlikely. Nor did he expect her to pay for anything. She felt no need to tell him about herself, or her situation, and he didn't ask. She didn't know if it was narcissism or lack of interest, but she was grateful for his incuriosity.

He was tall and fair, and a text-book fuck. His love-making was so technically good it was almost clinical. There was no passion, only proficiency. Gemma found it profoundly satisfying. For the next three nights she met him every evening at around the same time, when Boy had gone to bed. He taught her how to play black-jack and shoot craps. When her winnings exceeded fifty thousand, she became less cautious with her stakes. It was like toy money. Eventually she lost everything but the five thousand she had cashed in on the first night.

At around three in the morning, they would retire to his room. He had a king-sized waterbed. It was so ridiculously clichéd that Gemma wanted to laugh, but his kisses silenced her. On the last night he gave her underwear, luxurious and tasteful, an oyster satin camisole with hand-rolled edges and French knickers which she wore as he fucked her, his huge penis bunching the silk, pinching the soft flesh where her thighs divided.

In the early evenings, she taught Boy her new gambling skills, and he happily lost a thousand a night, as he had planned. During the day, as they sat by the pool, Gemma dazed by lack of sleep, only capable of sipping Coke and lying under a yellow umbrella, Boy relentlessly questioned her about her evening's activities. She felt mean, but she wouldn't tell him.

There was an unspoken agreement that she would not meet Herman during the day. On the last day, though, they ended up sharing a lift. They had already said their goodbyes. There had been no suggestion of exchange of addresses or keeping in touch. She was polite, as if he were just an acquaintance from the tables, but Boy guessed immediately. All the way home on the plane, and afterwards, he teased her about Herman the German.

It was all so distant, so unreal. Perhaps she had dreamed it? Gemma closed her eyes and fell asleep.

CHAPTER 13

Gemma was in the kitchen at Whitton House. Sun streamed in through the window and dust motes danced in front of her eyes. At first she thought she was alone. It was hot and silent. The house was completely still. Sweat trickled from under her breasts and armpits, soaking the thin cotton of her summer dress. She tried to open the door into the garden, but it was stuck.

She thought she heard a noise upstairs. The stairs creaked as she tiptoed up, not wanting to alert the intruder to her presence. The door to her parents' room was ajar. Gemma pushed it gently, but it flew back and banged. There, on the double bed, Estella lay sleeping. A dribble of vomit trickled from her mouth. The room smelt of decay. Suddenly Estella opened her eyes and smiled. Her skin was grey and papery.

'You're dead,' Gemma told her.

Estella's eyes closed again.

The noise was coming from down the passage. It was like the sound of an old rocking chair. Gemma crept along in the dark. She opened the door to Daisy's room. Some of the posters had lost their Blu-Tack corners and they flapped around in the draught. The room was empty.

She stood outside her own bedroom, shaking, then, unable to stop herself, she pushed the door open.

Oliver was lying in her bed. His black curly hair fanned out on the pink and white floral pillow, his head tipped back, eyes looking at the ceiling, ecstatic. Daisy sat astride him, her feet tangled up in the pink and white sheet. She was rocking up and down.

Somewhere deep in Gemma's chest she heard herself shouting, 'Why do you have to do it in my bed?'

But they didn't seem to hear her.

Gemma woke up sweating. The white cotton duvet felt as sticky and constrictive as a nylon sleeping bag. She threw it back and lay naked in the sunlight that streamed in through the bedroom window. Some of the sweat evaporated from under her breasts, cooling her, but the room felt airless. Gemma got up and opened a window. She could tell from the sounds of the market that she had slept too long. They were mid-morning sounds and the smell of hot oil from the kebab and chip shop told her it was almost lunchtime. She made herself try to remember the dream. If she acknowledged it, it might go away, stop haunting her, but she could only remember the pain of betrayal as she stood impotent in the doorway while her sister pleasured the man she loved.

She had thought that seeing Daisy again would help to bring her feelings to the surface and banish the nightmare. But it hadn't gone. If anything, it was more vivid. She lay sweating, feeling frustrated with herself and angry. It was no good. She had tried to paper over the cracks and forgive, but it wasn't working. She was going to have to see Daisy again and have it out with her once and for all.

Daisy lay in bed, the sheet pulled right up to her chin. She felt happy. She could hear Oliver juicing oranges in the kitchen. He brought her a tall glass. The juice took the unpleasant after-taste of spring onions from her mouth.

They had left the other solicitors drinking in the pub and gone to Chinatown for food. Oliver was on particularly good form. Daisy knew that he was delighted that she had come to meet him after work, even though he wouldn't say it to her. He ordered a whole crab dressed with ginger and spring onion and deep fried oysters with a tiny saucer of chili sauce. The waiter banged down the dishes on the table, bewildered by their refusal of rice or noodles. Daisy hadn't thought she was hungry, but there was a sheer sensual pleasure in sucking the flesh from the crab, her hands and cheeks covered in juices. She listened, eyes sparkling, to Oliver's imitations of Nigel, and thought how clever he was and how lucky she was to be with him. When Oliver was like this, she felt that same excitement, that same sense of danger and exhilaration as when she had first met him, and she saw that his face, lightened by humour and fun, was the same face she had fallen in love with, and not the angry one that so often glowered at her, its flesh weighed down by criticism and unexpressed frustration.

'It's a beautiful day,' Oliver said, climbing back into bed and smoothing back her hair from her forehead. She could smell the fresh tangy scent of oranges on his fingers.

'Shall we have a day out?' she asked. 'Let's go to Woodstock or something. Have lunch.'

'It'll be tea by the time we get there. What's up?' he asked, seeing Daisy's face scrunch up.

'I'm trying to remember where I left the car.'

'God, Daisy, you are hopeless. When we find it, it'll probably have had its wheels removed.'

'God, Lol, you've said that every time I've lost it in the last ten years and it's always been perfectly all right!' she replied, mocking his nagging tone.

'Well, it's such an old rust-bucket now that I doubt if anyone would want to steal it,' he replied tartly, unable to let her have the last word.

'You always say that too,' Daisy muttered under

her breath, adding, 'Well, do you want to go out or not?'

He was about to reply when the phone rang. Daisy picked it up.

'Hi! How are you this morning?' she said, instinctively turning on to her side, away from Oliver. 'We were just trying to decide what to do. Do you fancy coming to Woodstock for the day? Oh. No, it wasn't a definite plan, no.' She looked back to Oliver.

He motioned that he was going to have a shower.

'Well, yes, I'd love to . . . I don't know about Lol . . . Oh. All right . . . I shouldn't think he'll mind . . . Do you want to come here? . . . Where then? . . . Is it? We haven't really got up yet . . . OK . . . Well, Regent's is nearer for me. We could meet in the Inner Circle. There's a rose garden. All right then, I'll see you there.'

She put down the phone, got up and walked into the bathroom. Oliver was singing *La Donna e mobile* above the splashing of water.

'That was Gemma,' she shouted above the noise of the water. 'She wants to talk to me, says it's important. I said I'd meet her.'

'What about Woodstock?' Oliver shouted back.

'Could we go tomorrow?'

'Blast!' Oliver had dropped the soap. 'Your sister refuses to communicate with you for ten years and suddenly you're supposed to drop everything for a chat?' he shouted.

Daisy pulled back the shower curtain and looked at him through the steam.

'I'm sorry, but can't you see that it's exactly because she hasn't spoken to me for ten years that I feel I have to go?'

Oliver grunted and pulled the shower curtain across. 'You're flooding the floor,' he said.

*   *   *

Gemma was sitting on a bench staring at a flower-bed. She smiled as Daisy approached, and stood up, but she stepped back as Daisy went to kiss her.

Daisy began to tremble. Gemma had put on the cloak of coldness again. It was so strong you could practically touch it. Daisy's first instinct was to cry, but she sensed that Gemma would hate that more than anything. They began to walk side by side.

Each bed had a different species of rose. Some were already in full bloom, some didn't even have buds yet. There was a particularly beautiful yellow rose, with clusters of flowers at all different stages. The buds were dark gold, flecked with red, the flowers as they began to open clear citrus yellow, and the fully-blown blossom the palest lemon, almost cream. Gemma leaned forward to smell the blooms. A light, heavenly fragrance wafted towards her nose.

'Smell this. It's wonderful,' she said.

Obediently, Daisy leaned forward. The perfume was the same as the roses that clambered over the front of Whitton House.

'Mmm. Like home,' she said.

Gemma smiled at her, acknowledging something they had in common, then her face fell. She turned and stared into the distance, unable to look at Daisy.

'You do know that I love Oliver?' she said quietly.

Daisy wasn't quite sure that she had heard her correctly. She skipped ahead to her sister's side. What did she mean? Oliver had nothing but dismissive things to say about her sister. Surely they couldn't . . .

'I've always loved him,' Gemma was saying.

'What do you mean?' Daisy interrupted.

Gemma searched her sister's face, trying to find dissembling beneath the innocent surface.

'You didn't know, did you?' she said, at last convinced.

'What?'

'Daisy, I was in love with Oliver,' she said, exasperated. 'We were lovers . . . well, we had just started . . . and then you came along and took him away from me. I've hated you ever since.'

It took a couple of minutes for the pieces of information to sink in, then, as the horrible realization of what she had done flooded her brain, Daisy let out a wail. 'Oh Biscuit, why on earth didn't you tell me?'

'Would it have made any difference?' Gemma's voice was clipped, cold.

Daisy knew it was probably the most important question from her sister she would ever have to answer. It was her turn to walk ahead, looking at the flowers, unable to meet Gemma's pale blue eyes.

'I don't know,' she said eventually, honestly, 'I'd love to say of course it would. But I can't imagine my history without Lol. It's more than a third of my life. So in a way the question is a really strange one. Do you see?'

She looked at Gemma, who nodded, listening.

'You see,' Daisy continued, encouraged by the lack of reaction, 'if I had known that day that you were in love with him, then of course I wouldn't have flirted with him. But I didn't, and, that day, Oliver seemed like my destiny.'

She couldn't help smiling, remembering that first kiss. 'In a funny kind of way, he still does . . .' she added, thinking of him in the shower this morning, and frowned, 'but I wish you had told me. Why didn't you say? It's been awful not knowing . . .' At last Daisy could contain the tears no longer. 'Just awful,' she sobbed.

'Didn't you ever think?' Gemma continued, her voice warming slightly.

'I knew you hated me,' Daisy sniffed and felt her sleeves and her pockets for a handkerchief.

It was almost a reflex action for Gemma to open her

white leather handbag and take out a tissue. How many times had she done that in her life? Daisy never had a hanky, even at school, when she was always falling over and grazing herself.

'Thanks,' said Daisy, taking the tissue. '. . . I thought it was because I was hopeless about the arrangements when Daddy died. And then I got that letter from Estella and . . .' her voice trailed away, '. . . and then, when you didn't forgive me, I thought you had post-traumatic stress syndrome. It's the worst thing, Bisc, not knowing.'

She blew her nose loudly.

'Didn't Oliver tell you?' Gemma asked.

'No, I had no idea,' Daisy replied, her mind beginning to race.

Why hadn't Oliver said anything? Perhaps he hadn't realized how strongly Gemma felt. But he must have done. He had lived under the same roof as Gemma for a whole year. Gemma had always been sophisticated, but not that sophisticated. Only now she remembered how Gemma was when she had come home from France for Christmas. All her family, sitting at the kitchen table in Whitton House. It was the last time they had all been together. Gemma had been going on and on uncharacteristically about some bloke she was sharing with. Daisy remembered being annoyed. She was dying to tell Bertie and Estella all about France.

Oliver must have realized, she thought. How typical of him to be unable to accept some responsibility for events, to pretend it was nothing to do with him.

They walked side by side along the broadwalk in silence. A couple of youths on rollerblades whizzed past, darting in and out of the crowds. A large fat labrador made a half-hearted lunge at one of the boys.

Each new flower-bed contained a different blaze of colour. Purple pansies, petunias with pink and white striped bugles lifting towards the sun, blue lobelia cascading from ornamental urns. The colours danced. Everything around them seemed vibrant, and yet they walked silently, cocooned in a bubble of sadness.

Gemma didn't know whether she felt better or worse. She was still shaking. She supposed it must be a good thing to have unburdened herself of a secret that she had told no-one before, but she didn't feel relieved, only disorientated by the shift in the absolute reality she had created for herself. Was she mad, she wondered, to have thought that Daisy had known all along?

'Well,' said Daisy eventually, with a short wry laugh, 'Lol has certainly got something that all the Rush girls want.'

'What do you mean?' Gemma asked.

'You know that Mum tried to make a pass at him?' Daisy revealed.

'What? When?'

'After Daddy died. When we were all staying at Whitton. I must have told you . . .'

'We weren't really speaking . . .' said Gemma.

'Well, you know the veranda?'

Gemma nodded, eager to hear the story.

It was really a run-down greenhouse leaning against the back of Whitton House. Estella had insisted on calling it a veranda, or, in her more pretentious moments, the conservatory. There were shelves in it with potting trays and a few old terracotta pots. Estella was a feckless gardener. She loved the image of herself gathering cut flowers in a wooden trug, but she was impatient with the work that preceded it. Sometimes when Bertie received an unexpected royalty cheque he would hire a gardener from the village for the week, and Estella would play lady of the manor, ordering the poor man to dig out unusually shaped beds where she would plant the masses of bedding plants she had bought. For the first few days they would look wonderful, like the colourful abstracts in oils she sometimes painted, but then Estella would grow bored and forget to water them, and very soon the weeds would take over again.

'Lol loved the smell of the veranda,' Daisy continued, 'you know, that sort of geranium smell it had.'

Gemma remembered exactly. It was a sharp, composty smell.

'And there was that planter's chair . . .'

A battered relic of the colonies that Estella had found in a saleroom. The teak frame was solid and in good condition, but the wickerwork was frayed and full of holes. The chair had been left in the veranda until she found a man to repair it.

'It was a boiling hot day. Do you remember? Lol went into the veranda to read. He couldn't bear the oppressiveness of the house. He couldn't bear Estella's histrionics, and I was nearly as bad . . .'

'Where was I?' Gemma interrupted.

'You'd gone for a walk. I don't think you could bear to be in the house either. You were acting very strangely. You were really hostile and barely spoke to any of us. I thought it was because of Bertie dying, but I understand now . . . anyway, I think I must have gone for a rest, or something. Lol said he had fallen asleep, when suddenly he was aware of a shadow over him . . .'

Daisy was recounting the tale like a ghost story, part excited, part frightened.

'So, he opened an eye. Estella was standing right over him, staring at him in a peculiar way. He said she seemed to be transfixed by his body. He'd taken off his T-shirt in the heat, you see. She didn't even notice that he had woken up, so he pretended to be asleep again. He didn't want to talk to her. He thought she was hysterical.'

Daisy paused, remembering the way her mother kept bursting into tears in the weeks following Bertie's death. It had been very disturbing to see someone so strong reduced to such frailty.

'So what happened?' Gemma interrupted impatiently.

'Well, then she started to touch him, caressing his arms, his hands, his neck. Then, she took off her blouse and held his face against her breasts. Lol didn't know what to do. He told me that he felt he was suffocating with the smell of her perfume and her sweat in the heat of the veranda. He pretended he was beginning to wake up, and suddenly, as if she had just realized what she was doing, she let go of his head. He says it fell back with quite a crack against the wood, but you know how he exaggerates . . . "First she tries to smother me, then she tries to break my skull!" '

Daisy did a brilliant impersonation of Oliver's outraged voice. Gemma couldn't help laughing. 'He told me about it later that night,' Daisy went on. 'He thought she was really crazy. And, well, it made me feel a bit odd . . . That's why we left so soon . . .' She paused and looked at Gemma, addressing her directly. 'I'll never forgive myself for leaving her like that, leaving you both, but I didn't know what to do. Lol wasn't prepared to stay any longer in the house with her. I thought she had just gone a bit weird with the heat and the grief. I thought that she'd be OK in a couple of weeks. I had no idea she was going to . . .' Daisy's voice trailed off.

I can't talk about that now, Gemma thought. I can't have what I feel about Oliver all mixed up with Estella's death.

Her mind felt over-loaded and unfocused. Even though it was hot, she was shivering slightly. They were approaching the park gates. 'Shall we have lunch somewhere in Camden?' Daisy asked.

'I don't think I can,' Gemma said. 'I'm sorry,' she added, seeing Daisy's face fall. 'I just can't think about it all . . . it feels as if my brain is going to explode.'

'Shall we just keep walking then?' Daisy asked.

She couldn't bear to be parted again so abruptly. It was as though she had been emotionally stripped naked, then left to shiver. The last thing she felt like doing was spending the afternoon with Oliver.

'I think I'll just go home,' Gemma said, looking around for a landmark, not really knowing where she was.

'But I need to talk too, you know!' Daisy's voice was rising, 'Has it never occurred to you that I'm just as much a victim as you? You just ran away, and just because I did something wrong, you didn't even *think* how I'd be feeling. Yes, it's important for you to come to terms with what happened. I appreciate that. But can't *you* appreciate for a second that it hasn't been easy for *me* . . .'

Her voice suddenly cut out. She didn't want to row with her sister. She didn't even know where the words had come from.

'Not easy at all,' she said quietly, trying to regain her composure, to re-establish the traditional hierarchy: Daisy, the happy-go-lucky ne'er-do-well who got into trouble and Gemma the rational one who got her out.

'I did think about you,' Gemma said, but it was a half lie. She had thought about Daisy as the person who had betrayed her. If she had ever wondered how Daisy was coping, she replaced even the briefest speculation with the certain knowledge that Daisy was with Oliver, therefore Daisy must be fine. It was only since she had seen her again that she had begun to realize how Daisy had suffered too. There was pain behind those violet eyes. One of the things that Gemma was finding it hardest to deal with was the shame of having been so unfair to her own sister.

'I have been awful to you, and I don't know how to redeem that,' Gemma finally said, with a huge sigh.

'It's OK,' Daisy said eventually, 'it's not as bad as what I did to you.'

'Yes it is,' Gemma insisted.

'No, really . . .' Daisy stopped and began to giggle. 'Come on,' she said, taking her sister's arm, 'there's no point in us arguing and feeling guilty. We've both been horrible and selfish and unthinking, so why don't we stop all that now and be friends? I've missed you terribly.'

'And I you,' Gemma admitted, hugging her, with tears trickling down her face.

CHAPTER 14

It was obviously her weekend for having difficult moments with loved ones in parks, Daisy thought, as she tried to keep up with Oliver's step. He had been silent for most of the drive to Woodstock, and now, as well as not wanting to speak to her, he seemed not to want to walk beside her either. He had decided they would take the anti-clockwise route round the lake in the grounds of Blenheim Palace and he was setting a pace as if in training for the Olympics.

'It's quite chilly, isn't it?' she said, as she puffed along behind him.

'Not as warm as yesterday,' he replied, curtly.

She took his comment to mean that he was still annoyed about her spending the day with Gemma rather than him.

Gemma and she had lunched in a busy restaurant in Camden Lock, with Daisy expounding her hatred of street theatre, as a minstrel with a pennywhistle played 'Greensleeves' over and over again in the courtyard outside the restaurant. They had silently come to an agreement not to discuss the family anymore that day.

Gemma told Daisy a little about her job and explained how she was going about launching a new list of sassy women's fiction. Daisy suggested that she run a competition with *Cosmopolitan* or some other women's magazine to find new writers. It would generate publicity and mean that the cost of the launch was shared. She could see that Gemma thought it was a good idea, and that she was surprised Daisy had thought of it. Her sister hadn't realized how much she had grown up. Daisy had swelled with pride.

By the time she arrived back at the flat in the late afternoon, Oliver had gone out.

When he was in this sort of mood, Daisy wondered why anyone would love him, let alone both Rush sisters, but as they had driven past the signs to Oxford, she remembered how he was then, how Gemma must have seen him.

With his mysterious background and dark, brooding good looks, Oliver was like a classic romantic hero in a book. Even the way he spoke about himself came straight from a Victorian novel.

'I ran away to sea.'

How many people would say that? Especially, thought Daisy, rather uncharitably, when the truth was that a friend's father had needed a strong lad to help crew his luxury yacht on a holiday voyage to Bermuda, and asked if Oliver would like to come along.

The language Oliver used to describe the voyage evoked images of him climbing up rigging with a dirty, ragamuffin face. In fact, he had once let slip, the Atlantic had been as calm as a millpond and he had achieved a nut brown tan as he read *Ulysses* on deck. The only slight blemish to this luxury cruise had occurred when he fell asleep in the sun with a brass drinks coaster and a tumbler of rum balanced on his chest. He had woken up with a burning weal just below his breastbone which blistered badly and left a scar.

You had to know Oliver a long time before you realized that the stories he told about himself were greatly romanticized. The first time that Daisy had pointed out an inconsistency, Oliver had glared at her, 'You use your memory as a weapon,' he had said.

'I don't!' Daisy protested. 'It's just that I remember things better than you! If you're going to lie, you have to be consistent.'

She loved him just as much when she came to learn the truth about his life, and his stories, with their tendency to melodrama, began to irritate her.

He was the son of a Liverpool circuit judge. His father and mother were paragons of provincial middle-class behaviour. They had given Oliver every possible advantage in life. At eighteen, when he had achieved everything his father had ever wanted for him – a scholarship to Oxford to read law – they informed him that he was adopted. Oliver suffered a belated adolescent identity crisis, sailed across the Atlantic and spent the next few years bumming about the Caribbean, paying his way by coaching tennis to rich American children.

Associating with the rich in sight of the rampant Third World poverty of some of the islands had been, Oliver claimed, his real education. He eventually returned to Liverpool just as the Toxteth riots were brewing. He blamed his father, his class, and the government they had voted in, and decided to become what they would most hate and fear: a clever, left-wing radical lawyer.

It was an admirable enough story without the gloss of the sexual and political adventures that Oliver painted on, which made him seem like a cross between Alfie and Albert Schweitzer.

Sometimes Daisy wondered whether Oliver would have been a happier person if he had found out where he really came from. Being able to invent stories about his past made him seem very enigmatic and interesting to other people, but it had also given him the ultimate excuse for maudlin self-indulgence.

'You have no idea how it feels to be abandoned,' he would sometimes tell her when he was feeling particularly sorry for himself.

'Well, actually, I do,' she would remind him. 'At least you have one set of parents alive.'

Daisy looked at her lover striding out in front of her. At some stage in the last few years, she couldn't remember when, he had changed from being a boy into a man. There was a heaviness about his features now. His long lean thighs had become solid, his waist measurement had crept up. He was tall, but now he looked substantial too.

Would Gemma love him now, Daisy found herself wondering. She tried to picture them together. Gemma was so slim and pale. She had always been pale, and a bit floppy, like a rag doll. Now she seemed more sinewy, as if she worked out a lot, or as if her limbs were held taut by nervous tension, more like a porcelain doll with new elastic in her joints. She couldn't see them getting on. Gemma looked too clean, too ice-maidenish for Oliver's tastes. And he would be threatened by her sister's ability to close down her emotions and replace them with a protective coating of frost.

It felt a little odd to be picturing the two of them so objectively and dispassionately. How would she feel if Lol and Gemma *were* together, she wondered. The first sensation that came to her as she imagined the scenario was relief. She tried to put a stop on it, replace it with jealousy or pain, but the emotions wouldn't come. Relief. It was the same sensation she had woken up with a couple of weeks before, when, she now remembered, she had dreamt that Oliver had died in a car crash.

Horrified by her thoughts, Daisy ran to catch him up, linking her arm through his. 'I love you very much,' she said to him, as if saying it would make it true. She reached up to kiss his stubbly cheek.

He looked down at her disbelievingly. 'Do you?' he asked.

No! Daisy wanted to scream. This is terrible, I don't, and I can't be honest with you.

'Of course I do,' she said, and he squeezed her hand against his chest.

'Do you mind if I cancel our brunch?' Gemma asked, trying to stifle a yawn.

'Oh.'

She hadn't expected Jonathan to sound so disappointed.

'I mean, postpone,' Gemma added quickly. 'It's just that I've been through the emotional mill this weekend, and I just don't think I can see any more of my family.' She laughed, trying to keep a lightness in her voice. 'I saw Daisy and, well, we had a lot to talk about, and now I've got a lot to think about, if you know what I mean. I really am sorry.'

'That's OK.' Jonathan sounded very English and very mystified, as if what she were saying had nothing to do with him. He obviously wasn't used to hearing long psychological explanations as excuses for cancelling a meeting. 'We'll fix another time, shall we? Perhaps next weekend. The children are coming over and they say they want a barbecue. I've never done a barbecue before,' he said, sounding worried.

'It's the simplest thing,' Gemma responded, 'and I make a great marinade for chicken legs. I'll bring some.'

'That'll be great!' Jonathan said enthusiastically, the fact that she had just let him down now completely forgotten.

Gemma put down the phone with relief. She turned over and pulled her duvet right over her head. She desperately wanted to lose herself again in sleep. She had been sleeping so peacefully when her alarm woke her, the best rest she had had since returning to England. Now she was greedy for more.

She woke again at around five in the afternoon. She could tell it was late because the sun had gone round to the back of the house. She could remember nothing of her dreams. She felt renewed and refreshed, but very alone.

She showered quickly, pulled on her grey cotton sweat shirt and pants and trainers, and walked up through the mews, wondering which direction to run in. She found herself heading towards Westbourne Grove, then up over the railway bridge and under the motorway to Little Venice. She hadn't realized how the little bits of London that she knew fitted together. Yesterday, she had taken a cab to Regent's Park. It had spent half an hour sitting in exhaust fumes and cost nearly ten pounds. Today, running at a leisurely pace down the towpath she reached the park in approximately the same time. She ran round the Inner Circle and then through the Avenue Gardens with their blossom-heavy trees, and down to the Euston Road.

She stopped to get her breath, bending from the waist, her head hanging over her knees. She didn't want to go home right away but she had brought very little money and she knew that if she ran any further her legs would suffer all week. She hadn't taken any real exercise since she returned.

She looked around for landmarks, trying to place where she was. The Post Office Tower loomed a few streets away. She remembered Ralph saying that the street he lived in was near the bottom of the tower. His was exactly the neutral and relaxing company she needed. She decided to go looking for him.

He had just taken a sip of Pernod when she saw him.

'I was just thinking about you,' she said, approaching his table, 'but I didn't expect you to materialize in front of me! Is this where you live?'

'Well, this is my local,' he said, 'but I don't exactly *live* here.'

She laughed.

'Sit down,' he said. 'Do you want something to drink?'

'I'd love some water. Unfortunately I don't have any money on me, so it'll have to be tap.'

'I think I can stand you a Perrier.'

'Thanks,' she said, sitting down. As soon as she took the weight off her legs she realized how tired they were. 'Have you been working?' she asked.

'A little. I find it difficult to stay indoors when it's so sunny, but it looks so pretentious to bring your laptop out on to the street. So, I thought, hey, this is the one day of English summer everyone's been telling me about. I might as well enjoy it . . .'

He bought her a Perrier and a Pernod. Normally she hated aniseed drinks, but sitting at a pavement café it seemed appropriate. The alcohol went straight to her head. It was a pleasant sensation, and calming. She leant forward and picked up Ralph's sunglasses from where they were resting on top of the Sunday papers. She had noted and appreciated the fact that he had taken them off when speaking to her. She hated conversations with people wearing dark glasses. In New York she had once had a particularly difficult negotiation with an agent wearing Ray Bans. She always felt she would have paid less for the book in question if she had been wearing a pair of her own.

'They suit you,' Ralph said.

She tipped her face to the sun.

'Do you tan?' he asked.

'Yes, if I take it gradually. What about you?' She looked at his freckly face.

'Are you kidding? Lobster in five minutes. But I love the sun.'

'Me too.'

'Sounds ungrateful on a day like this, but it's what I miss living in England. Real weather. Here, there's just not much variation, in winter it's grey and cold and raining, in summer it's normally grey and warmish and raining . . .'

'Although it's often grey and cold and raining in the summer too,' Gemma said.

He laughed.

'Have you seen much outside London?' she asked.

'Not really. I went to Wales for a weekend. But it was grey and cold and . . .'

'I love the seaside,' she said. 'I've got an aunt who lives by the sea. I must go to see her soon . . .' she said, as much to herself as to Ralph.

She thought about asking him to go with her. She was slightly dreading visiting Shirley. She hadn't seen her since Ken died, and she was frightened that she would have become old and sad. With Ralph there, Shirley would have to be cheerful, and the visit might be less of a chore. But no, it wouldn't be fair on him. She realized that she had stopped mid-sentence and Ralph was waiting for her to continue.

'Would you like another Pernod?' he asked.

'I'd love one, but I mustn't. I haven't eaten today . . .'

'I've got some buffalo mozzarella at my place, and some tomatoes, I think. I could make you a salad?'

'That sounds delicious,' she agreed.

His flat was a studio. There was a kitchen area at one end with a table, but very little furniture in the rest of the room apart from a wrought-iron double bed, some state-of-the-art hi-fi equipment and a desk. The room was painted white and there was no mess. It almost looked as if he had tidied up in the expectation of a visitor.

'It's very neat,' Gemma commented.

'It was stuffed with furniture when I moved in. A friend helped me put most of it in the loft. And what is this English fixation with flowery wallpaper? It took three coats to cover it.'

She liked his austere taste, the choice of duvet cover (large blue and white checked natural cotton), the two yukka plants in undecorated brass skuttles, the row of fresh herbs growing in earthenware pots along the window-sill.

He prepared food with the same neatness and attention to detail, slicing through the sloppy mozzarella and the firm tomatoes with a small, very sharp knife, tearing each piece of basil carefully and arranging the green, white and red components in a circle on plain white plates. He trickled over green olive oil from a long-necked bottle, and sawed through a large round loaf, picking up a thick wedge of bread on the end of the bread knife and offering it to her. Then he opened a bottle of mineral water and poured it over ice and wedges of fresh lime in straight, tall glasses.

She felt at home in his flat. It was rather like the first apartment she had rented in New York. She had no furniture there either, although the reason for that was lack of funds, rather than pure good taste. She began telling him about it. He said that he had lived on Bleeker Street at around the same time. They must have been neighbours. They swapped anecdotes about which Korean grocery they used, and where the best cappuccino could be found.

He was nice, she thought, very nice. Normally the first time you saw a guy's apartment, alarm bells started ringing, but here she felt at home, calm and relaxed in the cool whitewashed room. He put some jazz on, not too loudly. If she closed her eyes she could have been back in the Village, the jazz filtering up from a nearby bar, a draught of warm city air with its collage of smells and noises drifting in through the open window, his soft American voice making pleasant, not too cynical, not too demanding, conversation.

If he had touched her then, her body would have yielded to him, skin meeting skin. She could feel her nipples contracting, sensitive as they brushed against the cotton wool softness of the inside of her sweatshirt. She glanced down, checking whether her arousal was obvious. His eyes remained resolutely on her face.

She got up, her chair grating across the bare polished boards. 'That was lovely. Delicious food.'

He nodded, getting up to open the door.

She didn't know whether to kiss him or not. After what seemed like minutes of embarrassed indecision she stood on tiptoes and made to kiss his cheek, at exactly the same moment he bent to kiss hers. Their noses bumped, and they both laughed.

Oliver had left the path and was walking over the fields towards the monument. Daisy thought she would stop for a while and wait for him by the bridge. He turned round. 'Come on!' he said.

'I think I'll wait,' she shouted, then seeing his look of impatience, changed her mind and decided to follow him.

There were only a few people left in the grounds, most having taken a short walk as a conscience-salving exercise before settling down to a copious cream tea at one of Woodstock's many tearooms. Oliver surveyed the park from the top of the hill, looking, in this pastoral setting, like the lord of the manor in a Gainsborough painting. Then he sat down in the shade of a tree and patted the ground next to him. Daisy went and sat down beside him.

'All this procreation', Oliver said, looking at the fields of sheep and lambs, 'is making me feel randy.'

'Is it?' Daisy giggled, then realizing what he was saying, 'Oh no, Lol, I don't feel like it.'

'Oh come on,' he said, slipping a hand up the side of her T-shirt, surreptitiously, 'you won't even have to take your knickers off.' He turned round and sat astride her knees, pushing her short flared shirt up to her waist and unbuttoning his flies.

'No, Lol, I don't want to,' she said. 'I can't. I DON'T WANT TO!'

His erection was raw and threatening. She found she couldn't look at it. She closed her eyes in resignation. With one tug he ripped away her pants and shoved himself into her, his mouth trying to kiss her mouth. Instinctively, she flicked her face round to avoid his lips, she didn't want to participate. His weight was pushing the backs of her bare legs into the twigs and roots around the bottom of the tree. She shifted her back to make it hurt less, a sign he took as submission, it made him come in two convulsive shudders. She watched his eyes rolling back like a shark's, and she thought, this is one of the last times we will do it. Ever.

CHAPTER 15

Daisy stared at the bucket of flowers. They were mostly dead. A couple of royal blue delphiniums and the gyp struggled on. She wished she had taken them out of their wrapping, arranged them properly, given them a better chance of life. She emptied the foul smelling dregs of water into the kitchen sink and threw away nearly all the stems.

She washed up Oliver's cereal bowl and cup, then wiped down the kitchen surfaces. It didn't need doing. Oliver was always meticulous in his cleaning. Daisy was rarely allowed to do the washing up, even if the thought occurred to her, because she always made a mess of it. Would she be able to cope, she wondered, if she lived on her own.

She wandered into the bedroom and made the bed. However much she tugged and smoothed, she could never seem to get the bottom sheet as flat as Oliver managed to. Often he would get out of bed and rearrange it, tutting and sighing despairingly at her work.

She opened the door to the spare room. It was perfectly tidy and no-one ever went in there anyway. Dusting it seemed pointless. The flat seemed huge and empty. The occupants of the rest of the building were out. She longed for some noise, some sign that she wasn't the only person on earth.

She went into the living-room and sat down at her

typewriter. She had completed all her outstanding commissions and ought to start thinking about ideas for the editor of *Cosmopolitan*, but she wasn't feeling inspired. She felt too depressed to start ringing round features editors and getting work. It was stupid being depressed, she told herself. She had worked hard recently, she ought to ring someone up and have lunch, or go to see an exhibition or a film. She opened the Sunday papers that had been delivered the day before, but not read, and looked at the entertainment section. An exhibition she had meant to see had just closed. The only sort of film she thought she could stand would be a slick American romantic comedy, but it was Cannes season and all the films she felt she ought to see were obtuse and sub-titled.

The person she most wanted to talk to was Gemma, but Gemma would be at work, and Daisy wasn't yet quite sure enough about the solidity of their reconciliation to want to disturb her there.

She stared out of the window. The surfaces of the puddles at the sides of the road were smooth and silver. The rain must have stopped. Daisy decided to go for a walk. She pulled on her Levi's jacket, shoving her hands in her pockets. The fingers of her left hand touched the still-wet stickiness of the torn knickers that she had hidden there yesterday. She pulled out the pants, holding them away from her as if they were contaminated, then took them into the kitchen and dropped them into the bin. She would have preferred to burn them, but she knew that if she held them over the gas with a pair of sausage tongs, she was bound to drop them and set the flat on fire.

She shifted uncomfortably at the memory of Oliver's sperm trickling down her legs as they walked back through Blenheim Palace Park towards the car. A chilly breeze had blown across the lake, lifting her short flared skirt up around her waist, displaying her naked bottom to the world. She didn't think that anyone had been looking, but it had made her feel degraded. As soon as they arrived back in London, she had run a hot bath, as if to wash the humiliation from her skin.

Daisy slammed the door behind her and headed determinedly down the street. As she reached the Heath it began to rain again. There was no-one around. The rain made her feel more secure walking on her own. It would have to be a pretty determined pervert to be out in this weather, she thought, trudging past the pond and up the hill, the path slowly turning to mud in the downpour. She stopped at the top of the hill and looked over a London shrouded in grey cloud. The rain was coming down so hard it flattened her hair and rivulets ran down her cheeks. Even her ears were filling with water. The downpour had muffled the sounds of the city.

Daisy found herself singing all the songs she knew with rain in them.

'It's raining, raining in my heart!' she shouted, surprising herself. 'Cry-aye-aye-aye-ing over you!' she yelled.

'Singing in the rain!' a voice squawked beside her.

Daisy jumped and turned round. It was a bag lady who had emerged from a hideout beneath a bush and was jumping from side to side. Her many layers of clothing were filthy, and the rain was bringing out their smell. Her teeth, beneath a peculiar cupid's bow smudge of scarlet lipstick, were yellow and gappy, but her pleasure at having found a companion shone through her smile.

'Come on love,' she said, grabbing Daisy's hand, 'let's have a dance.'

Despite the frayed plimsolls she was wearing, the woman could really dance. Daisy tried to follow her step.

'Happy again!' they both sang, 'what a glorious feeling, I'm hap hap happy again . . .'

As they came to the end of the number the woman sat down on the path, oblivious to the puddles, and breathless. 'You haven't got a fag, have you love?' she wheezed.

'I'm sorry,' Daisy said. 'Where did you learn to dance like that?'

'I was in *Diamond Lil* with Mae West,' the woman replied very seriously. For some reason, Daisy believed her.

'You couldn't spare any change, could you, love?'

Daisy found a soaking wet ten pound note in the back pocket of her jeans and handed it over. The woman looked at the note, then got up, unable to believe her luck, and hurried off without saying goodbye.

The rain was beginning to stop. One or two birds began to sing.

'I'm going completely bonkers,' Daisy thought, as she walked back down the hill with a big smile on her face.

Daisy sat on the bed wrapped up in her white towelling robe. She felt cleansed by the rain and the singing, and warmed by the hot bath she had taken. In front of her was a wooden box, intricately carved and fastened with brass hinges. She was trying to persuade herself not to open it. She tried to ration herself to one look per year, on Estella's anniversary, but on crisis days, she sometimes broke that rule. She always kept the small brass key on her keyring. It slid into the lock and the box opened with a satisfying click.

On top of everything was a neatly folded long silk scarf. It was red, with swirls of orange and purple. Daisy picked it up with the reverence a priest gives to the communion napkin, and sniffed. It still smelt of her

– a soft combination of Shalimar and sandalwood soap. Daisy carefully unfolded the scarf. There was a thick coil of her hair, long and black and shiny. Daisy smoothed it over her palm, then brought her hand to her cheek and inclined her head to rest against it. In the mirror on the other side of the room Daisy caught a glimpse of her reflection. Estella's lock of hair was longer than her own. It fell black against the white dressing-gown. It was luscious hair that had retained its sheen. As Daisy stroked it and coiled it round her fingers, she felt close to her mother again, remembering their last moments together.

When Gemma had found her dead, Estella's hair was greasy and matted with sick. When Daisy arrived home, the undertaker was already there, preparing to take away the body. Daisy had shooed him out of the room. She had taken a plastic bowl of hot water from the kitchen and her mother's favourite shampoo and washed her mother's hair as her body stiffened with rigor mortis. Then she had rinsed it and dried it and combed it through, so that it shone. It was their last time together. It had felt like an ancient ritual. Finally, Daisy had asked her mother's permission before taking a pair of nail scissors and cutting a swatch from the back, where it wouldn't show, she assured her. Only then had she called the undertaker back in to carry on with his work.

Daisy wrapped the hair carefully in the silk scarf and placed it by her side. She took the photograph from the box. It was taken on the Ponte Vecchio in Florence. They had snapped many photographs of each other all holiday, but on the last day Estella had realized they had none of them together. She had stopped a passer-by, a very handsome Italian passer-by, Daisy recalled with a smile, and indicated in loud, slow English, what he should do.

'He'll probably run off with the camera as soon as my

back is turned,' she said, scarcely lowering her voice as she returned to Daisy. They stood with their arms around each other smiling at the camera while he fired several shots. Then he brought the camera back to them.

'Thank you so much,' Estella had said, every inch the gracious Englishwoman abroad.

'My pleasure,' he had replied in a perfect Etonian accent and winked at Daisy before turning on his heels and walking away in the direction of the Boboli Gardens.

Their faces beamed at the camera, unmistakably related. Daisy remembered Estella's pleasure when people asked whether they were sisters, vanity battling with common sense and winning. Her mother was beautiful, but those dark, almost Latin looks did not age well. She did look fifty, Daisy thought. She knew that old age terrified Estella. Was that why she had killed herself? Because she couldn't bear to grow old? Daisy swallowed, trying physically to stop that train of thought from gathering momentum. She put the photo face down on the bed.

Underneath it was a small flat book, its boards almost falling from its spine. *Biscuit and Donut* by Bertrand Rush. There was a picture of the dolls and the title scrawled in her father's distinctive handwriting. Daisy opened the book and read the dedication: 'For my perfect daughters'.

She flipped through the pages, knowing the story off by heart. She was always slightly annoyed by how fat her father had made her look.

At the bottom of the box was the envelope. Thick cream vellum with 'Daisy' written on the front in black ink that had grown rusty with the years. Daisy knew she shouldn't open it.

My dearest Daisy,
How can I begin to tell you how much joy you have given me! I

know I haven't been much of a mother, but having you, my darling child, has been the greatest gift of all.

I hope you will never discover why I have to leave you now. I could not bear you to feel such pain, such responsibility. But it is far better this way. Trust me.

All I ask is that you enjoy your life: do everything you want, be everything you want to be. Do it for me. Your happiness will be my legacy to the world. Something I did right.

Don't be sad for long, darling one.

I love you more than life itself.

Estella, your mother

As if, Daisy sniffed, she knew any other Estellas.

She had always found the beginning of the letter perplexing, the end of it absurd. After the first few days of grief, the letter had made her very angry. How could her mother have been so stupid? How could she think that Daisy could ever be happy if she were dead? If she had chosen to die?

The coroner had taken the letter away as evidence for the inquest. In her anger, Daisy told him that she didn't want a copy. It was a stupid letter, she explained, typical of her mother at her melodramatic worst. But months later, after the inquest had returned a verdict of suicide, the letter was sent back to her. She started to read it obsessively, looking for hidden meanings, trying to understand. In the end, Oliver had tired of the constant soul-searching and sensibly suggested she put it away somewhere special. It could drive her mad, he said. So she put it at the bottom of Estella's jewellery box with her other mementoes, and she tried to read it only once a year.

But the passage of time had done nothing to soothe the agony of not understanding. Daisy folded it and put it back in its envelope. 'Why?' she asked her mother out loud. 'Why did you do it?'

Part Three

CHAPTER 16

Shirley tried to concentrate on her newspaper and block out the sound of Bethany-from-Age Concern's progress down the corridor. Tap, tap, tap went her white high heels on the lino.

'We're taking you all out to the superstore in a minibus!' she was shouting. 'Pick up at ten o'clock sharp. OK, Mrs Potts?'

Tap, tap, tap.

Shirley felt like pretending that she wasn't in. But she knew that if she did that, Bethany would only worry and call the warden. Then the warden would come along to check and then she'd have to come clean if she didn't want them opening up her door with the pass key. Bethany liked to keep an eye on things and she had developed a particular fondness for Shirley. Probably because I'm one of the only ones who isn't gaga, Shirley thought. Still, she was a good girl, really.

She sighed and thought for the umpteenth time that the sheltered flat had been a mistake. If she had her time again she wouldn't be pushed into it so easily. She hadn't felt as confident then, after she lost Ken. She'd realized that she'd have to sell the business. Frankly, it had been getting a bit much for both of them, but that didn't mean she couldn't take care of herself. She wondered why now she'd been persuaded to buy into the new sheltered development.

'You're on your own . . . No family to look after you

. . . It'll be the best thing . . . Then you needn't worry later . . .' they all said as if she was going downhill fast and would be decrepit before she knew it. But funnily enough, since Ken died she had felt younger than she had for years.

There were a couple of bills on the mat and an envelope with handwriting she didn't recognize, forwarded from the shop. Shirley started tearing it open.

Tap, tap, tap. With a sigh, Shirley put the envelope down on the telephone table and opened her front door.

Bethany looked like her name. Sort of sweet and fluffy in her pastels and soft angora. She had apple-round cheeks, a halo of white-blond hair, and a wide pearly smile. She was engaged to a nice-looking bank clerk, had been ever since Shirley had known her. Shirley knew the wedding plans down to the last buttonhole. As well as hearing them herself, she'd heard Bethany telling Mrs Potts next door all the details, the walls were that thin. The first time Shirley thought, how nice, how lovely and romantic that two young people in this day and age should want to go through with all that palaver. Now, Bethany's chatter grated on her nerves. Sometimes, when she popped in with *Brides* magazine, Shirley found herself fighting a strong urge to rip the glossy pages in half, and inform her that married life wasn't all about frothy white dresses and lily-of-the-valley-tiaras. Then she would wonder why she felt so impatient with the girl's dreams. After all, she and Ken had had forty good years, hadn't they? Everyone had their ups and downs, and they had had fewer than most people they knew. In a way, Shirley had thought, I might have preferred a few more hiccups . . .

'We're taking you all out to the superstore. Minibus arrives at ten,' Bethany chirruped.

'Thanks,' said Shirley, 'but I don't think I'll bother.'

'Feeling a bit under the weather?' Bethany enquired.

Why did she have to make up an excuse? Shirley wondered. The people from Age Concern did a good job, but why couldn't they leave her alone?

'They do have a lot of offers . . .' Bethany was cajoling.

There were certain things that old people were supposed to do that Shirley didn't want to be involved with. Counting the pennies, for instance. For heaven's sake, most of the people she knew were richer in old age than they'd ever been in their lives. And if they didn't spend it now, when would they? Shirley liked to treat herself. If she wanted to go to the superstore, she'd call a taxi, thank you very much, and she'd buy what she wanted, reduced or not. Like those expensive cartons of home-made soup. She wasn't going to sit in a minibus, waiting for everyone with hip replacements to haul themselves back in, comparing prices of tins and brandishing bargain loaves near their sell-by date.

As a matter of fact, she felt like saying, just to get the reaction, she didn't often eat in anyway. Quite a few of the restaurants in town did a lunchtime special and she'd discovered she liked eating alone, being served by a nice waiter, and leaving all the washing up behind. The first time she did it, she felt rather risqué, choosing a table at the back of the restaurant in case anyone who knew her passed by. These days she sat near the window, daring the likes of Bethany to walk past and notice her.

'There's nothing I need today,' Shirley said firmly, 'thanks all the same,' and she closed the door gently in the girl's surprised face.

Tap, tap, tap. After a moment or two Bethany's footsteps continued undaunted on her mission.

'We're taking you all out to the superstore!'

'What?' Mrs Bottomley was hard of hearing and she never would wear her deaf-aid.

'The SUPERSTORE . . .'

What on earth was she doing living next to Mrs
Bottomley, Shirley asked herself. Mrs Bottomley had
been old ever since she'd known her. She was a friend of
her parents', a different generation. That was the
trouble with old age. At twenty, forty seems older on a
different scale, but at seventy, ninety is just a different
degree of old age.

It was depressing if you thought about it, and there
was too much time to think about it. It was a lovely day.
Sunny, with a breeze. Stepping onto her balcony she
could hear the sea, which meant it must be choppy. She
decided to go for a walk along the Esplanade.

There was a girl with turquoise pedal pushers and a
lime green T-shirt, cut short so that it showed her
midriff. She was queuing in the ice-cream parlour with
a friend wearing a long Indian bedspread skirt and
clompy black boots. They say that fashion goes in
cycles, but Shirley thought that in the Nineties anything looked right, as long as you wore it with
confidence.

Stella had worn pedal pushers – white ones with a
skimpy black jumper stretched tight across her Playtex
Cross-Your-Heart bra. You're not going out like that,
Dad had roared, but Stella hadn't taken any notice,
sauntering out through the shop and letting the door go
behind her so that it didn't close properly and the bell
kept pinging, reminding Dad of her cheek long after
she'd disappeared.

The girls in front of Shirley turned round, licking
fondant swirls of ice-cream with dark lipsticked lips.
They all looked so knowing these days, Shirley
thought. These days Stella wouldn't stand out in a
crowd. She was always ahead of her time, that was her
trouble.

Shirley bought a Danish pastry and a cappuccino in a

polystyrene cup. Proper coffee, strong with froth on top and chocolate. It cost a pound and it tasted like it. The man serving put her purchases in a miniature brown paper carrier bag along with a soft white napkin. A bit of luxury. What would Bethany make of that? Shirley wondered, and smiled.

She sat on a wrought-iron seat on the promenade and looked down on to the beach. Nobody went in the sea these days and she couldn't blame them either. When the sky was blue the sea used to look blue too, but now it was the colour of a cup of cold tea. Still, it brought the crowds from the city for a whiff of salty air and roasting on the beach. Near naked bodies lay in rows, slick with oil, turning at intervals, like chickens on a spit. The sea breeze was deceptively cool. Shirley could tell it was burning weather. There were a couple of windsurfers in fluorescent pink wet suits, skimming the milky brown waves, falling in when they got close to the shore.

The trouble with being on your own was time. It seemed to pass so slowly. Shirley had given up wearing a watch. She was sick of looking at it, shaking it, thinking it was broken. She remembered, with a smile, the busy times at the height of the season, when she and Ken hadn't stopped. They'd be on the go all day, but hardly notice, until they lay down in bed at night and calculated out loud in the dark how long they'd been on their feet, only realizing as they tried to drift off how much their legs were aching. Nineteen hours, sometimes, because they'd be up at five to take delivery of the fish. But it flew by. And Ken would say that when he retired he'd sleep for a week, or longer if he needed it.

Sometimes Shirley wondered whether he would have enjoyed his retirement. What would he have done with the time? However long you slept, the hours of daylight still seemed to yawn before you. Golf was what retired men did in this town, but Ken had never played.

Perhaps he'd have learnt. Perhaps they'd have learnt together.

Hobbies were what you needed when you retired. There had never really been time for hobbies while they had the shop. When they weren't serving, they were scrubbing floors, draining down the fryers, changing the oil, beating the batter, doing the washing. It took a lot of soaking and rubbing to get the fat out of their aprons, even when they got an automatic machine. One thing she had been proud of – their clothes never smelt of fish and chips.

Then just when they had decided to sell up – they could see that they'd have to start doing chicken nuggets and burgers if they wanted to stay in business and Ken said he wasn't going to have any of that – he was bending over the freezer and had a massive heart attack. Lucky it wasn't the fryer, the undertaker had remarked, else he'd been done to a crisp.

They said it was a shame he never got to enjoy his retirement, but sometimes Shirley just wondered what on earth he would have done all day. When people asked him what he had planned, Ken used to say he had other fish to fry. It was the one joke Shirley could remember him making. But what had he meant by it? Other men went down the pub of an evening, or played cards, but Ken had missed out on all that, having a shop that didn't shut until after closing time. Perhaps the heart attack had saved him from years of decline and boredom.

Shirley shook herself out of *that* train of thought. Apart from her knees, which had seen better days, she wasn't declining as far as she could tell, and she wasn't going to let herself get bored. Gemma was coming down at the weekend. Now that was something to look forward to. And, she decided in a fit of optimism, she was going to buy herself a present – a hobby, if you like – why not? She thought about the house she had been looking at for the past few weeks. She would buy it. She got up from the bench and walked slowly up into the town.

There was bunting strung across Victoria Street. In a couple of weeks there would be a street party. The butcher had built a pyramid of Spam tins in his window. Fifty years since VE day. It felt longer.

Shirley had told the story of that day so often that she remembered herself in the third person as if she were a character in a film. She saw herself, very trim in her nurse's uniform, her hair cut in Greer Garson style, but pushed back from her face with a tortoiseshell Alice band. The girl in her memory wasn't the person she recognized as herself now. She was young and optimistic and carefree, remarkably, really, since she'd spent her first years as an adult tending to people who were injured or dying, the innocent casualties of war.

On VE day they all thought they had everything they wanted in front of them. Anything was possible. The world suddenly opened up, offering them everything they could imagine. People were dancing with the joy of it. For the first time as a grown up, she had felt safe.

Ken had come up with Stella on the train. They were waiting for her when she came off duty. He had been demobbed early because he'd broken his leg badly. He was all for joining the celebrations at home, dressed up in his demob suit, showing off the few words of Italian he'd learnt, and telling stories of his bravery to impress the neighbours. But Stella wasn't having any of that. She dragged him limping up to town – to surprise Shirley, she said, but they all knew her real motive. No party at home was going to be big enough for her. Stella wanted to be at the centre of things. And Stella usually found a way to get what she wanted.

Shirley stopped outside a shop on the corner of the High Street. It was in the window. The kind of house she had always dreamed of – square, solid and symmetrical, nothing too fancy, two up and two down, and roses growing round the front door. It seemed rather expensive for what it was, but she could afford it. People were always telling her to go on a cruise with her lump sum, but she could think of nothing worse than being cooped up with a lot of old people and second-rate cabaret artistes, playing bridge and feeling seasick.

The house was what she wanted. She could buy the furniture gradually – it really was expensive for what it was – and perhaps make some curtains herself. If it was ridiculous for someone her age, so what? She would say it was for her grandchildren, if anyone asked, which they usually didn't. Shirley pushed open the toyshop door.

'In here,' Shirley opened the door to her second bed-room. 'Just put it on the floor.'

The nice man from the toyshop deposited the large box. Should she tip him? Shirley didn't know whether he'd be offended.

'That's very kind of you,' she said, and it was, because he'd given her a lift home in his van too. 'Would you like a nice cup of tea?'

'No thanks, love,' he said, 'I'd best be getting back. I hope the kiddies enjoy their present. They're very lucky to have a gran like you.'

Shirley smiled back. If only he knew, he'd think she was barmy. Well, maybe she was. She saw him to the door.

The post was still lying unopened on the telephone table. Shirley took it to her armchair by the window. The bills weren't too bad. That at least was one advantage of a flat.

Shirley pulled a typewritten note out of the third envelope and as she read it her hands began to tremble. She looked at the envelope again. She hadn't noticed before, with all the crossing out, that they had used her maiden name. It wasn't really a letter for her at all, she realized. It was for her sister. They used to have the same initial.

That was a bit of a long shot, expecting her still to be there forty years on, Shirley thought. She got up and went to the kitchen. She kept a bottle of brandy, for medicinal purposes, in the cupboard under the sink. The shock, she thought, warranted a glass, even though it was still quite early in the day.

As Shirley sipped, her panic began to subside. If you thought calmly about the implications, she realized, you must come to the conclusion that they didn't know anything, really. The whole thing was best forgotten. She decided to pretend that the note had never arrived. She tore it up into tiny pieces and then set it on fire in one of Ken's old ashtrays.

CHAPTER 17

'So there was this kind of lightning bolt – like instant attraction between you, and then what happened?' Daisy asked.

She was finding it quite difficult to keep a straight face. The idea that anyone could be instantly attracted to either of these people was difficult to entertain. They were so fat that the two of them completely filled the squashy leather three-seater sofa in their living room, leaving no space at all for the two fat white cats that sat on their laps. You'd have to be family to consider either of them attractive, Daisy thought mischievously, but that, of course, was the whole point.

She was writing an article about relatives who had fallen in love with one another. She had aleady interviewed a rather poetic-looking young man whose equally willowy and beautiful aunt, twenty years his senior, had taken his virginity when he was sixteen. They looked such a perfect couple, she couldn't really see what was wrong with that, until Oliver had asked her whether she would have felt the same way if it had been an uncle in his thirties seducing his teenage niece.

Then there had been the American couple who were living in England because in America it was illegal to marry a first cousin. Daisy couldn't see what was wrong with that either. At least there would be no nasty surprises when the in-laws met each other.

And lastly Keith and Erica Pudding as she would call

them in her article (she had promised not to use real names). They were brother and sister who had been separated since infancy, adopted by different families. When Erica was thirty, she decided to trace her real family, and, on discovering that she had a brother, she tracked him down to a flat in King's Cross where she knocked on his door one rainy November afternoon, and *kerpow!* it was love at (virtually) first sight.

Daisy had written an article some time before about couples who looked like one another (following it with an article about people who looked like their pets), but Mr and Miss Pudding were something else. No wonder it was illegal to mate with your siblings. Daisy had a fleeting vision of what a Pudding junior might look like, and felt a bit queasy.

Between mouthfuls of Battenburg cake, and spraying a snowstorm of pink and yellow crumbs on their fudge-coloured deep pile carpet, Erica explained the trouble they'd had trying to get married. Somebody, she didn't know who but she had her suspicions, had told on them, she said, offering Daisy a custard cream. Then it was the social services . . .

'But why was it so important to get married?' Daisy interrupted, thinking that they could have avoided a helluva fuss if they hadn't been so determined to exchange rings in public.

'We're both Christians', Keith cut in, rather sanctimoniously, 'and we weren't prepared to live in sin.'

It was a long time since RE lessons at school, and Daisy had been sent out of most of those for being cheeky to the nervous vicar who taught the class last thing on a Thursday afternoon, but she had a feeling that incest was right up there on the scale of sins alongside sex before marriage. On the other hand, it can't have felt like incest to Keith and Erica, since they hadn't grown up together, and it was sad (as well as an extremely amusing anecdote she would have to be very strong to stop herself telling at dinner parties) that they should be caught out by their genuine belief in doing the right thing. Perhaps secretly they were so horrified by what they were doing, they were trying to sneak God's approval in another way, Daisy thought. What a terrible shame that they couldn't just have bumped into each other by chance at a bus stop, or something, and fallen in love, and nobody would ever have known they were brother and sister. Given that Keith spent most of his life with his bottom glued to the couch, however, that was an unlikely scenario.

This story, Daisy thought, composing copy in her head as she ran up Euston Road frantically waving at the only cab she could see with its orange light lit, wanting him to execute a U-turn and pick her up, illustrates perfectly how dangerous it can be to delve too deeply into your past. She smiled her most winning smile at the cabbie, and he smiled back, but drove on in the opposite direction.

Damn, she was going to be late. Daisy looked despairingly at the stationary queue of traffic all the way up the Hampstead Road. She would have to take the tube, which she hated, especially in rush hour. She had thought she would have enough time to do the interview, then come home and have a leisurely bath before putting on her party clothes and downing a large gin and tonic before going out again, but, as usual, she had miscalculated. She wished now that she had worn a dress to do the interview, but she had been late leaving the house for that too, and it was such a hot day she'd thrown on a white vest and cut-off jeans without really thinking about the evening. Now, if she didn't get a move on, Oliver would be angry when she arrived, or worse, ignore her all night.

The chambers that Oliver's firm briefed most frequently held an annual drinks' party in Gray's Inn

Fields. By the time Daisy arrived most people had been drinking Pimms for an hour or so. Daisy walked towards the crowd, trying to pick out acquaintances from the sea of bright pink sweaty faces. Why, she wondered as she grew nearer, did barristers never get their clothes cleaned, and why did they wear the same dark heavy suits throughout the year? The evening sunlight picked out the shine on each greasy collar and cuff, and the heat drew out a kind of beery smoky vapour that hovered around the gathering. Several of the men turned away from their conversations to look at her, and one young clerk wolf- whistled loudly, then tried to pretend he was coughing when he realized that she was not just walking past, but joining the party.

Daisy was wearing a sundress of crushed silk. The colour graduated from tangerine at the narrow ribbon shoulders down to rich scarlet where the fabric stopped mid-calf. As she walked, the colours shimmered like a flame. There hadn't been time to dry her hair properly, so she had wound an orange silk scarf round her head, keeping the mass of dark curls behind her ears.

She must look all right, she thought, because Oliver disentangled himself from chatting to the only female barrister in the chambers, and sauntered over to greet her. 'With the sun behind you, that dress doesn't leave much to the imagination,' he whispered, putting a proprietorial arm around her waist.

'Is it all right?'

'Gorgeous,' he kissed her cheek, nuzzled her shoulder, pretending to eat her bare flesh.

Daisy stood rigid. She tried to tell herself that she was just feeling embarrassed at being so publicly mauled in front of a bunch of perspiring lechers, but deep down she knew that ever since their walk at Blenheim, she had been turned off by any kind of physical contact with Oliver. She didn't think he'd noticed yet, but she was finding it increasingly difficult to fake pleasure when every time he touched her she was shaking inside with repulsion.

Oliver ushered her to the trestle tables that were serving as a bar. The white damask tablecloth was covered in a pattern of red wine spills. Daisy stared at it, trying to concentrate on anything that would banish the wave of nausea.

'Do you want the last of the Pimms?' He held up an almost empty jug.

'Yes, why not?' she took the glass and drank it down in two gulps, then fished out the mint from the bottom with her fingers. The fresh sharp taste helped a little. Daisy smiled and held up her glass for more and Oliver drained the jug into it.

'I think I've got some catching up to do,' Daisy said, feeling the hit of alcohol relaxing her a little.

'It's bloody strong, you know,' Oliver responded.

'Yes, I do know,' Daisy replied, slightly crossly. 'Oh look, there's Kathy. I'll see you later.' She left him standing alone, slightly bewildered.

Kathy was sitting some way away from the crowd on a wooden park bench. She was holding Alexander on her lap. 'Oh hello, Daisy.' It was clear from the way she spoke, very deliberately and slowly, that the glass of white wine by her feet was not the first she had consumed that evening.

'The babysitter cancelled at the last minute,' she continued, explaining the presence of the small child, and then looking at Daisy's dress and back at her own, which was a flowery cotton smock with food stains down the front. 'I didn't have a chance to change.'

'You look lovely,' Daisy assured her, sitting down on the bench. She did too. A kind of Madonna and Child by Laura Ashley.

'I think Roger would have preferred me not to come,' Kathy said softly, leaning towards Daisy to talk in confidence.

'Oh, I'm sure he . . .' Daisy started to say.

'You don't have to talk to me, you know. Go and enjoy the party,' Kathy interrupted.

'I don't enjoy these parties very much actually,' Daisy said, slightly alarmed by Kathy's mood change. 'One lawyer's ego is bad enough, don't you find?'

Kathy stared at her, 'I think Roger's having an affair,' she suddenly blurted out.

It was like that party game Scruples: Your friend's husband is having a very public affair and your friend is the only person who doesn't know. Do you tell her?

Daisy couldn't decide. It wasn't as if Kathy was really her friend anyway. She was Gemma's friend. Maybe Gemma could tell her. Daisy pretended to be deeply interested in her drink, and then looked towards the crowd as if she might not have heard what Kathy had said.

She could see Roger bantering with Nigel. Emily, his lover, was deeply involved in a conversation with the young clerk who had whistled at Daisy. They were about as far away from each other as they could be, but from time to time they caught each other's eye and exchanged knowing glances. The smugness of their betrayal infuriated Daisy. She looked back, about to tell Kathy the truth, but saw the little boy in her arms, his soft sleeping face a picture of innocence. She couldn't do it. She felt panicky. She found herself saying, 'I'm thinking of leaving Lol.'

She didn't know why she had told Kathy first, before anyone else. It was as if she couldn't accept a confidence from Kathy without returning an even greater one herself. Unable to tell Kathy the truth about her husband, she had to tell her the truth about something. But until that minute, Daisy hadn't even known that it was the truth.

She looked over to where Oliver was standing, and saw him suddenly as someone else might see him. Tall and slightly stooped, his face animated and intelligent, eyes holding those of his companion in that totally involved way he had which made whoever he was talking to feel privileged. Those black gypsy curls, so incongruous above his white shirt and well-cut grey suit trousers. He was so attractive, and he loved her as much as he was capable of loving anyone, she knew that. But she was going to leave him. She needed to, she realized, in order to grow.

He would never forgive her.

She turned back to Kathy, unable to focus, her eyes had filled with tears, mourning already for the loss of something she was choosing to relinquish.

Kathy reached out and took her hand, looking at her with concern, as if she understood the gravity of the moment. 'Are you sure?' she asked softly.

'I am really,' Daisy said, shaking the tears away, and smiling. 'I just don't know how to do it. You won't tell anyone . . . ?'

'Course I won't,' Kathy said. She seemed a lot more sober now. 'Have you talked about it with Gemma?'

'No, and I don't want her to know . . .' Daisy said quickly and firmly, searching Kathy's eyes, wondering whether to trust her, 'it would confuse things, you see.'

'I think I know what you mean,' Kathy replied. 'Have you thought about Relate?'

'No, look I'm not sure anyway,' Daisy said, suddenly standing up. How on earth had she got herself into this situation. 'Look, I'd better go and mingle.'

Daisy didn't remember the conversation until she was showering the next morning, trying to wash away the lingering cloak of alcohol with steaming water. Out of a dull haze of non-specific hangover anxiety, an acute memory of talking to Kathy sliced through her aching head, making her feel instantly and irrevocably guilty. Perhaps, she thought, scrubbing her legs with a loofah,

Kathy was so drunk that she would have forgotten. Perhaps she should ring her up and tell her she hadn't meant it. No, that would only make things worse if she had forgotten. Perhaps she should tell Oliver now. She didn't feel strong enough. She must. Daisy turned the shower to maximum strength. Needles of hot water stung her back. She closed her eyes. The sound of splashing water was so strong that for a moment it obliterated all thoughts from her mind.

'Daisy!'

She couldn't tell whether his voice was in her head or outside. She opened her eyes.

'Daisy!'

Oliver's head peered round the shower curtain. She jumped.

'For God's sake, Lol! You frightened me!'

'Jesus Christ. I do live here, you know. Who did you think it was?'

'I don't know.'

'How much did you have to drink last night? You were practically comatose in the taxi.'

When she left Kathy, she had mingled with a vengeance, smiling at everyone and making a determined effort to be charming, as if trying to make up for her momentary betrayal. She had laughed at all the lewd jokes and gently scolded the head of chambers when he pinched her bottom, and whenever somebody offered her a refill, she held up her glass for wine, or beer or whatever was going. She had no idea how long she had been standing making increasingly nonsensical conversation. She had no memory at all of the journey home.

'The trouble was that everyone else was so drunk, I felt relatively sober,' said Daisy, wrapping a white towel round her chest, 'and then when I started to feel a little bit drunk, it was too late, anyway . . . I didn't say anything, did I?'

227

'Well, you kept saying sorry, and kissing me.' Oliver was laughing, 'Actually, it was rather pleasant . . .'

Daisy squeezed past him and walked towards the bedroom.

'You must have a guilty conscience, or something,' Oliver called after her. 'Anyway, you were in no mood for my surprise.'

'What surprise?' Daisy called back, apprehensive, but unable to contain her curiosity.

'Get packing. We're going on holiday.'

'What? Where?'

'Two weeks in Crete. Sun, sea, sand and ancient history. I thought we needed a break . . .'

'But when?' Daisy stood in the doorway, still in her towel.

'Flight from Gatwick this afternoon.'

'But . . .'

'You haven't got any commitments . . . ?'

'Well, I've got to write up my relations piece . . .' And there was a film screening she'd been invited to and didn't want to miss.

'Take the typewriter and fax it back . . .'

Daisy felt very strongly that she didn't want to go, but her hung-over brain couldn't think of an excuse quickly enough. 'But it's lovely weather here,' she offered pathetically.

'No beach, though,' Oliver smiled. 'Come on, get packing. All you'll need is a couple of bikinis and some shorts. I'll make some coffee. And Daisy,' he said as he disappeared into the kitchen, 'take that dress you were wearing yesterday. I fell in love with you all over again when you turned up at the party . . .'

It was such a beautiful thing to say, and it made her feel ungrateful and wretched. She felt the tears cloud her eyes as she pulled down a small suitcase from the top of the wardrobe.

CHAPTER 18

The bit of the journey that Gemma most liked as a child was when the train pulled out of Victoria and, gathering speed, trundled over the Thames. It was like coming out of a dark tunnel into light. It was the moment she knew her holidays were really beginning and no-one could change their mind or bring her back.

It had become tradition for her to go by herself on the train ever since the second time she went to stay with Shirley and Ken. Her father was going to take her, but the the car had broken down, so the whole family accompanied her to Victoria, planning to go to the coast for the day, then leave Gemma with her aunt for the rest of the week. But as their departure time grew nearer Estella felt the onset of a migraine. There was no way, she said, that she could board a train crowded with holidaymakers – the sneer in her voice branding holidaymakers worse than animals. Bertie had offered to take both the girls, but Estella had looked so pained that he quickly changed his mind and they were all about to turn round and go home when, joy of joys, he suddenly asked, 'Well, why can't Gemma go on her own? Shirley's meeting the train, isn't she? She's a sensible girl.' Gemma could remember exactly the way he looked at her, a gentle conspirator, and winked.

'Me go too, me go too!' Daisy jumped up and down, her shouts getting increasingly menacing.

'No. Gemma can't possibly look after Daisy as well as herself,' Estella said wearily.

Gemma looked at her mother. It sounded as if she was tacitly giving her permission. She kept very quiet, knowing that the slightest thing could spoil it.

'Well, then, my girl,' Bertie said, taking her hand and marching her smartly towards the platform before Estella could change her mind. 'You will be careful,' he said, putting her into a carriage with lots of people.

Gemma nodded, hardly daring to speak.

Bertie asked the lady next to her to keep an eye on his daughter, and she smiled and said she would, if she had an eye free, because she had one on each of her boys.

'What will you do if Shirley's not there?' he asked, suddenly worried as he kissed her goodbye through the open window.

'Wait until she comes, and if she doesn't, I shall ask a policeman to help me,' Gemma replied solemnly, and then the whistle blew and the train was moving.

Her father ran down the platform waving, which embarrassed her a little because everyone in the carriage was watching. And then he was gone. The train was pulling out of the station, and Gemma felt a lump in her throat, but she didn't cry, because this, she was acutely aware, was her first adult adventure.

Gemma sighed, the long slow exhalation of air making her realize she had been holding her breath. The carriage was packed. The sudden hot spell had made everyman and his beach ball head for the coast at the Bank Holiday. As the train chugged across the river a welcome breeze blew in through the open windows, but even that was warm, sultry air, not at all the weather she remembered in England.

She could feel the hard, bristly seat patterning the backs of her legs through her fine linen trousers. It was like sitting on a doormat. Opposite a little boy slurped at a hamburger, melted cheese and ketchup dripping off his hands perilously close to Gemma's handbag. Gemma whipped the bag onto her lap and closed her eyes, trying to block out the heat, the noise and the almost putrid smell of cheap fried meat.

She was trying to work out why, when she had only happy memories of visiting her aunt, she was now feeling vaguely apprehensive. The night before she had been on the point of cancelling, and had got as far as ringing Shirley, but when she heard the excitement in her aunt's voice, she pretended that she was only ringing to confirm that she was coming. She couldn't bring herself to disappoint her.

Perhaps, she wondered, she was nervous because she had never seen Shirley without Ken. Shirley might have liked her to fly home for Ken's funeral, but it hadn't even occurred to her at the time. Shirley wasn't the sort of person who would bear a grudge, though.

Perhaps she was just afraid of seeing her aunt grown old. Gemma didn't have much experience of old people, and although Shirley's letters were always bright and cheerful, the handwriting was getting shakier and she seemed to be living in an old people's home.

Gemma sat up straight. She wished there had been time to buy a magazine. She needed something to concentrate on. Her head was a jumble of thoughts and memories and vague worries. She looked around at her fellow passengers and felt she didn't belong there.

Maybe, she thought for the thousandth time, coming home had been a mistake. She wasn't settling in to life in England as she had hoped to. It was as if she were in a state of transition, standing in the wings waiting for a cue to go on. To be what, though? Different? The same? Herself, whatever that was?

Ironically, it was with Daisy, of all people, that she felt most at ease. There had been one moment over

231

lunch in Camden when she had relaxed completely, and ceased thinking for a moment about how she should be. Spontaneously, they had both stopped talking for a few minutes, only the chink of metal on china disturbing the sense of peace between them as they spooned *crème brulée* into their mouths and watched the milling crowds outside.

Daisy, needless to say, had not been able to tell her anything about Shirley. Daisy was not close to her aunt and never had been. In fact, Gemma thought wryly, the only reason that she herself had grown to know Shirley was because her mother liked to have Daisy to herself for one week of the year.

The yearly visits, usually at the beginning of summer, began when Gemma was ten. Until then, she had only vaguely known that her mother had a sister who always sent a Christmas card, usually a crude Victorian snow scene with a horse and carriage. Every year there was the same message, 'Best wishes to you and yours, from Shirley and Ken.'

She could remember her mother's face as she tore open the cheap envelope, turned her nose up at the picture and relegated the card to the back of the mantelpiece, behind the rows of more tasteful cards. She never did find out whether Estella sent one of the brightly-coloured abstract cards she designed in return. She used to think that if she did it might look just as out of place on her aunt's 1950s marble-effect mantelpiece as hers did on their elegant, Georgian one.

Then when she was ten, Gemma caught chicken-pox, which wouldn't have been significant at all if it hadn't coincided with the only time she could remember her father being away. A studio in Hollywood had noticed his work and had great plans for animations based on it. A first-class air ticket had arrived in the post and there was so much excitement in the house,

Gemma remembered, you could almost touch it. They were going to be rich!

The day after they waved him off at Heathrow she fell ill. It was a bad attack, and even after the infection ceased to rage she was still covered in spots and felt very poorly. Lying in bed, feeling too ill to read herself, she missed him terribly. She spent what seemed like endless days staring through tear-filled eyes at the illustrations that papered her walls, wishing that he were there to soothe her with a story.

Estella just about managed to cope when one child was ill, but when Daisy succumbed to the virus too, she ran out of patience. One evening as Gemma crept downstairs to get herself a glass of milk, she heard her mother on the phone. She was thanking someone. Her voice sounded odd, she was employing the sort of vowel sounds she herself would call 'rather common'.

'You'll come for her on Sunday? Oh, thanks, Shirl, you've really saved my life . . . She's a lovely little girl, really, just a bit sorry for herself . . .'

Gemma automatically assumed that she was talking about Daisy, but the next morning, her mother came into her room carrying a glass of freshly squeezed orange juice. She had sugared the rim and slotted a slice of orange over it like a cocktail. 'Would you like to go to the seaside, darling?' she asked, sitting down at the end of Gemma's bed and smiling indulgently at her.

'When?' Gemma had responded warily.

A flicker of annoyance crossed her mother's face. She looked about to be cross, but composed herself. 'At the weekend. I thought you might like to recuperate with your Aunt Shirley. My sister,' she added. 'Her husband's going to drive up the refrigerated van to collect you,' she said, as if in explanation.

Gemma pictured herself shivering in a kind of igloo interior on wheels.

'Is it to stop the germs?' she asked.

'Germs?' Estella looked alarmed. 'No, no, it's for the fish,' she said then, understanding, and added, 'You'll be nice and warm in the front.' Before Gemma could ask any more questions, Estella got up and said, 'Well, that's settled then,' and went to attend to Daisy.

Gemma felt her head jerk upwards suddenly. The little boy opposite giggled as she took out her handbag mirror and checked her appearance. She hoped she hadn't been snoring. She must have been asleep for over an hour. Outside the South Downs were flashing past and the air in the carriage was fresher as they approached the coast. She began to feel quite excited.

Shirley was waiting where she had always waited, under the clock. Apart from the walking stick, she looked remarkably the same as she had ten years before. Her hair was, if anything, less grey, and it had been newly permed. She looked as if she had lost a little weight, but when Gemma hugged her she felt as comfortable as ever and her cheeks were still soft and fleshy to kiss, and still smelt of carnation soap. Gemma held on to the embrace for several minutes. This, she thought, truly feels like coming home.

'Well,' said Shirley, holding her out at arms length before hugging her again, 'you do look a treat!'

How could she have forgotten how Shirley spoke? Whenever a word ended in 'l', Shirley would add a 'w'. So 'well' became 'wellw' and when she spoke of her sister it was always, Gemma now recalled, 'Stellw'. She found she was smiling.

'Well,' said Shirley, 'what's it to be? Are you hungry? I hope so because I've made us a picnic.'

Strangely, Gemma was, for the first time in weeks.

'I went to Marksies on my way.' Her aunt held up a familiar plastic carrier bag and pointed to the exit. They started walking slowly out of the station.

'I remembered you liked egg, but I got a couple of

others too,' her aunt continued, 'and some iced buns, although looking at you I don't suppose you eat a lot of buns these days. They do lovely stuff, you know, it's not worth making it yourself. I mean, what would I do with the rest of the loaf? I don't do much cooking now,' she went on. 'When Ken died, I thought, that's it, I've cooked my last chip . . .'

How could she have wondered what they would talk about? Gemma asked herself, delighted.

'And I had. I haven't even opened the deep fat fryer I got as a flat-warming present. Mostly it's the microwave. That is,' she concluded, with a wink, for effect, 'when I'm not eating in restaurants. Let's save our legs.'

The cab dropped them at the entrance to the Memorial Gardens. It was slightly early for lunch and they found a free bench next to the resort's annual Painting in Flowers. This summer it was a Union Jack with '1945–1995' underneath, planted in red salvia, blue pansies and white asters.

'Spread yourself out a bit,' Shirley advised. 'It'll get crowded soon, and we don't want anyone bothering us, do we? That's right. Now, choose what you want. I got you egg and cress, like I said, but there's some fancy chicken too . . .'

Gemma didn't really care what she was eating, she was enjoying Shirley's chatter so much.

It was as if there had been no gap. All the time she had been away, Gemma thought, looking at the ample figure in her turquoise jacket and pleated tricel skirt, Shirley has still been my aunt, still loving me, still sharing all that history.

'I used to come for a walk in the Gardens every day when we had the shop,' Shirley was saying. 'Well, I had to grab a bit of peace after lunch, before the evening rush. Ken used to have a doze upstairs, but I liked a bit of fresh air.'

And when her niece came for holidays, she had always accompanied her. She remembered pointing to the flower-bed, teaching her the names of flowers. Gemma was always such a good little girl, happy to walk along beside her, holding her hand, not rushing about like the boisterous kids who played on the swings at the far end.

How has Stella ever managed to produce such a child, she used to ask herself.

And now she was all grown up. Very sophisticated looking, like one of the women in a fashion magazine. Shirley saw the way passers-by looked at her, then looked again.

'Do you miss the shop?' Gemma was asking.

'What? All that work? You must be joking . . . though the company was nice,' she added a little wistfully.

Gemma noticed that her aunt's eyes were watery. One of the things she most liked about her aunt, she realized, was that she never complained. She possessed a naturally happy temperament. She would have made a really lovely mother. She remembered with a sharp stab of guilt the one time she had asked Shirley why she didn't have any children. Her aunt had smiled, a sad smile, and said gently that it wasn't very polite to ask people that. Gemma had felt terrible for days, and tried to make it up to her by drawing her lots of pictures of flowers and other things she liked.

'You see, girl,' her aunt was saying, 'when you get old, they expect you to be with old people all the time. I liked seeing the world go by. That's what I liked. Still, can't complain. Not on a lovely day like this. Not with you here. Have another sarnie.' She delved into her carrier bag and came up with another cellophane packet.

'They always do a nice display.' Shirley nodded in the direction of the flower bed. 'That's one thing that hasn't changed. They keep it nice.'

An image of Stella lolling around up by the swings shot through Shirley's mind. Flirting and smoking with the boys who'd come home from war. She was only a child really, though she never was like a child for long. As far as Stella was concerned, the flowers in the park were for picking. She presented a bunch to their mother one Mother's Day and didn't half get a hiding. After that, she seemed to take revenge on the Gardens, and when their dad, reading a report in the *Gazette*, asked who on earth would be so stupid as to trample the annual floral display (that year, she remembered, it had been a clock whose hands, planted in yellow primulas, showed ten to two), Shirley had had to bite her tongue hard to stop herself going red and giving away the culprit.

'That says it all about this bloody dump, Shirl,' Stella had said, pointing at the clock before it was mysteriously vandalized. 'Time stands bloody still here.'

Shirley brought herself back to the present. 'Your mother and I,' she said, biting into the last sandwich, 'was always chalk and cheese. Didn't stop us loving each other, though . . .' she added firmly.

'Were you close when you were young?' Gemma asked, shocked by her aunt's sudden mention of Estella.

'Close? Oh yes, we was always close. Didn't see a lot of her after she left home, but we wrote each other letters and we talked, well, when she got married and had a phone . . .' Her aunt stopped talking mid-sandwich, noticing Gemma's look of surprise and added, 'Didn't you know that?'

'Er, not really,' Gemma stammered.

She had always assumed that the phonecall she had overheard was the only one Estella had made to her sister, and then only because she was desperate. Now she realized that was ridiculous. How else had her annual trips been arranged? But close? She couldn't imagine that Estella had felt close to Shirley. For one thing, she must have been livid that her sister always called her 'Stellw', when she insisted on 'Estella', having added the first 'E' when she left home, even from her children. Perhaps Shirley was getting old after all and remembering things wrongly.

'Poor old Stell . . . I wish I could have made it better for her . . .' Shirley continued, 'I do miss her . . .' She was staring into the middle distance, then she took Gemma's hand and squeezed it hard.

Gemma squeezed back, then let go, feeling slightly fraudulent because she was never conscious of missing Estella. She was, she thought, often aware of her absence, because major decisions were rather easier without Estella's views to contend with, but if she ever really tried to think about her mother fondly, she found herself almost immediately stiffening with fury.

'Are your knees up to a walk along the front?' she asked Shirley, collecting up the sandwich wrappers and walking to the nearest bin with them.

After the relative tranquillity of the Memorial Gardens and the shade of its big trees, the seafront was scorching and writhing with people. Gemma took Shirley's arm and negotiated a path along the promenade, dodging over-excited dogs and children brandishing virulent-coloured lollies. They paused to look over the railings and down at the bodies slowly barbecuing on the shingle.

'I should have bought my bikini,' Gemma remarked, slipping off her linen jacket to reveal a simple white cotton camisole.

'They say it's bad for you. You'll burn, you know,' her aunt looked anxiously at Gemma's bare shoulders.

'Just a few minutes,' Gemma said with a laugh, remembering how she used to plead to go uncovered as a child.

There was too much noise for comfort. Gemma put her arm through her aunt's and they walked slowly in companionable silence, until they came to the terrace of shops where Ken and Shirley's fish and chip shop had been.

'Oh what a shame!' Gemma said, stopping in her tracks.

Where there had been clean blue and white tiles, there was now garish plastic, and instead of the sign painted on the window saying 'Smith's Fish', there was now a neon loop reading 'Bu ger Ke ab Fri s'. Inside, under lurid photographs of fast food, a kebab spike with raggedy pieces of meat turned slowly, and bits that had already been cut languished in the fat that dripped into a metal tray beneath. The Formica shelf where people used to salt and vinegar their newspapered dinners had been replaced by a fruit machine, and, upstairs, the maisonette, in which she had whiled away so many happy hours just staring out to sea, was now an Entertainment Lounge, filled with more fruit machines and video games. An electronic din of beeps and sirens assaulted their ears as they drew near.

'Well, they paid me a good price for it,' Shirley said, resolutely. 'I don't often come this way. Don't like to see it, really.'

'Oh, I'm sorry,' Gemma said.

How could she have been so thoughtless? She had assumed it was Shirley's knees that had made her hesitate before agreeing to a walk along the prom.

'Come on,' she said, trying to make up for her blunder, 'let's have tea at the Royal. My treat.'

'Are you enjoying your job, then?' Shirley asked, selecting a pastry with strawberries on top from the three-tiered cake stand the waiter had placed in front of them.

Gemma had just bitten into a tiny coffee éclair. The

239

marriage of whipped cream, sweet fondant icing and choux pastry was sinfully delicious. She let the flavours melt in her mouth.

'Yes. I am, I suppose.' The office was the one place Gemma felt totally confident in herself.

'And you've got yourself a nice place to live?'

'Yes. It's not permanent. I'll have to think about buying somewhere soon.'

'Anyone nice around?'

It was about as subtle as Shirley ever got when asking about boyfriends. Gemma hated to disappoint her. An image of Ralph sprang to mind, which surprised her. She liked him, but he wasn't her type, really. Before she had a chance to answer, Shirley said, 'I was ever so sorry to hear about your husband. I mean, I know you was just friends, but you lasted longer together than most people these days . . .'

Gemma had written to her explaining that it wasn't a proper wedding, but she had never told her everything. She hadn't been sure what her aunt would make of it.

'Yes. He was my best friend . . .'

Shirley leant across the table. 'Was it AIDS?' she asked, in a confidential whisper that wasn't quite as quiet as she imagined. Two elderly ladies at the next table looked at each other and shifted in their seats.

Gemma sat back in her chair and nodded.

'I thought so,' Shirley said understandingly, 'reading between the lines. Some of them are lovely people, I'm told. Very sensitive. What a shame. And here we both are widows.'

If anything, Gemma was more shocked by the fact that Shirley was prepared to speak about Boy and Ken in the same breath as husbands than that she had guessed he was gay.

'Poor Uncle Ken,' she said, trying to regain her composure, 'I keep thinking that we'll go home after our walk and he'll be there . . .'

'Yes, it took me ages to get used to it. I won't say get over it, because you never do, do you?' her aunt said, helping herself to the wedge of Black Forest gâteau. 'I think it was easier with him,' she continued, 'because I saw him die. One minute he was as happy as Larry and the next, oops, he was over, and that was it. Well, he had a good life and a quick end, and what more could you ask for? Now, it's different with Stell, you see, because I still dream about her. I never dream about Ken. He's at rest . . . but Stell. I still think there must have been something I could have done . . .'

'No, I'm sure there wasn't, Auntie,' Gemma said automatically, and reached out for her hand.

'I don't know, Gem. Not a day goes by when I don't think about it,' Shirley mused. 'Was she ringing to say goodbye, or was she asking for help, and I didn't know . . .'

'When?' Gemma asked impatiently.

'When she rang. The night before she . . . you know . . .'

'Estella rang you?' Gemma was incredulous. If Shirley had told her that Estella had put a call through to the Prime Minister, she couldn't have been more surprised.

'Yes, she was in quite a state,' Shirley continued, ' "Shirl," she says, "I've ruined all my children's lives." That's rubbish, I said. You've given them wonderful lives. But she wouldn't have it. Crying. I couldn't make her stop, then Ken says, "Is she drunk or something?" and I told her, "Stell, go to bed, we'll talk in the morning," but we never did . . .'

Two fat tears rolled down Shirley's round face. She started to delve about in her handbag.

'Here,' Gemma handed her a clean tissue.

'Course, Stell would never be told. Never. If she was determined to do something, then she did it . . .' Shirley sniffed and looked around the room, focusing on anything to stop her weeping. It wasn't right to make a scene here, not in The Palm Court.

They used to hold tea dances here. She remembered slipping past the uniformed doorman with Stella, hiding in the folds of one of the dusty eau-de-Nil velvet curtains and silently watching the posh folk sipping their tea from delicate porcelain and taking slow graceful turns on the dance floor. And Stella whispering, 'When I grow up, Shirl, I'm going to be one of those people.' Then she sneezed, giving them away, and the head waiter booted them out, and Stella shouted at him down the street, 'Piss off. You're only a bloody servant anyway.' She was cheeky. But she got away with things, because people said she looked like Elizabeth Taylor in *National Velvet*.

'Anyway,' Shirley said pulling herself together, 'we can't bring her back now.'

'No.' Gemma agreed and waved at a waiter for the bill.

'What were you doing on VE Night, Auntie? Do you remember?' Gemma asked as they puffed up Victoria Street.

'Clear as if it was yesterday. I've been thinking about it a lot recently. All these reminders . . .' Shirley pointed at the tiny red, white and blue flags fluttering above their heads. 'I was in London, of course, well, we all were that night. Ken was just home and Stell dragged him up to meet me from work. I don't know how she managed it. Dad was usually strict with her. But that night nobody was in a mood to refuse anybody anything. He regretted it later, though, the miserable old sod . . .'

'Why?' Gemma asked.

'Well, that's when it all started really. Stell saw what she wanted that night – London, life, men – she was only twelve, but she looked much older, and after that, well, there was no controlling her . . .' Shirley smiled at her memories.

'We all linked arms, so we wouldn't lose each other and we went everywhere . . . Shaftesbury Avenue . . . Piccadilly Circus,' her breathless recollections made the names sound as exotic as Xanadu. 'There was a bloke playing the trumpet and we danced. All the soldiers had eyes for Stell . . . of course . . . and she danced 'til she dropped. "Cor blimey," says Ken, "she's going to be a heartbreaker, Shirl . . ." '

'And was she?' Gemma asked, fascinated.

Shirley paused for breath. She leant on her stick and looked at Gemma as if wondering whether to trust her. 'Course, you don't know any of this, do you? Stell didn't tell you anything, did she?'

'Not really,' said Gemma, wondering how to explain without sounding rude. 'I don't think she wanted anyone to know about her background . . .' She remembered Estella's forbidding look whenever she asked about her childhood.

'Well, she was probably right,' Shirley said, 'it's probably best left alone . . .' She started walking on.

'No, tell me . . .' Gemma was tingling with curiosity.

'These days it wouldn't seem like anything, really,' Shirley said, 'but those were more innocent times . . . come on, you'll miss your train . . .'

Gemma looked at her watch. She was half inclined to say sod the train, tell me all about my mother, but she had promised Jonathan she would help him with his barbecue, and she couldn't let the children down.

'I haven't even seen your new flat,' she said, as she leant out of the train window to kiss Shirley goodbye. 'Can I come again soon?'

Shirley smiled; it was the question her niece had always asked when she put her on the train.

'Of course you can,' she said, 'whenever you like!'

'She seemed in very good form, considering,' Gemma shouted from the kitchen.

She inspected the last leaf of a cos lettuce closely, decided she had rinsed it enough, and put it in the spinner with the rest. Then she picked up the jar of vinaigrette and shook it vigorously.

'She wanted to talk a lot about Estella. But I suppose that's only natural. It's funny, I was beginning to get quite a different picture of my mother . . . I think she must have caused some scandal . . . and then it was time to go. I think I'll go down again soon. I'd love to know . . .'

'What?' Jonathan stuck his head round the door. His face was covered in soot. 'Do you think it's meant to blaze like this?' he asked, looking at the flaming barbecue with some trepidation.

'It'll die down in a minute,' Gemma reassured him. 'Now where are those drumsticks?'

'Daddy, Daddy, Daddy!'

'Yes, David.'

'Will there be burgers, Daddy?'

'No, darling, I think that Gemma's making some delicious chicken.'

'Don't like chicken.' The little boy sounded quite determined.

'Well, you've never had chicken like this,' his father said, equally firmly.

'Is it from America?'

'Well, yes, in a way,' Gemma replied.

'Daddy, will we have chips?'

The relentless questioning went on for several minutes, then suddenly the little boy was distracted by the cat from next door who was stalking a blackbird on the lawn.

'Who'd have kids?' said Jonathan apologetically.

'He's lovely,' Gemma said.

244

'Have you ever . . . ?'

'Thought I would like some? I don't know. I think one probably has to find the right man first,' Gemma replied lightly.

'And you've never thought . . . this is the one?'

'Well, yes, but . . .' She had imagined little boys with Oliver's curls and Oliver's eyes. 'But he fell in love with somebody else,' she said. 'Shall we put some chips in the oven for them? Somehow I don't think jacket potatoes are going to do the trick . . . oh thanks!'

Jonathan had poured her a glass of Rioja. 'Come and sit down in the shade. You must be exhausted.'

'I don't feel at all tired, actually,' Gemma said, relaxing into the padded lounger nevertheless. 'My mind's buzzing. It was kind of weird talking to Shirley as an adult. I mean, I know I was over twenty when I left, but my relationship with her was still very much the one I'd had when I was little . . . Today, well, it was different. It was as if she had been waiting for someone to talk to about my mother . . . However much I tried to change the subject it kept coming back to that . . . and by the end, "wellw", as she would say, I was hooked . . . I looked at Shirley and that ordinary little seaside town, and I thought that Estella was a pretty remarkable self-invention with all her airs and graces . . .'

'Yes, I don't think you'd have known that she was brought up in a fish and chip shop in some run-down resort, you're right . . . Maybe that's why she was always so cross and defensive.'

'I was thinking on the train back, maybe she hated me because I was desperate to be ordinary . . . when I think of it now, I used to come back from Shirley's and whinge on about wanting to live there . . . it must have driven her mad . . .'

'She didn't hate you, Gemma . . . I think she just found you harder to love than Daisy because you were such a solemn little girl . . . judgemental almost . . . perhaps she thought you had sussed her out.'

Gemma saw Estella's face, that searching look she had, as if she were trying to see what she was thinking. Had that forbidding face been frightened of her? Surely not. In the smoky heat of the barbecue, Gemma shivered.

She couldn't sleep. Whenever she closed her eyes she saw her mother, not dead, not lying as she had found her, sprawled across the bed like a giant rag doll, but alive, very much alive, and young and smiling. She was wearing a dress with a tight bodice and a full skirt. Gemma couldn't tell what the colour was because the image was in monochrome. She sat up in bed, realizing that she was thinking of the photo that always fell out of her mother's album, the one that had been stuck to the first page until the glue aged and cracked, the one above the caption that read, in careful looping handwriting: 'The first day of my life. I leave home.'

She was standing in the station, Gemma realized, about to board a train, the long platform stretching away behind her. Her posture was all confidence and defiance, a full-bosomed, hourglass figure with a cinched-in waist. She was beautiful in an Ava Gardner-ish way, with dark exotic eyes and a face much too ripe for her seventeen years. Who had taken that photo, Gemma wondered, and, now she thought about it, who had bought her that provocative New Look dress?

Perhaps Daisy knew. Daisy had kept the album, she was sure. Gemma switched on the bedside light and looked at her watch. It was after one o'clock, too late to ring now. She would try in the morning.

CHAPTER 19

RELATIVE STRANGERS: Daisy Rush meets three couples who put the relation into relationships, Daisy typed. Perhaps that was too facetious? Well, if it was the editor could change it. It was too hot to think of another title.

She pulled her copy out of the typewriter. Now there was the small matter of finding a fax machine. It had taken her long enough to find an adaptor plug in the town and she had been amazed when she finally plugged her typewriter into the socket which hung out of the wall of their apartment that the machine didn't blow up. She had seen a fax in the office of the apartment complex, but she didn't know what reward the caretaker would demand in exchange for her using it. She would need a chaperon, but Oliver was asleep by the pool under a copy of the *International Guardian*. She didn't want to disturb him.

Daisy slipped on a large T-shirt over her bikini top and cut-off jeans, and pulled Oliver's baseball cap onto her head. Then she let herself out of the apartment, only realizing when the door slammed behind her that she had left the key inside.

On the whole, she thought, stepping out into the blazing sun, it has been a good idea to get away. There was always an element of potluck in the kind of late booking holidays Oliver liked to spring on her. She squirmed, remembering two weeks in Lanzarote trapped by a desert wind in a ghastly hotel with a convention of Elvis Presley impersonators. On the last day the wind had dropped and they had toured the island in a coach only to discover that they had been staying on a lump of live volcano. She had thought, looking at her fellow passengers boarding the charter at Gatwick, that this latest holiday was going to be a repeat, but when they were divided up at Heraklion airport a coach took the disco bunnies east, and Oliver hired a jeep and drove west. The town they were staying in had a kind of Venetian charm, and although the waterfront restaurants with their hanging lanterns were expensive, the food was good fresh seafood, miles away from the hunks of charred flesh Daisy normally associated with Greek cuisine.

Their apartment was the top half of a white cube, with bougainvillaea dripping from the steps up to the door. There was a hard double bed on which they had slept soundly, a crucifix with a tiny red bulb glowing above their heads, the bouzouki music from the nightclubs too distant even for Oliver's sensitive ears.

His only complaint had been about a small visitor to their room. The first night as they were drifting off to sleep Oliver had said, 'There's something I've been meaning to tell you.'

She had remained silent.

'I've . . . Jesus Christ, there's a bloody mosquito in here.'

He had leapt out of bed, switched on the light, and grabbed the ringbinder notebook from her bedside table. Thus armed, he spent most of the rest of the night chasing the insect round the room, with Daisy laughing and laughing as his long naked body lunged and leapt, and as he finally crushed the offending body against the wall above the bedhead, leaving two splashes of blood like stigmata on the whitewashed surface.

He never did get to complete his sentence.

Daisy walked through the streets towards the harbour. A couple of leather-faced old women tried to wrap lace shawls round her shoulders and she managed to convey admiration for their work with smiles, whilst pleading poverty by pointing at her shorts. By the end of the holiday, she thought, I shall probably have made the mistake of buying one, thinking of the drawerful of clothes she never wore at home that had been purchased on Mediterranean holidays. It must be something to do with seeing them every day, she thought. By the end of two weeks you're brainwashed into thinking that there are no clothes in the world other than those that hang from every stall. Perhaps this time I could satisfy the consumer urge by confining myself to a triangular cotton headscarf with tiny gold discs sewn on to it, she thought.

'Fax?' she asked the ladies, imagining that the word must be international, 'Faxee?' she tried again, remembering that whatever the vowel combination, it always seemed to sound like 'ee' in Greek.

Daisy followed their hand signals to the harbour where a line of ancient dusty Mercedes, their leather seats worn to a shine, stood in the sun. A huddle of cab drivers were smoking and sipping tiny cups of coffee in the nearby café.

She decided to find the restaurant where they had eaten delicious calamares and where the waiter spoke passable English. He gave her complicated directions which led her back to the office at the apartment development where they were staying. The fax went through first time much to the delight of the caretaker and his wife who was the only person who had bothered to read the instructions for the machine and knew how to work it. Much relieved, Daisy went to find Oliver. He was still sleeping. His skin tanned easily, and his chest was already brown except for his sickle-shaped scar that had turned deep pink in the sun. Daisy shook out her towel and lay down next to him in the shade.

'Come on, let's go for a drive,' Oliver rolled over and watched her rubbing oil on her arms.

'But I'm hot.'

'You shouldn't go for long walks in the midday sun. You've burnt the back of your neck,' he told her.

'Let me have a doze.'

'No, come on. The south of the island is the best bit. They say the north is like Europe, the south like Africa. There are banana plantations,' he added, as though offering a bribe.

After a few days in a new place, Oliver became a walking guidebook. Daisy sighed. She liked the warmth of Europe. She wasn't sure she wanted the sweaty heat of Africa, and she had never been particularly keen on bananas, but she knew there was little point in arguing.

This is a metaphor for my life, she thought, as the jeep bounced along. Oliver's in the driving seat and I'm doing something I don't really want to do because to object would cause a fuss and a temper far greater than the discomfort I am putting up with.

Perhaps that was how every couple worked. Certainly there had been the same dynamic in her parents' relationship, except that it was Estella who called the shots.

Daisy couldn't decide whether what she was feeling was just a passing phase of doubt that anybody would go through after years in the same relationship, or something more fundamental. She had no-one to discuss it with.

She had never been very good at making girlfriends, she realized. When she was young she told Gemma everything, and she didn't need or want to join in the girls' talk about bra sizes and tampons at school. Then, after Gemma left, Oliver became her sole confidant.

She had felt totally relaxed sharing all her innermost thoughts with him. But when it came to her anxieties about him, she had no-one. Since Gemma's confession, talk of Oliver was off limits. Perhaps Kathy had been right. Perhaps Relate was the answer. She looked at Oliver's profile. Anyone would think her mad to give him up. But if she didn't say something soon she would burst.

'I'm thinking of going to see someone at Relate,' she blurted out suddenly.

'Another relationships' article? Why don't you write about something serious? You're wasting your talent as a journalist . . .' Oliver overtook an old man riding a donkey, and put his foot down. A spray of gravel shot up from the wheels, stinging Daisy's bare arm.

'No, I didn't mean for an article,' she said, hoping that he would catch on and stop making it so difficult for her. Oliver began to sing 'The Anvil Chorus'.

'I meant . . .' Daisy was having to shout, 'I meant because I want to talk to someone about our relationship . . .' There, it was out.

Oliver continued to sing. At first she thought he hadn't heard, but he finished the verse and then said, 'Why don't you talk to me about it? I've been waiting for you to say something. It's obvious you're not happy . . .'

At first she was furious. If he had known, why hadn't he said something before? But then, why hadn't she? She felt completely thrown. It was as if he had wrested power from her again. She decided to employ one of Oliver's tactics and say nothing. They drove along in complete silence for several minutes, then Oliver said, 'Look, windmills!'

'Bugger the windmills,' Daisy said. She felt stupid. Now everything that she had wanted to say carefully would sound petulant. She stared straight through the windscreen. The wind was blowing great clouds of hair around her face. 'I think I fell in love with you too young,' she began, 'and now I feel trapped.'

'God, Daisy, you're beginning to sound like one of the trashy magazines you write for.'

'Why do you always have to belittle me?' she screamed at him suddenly, daring him to look at her. He turned away from the wheel and she saw that he was shocked by her shouting.

'I'm sorry,' he said simply, 'I just don't want to lose you.'

'But why do you try to undermine me then?' she asked quietly.

'I don't know,' he said, 'maybe it is my fear of being abandoned . . .'

'Don't you see that everything isn't always to do with *you*,' she said, her voice rising, 'I want to talk about *me* . . .'

'Well, tell me all about you, then.'

Of course, then she couldn't think of anything to say.

The jeep lurched down the cliffside. Daisy closed her eyes. There was no edge to the road. Any minute the track was going to crumble, and the jeep would go down with it. How long would it be until they were found and identified, she wondered. How long before Gemma knew that she and Oliver were dead? Poor Gemma would probably think that at least they had been happy during their last moments, but how wrong she would be. They had spent the last hour driving in stony silence, and now Oliver seemed to be punishing her by taking this reckless route.

I don't want to die like this, Daisy thought.

'You're very near the edge,' she told Oliver.

'I know,' Oliver said, putting the jeep into the lowest gear. He didn't sound at all sure. She realized that he was almost as frightened as she was.

'We can't go on,' Daisy said.

'What do you want me to do, execute a three point turn at this point?'

She shut up.

'It'll be worth it when we get there,' he assured her more kindly.

If we get there, thought Daisy, her eyes closed.

When she opened them again, the road had flattened out, and they were almost at sea level. The track ended by an unfinished two storey building with a terrace. Under trellises of vines with grapes hanging down like baubles from a Christmas tree, a couple of tables were set with white cotton tablecloths for lunch.

'What a peculiar place for a restaurant,' Daisy said, getting out of the jeep, pulling her T-shirt away from the back of the seat where it had stuck with sweat.

The choice was octopus grilled and served with lemon wedges, or octopus stewed with tomatoes and potatoes.

The proprietor joked about the pallor of Daisy's complexion and brought her ouzo in a little glass like medicine. Oliver started on a bottle of retsina. Daisy began to feel a little better. She smiled at Oliver, feeling warmer towards him. 'I can understand the war,' she said.

'What?'

'You feel closer to someone when you've shared a near death experience.'

He laughed. 'I am sorry. The map made it look like a better road. But the octopus is good, isn't it?'

'I'm not a great octopus *cognoscente*,' Daisy said, and it sounded so pompous, they both giggled.

They spent the afternoon lying on the tiny stretch of sand under the shade of an umbrella the restaurant proprietor insisted on lending them. Apart from the gentle lapping of waves, it was quiet, perfectly quiet. Daisy felt that they were in some magical place near the edge of the world, a place that had nothing to do with reality. She was content to lie there, suspended in time, thinking of nothing. She felt safe now. The fact that they had survived the descent down the cliff seemed like an omen. She had thought she was going to die, but now she felt so relieved to be alive, nothing seemed to matter very much.

'I do understand', Oliver said out of the blue, 'why you would want to leave me, but I don't want you to . . .'

Daisy stared up at the word Cinzano.

'I think I just need some time on my own,' she said vaguely.

'OK,' Oliver leapt up. 'I'll move out when we get back. Now, I'm going for a walk.'

It was what she wanted, wasn't it? Daisy watched him clambering along the rocky shore, bending from time to time to pick up a suitable stone and skim it out to sea. She knew she should be feeling relieved that in the end it had been Oliver who had said it. Instead she just felt numb.

It was as if she had been in a room with a flickering candle that made shapes and shadows on the walls and ceiling, ever-changing patterns in the soft eddies of air. Then suddenly she had leant forward and blown the candle out. And she could see nothing, nothing at all, until her eyes became accustomed to the dark.

CHAPTER 20

'Hello. We can't come to the phone . . .'

The answerphone again. She wished that Daisy had recorded the message. Every time she rang she was thrown when she heard Oliver's voice.

It was probably a bit early for Daisy. She had always been a late riser. Gemma imagined her sprawled across Oliver's chest in post-coital slumber. The phone was ringing. Daisy raised her head and said with a yawn, 'Oh, let the machine pick it up.'

Gemma decided not to leave another message. She had left two during the week. It was peculiar that Daisy hadn't called back. For a second she wondered if something was wrong. Then she smiled. Ten years without speaking to her sister, and now she was anxious after just a few days. Just as she put down the receiver, her phone rang.

'Yes?'

'Sorry. Is this a bad time?' Ralph asked.

'Oh hi! No. Not at all. How are you?'

'Good. I know it's short notice, but are you doing anything today, because I have the loan of a car and I wondered, since we seem to have some sunshine, whether you'd like to go out for lunch?'

He sounded as if he had rehearsed the casualness of the invitation until he got just the right balance of eagerness and nonchalance. She was touched. It was rather nice to be so transparently liked.

'I'd love to,' she said.

'OK, gimme your address and I'll be there in half an hour.'

He wouldn't tell her where they were going. When they left London on the A2, she thought of Kent. There was an oysterage at Whitstable she had read about on the train back from Shirley's the weekend before. It had been a great write-up. Perhaps Ralph had read it too, but they sailed past the turning. Perhaps he was taking her to Canterbury. It was the sort of place, a cathedral town with history, that Americans liked, but they didn't turn off there either. It wasn't until they were sitting in a queue of cars waiting to drive on that she realized they were about to enter the Channel Tunnel on Le Shuttle.

'But I haven't brought my passport!' she said.

He held up a dark blue wallet she recognized.

'I thought you were the sort of woman who would keep her passport in her bedside drawer,' he said, and she remembered that he had wanted to use the bathroom when he picked her up. 'Nice photo too!'

She felt slightly annoyed.

'Don't worry,' he said, 'I thought I'd just follow a hunch. If it hadn't been there, I promise I would have asked you. But that would have spoiled the surprise. You haven't been in the tunnel before, have you?'

'It's only just opened, hasn't it?'

'Yes.'

He looked at her like a child seeking approval, after doing something naughty.

'It's a lovely surprise,' she said, 'but you should have asked me about my passport.'

Then they were moving, and sitting side by side in the car in the tunnel felt oddly intimate. Gemma sat rigidly in her seat as if any chance touch of knee or hand would produce an electric shock. When they emerged she exhaled as if she had been holding her breath the whole way through. She realized that they hadn't spoken.

'Were you frightened?' Ralph asked.

'A little. Not as much as I thought. What about you?'

'The same,' he said, 'now, are you desperately hungry, or shall we drive somewhere off the beaten track?'

'It's still early,' Gemma said, looking at her watch. She couldn't believe she was in France so soon after getting up. 'Let's drive. Excuse me, but I think you're on the wrong side of the road.'

Ralph swerved the car. 'I've just gotten used to driving on the wrong side,' he said.

'You're doing well,' responded Gemma and he rewarded her with a disarmingly open smile.

They drove due south for an hour until the little road they had taken ran out at a fishing village. After perusing a couple of menus, Ralph sauntered over to some fishermen who were rolling up their nets on a jetty and they pointed at an unpromising-looking café.

The waiter wiped down the vinyl tablecloth and plonked a plastic basket of bread and cutlery between them.

'You do like seafood?' Ralph asked her as he chatted through the various options in fluent French. She didn't know why it should surprise her that he spoke the language so well.

'I think I would have told you by now if I didn't,' Gemma replied, smiling.

He ordered the biggest tray of *fruits de mer* she had ever seen. There were a dozen oysters, a whole lobster, piles of shrimp and winkles to be eaten with a pin.

'Now,' Ralph picked up a bowl of yellow mayonnaise and sniffed it, 'this has a lot of garlic. I'm talking bulbs here, not cloves, and I'm not going to taste it until you have solemnly sworn to have some too, because otherwise the car is going to be a very unpleasant place for one of us . . .'

Rising to the challenge, Gemma took her fork, scooped a blob straight into her mouth, and grinned at him. It was oily, garlicky, delicious. Then they set about the task of demolishing the food in front of them, washing away the salty taste of the sea with crisp white wine.

'This was a wonderful lunch,' Gemma said, having tipped the oyster she was saving for last down her throat, 'thank you so much.'

'You're welcome,' he replied, and she realized how much she missed that simple response Americans always use and English people think is superfluous. She felt easy with Ralph. She liked his company. He had an offbeat way of looking at things, and he was also kind. 'Never mind about their looks,' she could hear Shirley saying, 'what you want is a kind man.'

He was also, she found herself thinking, gazing at his back as he chatted with the waiter, rather attractive. She hadn't thought so when she first met him. She liked men dark and brooding, and Ralph was red-haired and open. She had taken his broad smile to indicate a lack of subtlety, but there hadn't been any evidence to support that. How many men she knew would think of taking her to a French fishing village for lunch, she asked herself. He had a good body too, a swimmer's body with broad shoulders and slim hips. His Levi's fitted him perfectly and there was no trace of a dreadful buttocky bum that spoiled the back view of so many American men.

She thought she would quite like it if he asked whether she wanted to spend the afternoon in bed. They had passed a rickety little hotel when they were looking for a restaurant and she was so far on in her imaginings that she was almost disappointed when he returned to the table with two little cups of dark coffee and suggested they go for a walk.

'I need to work off some of that wine,' he said.

Yes, thought Gemma, jumping abruptly back to reality, I think I do too.

'What are you writing about at the moment?' she asked him as they ambled along the beach. The tide had gone out a long way, leaving the harbour and most of the estuary a mud flat. She had met many writers, but none as reticent about his work as Ralph was.

'Oh, this and that.'

'Don't you like talking about your work?'

'Have you ever met a writer who doesn't?'

'Well . . .'

'Exactly. Your typical novelist – he goes on and on for an hour or so about his book,' Ralph looked down at her and smiled, 'then he says, but that's enough about *me*, what did *you* think of my novel?!'

'But you're not like that,' she protested. 'Anyway, I asked you and I'm interested.'

'My first novel was one of those, most dreaded words, a coming-of-age novel about a boy growing up in a stifling atmosphere. I thought of it as a kind of *Great Gatsby* meets *Love Story*,' he said self-mockingly, 'and now I'm working on a novel about a young man who spends a summer as a gardener in the Hamptons . . .'

'Is that your background too?'

'Well, of course. You don't think I have an imagination, do you?' he laughed.

'I didn't mean . . .'

'I know you didn't. I'm sure you've heard it all before. It's not really me, and that kind of thing. I think most writers are pretty disingenuous about that. If anyone ever asks me whether my writing is auto-biographical, I always say, yes, completely, what else do I know about?'

'I'd love to read them,' she said simply, meaning it.

'I'll give you a copy of the first. I'm still in the middle of *The Garden Summer*.'

'It's a good title.'

'Doesn't sound too much like a gardening manual?'

'Not with the right cover.'

'You mean you *can* tell a book by its cover?'

'Yes,' she laughed, 'I think you ought to be able to, anyway. That's really all most people have to go on. Was your first book successful?' She vaguely remembered seeing a short, favourable review in the *New York Times*.

'Well, let's put it this way, I couldn't live on the money.'

'So how do you support yourself?' she asked, before it occurred to her that it was probably a rude question.

'Well, actually, I'm quite rich.'

The way he said it, with a hint of apology in his voice, made her think that he didn't tell most people that. She found his honesty endearing.

'Not as rich as I could be if I did what my folks wanted me to do, but I haven't annoyed them quite enough yet to be cut off entirely,' he explained, 'although I expect the third novel I write will probably get me disinherited immediately.'

'Don't tell me . . . it's about the rich parents of a boy who grew up in a stifling atmosphere and worked as a gardener one summer in the Hamptons.'

'You got it!'

She looked up into his face and her eyes met his. They were sparkling with good humour. She had an almost uncontrollable urge to hug him. She skipped along beside him, feeling very happy.

'Why are you living in England?' she asked.

'Well, there are no distractions here. I find it easier to write. And I like the English. I speak their language . . .'

'You speak pretty good French too.'

'My mother is French.'

Of course. Only now she realized why Ralph's name

260

was familiar. His father was a major financier and his mother was an ex-model who now devoted herself to building a collection of 20th-century art. Gemma had seen her pictured in *Hello!* magazine modelling a range of swimwear based on her seven Mondrians. No wonder he wanted to live in anonymity in London.

Having lived with Boy she thought she understood what it was like to have ghastly rich parents. But Ralph appeared to be far less neurotic than Boy. She frowned, wondering suddenly whether the fact that he was walking along next to her, yet so fastidiously not letting their hands touch, meant that he was gay. The thought hadn't occurred to her before, but it would explain why he was so easy to be around, and yet why there was a physical awkwardness between them. She remembered how sensitive he had been when she had told him about Boy on their first meeting, how concerned.

The mud was getting too wet to walk out further. Ralph picked up a stone and skimmed it across the water. Gemma smiled. Why was it, she wondered, that any man on any beach was programmed to pick up a stone and skim it out to sea?

'I know a great patisserie in Le Touquet,' Ralph said, turning round to face her. The sun was behind him and his hair was a copper halo around his face. 'Shall we have tea before we head back?'

'It's been such a lovely day,' Gemma said, licking her forefinger and dabbing the last flake of *mille-feuille* into her mouth. 'I feel miles from home, as if I've been on holiday for a week. I don't want to go home!'

Ralph was thoughtful for a few seconds, then he said, 'Well do you have to? Do you have plans for tomorrow?'

'Not really,' Gemma said, panicking slightly. It had been something nice to say, not really a proposition.

'Well why don't we stay? We could have dinner, some good wine. There's a hotel on the beach. It's functional, nothing more, but you can hear the sea all night. It's like being in a bunker on the sand dunes.'

'Do you come here a lot, then?' It had been such a special day, she somehow hated the idea that he did this every weekend.

'I have a friend who likes to gamble. I've been a couple of times with him,' he said.

So, he was gay. Well, fine. It made things so much more straightforward.

'All right,' she said, 'but you must allow me to buy dinner.'

They checked into the hotel. The good weather had brought out the crowds and there was only one room left. She saw Ralph's look of concern as the receptionist explained, then he turned to her and asked if she minded sharing.

'There are two beds,' he said.

'Well, as long as you don't snore,' she said, laughing and wondering why he was making such a fuss.

Ralph was sure he knew where the restaurant he wanted to go to was but he couldn't remember its name, so he decided to find it on foot and make a reservation, while Gemma went shopping for toothbrushes.

A camisole made of rose silk satin had caught her eye earlier in the window of the extremely chic lingerie shop next to the patisserie. She had thought then that it would be ideal as an evening top. She retraced their steps. Her linen suit was a little crumpled after the day and the bottoms of the trousers had watermarks from walking on the beach, but it would do. Her black cotton vest felt sweaty and she wanted something to change into. The camisole, she calculated as she twirled in front of the elegant cheval mirror behind the pink and white striped curtain at the back of the shop, cost a week's salary, but it was bias cut and perfect in its simplicity. Having made the decision to buy it, the matching panties seemed relatively inexpensive.

Gemma was showering when Ralph returned to the room. She came out of the bathroom wearing her new purchases and with a large white hotel towel wrapped round her head like a turban. Ralph whistled. She bent forward and began to rub her hair dry. There was a knock on the door. 'I asked for an iron,' she explained, and Ralph disappeared into the bathroom as she ironed out her suit, still clad in her underwear.

'You look drop dead gorgeous,' he told her as they stepped out into the cooler evening air, and Gemma remembered with a pang of sadness how nice it was to be with a gay man who appreciated clothes and fabrics and had no inhibitions or hidden agenda about issuing compliments.

'I don't think I've ever eaten so much in one day,' Gemma said, folding the menu, 'but I think I'll have a steak nevertheless,' she giggled.

They had stopped for an aperitif at a bar which had lace curtains stained ochre by years of Gauloises' smoke. Then they hadn't been able to resist another, and another. And now, in the restaurant, Ralph was ordering wine.

She hadn't felt as happy in anyone's company since she left New York. She could tell that Ralph liked her, really liked her, and she really liked him. Her earlier twinge of disappointment that he was not, after all, a potential lover, had vanished as it dawned on her with delight that she was making a new friend. The early stage of friendship: conversation, seeing eye to eye on important things, laughter, was one of life's great pleasures. The early stage of a relationship: waiting for the phone to ring, fine judgements about how keen or cool to appear, suppression of optimism and expectation of failure, was, in her experience, more like torture.

Having given her sharp sketches of his family, now he wanted to know about hers.

'Well, as a matter of fact, I suppose I'm quite rich too,' she said, echoing his earlier admission, 'but only because my father died of cancer when I was twenty-one and my mother committed suicide a month later . . .'

'Ah, Gemma, I'm so sorry . . .' A look of real pain crossed his face.

'Thank you.' She never knew what to say. On occasion she had found herself saying it's all right, knowing that the information was more of a shock to the recipient than it was to her. She didn't tell many people.

'I didn't get on with my mother,' she continued, feeling that she could tell him anything, 'not that that made it easier. I think sometimes it makes it worse. I mean, I can think about my father fondly and I feel sad, but whenever I think about my mother I feel angry and then guilty for being angry . . . does that make me sound horrible?'

'Of course it doesn't.'

'I went away to the States and tried to make a new life, and I succeeded in a way. But then that all went wrong too, and I thought I'd come home. I thought that I had got over everything and I could start afresh here. I thought I was good at starting afresh, you see. But now I'm back, I find that all the things I left behind are still here, ten years later, and I'm having to deal with them and this time I know I can't escape . . . and sometimes,' she felt a tear roll down her face, 'I just feel so lonely . . . I'm sorry . . . this is self-indulgent and that is what I most hated about Estella.'

'Estella was your mother?'

'Yes.'

'Great name.'

'Well, like lots of things about her, it was made up,' Gemma said cruelly. 'Her real name was Stella and she grew up in a fish and chip shop, but if you'd have met

264

her you'd have thought that she had grown up in a palace.'

'Her mother was an Indian Queen and her father was the Emperor of China?'

'Yes, where's that from?' Gemma knew the quote but couldn't place it.

'*Wuthering Heights*, it's Heathcliff.'

'Of course it is,' Gemma remembered, thinking how apposite the quotation was, 'yes, Estella would have loved to be compared to Heathcliff – she was dark and tempestuous and romantic, I suppose . . .' She smiled at him.

'She sounds rather wonderful,' Ralph ventured.

'Well, you know, she probably was. Everyone else always thought so, but it's taken me ten years after her death to see that she was quite an extraordinary woman. Maybe I'm getting through the stages of grief my friend Kathy says I have to go through . . .'

Since she had seen Shirley, it *was* beginning to get easier to think about Estella, Gemma realized.

'What did she do?' Ralph asked.

'Well, she could have been a very good artist, but she was lazy. She dabbled, really. My father supported her.'

'Did you inherit any of that from her?'

'What, the laziness? Not that, I think, and certainly not the artistic flair.'

She remembered Estella reading her school report. 'Gemma's drawings are neat and tidy,' she had read out loud, laughing. Gemma winced.

She waved at the waiter for the bill. They sat in silence while she carefully filled in a tip on the credit card slip and signed it. Then she looked at him and saw that he was waiting for her to continue.

'She took a bottle of pills,' she said. 'I found her.'

'No wonder you're angry,' Ralph replied, helping her into her jacket.

'Come on,' she said, taking his arm for stability as much as friendship, 'let's go back to our bunker in the sand dunes.'

Ralph showered first and by the time Gemma had finished brushing her teeth, he had turned off the light and was lying covered in bed. She noticed that he had left her the bed by the window. She took off her trousers and climbed into it.

'D'you mind if I open the window?' she asked a few minutes later, quietly in case he had fallen asleep.

'Go right ahead,' he replied immediately, obviously very awake.

The noise of the waves crashing only yards away was loud but soothing.

Gemma lay on her back with the sheet and blanket pulled up to her chin, looking out at the clear starry sky. There was only a wisp of moon but her eyes soon became accustomed to the darkness. She liked lying there next to her new friend. She felt safe. 'It's like being in a dorm,' she said.

He didn't reply for a few moments, but she could sense in the air that he wanted to say something. 'Gemma, I don't know quite how to put this,' he finally said, 'but I have a hard-on like the Eiffel Tower.'

She caught her breath, 'But I thought . . .'

'What?'

'You . . . gay?' she stammered. Her heart had started to race.

'Whatever gave you that idea?' he sat up.

'You're not?' she said, delighted.

'No.'

'Oh God,' she said, clambering out of her bed, 'what a relief!'

'You're so fine,' he whispered to her as his tongue stroked soft circles on her breast, coaxing each nipple

266

alternately until they were so hard that she was arching towards him, wanting to pierce his chest with hers.

'Open your eyes,' he said, and he held her head in both his hands and looked at her. She looked back, her body twisting with pleasure under him.

'Please,' she said, 'oh please, please . . .'

He rolled a condom over his penis, quickly and expertly. No embarrassed fumbling.

Then he kissed her forehead, her eyelids, her neck, while his fingers played with her clitoris, and she could feel the climax rising, lifting her back off the bed, the pleasure so acute it was unbearable unless he would share it with her. She climbed over onto him and held his hair in her hands, then she inched herself down onto him and when he filled her completely and gasped, she began to move, deliberately at first, then out of control, pleasuring herself with him until his eyes closed and he squirmed, and she felt the strange sudden change from red hot to molten inside her.

They lay locked together for a couple of moments, sweat and breath intermingling, then he withdrew, carefully, checked the condom, then kissed her nose.

'You', he said, 'are my fantasy woman.'

And the word made her think of Oliver, and she found that she couldn't see his face.

It was a tiny bed for both of them, but when she woke snuggled into his chest, she felt as if she belonged there. The sun was streaming in and she could hear children shrieking on the sand.

'We've missed breakfast, but I didn't want to wake you,' Ralph said.

She put her arms around his chest and squeezed and was reassured to feel him drop a kiss into her hair.

She didn't want to leave the room, the plain little twin room that could have been in any hotel anywhere, but felt the most special place in the world. She was afraid that outside the magical spell that had made them do wonderful things to each others' bodies would be broken. She craved the reassurance that there would be more nights like this, but she knew not to ask.

She retrieved the black vest she had rinsed through from the towel rail in the bathroom. It was still damp but she put it on. She thought she would keep the rose camisole just as it was – scrunched up and smelling of sex – and put it in a box to remind herself of a beautiful night. She brushed her hair and went back into the bedroom. Ralph was still staring at the ceiling.

'What are you doing for the rest of your life?' he asked her.

CHAPTER 21

Curiously, she could understand Stella better now, at nearly seventy years old, than she ever could when she was young.

She had never been much of a risk taker then. Nor had Ken. Or perhaps she had, originally, and marriage had ground it out of her. Perhaps she had married him when she was too young. She'd never known anyone else. She was a child when he left for war and five years later she wasn't much more than a child still, although she had seen a lot of grown-up things in between.

He'd proposed that night, VE night, on the train home, with Stella snoring between them. And she had accepted without hesitation. They had to keep it their secret for years. Dad was strict enough about courting. She knew he'd never give his permission to marry until she was twenty-one. So she had been a good daughter, donning a blue and white checked overall and taking over Mum's role at the till, and Ken had got himself a nice job driving a delivery van. And when the right time came they did it all properly.

Ken asked Dad for her hand, and Dad was delighted. He could want no finer son-in-law, he said, and he'd be happy for him to take over the shop in due course. That was a surprise.

So there they were with their whole lives sorted out, and she had only just been given the key to the front door.

'You're mad,' Stella said, when she told her. 'What d'you want to marry the first man you've ever kissed for? And I bet kissing's all you've done too.'

Shirley told her what Dad had said about the shop. She was a bit nervous about that. What would Stella have, if she and Ken had the shop? It's not my idea, she told her sister.

'Take the bloody shop. I'm out of here as soon as I can,' Stella said, 'Oh Shirl, I do love you, and Ken isn't too bad, but are you really sure you're doing the right thing?'

'Will you be my bridesmaid?' Shirley had asked her.

'As long as I don't have to wear pink,' Stella had said.

But by the time the wedding came she was long gone.

Shirley stared at the letter in front of her. She turned the envelope over and read it again and again, willing it to change in front of her eyes, but it was addressed correctly. It had her name on it, her married name. This time she couldn't just tear it up and pretend it hadn't arrived. She knew that wouldn't be the end of it, now. Not if they'd got this far. What was to stop them coming round and confronting her?

The past was catching up with them all. She had somehow known it would. What with all the fuss about VE day, and Gemma coming home. What goes around comes around.

She had thought about telling Gemma everything, but in the end she had chickened out. Gemma was still vulnerable, still smarting with the loss of her husband, still, Shirley had noted, reluctant to discuss her mother. And there hadn't been time to explain. Maybe next time she came. Or maybe not. Shirley shuddered.

Perhaps the best thing to do would be to reply saying that she didn't want to be involved. She couldn't see the point of it. Not now. Things were best left as they were. It could only lead to more pain, she would warn. She sat down and tried to compose a letter.

'I'm trying to decide on lettuce or scallop shells,' Bethany said, her voice rising at the end of the sentence to indicate that she would welcome an opinion. She had popped in to see how Shirley was because, she said, she thought Shirley had been looking a bit peeky recently.

'Lettuce or scallops?' Shirley sighed and tried to give the matter her proper attention, 'I thought you'd decided on a nice salmon in aspic with cucumber slices all over to look like scales . . .'

'Oh, you haven't been listening,' Bethany chided, in her I'm-patient-with-old-people voice. 'I was talking about the icing on the cake.' She smiled her I'm-lovely-with-old-people smile. 'Maybe you're tired?' Voice full of concern.

'Yes, I am,' Shirley said, a bit too quickly, and Bethany looked quite put out as she gathered up her glossies and left.

She needed a bit of peace and quiet. Normally she had too much peace and quiet for her liking, but today, after the morning's post, she hadn't been able to settle.

She slid open the glass door of her balcony and scraped the white plastic armchair across the concrete floor into the last triangle of sunlight. As soon as dusk fell there would be fireworks on the beach. She could hear the hum of a distant crowd gathering. She would have a nice view of it.

The last time the town had fireworks was on VJ night. Stella had begged to be allowed out, but Dad had said they needed all hands on deck because people would be hungry afterwards. She could remember the look on her sister's face as she defiantly poured a pail of chips into fat that wasn't yet hot enough, and her dad walloping her with a slotted spoon. If only he had been big enough to give her some freedom. You couldn't put someone like Stella in a cage.

She had tried to tell him that all her little sister wanted was a bit of harmless fun, but she hadn't been very brave. He was a bit of a bully and she hadn't wanted to offend him.

'We should have stood up to him,' she'd said to Ken, years later, after Dad died, 'then Stell might have trusted us more.'

'Trusted us?' he'd replied. 'What about us trusting her? What about that then?'

And he'd sounded so much like Dad, she could have hit him.

Still, rest in peace, he was a good man and it was no good blaming him for everything.

'If you were here now, Stell, what would you do?' Shirley whispered into the night air. 'I know I promised, but it's going to come out. I can't stop it. There's nothing I can do, except make it easier. I might be able to make it easier for everyone, you see . . .'

A palm tree explosion of red and green stars burst high in the sky above the sea. A loud bang. Shirley smiled to herself. If she weren't so sensible, she'd take it as a sign.

She had always kept Stella's secrets. Little ones at first: pennies she stole from the till to buy sherbet sweets, cigarettes she smoked under the dripping iron legs of the pier, kisses she exchanged with the rough boys who ran the waltzer when the fair came to town on Easter Bank Holiday.

She had known about Mr Blair too, she could never bring herself to think of him as Laurie, long before anyone else did. He was the first male teacher they had ever had at the school. And the last, for a long time after. He wore rust-coloured corduroy trousers, and for a few weeks after he arrived, the town could talk of nothing else.

He joined the school just as Stella went into the sixth form. Dad never forgave himself for letting her stay on. It was much against his will that she had in the first place. The headmistress herself had come down to the shop to see him. Stella was an unusually talented girl, Shirley had heard her saying as she made the tea in the back kitchen, Miss Reid's loud voice booming through the wall. She was college material. Dad didn't believe in college, especially not for girls, but Miss Reid wasn't used to being challenged and she wouldn't leave until she got her own way. She stayed so long, Dad called Shirley in and asked her to make up a nice fish supper for Miss Reid, even though she was on her own serving in the shop.

All the girls fell in love with Mr Blair, even though he had a glamorous wife who drove a white car. There never had been such a demand for Art. Dad wouldn't countenance Stella changing her subjects. It was bad enough, he said, supporting her while she wasted her time learning languages, he was not going to keep her while she painted pretty pictures. Even Stella could see that one was a losing battle. She took to staying on for Art Club after school. Studying in the library, she told Dad demurely, smiling into his face and putting two fingers up at his back as soon as it was turned.

Shirley knew. She could see it coming. She had seen the way Mr Blair looked at her on school sports day. Stella with her long legs scissoring over the high jump, triumphant.

'Promise you won't tell,' Stella had whispered, 'promise, Shirl.'

She had promised. She thought it was a crush. Stella would get over it and no harm done. Mr Blair would come to his senses soon enough.

'Just be careful,' she told her sister, not really

knowing about these things, but feeling, as the older, engaged one, that she ought to say something.

'Oh don't worry about that,' Stella assured her, 'I've got no intention of getting up the spout.'

She showed her sister a large compact case with a Dutch cap in it. Shirley was so shocked she never even asked where she got it from. Those days they wouldn't give you anything unless you were married, and sometimes not even then. She and Ken wanted to wait a bit before they started a family. When she went to see the doctor, a few weeks after the wedding, he had been very disapproving, said he'd have to speak to Ken too. It was all so embarrassing they hadn't gone back. As it turned out, they'd never needed anything anyway. When she'd seen the same doctor a few years later to ask why she didn't seem to be falling pregnant, he'd given her a funny look, as if he remembered the earlier visit, as if infertility was somehow her punishment for asking.

Then there was the secret Stella had made her promise to keep on her wedding day. It had made Shirley sad. At last Stella seemed to have found a nice man, someone who would look after her. A bit old, perhaps, but still attractive. She had liked Bertie immediately. She was sure he would have understood. But Stella said no, that's in the past now and I'm starting a new life.

How many times could you start your life again, Shirley had wondered, but she had promised nevertheless.

'Cross your heart?' Stella said, standing outside the register office in the freezing cold before she went in to take her vows.

'Cross my heart and hope to die,' Shirley had chanted dutifully, like a little girl, even though she was all of thirty-five by then.

*   *   *

The frenzied finale sounded like machine gun fire. The sky was ablaze with gold and silver cascades, and smoke that lingered white in the air long after the brilliance had disappeared. Shirley realized she was cold. She went inside, put on a cardigan, and poured herself a large brandy.

Then she picked up her phone and dialled Gemma's number.

CHAPTER 22

**Seven things to do when your lover leaves.
You're feeling down, don't know what to do
with yourself? Here are some suggestions. One
for every day of that first, difficult week . . .**

Daisy was sure that she had read a thousand articles
with lists of valuable tips. She thought she might write
one of her own:

1. Eat plenty of citrus fruit.
Citrus fruit and green leafy vegetables were a
universal women's magazine panacea.

So far, Daisy had breakfasted on white chocolate
Magnums on the way back from the paper shop and
sent out for pizza at night.

She felt so very alone that on one occasion she had
almost been tempted to ask the pizza delivery boy in to
share the Capricciosa with extra pepperoni with her.

The last ten days of the holiday had been almost as
frenetic as the first ten days of their romance. It was as if
they had been liberated by the decision to separate, and
they had fallen on each other with a kind of desperate
hunger, trying to devour as much of one another as
possible before they parted.

As night fell on the drive back from the octopus
restaurant, Oliver had suddenly turned off the road
down to a deserted little beach. The water looked so

inviting with its sparkle of phosphorescence that they had peeled off their shorts and dived into the shallow waves, splashing each other and laughing like children. That night they made love and it felt wonderful again, almost illicit on their monk's bed with its crisp laundered linen.

Each day Oliver found somewhere new for them to explore, and each night they returned to their beach and bathed naked. On the last night they made love there in a dip in the sand, licking the salt from each other's bodies, and Daisy had not known whether it was sea she was tasting, or tears.

And now he had gone. An hour after they returned from the airport he had walked down the street with a suitcase, not looking back, not waving at her, hailing a cab, going where? It was almost as if he had planned it. It felt so final.

Daisy had sat on the floor in a pool of evening sunlight and cried until she could cry no more, then she had a bath and went to bed, huddled on her side. It felt too soon to lie comfortably in the middle, to encroach on his territory. She realized that she hadn't spent a whole night without him since the day they met.

2. Change the furniture round. Have a spring clean.

The first morning she went to Harvey Nichols and bought herself an entirely new set of bed linen. Adapted from a Picasso painting, the duvet cover had bold primary colours in big splashes. She bought matching cornflower-blue pillow cases and sheets. Tasteful but loud. Oliver wouldn't have liked them and, more importantly, they didn't need washing every other day.

3. Hire a weepy video, buy a box of Kleenex and have a good old cry.

The selection at the paper shop wasn't very

comprehensive. Daisy settled on *Terminator 2, It's nothing personal*, but it didn't seem to do the trick.

4. Join a health club.

It was hot, hotter than it had been in Greece. The weather was breaking records. It was all too easy to take a book to the Heath and lie on the grass dozing and occasionally turning a page. But after a few days Daisy decided that it was work that would get her through this unreal patch before she could start her life again. She decided to ring round her favourite editors and take whatever was offered.

'Oh Daisy, I'm so glad you rang. Really? How was it? How's your tan? Great. Look I've got a freebie at that American gym that's just opened. I need someone who'll look good with their clothes off.'

Join a health club, Daisy thought and smiled. Well, as long as it was only for one day.

A PR girl immaculately dressed in white jeans and a white sweatshirt with the gym's very discreet dark-green logo embroidered above her pert left breast met Daisy at the door and introduced her to Marlon, a black man with most of his head shaved apart from a square pad on top dyed orange.

'Marlon will be your personal physical instructor for the day,' she said, without a trace of irony.

Immediately Daisy knew that the maroon track suit that she had had since school was not going to be allowed in the building. Just as there were some gentlemen's clubs in town that still insisted on gentlemen wearing a tie, there were some sports' clubs, Daisy thought, where you couldn't gain admittance unless you were squeezed into a strange leotard that looked like a swimsuit at the front but for some reason disappeared into a thong up your bum, so that even though you were embarrassed already about showing your buttocks, now you had to draw attention to them by pouring yourself into some cycling shorts which stopped just where your thighs were fattest. And if that wasn't enough humiliation, the shorts had to be fluorescent pink or roadsign orange or . . .

'We only have *Margarita* in your size.' The PR had taken her into the club's equipment shop and was holding up a pair of lime-green shorts in one hand and a black and lime-green zebra-striped cutaway leotard in the other.

Daisy skulked in the changing rooms for a long time, wondering how she could get out of the assignment. She knew there was no escape through the door into the gym. Marlon was waiting there for her. The PR was guarding the exit to the real world. Daisy turned to look at her side view in the wall of mirror. Better, she thought, than the full frontal, or maybe she was just getting used to it. Think of the sauna after, she told herself, took a deep breath, pulled in her tummy and pushed open the door.

'Try twenty of those,' Marlon said, and left her leaning over the triceps machine wondering how she was going to manage five.

He hadn't believed her when she had told him that she wasn't very fit. He had asked her what her exercise routine was and for some reason she hadn't wanted to admit that she did absolutely nothing. 'I used to go to aerobics,' she had offered pathetically, thinking of the one time she had been after which she had decided that aerobics couldn't be intended for girls with breasts.

Daisy observed the other clientele. Beautiful people. For a moment she wondered whether they had bussed in a coach load of perfect bodies for her benefit. A photographer from the magazine was arriving later. Daisy wiped her forehead with the back of her hand, realizing too late the purpose of the matching towelling headband that the PR had offered her and Daisy had turned down, thinking that she would look enough of a fool as it was.

Why did the men grunt? Daisy wondered. Was performing scissor-movements with your legs or pulling down bars with weights attached a form of suppressed masturbation? If you closed your eyes and listened you would think you were standing on the landing in a brothel with unnatural acts going on all around you.

Opening her eyes again, Daisy couldn't decide whether she really disliked the blatant narcissism she saw all around her or whether she was just jealous. She took a couple of notes, and began to think how she would describe the place to Oliver, then realized with a stab of fear that she wouldn't be telling him. She had always used Oliver to practise her copy. If she liked the way a sentence came to her she would say it to him and if he smiled, that kind of admiring grin, then she knew it was OK. Often he had the quickness of mind to make a pun better, or to point her to a quotation that would perfectly illustrate what she was trying to say. What was she going to do without him? She wished the photographer would hurry up. Marlon was sauntering back towards her and it was all she could do to stop herself fleeing in tears.

They had given her the lime and black zebra-print leotard. They had even put it in a white cotton tote bag with the club's logo printed on it. It hung like a lead weight from her shoulder until she decided to consign the bag, contents and all, to a rubbish bin.

Over a jug of freshly squeezed ruby grapefruit juice (citrus fruit, Daisy thought with relief), the PR had insisted on 'taking her through' the club's brochure, complete with its list of beauty treatments and therapies. So, thought Daisy, I have done the health club and the citrus fruit. If I had pushed it, I probably could have had a facial too, which took care of number 5, but, it didn't really begin to fill the space in her life where Oliver had been and now wasn't.

6. Change your image. Now's the time to experiment with new make-up, that haircut you've been thinking about.

Her hair was taking ages to dry even in the heat. Daisy was sure it was making her hotter and more bothered. And she was within a stone's throw of Trevor Sorbie. She needed a boost after seeing her lime-green thighs in all those mirrors. A couple of hours of flattering chat about the thickness, the bounce, the depth of her hair colour would be very nice. Perhaps she should do something really different. Hold on. Daisy made a bargain with herself: if they had an appointment straightaway, she thought, I'll have it done. If not, it's not meant to be.

One of the male stylists had just had a cancellation. Daisy emerged with the bulk of her hair in a bag. He'd asked her if she wanted to keep it as he held up the thick ponytail he had gathered together in his left hand. She said yes, not really expecting him to cut it all off straightaway. She had thought it would be snip snip snip, how's that? Instead it was scrrrunch, that wonderful sound of very sharp scissors cutting through cloth. When she opened her eyes her hair was being taken away to be tied with a ribbon by a helper and Daisy looked in the mirror and thought how white her neck was compared to her deeply tanned arms.

He kept on cutting until there was only about an inch left. Then, in that casual way that hairdressers have which is impossible to replicate at home, he ran some gel through his fingers and patted it on. All that was left on her head was a cluster of little damp-looking curls.

7. Treat yourself to something new to cheer

yourself up, it need only be a pair of sunglasses,
a headscarf . . .

Daisy felt like a totally different person.

'It makes you look thinner,' her stylist said, choosing
exactly the right compliment and confirming what
Daisy was hardly daring to think.

She managed to get to Whistles before it closed and
bought herself a very short ivory silk dress with a
pattern of red poppies, and a pair of cream suede shoes.
She had tried the dress on when she had hair, but it had
made her look like an overgrown child; now, with her
much more masculine silhouette, it worked. She
stuffed her jeans and T-shirt in the bag with her hair,
and walked out of the shop feeling fresh and light and
altogether more optimistic.

She didn't think that those articles with their ego-
boosting advice ever included:

8. Get completely plastered with a notorious womanizer you work with . . .

Daisy woke the next morning with a horrible guilty
feeling. Before opening her eyes she felt on Oliver's side
of the bed and was relieved to feel only sheets and an
unslept-on pillow. As she sat up the headache attacked
her like a surprise shot from a sniper and made her keel
over into the pillows. Half an hour later, Daisy dragged
herself to the bathroom and got the shock of her life
when she looked in the mirror. Then she remembered
the haircut the day before.

Patrick had been walking down the stairs of the *Sixpack* offices as she began to ascend. All she had wanted
was someone to tell her how nice she looked, and to
share a plate of pasta with her.

He looked her up and down and informed her that
she looked like a very sexy principal boy, which was a
good start. Then he took her to the Groucho and plied
her with Whisky Sours. Maybe it was the fact that she

hadn't eaten all day, or maybe the dehydrating sauna, but she got drunk very quickly, and found herself necking in a cab heading south of the river towards his home in Battersea.

Daisy turned on the shower.

At least she had had the presence of mind to stop short of going into his house. She thought she remembered several minutes' conversation as she refused to budge, he tried to coax her out, and the taxi driver got increasingly impatient for his fare. Finally, she slammed the door and gave the cab driver her address, and she thought she could remember speeding through Hyde Park with him muttering about how he was on his way home and that would be the last time he picked up outside that club. The fare had been over forty pounds and she must have been drunk because she had felt obliged to make it up to fifty, cleaning her wallet out of cash.

Through the fog of hangover, Daisy made a mental calculation. In total, the day before had cost her almost three hundred pounds, which was probably more than she would make from writing up her freebie at the gym. And now she felt terrible, she had a silk dress that needed dry-cleaning and the phone was ringing. The answering machine had picked it up before she could get to it.

Patrick said, with a bit of a smirk in his voice, that the Groucho Club had just called to tell him that his companion had left a carrier bag with some clothes and an animal in it. Daisy didn't bother to pick up the receiver.

The red eye of the answerphone blinked at her. She played back her messages. Gemma had rung again. She would have to ring her back. She couldn't keep putting her off. She had delayed calling since she got back from Crete because she didn't know how her sister would take the news of her split with Oliver. She couldn't think how she would tell her.

At the moment she couldn't think about anything.

There was a message for Oliver from a woman called Caroline, and one from Cal Costelloe. 'If this is Daisy Rush's answerphone', it said, in a rather clipped tone, 'could she ring me.' He left a number.

From the sound of his voice, Daisy thought he must be ringing to complain about her article. It was in the magazine's next month's issue which was now in the shops. She had only flipped through quickly in the newsagents since she had long thrown off the habit of checking whether her copy had been subbed. The photograph they had used was really nice, so she didn't know what his problem was. And how had he got her home number anyway? Patrick. It must have been bloody Patrick. She breathed another sigh of relief that she hadn't actually succumbed to him the night before. Although why she was being so Victorian about it, she didn't know.

She had thought that she might try going to bed with some men. She thought that she might add '*have a string of one-night stands with people you hardly know*' to her list of things to do when a lover leaves. It might be fun to be a bit promiscuous for once, but when the opportunity arose, she found she hadn't wanted to at all. Not with Patrick anyway, she told herself. For all his lascivious flirting, she didn't actually think he'd be up to much in bed.

Daisy sat down at her typewriter and started to bash out a piece about the gym. However much she tried to make it a thinly disguised piece of advertising copy, which is what the editor wanted, it kept coming out like a bird's eye piece for *Six Pack*. She knew that wouldn't do. Not least because she doubted whether Patrick would want any more pieces from her after last night's lack of performance.

It was no good. She knew that if she didn't start a piece in the right mood, she might as well abandon it for a day or two. Daisy got up and looked in the fridge. The only thing to drink was tomato juice and when she poured that out a lump of grey mould plopped out into the glass too. You're going to have to get a grip, she told herself, picked up her car keys and walked purposefully out into the street. After a quarter of an hour or so, she remembered where she had last parked the car.

Daisy unpacked the last carrier bag. A pan of water was boiling on the hob, a packet of fresh *paglia e fieno* was sitting on the work surface next to a pot of pesto sauce (no heating required). Even an idiot could cook a decent meal these days, Oliver was always saying, and he was right. Feeling rather pleased with her efforts, Daisy tore open a bag of green salad and arranged it on a plate, slit open the pasta and put it in the water.

Then the phone rang. 'Is Oliver there?' a pleasant female voice asked.

'No, I'm afraid not,' Daisy replied.

'Is that Daisy?'

'Yes.'

'It's Caroline Thomas. I know that Oliver's told you what I'm doing . . .'

Daisy didn't know why she chose to reply as she did. Maybe it was a journalist's instinct to pretend she knew more than she did. Maybe she was just nosy. 'Yes,' she said, adding for good measure, 'how are you getting on?'

So Caroline told her what had been happening, and Daisy listened in silence. And at the end she said she was pleased that Caroline was making good progress, and she would get Oliver to call her himself. Then she put down the phone and felt very sad that Oliver had not even mentioned what was going on. Especially since he had obviously wanted to. He had told Caroline he had.

Daisy remembered all the thoughts she had been

keeping secret from him over the last weeks, and she thought guiltily about how temperamental she had been, how difficult to live with. So difficult that he had felt unable to tell her about a profound and grave decision he had made.

They used to be so close, and now, oh Lol! What had happened to them?

Daisy wept and wept until she remembered the *paglia e fieno*. She dashed to the kitchen where the stove was covered with scummy pasta water that had boiled over, and the pale green and white strands were turning hard and brown on the bottom of the red-hot pan.

CHAPTER 23

'Oh. I see. Gemma, it's your Auntie Shirley. Could you give me a bell? That's right. Oh. Hope you're well. Love from Shirley.'

Gemma smiled as she played back the message, the first on her new answerphone. Shirley obviously wasn't used to machines. Gemma wondered when she had left the message. It was the first evening she had spent at home for three days.

She had rushed in to pick up a few clothes while Ralph waited for her in the car on Sunday evening. Since then she had been staying in his studio. It was a ten-minute walk to work, a five-minute run home at lunchtime, half an hour to make love, fifteen minutes to sit up in bed eating the delicious lunch he had prepared for her, five minutes to shower and ten to walk back to the office with a great big smile on her face.

She noticed that people were smiling back at her. Maybe it was the weather, or maybe when you were in love you had a kind of aura around you and people knew. She couldn't remember being so happy. Decisions were easier to take because they somehow didn't seem to matter so much. She felt she had a lightness of touch, a confidence she had been missing since she returned to England.

The intensity frightened her at first. She kept expecting it to vanish, for a cloud to pass over Ralph's sunny mood. She hadn't dared to tell him what she was feeling in case he grew scared and ran away. Then, on the third night, when they were making love, the sensations were so completely delicious she felt the dreaded words bubbling up inside her. 'I think I love you,' she said very quietly, allowing herself the 'think' as a get-out later.

'I know I love you,' he replied immediately, and it felt so wonderful, so exciting, her smile broke into a laugh and he joined in, and they laughed and laughed until they were both panting for breath, and then he held her very close until she drifted into a light, dreamless sleep.

Tonight she had some reading to do and Ralph had been invited to a party by his publisher. Gemma took off her dress and put it on the large pile of clothes for the dry cleaner, thinking that if she didn't take them in soon she would have to buy some new outfits.

Even after dark it was still very hot. She peeled off her underwear, put it in the washing machine and started the programme, then she put on her lightest robe, white poplin with yellow rose sprigs embroidered round the edges, and settled down on the sofa with the phone.

'It's me, Shirley,' she said.

'Oh Gemma,' Shirley sounded flustered.

'Is anything wrong?'

'No, no. Well, I wondered if you'd like to come down at the weekend. I've got something to give you.'

'Of course.'

'I'll need to explain . . .' Shirley interrupted.

Gemma smiled. 'Can I bring someone?' she asked, flicking absently through a manuscript with her free hand.

'What do you mean?'

'There's someone I'd like you to meet,' said Gemma, amazed that she was having to spell it out.

'Oh, I see. Well, I suppose . . .'

'He's very nice,' Gemma said, thinking how much Shirley would like Ralph.

Shirley liked Americans. The GIs looked smart in their uniforms, and they were always clean, she had often said. 'Well . . .'

'We'll come down on Saturday and take you out to lunch,' Gemma said. 'Bye now!'

And she put her finger on the telephone rest to disconnect the call.

She rang Daisy's number and got the answerphone again. She didn't think she could begin to leave a message for her. She rang Kathy but she was engaged. So she rang Meryl who, because of the time difference, was still in her office. She had been bursting to tell someone since the weekend, but it wasn't the sort of giggly girls' conversation you could have at work, or really in front of Ralph.

'Guess what?' she said, after they had exchanged hellos.

'You've found the man you're going to spend the rest of your life with?' Meryl asked, wearily sarcastic.

'Well, maybe,' Gemma said.

'Omygod! . . . He's American? Jesus! He's what? And he's rich, I suppose. He is? You bitch!'

Shirley was toying with her lemon sole.

'I'm sorry, Auntie,' Gemma said, remembering what her aunt had said about chips and thinking belatedly that a fish restaurant was perhaps not the best place to take her for lunch, 'perhaps you'd like to change it. I think I saw a steak on the menu.'

'No, no,' Shirley replied, 'this is lovely . . . I'm just not feeling very hungry.'

Gemma was concerned, but also disappointed. She had spent the train journey down telling Ralph what a wonderful character Shirley was, but ever since they

289

had picked her up at her flat, she had been quiet, reticent almost.

'Have a dessert then,' Gemma urged. 'Look, there's a triple chocolate mousse, or home made treacle tart.'

'I don't think I'll bother, thanks.' Shirley put down her knife and fork and sat back in her seat. She looked from Gemma to Ralph and smiled wanly.

Something must be wrong, Gemma thought.

'Can I make a suggestion?' Ralph asked. He had been quite quiet throughout the meal, 'I've never been on an English pier, and I hear that the one you have here, Shirley, is the finest on the South Coast. I'd like to take a look at it, so maybe I'll join you later back at your flat. How does that sound?'

'We could come too,' Gemma said, then caught his eye.

'I'm sure Shirley's seen enough of that pier, Gemma,' he said.

'Well,' Shirley brightened considerably, 'you're right there, Ralph. Gemma and I will just walk back slowly, shall we?'

'I'll see you later,' said Ralph, and set off quickly.

'Well, he seems very nice,' Shirley said, crossing the street so that they could walk in shade. Away from the seafront, shops were closed and there were few people about in the back streets.

'Yes, I think he is,' Gemma smiled.

'Known him long?' Shirley asked.

'Only since I got back . . . we met a few times, just as friends, and then last weekend he took me to France, and . . .'

'He has swept you off your feet, hasn't he?' Shirley said, stopping to get her breath.

'I suppose so,' Gemma blushed.

'Sounds like one of those books you publish,' Shirley said.

Gemma laughed, 'Yes, it's all a bit too good to be true.'

'Well, as long as he's kind', said Shirley, setting off again, 'and he's not married, is he?'

'Course not,' Gemma replied, shocked.

'Well then.'

Gemma thought it sounded as if she had given her her blessing.

'Now, what is it that you wanted to tell me?' she asked, belatedly realizing the reason for Shirley's uncharacteristic behaviour.

Shirley took a deep breath, 'How are you getting along with that sister of yours, these days?' she asked.

'I think we're friends again,' Gemma said cautiously. 'A long time ago she did something terrible to me and I didn't think I'd ever forgive her, but I'm beginning to. We have talked about it, at least. I don't think she meant to hurt me . . .'

How history repeats itself, Shirley thought. 'What I'm going to tell you affects her too, you see,' she said, 'but I don't know her very well, so I thought I'd tell you . . .' She looked at Gemma. 'I do know how you feel, you know. Stell did something I thought I'd never forgive her for too, but I'm glad I did. You can't bear a grudge all your life. It's like poison. It spoils everything.'

'What was it she did?' Gemma asked.

Shirley was looking at the pavement. For a moment Gemma thought that she hadn't heard the question. Then she sighed and stared into the distance. 'She took something from me that I wanted very much . . .' she said, 'but I can't start there.' She brought her gaze back to Gemma. 'I'd better start at the beginning . . . And Gemma . . .'

'Yes?' It was a boiling hot day but suddenly she felt cold.

'I know you'll have questions to ask, but hear me out first of all because this is going to be very difficult for me. I promised I wouldn't tell.'

Part Four

CHAPTER 24

April 1951
Dear Shirl,

Laurie's out seeing someone about a job, and I'm meant to be cooking tea. I looked at the bit of mince he managed to find and the vegetables and thought what the hell am I meant to do with that? So I've peeled everything and put it in a saucepan with some water. Is that how you make stew? I wish you were here to tell me.

We've found somewhere to live now – all correspondence welcome! It's lovely, I can't tell you how happy I am. There are cherry trees in blossom all around this area. It's called Notting Hill Gate in the Royal Borough of Kensington, if that means anything to you. The house we live in must have been very grand once, and now it's divided up into bedsits. The ceilings are high and there are flowers and leaves carved round the edges. We've got a lovely room and everything we need. There's a bathroom on our landing. We told them we were married and Laurie bought me a ring. It's a silver one, very plain, and I wear it on my wedding finger. There's lots of different types here, and I don't think most of them would care, anyway. That's how London is, you see, more cosmopolitan.

How are your wedding plans going, by the way? I'm sorry to let you down about the bridesmaid thing, but I don't think Dad would like me turning up like Banquo's ghost at the feast in Macbeth. I'd have to wear red or something! What are they all saying? Don't answer that, I can guess . . .

I've got a job now. I'm a server in the Lyons Corner House

*at Charing Cross. Do you remember where that man was
playing the trumpet on VE night? Well, it's near there. I'm in the
self-service bit. I mostly do the sweet section. We make sure
there's plenty of everything out. I have to make up knickerbocker
glories. It's two sorts of jelly, fruit, then ice cream and a swirl of
red stuff on the top, and you have to do it in the right order. They
watch you pretty carefully. I did one wrong the other day, so I ate
it when no one was looking! I'd prefer to be a waitress because
the tips add up, but you have to know silver service for that, and
those trays are pretty heavy and you'd have to bite your tongue if
anyone started getting high and mighty. It's quite fun working.
The money's not bad, and I get my food. That's lucky, because if
it were down to me, Laurie says, we'd both starve to death!*

*Laurie says it's only temporary. We're off to Paris as soon as
he sells a picture. Paris, Shirl, can you imagine? I can't get
over living in London yet. I walk around with my eyes looking
up. I work Saturdays but on Sundays Laurie takes me to a
gallery. It's wonderful, Shirl. You'd never know how many
foreign pictures there are.*

*I know you disapprove, but I hope you'll come round to
liking Laurie one day. I wish he wasn't married too. So does
he! Honestly, his wife will be all right because she's got money
on her side – she kept reminding him of that and he didn't like
it, I can tell you. Well, we're poor and blissfully happy
together, like in a novel.*

*Hope your big day goes off well, Shirl. Send my love to Ken
and write to me, please Shirl.*

Love from Estella
P.S. I decided to call myself Estella. Sounds nice, doesn't it?

Gemma folded the letter very carefully. It was cheap
rough-lined paper torn from an exercise book. It felt as
if it would turn to dust if mishandled. She put it back in
its envelope and returned it to the shoe box on her lap.
How strange that Estella should have lived in Notting
Hill. She knew the street. It was five minutes' walk
away from where she was living.

Ralph was climbing into the carriage with two polystyrene mugs of coffee. He smiled at her.

'I thought you were going to miss the train,' she said, as the whistle blew and they started pulling out of the station.

'Anything interesting?' Ralph nodded at the shoe box.

'It's my mother's letters to Shirley,' Gemma said. 'I don't think I ought to read them without Daisy, but I couldn't resist looking. Shirley told me the big secret they'd been keeping all their lives. Estella eloped with her art teacher when she was seventeen. Caused a huge scandal in the town. She never came back, but she wrote to Shirley, and, for some reason, Shirley wanted us to have the letters now . . .'

'Perhaps Shirley feels she's getting too old for secrets. She seems like a pretty upfront lady.'

'Perhaps,' said Gemma a little sadly. 'She's nice, isn't she?'

'She's a lovely woman,' Ralph said, 'going a little crazy, maybe, but lovely . . .'

'Why do you say that?'

'When I went to the bathroom I opened the wrong door . . . it must be her bedroom. There was a doll's house in there with the front open. It looked as if somebody had been playing with it . . .'

'Really? How sweet! I don't think that's crazy,' Gemma protested, 'I love doll's houses . . . why shouldn't she?' she added protectively.

'No reason, I guess. Did Shirley have any children?'

'No, she didn't. Oh I see, you think she's making the dolls into the family she never had . . . Trust an American to have a psychological explanation for everything,' Gemma teased. 'It's such a shame because I think she would have loved to have had children.'

'She obviously loves you very much.'

Gemma smiled.

'She kept a very beady eye on me, I can tell you,' Ralph added.

'I think you passed, though.' Gemma reached across the table and took his hand.

May 1951
Dear Shirl,

I thought about you today on your wedding day and I was hoping that you had a lovely day (and night! You can tell me honestly now, Shirl, was it really your first time?). I don't know whether I'd like to be married or not. Laurie says that it's very bourgeois (I think that's how you spell it). I just wish he'd make up his mind whether he wants me to pretend to be his wife or not. The other day we went to see some friends of his who live on a kind of farm thing and make pots (sorry, throw pots, the correct term as I'm constantly being told – sometimes it feels like living with a teacher – ha, ha!). They asked me how long I'd known Laurie and so I started telling them about how we were married, just like we'd agreed, and Laurie interrupted and said, don't be so stupid Stella, and it made me feel really small. Then we went for a walk and I was cross back because he's meant to call me Estella. He thinks it's a joke. I don't know how he does it, Shirl, but he manages to get a laugh in there sort of in his voice behind that E. Anyway, we kissed and made up. Laurie can always make me laugh, Shirl, and I think that's the most important thing.

I got talking to the lady whose farm it was, Georgina, she's called, and she told me that she wasn't married to Jack who she lives with either. She was very nice and I hope we go to see them again soon. She baked us a cake with dates and walnuts in it. It's a bit heavy, but it fills you up.

Laurie's teaching a WEA course two evenings a week now. We can use the money. I said I'd like to be in his class, but he said don't be ridiculous, so that was the end of that. But I'm learning a lot about life, Shirl. Much more than I ever learnt at school.

Please write to me, Shirl,
Love from Estella

She couldn't recognize the person writing the letters as her mother, and yet the emotions, the apprehensiveness she sensed hiding just behind the jolliness, felt very familiar. Gemma took the next sheet out of the shoe box and put it face down on the photocopier.

It was peculiar, she thought, how important the letters had suddenly become to her. The day before she had not known of their existence, and yet, in the night, her hand kept straying from under the sheet to feel that they were still on the floor by the bed. If it hadn't been for the fact that Ralph was sleeping next to her and she had told him that she was saving the letters to share with Daisy, she was sure she would have been up all night reading.

This morning, she hadn't been able to think of a safe enough place to store them and so she had brought them into work and was spending her lunchtime photocopying. The shoe box was pretty full, but she was gradually getting through the pile, replacing each letter in its envelope before she had a chance to read too much of it.

June 1951
Dear Shirl,

I was so happy to get your postcard. I didn't think you would give up on me, although it's been such a long time, I was beginning to wonder. Write properly and tell me all about the honeymoon. Torquay looks very nice. I didn't know there were palm trees in England!

Laurie and I had our first row, Shirl. He was cross because I bought myself a jacket. I know I shouldn't of, but I saw it every day in a window from the bus. It's dark green corduroy, and I spent every penny I own (including the money you leant me in case of trouble, don't worry, I'll pay you back) and Laurie said I was irresponsible. Well, who's paying the rent then, I said to him, because I'm bringing home more than he is. Well, that did it, Shirl. We shouted the place down. He

stormed out and I thought he'd gone for ever. But then he came
back and we made up. He said he loved me and he's never
loved anyone else, and that's the way it is for me too. I never
knew that love could hurt you so much. He sketched me crying.
He says it's very good. I said you're not going to show that to
anyone are you, but I think he will.

I'm still working at Lyons. There's all sorts of people there
and at least you get your food. You can have a bit of a laugh
with the girls. You think I'm bad, Shirl, you should see how
the girls on breakfasts arrange the sausage and tomato on the
plate!

Write and tell me how you are, Shirl.
Love from Estella

Gemma smiled. At last the breathless girl writing the
letters was beginning to sound a little like her mother.
Estella loved clothes and she couldn't resist rich
colours. Gemma remembered a dark green corduroy
waisted jacket with padded shoulders and two of the
buttons missing. It had gone to Oxfam along with lots
of other clothes, all the deep bright colours of a
stained-glass window. She had been ruthless with her
mother's possessions as she had cleared out Whitton
House. When Daisy finally turned up to lend a hand, all
the wardrobes stood empty. It was just as well because
Daisy, being Daisy, would have kept everything.

Where on earth was Daisy now? Gemma had left
several messages but her calls weren't being returned.
She pushed the microphone button on her desk phone
and punched out her sister's number again. It rang once.

'Yes?'

His voice made her jump. He sounded impatient, as
if he were taking the call at work, not home.

She had imagined the moment she spoke to him
again a million times, but she was still completely
unprepared. She picked up the receiver quickly. She
felt better able to deal with him trapped inside the

receiver than talking out loud, disembodied, in her office. 'Is Daisy there?' Gemma stuttered, trying to compose herself.

'She's not. Hang on . . .' Oliver had lost most of his Liverpool accent but he still pronounced the silent 'g' at the end of words, 'If I can find something to write with, I'll take your name and number.'

She heard some shuffling of papers at the end of the phone and Oliver, unable to find a pencil, swearing under his breath.

'Oliver? It's Gemma. Just tell her I called.'

'Gemma?' Was he surprised, pleased, displeased? Gemma waited for some indication, her heart beating in her mouth. She felt sure he could hear it.

'The thing is, Gemma, I won't be seeing her,' he said impatiently. 'I've just come back in my lunch hour to pick up some things. She's turned me out, as I'm sure you know.' His voice became slightly menacing.

She didn't think she could have understood. 'What do you mean?' she asked.

'Daisy and I are no longer living together,' he said slowly and deliberately, as if talking to a child.

'Oh.'

'News to you, was it?' he queried sarcastically, adding, 'It's just coincidence, is it, that this happens when you come home?'

She had forgotten how nasty he could sound when he was angry. What was he implying? 'Yes,' her surprise was so apparent, his tone changed.

'Oh . . . well, sorry Gemma, I just thought . . .'

'So where are you living?' she asked, still pinching herself.

'On people's floors at the moment . . . Look, I'd better go. I hear from Daisy that you're well.'

'Yes.' She tried to think of something to say.

'And you? Are you well?' she asked.

'Well? I've been better, Gemma.' Then, perhaps

realizing how unnecessarily hostile he was sounding, his tone softened, 'Yes, I suppose I am well. Look, I can't talk now. Call me at work sometime. Let's have a drink, catch up on old times . . . See you, Gemma.'

'See you,' Gemma said, but the line had already gone dead.

She held the receiver for some time, uncertain whether she had imagined the conversation. Then a recorded voice started shouting, 'The other person has now cleared!' down the line at her.

Her stomach felt fluttery, as if she were about to walk into an important interview. She swallowed, and went to the Ladies' Room. Her face was perfectly pale, not the lobster colour it felt. She washed her hands and brushed her hair. Then she went back to her office, picked up her messages and returned every outstanding call. That afternoon she got through more work than she had done in the entire previous week. She didn't want to allow herself a single second to think.

Gemma got off the bus two stops before her usual one. She walked up the crescent and stopped outside one of the large white semi-detached houses. There was only one bell next to the shiny green front door with its brass lion knocker gleaming in the sun. The house had obviously been converted back from bedsits into a grand residence once again. A huge wooden rocking horse stood in the bay window on the ground floor. Gemma peered down into the basement. The kitchen was expensively fitted in beech and stainless steel. A frame with a set of gleaming copper saucepans hanging from it was suspended above the solid refectory table. A little boy was crayoning on a huge sheet of white paper. He looked up from his picture and waved at her.

Gemma walked past the house and crossed the road. She looked back and wondered which room her mother was sitting in when she wrote to Shirley. It must have been on the raised ground, or the first floor, she thought, because of the high ceilings she described with their decorated cornices. Gemma narrowed her eyes and tried to imagine the house when it was shabby, the stucco falling off round the windows, peeling black paint on the front door.

A woman looked out of the first-floor window and saw her watching the house. With one movement of her hand, she reached to the side of the window and let a dark green bamboo blind drop in front of her face.

Gemma turned and walked away smartly, a carrier bag of her mother's letters and their photocopies in each hand. She dumped them in her house then carefully double-locked the door while she nipped out to the market for shopping.

She was cooking dinner for Ralph. She bought a leg of spring lamb, a bulb of new season garlic and some potatoes that looked as if they had been dug that morning, the earth on them still fresh and red. It would be the first time she had cooked for him and she wanted it to be simple but good, like the delicious food he had prepared for her.

She was tucking a sprig of rosemary under the meat when he arrived.

'Smells wonderful,' he said, standing one of the bottles of wine he had bought in France on her table, and presenting her with a bunch of violets. Gemma put them into a chipped painted mug at the centre of the table.

'How was your day, honey?' he asked her, giving her shoulders a quick massage as she bent over the sink, scrubbing the dirt off the potatoes.

'Mmm. Fine. And yours?' She felt her neck and back relax even though she hadn't been aware that they were tense.

'Not very productive. You fill my imagination . . . it doesn't leave room for much novel-writing . . .'

303

Gemma turned and kissed him, 'How very corny,' she said.

'Well, exactly. I'm beginning to sound like the kind of writer who composes verses in Mother's Day cards.'

'Perhaps I should commission a book from you for my new series?'

'I thought you'd never ask! I've been dying to write something steamy. I would use a pseudonym, of course,' he joked. 'Have you thought of a name for it, yet?'

'Yes. You provided the inspiration, actually . . .' – he looked slightly dubious – 'with those flowers you sent me on my first day. I thought I'd call it Tiger Lily. Sounds sexy, don't you think, but not seedy, and goes with the general flower theme of the company.'

'Inspired!' he said.

'I'm thinking of taking Daisy up on one of her ideas. She suggested running a competition in one of the magazines she writes for to launch the list . . .'

'Sounds good . . . did you manage to reach her, by the way?'

Gemma loved the way that Ralph listened and remembered things that were important to her. It continued to surprise her that he did. She had never met a man who had tuned in to her life like that.

There were times, especially when he had no lover of his own, that Boy had been obsessively interested in Gemma's private life, but that was prurience rather than concern.

'No, I still haven't,' Gemma replied.

She would have told him about talking to Oliver, she knew she would, if Ralph hadn't stepped outside into the garden to admire her tubs of flowers.

CHAPTER 25

December 1951
Dear Shirl,

It's been a long time since I wrote to you. I thought maybe Dad was intercepting the letters so I stopped. But I do miss you, Shirl. I wish you'd write to me.

In the summer Laurie sold a couple of pictures and we went for a holiday in Suffolk with some other friends of his who are painters too. They wanted me to be a life model (that's nude if you didn't know). I didn't mind but sometimes it makes me feel funny that my bare body's hanging on walls all over the country. At least the weather was warm, which is more than I can say now.

We soon spent the extra money, and we haven't got to Paris yet. I don't mind, though. I quite like my job. Not the serving food to the bloody general public (I could have done that at home!), but all the different types you meet who work there. Everyone has a story to tell. There's a bloke who was in a concentration camp, Shirl. He lost his wife and children and he's ever so sad. There are some soldier boys too on leave and making a bit extra and we have a laugh, but you have to be a bit careful because some of them have wandering hands. I've got some friends too. A couple of times we've been to the cinema together.

Laurie left me for a while. I think he went back to his wife because when he came back he had new clothes. Perhaps you saw him, or perhaps he wouldn't dare set foot there again? Anyway. I thought if you saw him, then you'd probably *wonder what had happened to me, but I didn't hear from you, so I thought you couldn't have seen him. To be honest with you, Shirl, I didn't know what to do. I just sat and cried for a long time. Then I just continued on as usual and one day I came home and Laurie was sitting on the bed asking me to forgive him. I love him, Shirl. I couldn't turn him away.*

Laurie's usually out teaching in the evenings. When I'm on late shift, I come home and go straight to bed, but when I'm on early shift I go to the library because it's warmer there. I'm reading all about the History of Art.

Happy Christmas to you and Ken, Shirl.

Love from Estella

'Laurie sounds like a bastard,' Daisy said, 'doesn't he?'

It was Saturday afternoon. They were sitting cross-legged on the floor in the middle of Daisy's huge living-room, each with a pile of letters beside them. Gemma had the originals, Daisy the photocopies. They were reading each letter simultaneously. Three-quarters of a pizza left over from their lunch sat in its box uneaten. They had been too absorbed to feel much like eating.

'Well, I suppose it must have been very romantic,' replied Gemma. 'Do you think there's a picture of him in her album? Do you still have that album?'

'Of course I do.'

Daisy went to find it.

It was bound in hide that had been worn to a shine like a conker. She put it down on the floor between them and opened it. The picture of Estella in her New Look dress fell out: *'My life begins. I leave home.'*

'She was so pretty,' Daisy said. There were tears in her eyes.

'Yes, wasn't she?' Gemma took her hand. 'Actually, she looked just like you did before you cut your hair,' she said, acknowledging Daisy's new look.

'Don't you like it?' Daisy asked nervously.

'I think it's wonderful,' Gemma said and smiled at her. 'It really suits you.'

Daisy beamed.

'Come on,' Gemma's eyes went back to the album, 'turn over.'

The photo on the next page was properly secured with paper corners. It was a black and white portrait of their parents on their wedding day. Estella was wearing a dark coat with an orchid pinned to the collar. Bertie was wearing a black polo-neck shirt. They looked very happy together.

'I didn't think I could remember any pictures of the in-between bit,' Daisy said, 'but there must have been thirteen years between these two pictures . . . how strange to start an album and then not put anything in it.'

'But she didn't start the album then,' Gemma reasoned, 'she can't have done. For one thing, she didn't have the money for something like this.'

She fingered the expensive leather cover and the semi-lucent parchment leaves that covered the photos on each page.

'You're right. You'd make a much better detective than me,' Daisy said, admiringly, 'but what a shame! I wanted to see what Laurie was like.'

'Turn to the back,' Gemma said, suddenly remembering something, 'I'm sure there was a picture of her school.'

There were a few pictures in a cardboard folder at the back of the album, one of which was folded in half. It was a wide picture of several hundred girls in gymslips. A row of forbidding spinster teachers sat in front of them, and there, just to the left of the headmistress, was a man glowering at the camera.

'I never noticed him before,' Daisy said, 'I was always looking at the two pictures of Mum . . .'

Estella appeared at both ends of the row of girls

standing at the back. She told her daughters that she had run from one to the other while the camera was panning round. On one side of the photo she looked serenely beautiful, on the other she was slightly out of focus, smiling wickedly at the camera and bits of her hair had escaped her ponytail and were a blur around her face.

'Perhaps Estella was trying to distract us from asking about him. I always wondered why she kept the picture when she said she hated school so much,' Gemma said, peering at the man's face.

'He is rather delish,' exclaimed Daisy. Laurie had a mop of dark hair swept back from his face. He was holding a pipe. 'He looks like a French existentialist, or something, like he should be advertising Gitanes in a Fifties retro campaign.'

'Except that he was the real thing. This must have been just before they eloped,' Gemma said. 'Look, it's summer 1950.'

'How typical of Mum to outrage the entire town!' Daisy said, with admiration.

'Yes,' Gemma agreed.

But it wasn't Estella's elopement that had come as a shock to her, exactly, more the youthful tone of the letters to Shirley. It reminded her of a phrase Shirley had used. Those were more innocent times, she had said. And even though Estella had been less than innocent in some ways, her voice was young and unsophisticated, completely free of the weary cynicism she had adopted later.

'Do you think she kept this picture as her one memory of Laurie, Gem?' Daisy asked. 'Do you think she got it out and looked at it from time to time and remembered her first love . . . ?'

'I suppose so.' Gemma thought that Daisy was treating the whole thing very lightly. It was as if she were talking about a romantic film she had seen, rather than witnessing the unravelling of a life. It was beginning to irritate Gemma.

'Why didn't you tell me you had split up from Oliver?' she suddenly asked.

'Oh. I don't know really. I thought you'd think I was stupid . . .'

Gemma picked up the next letter and began to read.

January 1952
Dear Shirl,

  Happy New Year!

  It was such a lovely surprise to see you before Christmas. I can't tell you what a shock I got when I saw you peering over the top of the Winter Wonderice Cake! I hope you managed to get a few presents. I thought after, what would happen if you went home with nothing when you told them you were coming up for Christmas shopping? You looked very well-to-do. Quite the married lady in your new costume.

  I saw our room through different eyes after you left. I looked around and thought how it must have seemed to you. I know it's a bit shabby and everything, but we're happy, and that's the main thing. Laurie was disappointed he missed you.

  We spent Christmas with Georgina and Jack, thank God, so we got some nice food, even though they are vegetarian. Laurie gave me a scarf. It's got all different coloured bits of velvet sort of carved out of silk. It's from the 1920s. He got it in a junk shop so it's a bit dirty but I gave it a gentle wash in cold water and it's come up OK. We went to a party at New Year and I wore it with my black slacks and a black boat neck top I bought. There were lots of artists and somebody said I should be a model and kept trying to kiss me, and Laurie said, she is a model, my model actually and keep your hands off!

  My New Year's resolution is to learn to smoke. Everyone does it and it makes you look older, but the taste makes me feel a bit sick. What's yours?

  Please sneak up to London again soon, Shirl, and good luck with you know what. I'll be the naughty aunt who teaches your children bad ways!

Love from Estella

'Do you think Shirley was pregnant?' Daisy asked as they simultaneously put down the letter.

'Either that, or trying, I should think,' Gemma said.

'In those days, people didn't *try*, did they?' said Daisy. 'I mean they didn't have contraception, did they? I thought they just did it and hoped for the best.'

'It's only a generation ago . . . I'm sure they did have contraception,' Gemma said, 'just not the Pill.' She found it strange that neither of them had the faintest idea about such a recent piece of social history. It was one thing she wasn't sure she could ask Shirley about.

'Do you want to have children?' she asked Daisy.

'Not at all.' The answer was immediate. 'What about you?'

'I don't know, really,' she smiled, thinking of Ralph, who said he would be waiting in bed for her later that evening.

'Well, that sounds quite a lot like yes,' Daisy said, leaning forward excitedly, 'and you keep having a little smile to yourself. Are you in lurve, or something, Biscuit?'

Was she in love? Gemma didn't know. What she had with Ralph felt wonderful, beautiful, secure. It gave a kind of confidence she had never felt, a certainty about herself. But love wasn't like that, was it? Love was something she associated with despair. Love was the small hard feeling of pain she had felt when she spoke to Oliver on the phone. Love was what Estella had felt for Laurie. For the first time in her life she was feeling a kind of empathy with her mother.

'Well?' Daisy asked.

'Maybe,' Gemma said, and she thought of Ralph's face and how disappointed he would be to hear that response, and she felt a shiver of betrayal.

Daisy knew better than to ask a lot of questions. She could feel Gemma closing up like a frightened sea urchin. Love, she realized, was one thing that they couldn't yet talk about. Gemma was still raw, still hurting about Oliver. Perhaps she thought that if she revealed too much, Daisy would run off with this man too. With huge effort, Daisy contained her curiosity.

'Why did you split with Oliver?' Gemma asked her.

'I don't know, really,' Daisy said, then seeing that her response was making Gemma's knuckles clasp the photograph album so tight they were becoming white with fury, added, 'well, I do. I just think I grew out of him. By the end, we were hardly talking to each other. I don't mean not speaking in anger, I just mean not telling each other the important things . . .'

'Like what?' Gemma asked, trying not to mind that Daisy could be so casual.

'Oh, I don't know,' Daisy said, then added quickly, 'well, for instance, he hadn't even told me that he had finally decided to trace his real mother. I only found out by accident.'

'What do you mean, his real mother?'

'His birth mother, I think they call it . . . Didn't you know Oliver was adopted? God, I'm surprised. He was always holding it over me as a kind of threat.'

'A threat?'

'Yes, you know, his fear of being abandoned again. It made me so guilty it took me months to suggest that we separate.'

Gemma felt tears come to her eyes. If she needed final proof that she meant nothing to Oliver, there it was. He had never talked about being abandoned to her. He had been intriguingly elusive about his background, but she was sure she had never known he was adopted. She had obviously meant nothing to him.

'Not that I'm saying it was all hell,' Daisy was saying,

feeling that she had perhaps sounded disloyal. 'I mean, in a way, I'll always love him, because he was my first love, but now, even though I miss him and I feel terribly lonely, I do feel more myself . . . I know I'm going to be all right without him, and that,' she added, 'is a wonderful feeling.'

It was the first time that she had expressed the confusing combination of emotions that had been overwhelming her since Oliver took his suitcase and walked down the street. It was the first time she had realized that she would recover. 'Come on,' she said, 'let's continue with the young life and loves of Estella Smith. Sounds like a Victorian novel, doesn't it?'

Gemma picked up the next letter, then looked at her watch. 'Oh God!' she said, suddenly remembering, 'I'm meant to be going to a film with Kathy. I'm late. She'll be waiting for me.' She began to gather her things together.

'Oh.' Daisy's heart sank at the prospect of another evening without company.

'Please don't read any without me, I'll come back tomorrow,' Gemma said, making her way to the door. Then seeing a look she recognized cross her sister's face, she added warningly, 'I mean it, Donut. I kept these letters a whole week without peeping. Now you must do the same for a few hours.'

'All right,' Daisy agreed reluctantly.

'Promise?' Gemma asked.

'I promise,' Daisy said, 'Cross my heart, I promise, Biscuit.'

CHAPTER 26

Kathy was standing by a pink neon sign that said 'Pick'N'Mix', staring absently at the wall of perspex boxes filled with shiny wrapped sweets. She was wearing a shapeless blue dress that didn't suit her and made her look washed out. She didn't see Gemma rushing towards her and she was visibly startled when Gemma went to kiss her. 'I'm so sorry,' said Gemma breathlessly.

'Oh, that's OK.' Kathy looked innocently delighted. 'I was beginning to think you'd forgotten . . .'

'Did you get the tickets?'

'Yes. We haven't missed anything. Just adverts. The main programme doesn't start for a bit.'

They pushed past the popcorn queue and handed the tickets to an usherette, then Gemma said, 'Actually, do you really want to see this film?'

Kathy replied, a little warily, 'What do you mean?'

'Well, it's so rare I get to see you on your own, why don't we just have a nice meal and chat?'

A huge relieved smile spread over Kathy's face. 'What a great idea!' she said, and gave Gemma's arm a squeeze. To the astonishment of the usherette, they executed an about turn and walked purposefully out of the cinema, arm in arm.

Although it was beginning to get dark, it was still hot, and the air was steeped in aromas of food. 'Char siu pork,' said Gemma, inhaling a lung full of the sweet barbecue smell. 'Do you fancy Chinese?'

'Anything, really,' replied Kathy.

They managed to get a table by the door in Mr Kong. The restaurant was busy and a queue was forming beside them. They had to talk quite loudly to hear one another, but all the other diners were far too absorbed in their food and their own conversations to be bothered about listening in.

Kathy took one look at the menu and handed it over to Gemma. 'You order. I'm sure you're much better at it than me.'

It wasn't the first time Gemma had noticed that Kathy seemed to have lost her confidence over the years. When they were at Oxford, Kathy had had strong views about almost everything. Gemma seemed to remember that she had been particularly vociferous on the subject of chilli prawns. She ordered some, along with several other seafood dishes.

'Do we have to use chopsticks?' Kathy asked, looking worried.

'We don't have to do anything we don't want to,' Gemma replied, and asked for two forks so that Kathy wouldn't feel uncomfortable using one on her own. 'So, how are you?' she asked.

'Oh Gem,' Kathy said, tears filling her eyes as if they had been gathering there, waiting for sympathetic company to release them, 'I think Roger's having an affair . . . well, I know he is, really, you know how you know these things? I don't know what to do . . . I've done all this bloody Relate training but when it's your own husband it isn't much help.'

Gemma took a deep breath and felt herself doing the human equivalent of changing gear. What she had wanted to do was spend a giggly girls' evening talking about Ralph and telling Kathy about Estella's letters. She had been looking forward to one of the great talks they used to have together, where by the end of the evening everything seemed to have been put in perspective. Kathy was good at getting to the point, seeing it clearly, saying things that were sometimes obvious, but always useful.

In Gemma's opinion, friendship was rarely equal. There was usually one party whose function was primarily to listen and one whose it was to talk. In the end, it balanced itself out because you could be a listener for one person and a talker to another. She had explained this theory once to Boy, who had said immediately, 'Yes, you're right. It's a bit like smoking. You never cadge cigarettes from the person who borrows from you, but you do cadge from someone.' From then on, Gemma had never been able to embark on a bit of soul-searching without thinking about Boy lighting up a Marlboro.

In most of her friendships, Gemma was the one who sorted things out, but not with Kathy. The dynamic of their friendship had always been that Gemma was the one with problems, Kathy the one who sorted them out. That was what made that relationship so very precious to her. Gemma didn't know whether it would work the other way round. Kathy wasn't supposed to have problems. For a moment she felt almost irritated, but then she looked at Kathy's face, the same patient, trusting face that was now so openly asking for her help. She pulled herself together. 'Are you sure?' she asked. 'Who with?'

'Yes . . . and I don't know. I don't want to know, actually . . .' Kathy sighed. 'Actually, I don't really mind *per se*, I mean, I don't mind if he fucks someone else. I mean, I haven't been feeling much like sex since Alexander was born. In a way, it's quite a relief from that point of view . . . but I'm frightened of it being more . . . I'm frightened of losing the house.' She started crying again. 'The children need two parents . . . I don't want to be on my own . . .'

'It's OK, it's OK,' Gemma stretched across the

table, 'you won't lose the house. Look, however much of a bastard Roger's being, he wouldn't do that. He loves the children. And well, he's . . .' – she thought of a nice way of putting it – 'he's too conventional to leave . . .'

'You think so?' Kathy wiped her eyes. 'What do you mean?'

Tread carefully, Gemma told herself. 'I'm sure that he wants more than anything else to be a married bloke with two kids,' she said.

'What, you think he hasn't got the imagination to go?' Kathy smiled through her tears.

'You said it,' Gemma replied reluctantly.

'Oh Gem, I knew you never liked him . . . but I didn't realize just how much!' Kathy was laughing now. 'Well, that does make me feel better. My husband's having an affair, but we'll be all right because he's so bloody boring!'

'Do you still love him?' Gemma asked. It was the politest way she could think of asking why Kathy was still with him.

Kathy looked at her and sighed. 'It's not something I even think about,' she replied carefully. 'Oh Gemma, I do believe that you still think that being in love is the most important thing . . . being swept off your feet by mad passion. It doesn't last, you know. In the end, it's not Cathy and Heathcliff on the moors, it's Kathy and Roger and the mortgage – oh that's quite good!' She laughed at her own unintentional pun. 'And love becomes a certain shared pride when your kid gets her lines out in the nativity play,' she elaborated, 'and sex is a function you perform when one of you is freezing cold in the night, after getting up to change a nappy, and cuddles up for a bit of warmth . . .'

'God, you're making me so envious!' Gemma said, only half-believing it. She'd heard the same sentiments, perhaps not so forcefully expressed, from several people she knew with children. But surely it didn't have to be like that?

'And you know the one thing that makes us all suckers? The one thing that makes us all think we're different? It's that we all think that we discovered love, that it happened to us for the first time, don't we, Gem?'

Daisy tore off a piece of pizza. It was cold and rubbery. She took it into the kitchen and put it in the microwave for a minute, then took it out. Now it was warm and rubbery and even more flaccid than it had been before. She took a large bite then yelled as a burning spot of cheese attached itself to the roof of her mouth. She dumped the pizza in the bin and drank the rest of the Coke straight from the bottle. The inside of her mouth felt raw.

She picked up *Time Out* and started leafing through the movie section, wondering what film it was that Gemma and Kathy were going to see. She felt quite in the mood for a movie herself. It wouldn't have hurt Gemma to invite her along too, she thought, slightly put out. Gemma had always been rather possessive about her friends. In fact, Daisy thought sulkily, that was exactly why they had got into such a muddle about Oliver. If Gemma hadn't been so bloody secretive, then she would have known that he was forbidden territory. And then . . . how different everything would have been if she and Oliver hadn't fallen in love. She would have gone to university. Gemma would not have gone to the States. They would have cleared out Whitton House together. Or maybe they wouldn't have sold it at all. She imagined herself wearing a large straw hat, watering the runner beans in the old walled garden.

It was strange that one day could so alter the rest of one's life. If she hadn't fallen in love with Oliver, she might have been a completely different person. A career woman with smart clothes like Gemma, or married to someone she met at university like Kathy? Or didn't it work like that? Was she destined to end up as a vaguely dissatisfied journalist with a handsome, intelligent and overpowering boyfriend? Or, she reminded herself, a vaguely dissatisfied journalist who lived on her own now.

And what would Gemma be? The same serene, but desperately vulnerable woman whose face shone with a kind of wholesome beauty but whose eyes spoke of loss. Or would she be the confident publishing wife of a well-to-do solicitor, with a three-storey Georgian terraced house in Islington and impeccable left-wing credentials, a couple that gave the chattering classes something to chatter about?

'The Day that Changed My Life', Daisy scrawled on the top of the pizza box. It would make a great theme for an article.

She picked up *Time Out* again, feeling sorry for herself. She definitely wanted to go to the cinema, but she couldn't think of anyone to go with. The Screen on the Hill was showing a film set in India during the Raj. She quite fancied seeing it. It was the kind of film that Oliver hated.

Suddenly it occurred to her that she didn't *have* to go with anyone, and the film was starting in just ten minutes. Daisy changed her T-shirt and automatically went into the bathroom to brush her hair. She still hadn't got used to seeing her shorn crop and, after almost a week, it still came as a lovely surprise because it just looked right and didn't even need a comb pulling through it.

The cinema was air-conditioned and blissfully refreshing. Ticket in one hand, and oversized paper cup of Coke in the other, Daisy went straight to the front row and plonked herself down in the middle seat. This was wonderful. No arguing about how far back to sit, and she could see the screen. Daisy had once been prescribed glasses for her short sight. She kept one pair in the car, but the other she had lost almost immediately and never bothered to replace. She slurped on her Coke and found herself laughing out loud at one of the adverts, then looking over her shoulder apologetically, as the man behind her tutted. Oliver would have been livid. She could almost hear him muttering about succumbing to the blandishments of capitalism. Perhaps she was after all, as Oliver had accused her in one of his darker moments, just an intellectual lightweight. Well, what the hell, thought Daisy, wishing she had brought a jacket as the titles began to roll and the chill of the air-conditioning began to bite, leaving goosebumps on her bare arms.

She hadn't expected to see Cal Colstelloe. He rose up like a giant in front of her, wearing a soldier's uniform and looking rather surly. 'May I have the pleasure of the next dance?' he asked her.

'You bet,' said Daisy, under her breath. There was a warning cough behind her. 'Oh, Major Short, I'm afraid my card is full,' said the blond actress.

Cal clicked his heels together formally and skulked off, no doubt to perform some nefarious deed in revenge for his dismissal.

Why, Daisy wondered, did they always seem to cast him as a baddie? His face was rather mischievous, but once you knew him he was really about as bad as a fluffy toy. Daisy giggled. Major Short, indeed. The man behind her hissed. Daisy settled down. The plot of the film was pretty dull and Oliver would have been right to call it a chocolate box view of India. If it hadn't been for the prospect of seeing Cal Costelloe in his safari suit and topee again, she might very well have left before the end.

*   *   *

Gemma speared a piece of squid with her fork. After Kathy's impassioned outburst about the frailty of passion, she had rather lost her appetite. At least Kathy seemed a lot more cheerful now, although Gemma didn't really think she had contributed much comfort.

'I don't know what the solution is,' she said.

'I think there probably isn't a solution,' Kathy replied buoyantly, 'but I feel a lot more able to cope now. Maybe the holiday will help sort it out.' They were leaving for two weeks in Sardinia with the children the next day. 'Thank you.' She smiled at Gemma.

'You're welcome,' Gemma said automatically.

'What about you, Gem?'

It didn't feel right to talk about Ralph now. Gemma's grasp on her own feelings for him felt tenuous enough. In her mind, Gemma wrapped her thoughts in tissue paper and consigned them to a brown cardboard box with FRAGILE stamped in red across the sides.

'Well,' she began, 'I've had quite an interesting week . . .' She began to tell Kathy about Shirley's letters from Estella.

Kathy listened, fascinated.

'But how come you're only in 1951! I don't know how you had the self-control to wait to read them with Daisy,' she marvelled.

'No, I don't either,' Gemma smiled, 'but it is fun reading them together. It feels right, somehow.'

'Yes,' said Kathy, understanding. 'How is Daisy, by the way?'

'She seems fine. She and Oliver have split up, it seems . . .'

The calm way in which she said it belied the turmoil that she felt inside whenever she thought about it.

'Yes, I know,' Kathy said, 'she told me a while ago that they were going to.'

'She told you?' Gemma pretended to be deeply

interested in the hotpot dish of pork and shellfish. The familiar poison of jealousy was seeping into her circulation. What was Daisy up to? Why had she told her best friend, and when? Had she already decided to ditch him that afternoon in the park, when Gemma had had to summon all her reserves of courage to admit that she had loved him all her life. Was Daisy thinking of leaving him then? Had Gemma humiliated herself for nothing? Was Daisy secretly laughing at her? No, she told herself. That's all over. You have forgiven Daisy. This has nothing to do with you.

'I wonder why she told you and not me,' she said, as levelly as she could.

'Oh, she told me not to tell you, although you would have found out soon enough because he's camping out in our spare room while we're away. Roger asked him, I don't know why. I always thought they hated one another,' Kathy said, not realizing that every word she spoke was making the situation worse.

Conspiracy slithered in below betrayal on the list of Daisy's misdemeanours, and now Kathy, her best friend, had been dragged in too. Gemma put a cooked oyster into her mouth. It was cold. The taste of the sea, the cold glutinous sauce, the chewy, muscly texture that she couldn't seem to swallow, the noise in the restaurant – she thought she was going to be sick. Stop it, she told herself. It doesn't make any difference any more. Oliver is nothing to you. He never was.

Gemma took a deep breath. 'I think I'm beginning to understand Estella better now,' she said, reverting to their earlier conversation, 'it's kind of like watching a film. There's this young beautiful, trusting girl who falls in love with an older man – that's the first quarter of an hour, and you know, just because the film is two hours long, that something's going to go wrong because otherwise there wouldn't be a story . . .'

'And in this case you know the ending,' Kathy said.

'Yes. Well, I know that she changed . . . but somehow it's very comforting to know that she was kind of unsophisticated before she became so bloody worldly. Sad, too . . .'

'I thought that side of her was always there,' Kathy remembered. 'I know that you used to cringe when she came up to Oxford and all the men we knew fancied her, but I always thought that was a genuine kind of charm she had. She was lovely to us when we were doing up the house,' she added.

'Yes, I suppose she was,' Gemma admitted. 'I suppose I always felt she was trying to muscle in on my experiences . . . and now I think, well, why shouldn't she, after all? She didn't get the chance to go to Oxford. She didn't have the luxury of being a sulky teenager like I was. She had no home . . . I know she *chose* that, but there was obviously no going back if she decided she had made a mistake. She had to work making knicker-bocker glories, for God's sake . . . and, do you know, the thing that I most like about her then is that she made them cheerfully. Everything was an adventure for her. It seems really peculiar, but the letters have made me see how cynical and spoilt I am . . . and that's what I always thought *she* was . . .'

'I'm dying to know what happens,' Kathy said, then realizing that it was perhaps an unfortunate choice of words, she stuttered, 'I mean . . . I didn't mean . . .'

'It's OK,' Gemma reassured her, 'I know you didn't mean . . .'

Daisy bought a large portion of chips from the fish and chip shop and shook salt and vinegar vigorously all over the paper. She couldn't imagine why she hadn't gone to the cinema on her own before. It was so much easier. You could watch the film, form your own opinion, eavesdrop into other people's conversations on the way out, buy a great big bag of chips and eat them walking down the street. You could fantasize about the hero (well, in this case, the bit part), hum the theme tune, even wipe your greasy fingers on your jeans, with nobody to nag at you. She resolved to go regularly.

The neighbour with the steel guitar was playing 'Albatross' by Fleetwood Mac. She could hear it down the street. When she opened the front door the music stopped and he put his head round the door of his flat as she went past. He had obviously been listening out for her.

'Hi, Daisy!' he said, casually, as if they had bumped into one another unexpectedly. 'Oliver's moved out, right? I saw him collecting some stuff . . .' he went on.

Daisy nodded, waiting for him to get to the point.

'I just wanted to say that, like, if you ever need company . . . you know,' he smiled at her.

'Oh thanks,' Daisy said, 'but I'm rather enjoying being on my own.' She skipped up the stairs, leaving him with his mouth hanging open.

She supposed it was a genuine enough offer, but there was something about him she found slightly repellent. She had never liked beards, but one that actually required a lot of trimming to keep its monkish pointed shape seemed particularly silly. And he was ginger, which was fine, she supposed, but was it really necessary to make such a thing about being ginger? His hair was long and ginger and his stupid beard was ginger too. She hadn't seen him naked, thank God, but she would have taken a bet on him having tufts of ginger hair on his shoulders, and ginger pubes. He always wore ginger clothes too, and, in winter, he sported a leather jacket the colour of diarrhoea.

There were no messages on the answerphone. Daisy walked from room to room, carefully avoiding the living-room, trying to think of something to do. The hot evenings seemed to be making her feel livelier rather than sleepier. She switched on the electric fan in the bedroom and lay down on the bed with a book. The novel, which had attracted an unprecedented advance from its publisher, was the most talked about book of the year. Daisy knew that it wasn't going to be cool to say for much longer that she hadn't yet read it, but she couldn't concentrate. She put the book down beside her, switched off the light and tried to drift off to sleep, lulled by the whir of the fan. Every time she closed her eyes she saw an image of the very thing she was supposed to be avoiding until Gemma returned: the two piles of letters lying on her living-room carpet.

Daisy ran herself a cool bath and poured in a lot of aromatherapy oil, but she couldn't seem to relax. She kept wondering whether she had left a window open in the living-room. If she had, and it rained in the night, there was a possibility that the original letters would get damaged. She convinced herself that it would be irresponsible not to go and check.

One of the windows was open and although it would be a driving hurricane that allowed rain to jump in and across at least ten feet of room before spattering the letters, Daisy thought it would be best if she picked them up and put them in the shoe box on the dining table out of danger. She gathered them together and, holding them at arm's length, endeavoured to put them into the box without looking. Inevitably the uneven pile tottered and several of the letters slid to the floor. Daisy was about to attempt the manoeuvre again when one word written in capital letters screamed out of the telegram which was lying face up on the floor, and Daisy's resolve collapsed.

They had spent an hour trying to get a cab. Piccadilly Circus at midnight on a Saturday was thronging with people like Times Square at New Year. Kathy was getting increasingly anxious as she still had holiday packing to do for the next day.

'Is it always like this?' Gemma asked, as yet another troop of teenagers in wild Gothic make-up pushed past them.

'I don't know,' Kathy said, 'I'm rarely out at this time of night. How do they afford it?'

'God, it makes me feel middle-aged!' Gemma said, horrified.

'I'm sure, according to them, we are middle-aged,' Kathy replied, unperturbed.

When they eventually hailed a cab it seemed only right to let Kathy take it. Gemma caught a night bus.

The London she remembered hadn't been like this, Gemma thought. When she was a teenager it was considered the height of wildness to wear a boiler suit and see a punk band at the Marquee. A couple of girls she had known at school had worn safety pins through their pierced ears and lots of mascara. They had been expelled. For the rest, make-up was a bit of mauve Rimmel eye shadow and some tawny blusher. Nothing like the white pancake and black lipstick that the girls at the back of the bus were wearing. Underneath all that paint, were these girls in their micro-skirts still worrying about spots, intimate deodorants, and heavy petting? Or did they take all that in their stride these days? Was each generation a bit like what Kathy had said about people in love – each thinking that they were the first to discover sex and wildness and rebellion? How depressing! Gemma stared out of the window, seeing nothing as the thoughts free-fell through her head.

Ralph was asleep in her bed. The light was still on. He had obviously been waiting for her. Gemma smiled at him, loving his even breathing, the fact that he was there.

She switched the light off and went downstairs to get a glass of water and saw the light blinking on her answerphone. She smiled. She liked the fact that Ralph

325

didn't answer her phone, that he respected her boundaries. She pressed the playback switch and turned the volume down. 'Biscuit, guess what?' said Daisy's excited voice, 'Get over here as quickly as you can tomorrow. Estella had a baby!'

CHAPTER 27

June 1953
ITSABOY.
BOTH OK.
COME SOONEST. E.

'It fell out!' Daisy said as Gemma handed her back the yellowing piece of paper.

'What do you mean, it fell out?' Gemma asked her. The telegram must have been stuck to another page when she was photcopying as this was the first time she'd seen it.

'I was picking up the pile of letters to put them on the table safely and it fell out. Honestly, I didn't read them, Gem.'

Even as she said it, Daisy thought it sounded an unconvincing explanation.

'Just give me the originals,' Gemma said, holding out her hand.

'Oh, don't be like that. I've been dying for you to get here. I want to read all the rest with you again.'

'Again?' Gemma raised her eyebrows.

'I mean again like yesterday. I haven't read them, honest . . .'

Ignoring her, Gemma picked up the pile of letters, put them into the shoe box and tucked it under her arm. 'Bye,' she said, without looking at Daisy.

'Oh Gem, don't go. Why do you have to be like this?' Daisy stood in her way.

'Because you spoil everything,' Gemma told her.

Daisy's lip quivered. She told herself she wouldn't cry. 'I swear that I haven't read them,' she said.

'I don't believe you,' Gemma said evenly.

'Are you calling me a liar, then?' Daisy's voice rose. 'Because I'm not a bloody liar and I won't be called a bloody liar. I'm twenty-eight, Gemma. I'm not your little sister any more, you know. If I say I haven't read the bloody letters, I haven't read them . . . and in any case, what gives you the right to set the rules about the letters anyway? They're mine as much as yours!'

'So you *did* read them,' Gemma pounced.

'No . . . only a couple . . . no . . .' Daisy faltered.

'What gives me the right is that Shirley entrusted them to me. As a matter of fact, they're not mine or yours, they're Shirley's, and she asked me to ensure that we read them together. That was her wish, not mine. If I had wanted to I would have read them all in the week when I was trying to get you on the phone.'

'Why do you always go so cold when you argue?' Daisy asked her. 'How come you're so logical and clinical? I hate it.'

'Well, tough,' Gemma said, icily, but she was boiling inside.

'Look, it's too early for this,' said Daisy, suppressing a yawn. 'Have a cup of coffee, sit down. Come on, Biscuit . . .'

'Don't call me that!' Gemma suddenly shrieked and stamped her foot.

'It's only a term of affection,' Daisy was taken aback.

'Well, I don't feel very affectionate at the moment. I'm going. Get out of my way!'

'Don't boss me around in my own flat!' Daisy said, suddenly very angry too, 'I've just about had enough of you loading guilt trips on me. I'm not going to feel guilty about this. You're not going to make me because I've done nothing that any normal person wouldn't do, and just because you're so bloody pious . . . What do you think you are, a bloody nun, or something? Does it ever occur to you that I've got feelings too, or are feelings just the things that you have that you bottle up like vinegar for years and then pour all over me and expect me to feel as sour as you?'

'Oh shut up!' Gemma said, and tried to push past her.

'No, you shut up . . .' Daisy pushed her back, 'Did it ever occur to you that I might be feeling bad because I've broken up with my boyfriend, or can you only see it as something to do with you? Are you so selfish . . .'

She had finally hit a nerve. 'ME? SELFISH?' Gemma shouted, 'God, that's rich from you . . . you didn't even bother to tell me that you had split up with Oliver . . . you must have known how it would make me feel . . .'

'No, actually, I was thinking about my life and not about you at the time, and if that's selfish, I'm sorry, but since you haven't been part of my life for the last ten years of it, I've kind of got used to thinking things out for myself . . .' Daisy stopped suddenly, amazed by everything she was saying. She had never spoken to her sister like this before.

'Have you finished?' Gemma asked her, pushing past her and letting herself out of the flat.

Her coolness made Daisy explode. 'No! And you know something, Gem, you can't blame me for everything, you know. I didn't know about you and Oliver. And . . .' There was no stopping it now, although she knew even as the words were in her mouth that she shouldn't let them out. 'I couldn't help it that Mum loved me more than you, or that she wrote me a letter and she just left you a stupid note . . .'

Gemma turned her back on her, put both hands over her ears and ran down the stairs.

'. . . It's not my fault . . . I've always loved you,' Daisy screamed after her.

The front door of the house slammed. Daisy threw herself on the floor, thumping the carpet with both hands like a two-year-old having a tantrum. She didn't know how long it was before she heard a soft knocking at her door.

'Gem?' she asked, wiping her eyes on the towelling sleeve of her dressing gown. Gemma had arrived so early, she hadn't had a chance to get dressed.

'It's Bob from downstairs,' said the ginger neighbour, 'is there anything I can do?'

'Yes,' Daisy shouted at the door, 'piss off.'

'I've ruined all my children's lives!'

Gemma had known there was something wrong with that sentence when Shirley told her about Estella's last phone call, but she hadn't been able to figure out what it was. Of course, if you only had two children, then you would say both. If you said such a thing at all.

You didn't ruin my life, Gemma suddenly thought. You did some things that made me hate you, but you didn't ruin my life. And you certainly didn't ruin Daisy's, until you killed yourself . . . so why did you say that to Shirley?

Gemma stared out of the taxi window at the canal boats of Little Venice. It was still early, but the sun was already hot. People were eating breakfast on deck amongst painted pots of bright red geraniums. The scalded treacly smell of coffee wafted in through the cab window as they pulled away from the traffic lights.

Gemma's mouth was dry and she felt bruised by the row with Daisy. She hoped that Ralph was going to greet her at the door with a steaming cafetière of freshly brewed coffee, and a hug. She wasn't sure that he had really understood what her mission was when she climbed over his sleeping body at daybreak and whispered where she was going.

Then she changed her mind and hoped that he had already left. She knew he was supposed to be going to play softball and do some male bonding with the team from *Sixpack*. She had most definitely not been invited, which was just as well because she needed the day to herself. She wanted to sit and read all the letters thoroughly, starting at the beginning, resisting the temptation to skip to that telegram with its intriguing message. She wanted to find answers to all her questions, without having to explain anything to anyone. By the time the cab drew up at the top of the mews, she was already impatient for Ralph's departure, and it showed.

'Aren't you being a bit hard?' Ralph suggested after Gemma's perfunctory explanation of what had happened.

'You don't know Daisy,' Gemma replied crisply.

'True. But if she didn't read the other letters . . . even if she did . . . it's not such a big deal, is it?'

'It is to me.'

'I see.'

'What's that supposed to mean?' She was immediately on the defensive.

'Nothing . . . listen, I'll leave you to get on with your reading,' he volunteered, 'I'll call you this evening.'

Gemma softened. Maybe she had been precipitate. Maybe it wasn't such a big deal. She followed him to the door and wrapped herself around his back, 'I'm sorry,' she whispered into the nape of his neck.

'What for?' He turned round, held her hands and looked into her eyes.

She held his gaze for as long as she could. 'I'll see you later?' she said.

'Yes.' He walked up the mews without turning back to wave.

March 1952
Dear Shirl,

I was so sorry to hear your news. I'm really keeping my fingers crossed for you.

We've been through a bit of a bad patch too. Laurie spends a lot of time with his friends and he's not very good with money. Whenever I tell him that we've got to be careful, he says I'm a typical shopkeeper's daughter, and that makes me feel mean. He says he's going to have an exhibition soon, and he says we'll have more money than we know what to do with then. But when is this bloody exhibition we keep hearing so much about, I ask him, and he says I've got no faith, which isn't fair. I know that Laurie's paintings are really good, but so were Van Gogh's and he died a pauper.

I was thinking about doing some painting, too. He used to say that I was really good at school, but when I suggested it, he just laughed. So who's got no faith then?

Secretly, Shirl, I think that Laurie is a bit of a snob, even though he calls himself a socialist, because he doesn't like me telling his friends what I do. There's a very nice man called Leo who owns a gallery and he says I shouldn't worry. He said that Laurie's a bit immature, which made me laugh because he's fourteen years older than me, so what does that make me then? I don't think Leo realizes.

My friend at work says, 'Why don't you get yourself a good man, a nice girl like you?' Do you remember I introduced you to him? He's the one who wraps up the knives and forks in a serviette and he lost all his family in the war. But Laurie is good really, I told him, he's just frustrated because his talent isn't being recognized. He said Laurie was a lucky man to have a nice girl in love with him. Nice girl! NB, Shirl. Anyway, at least I made him laugh.

Must close now. I can hear Laurie coming up the stairs.
Love from Estella

Gemma filled the kettle. She was pleased that her mother had a friend at work. She was beginning to feel very protective towards her. She made herself a cup of coffee, then sat down at her desk again and picked up the next letter.

June 1952
Dear Shirl,

I'm feeling a bit low, so I thought I'd write to you, even though you owe me a letter. Don't worry. I know you've got other things on your mind. Do you think you're working too hard in the shop? You're on your feet all day, so maybe you never give a baby the chance to get going. I hope there'll be good news soon.

I want to ask you something, and I wish you were here sitting next to me so we could talk about it. My question is this: when you love someone, do you think you ought to do anything in the world for them?

Here's the whole story: there's this man called Leo who owns a gallery. I can't remember whether I've told you about him before. He's really kind to us and he's always taking us out for drinks and things. Well, a couple of weekends ago he took us to a party in this big stately home kind of place that some of his friends own. It had a swimming pool. Everyone was drunk and a lot of us ended up skinny-dipping in the pool. I lost Laurie half way through the evening and when I found him, he was writhing about under a rhododendron bush with a really tarty piece called Mandy. I was so upset I went crying to Leo. Anyway, I must have been half cut because I don't know how it happened but Leo ended up kissing me and he was trying to get me to go the whole way with him. He said he'd give Laurie his exhibition if I did. Well, I like Leo, but I don't like him in that way, if you know what I mean, so I said no, but then I told Laurie later and he was really cross and said I should have done if it meant he got his exhibition. I don't know what to do now. I can't believe Laurie wanted me to do that. He says he can't believe I'm so selfish. I'm frightened of losing him now, but it seems all topsy-turvy like Alice in Wonderland. Am I being stupid, Shirl? I haven't told anyone else. Please write soon.

Love from your loving sister, Estella

Don't do it, Gemma thought, picking up the next letter hurriedly.

July 1952
Dear Shirl,

Laurie's gone again. I've only got myself to blame. If I hadn't kept putting pressure on him and asking where he was spending his evenings then he wouldn't have gone. The thing is, I try to understand him and give him lots of freedom, but then sometimes I just become petty and small-minded and jealous. I don't know if I'll ever get it right. When I'm out with Laurie's friends I know that people think I'm a good catch for him, but sometimes at home it all goes to pieces and Laurie says I'm showing my age and background. Anyway, I'm feeling a bit down in the dumps. I know you will say that I mustn't have him back again. You're probably right. But I can't promise. I love him so much, and know that I can be right for him if I can just control those silly feelings I get. That's if he ever comes back. This time, I don't know if he will.

I'm always thinking about you and wishing I could see you and have a good, long chat.

Lots of love,
Estella

Laurie, it seemed to Gemma, was one of those people who liked to call themselves angry young men, which was just another name for a misogynist who systematically undermined the women who loved them. As each month passed, it was apparent that Estella's confidence was declining. There was still the spark of fiery independence in there, but Gemma could feel her becoming drained. Don't have him back, she told her mother. Go and find someone lovely who will appreciate you, like Bertie. But she knew that Estella hadn't met her father until years later.

She picked up a postcard of the Sacré Coeur.

July 1952
Well, we finally made it to Paris. Leo drove us here and we're staying in Montmartre, which is the bit where the artists live. It's a wonderful city and very romantic. I could live here forever, so it's a pity it's only for the weekend! Yesterday we ate oysters sitting in the street outside a café!

Love from Estella and Laurie

Gemma remembered her seafood lunch with Ralph. She was beginning to get hungry but she didn't want to interrupt the flow of the correspondence.

August 1952
Dear Shirl,
Well, Laurie finally got his exhibition. It's going to happen in November and after that our lives will be different. Maybe we will even go and live in Paris. It is so beautiful there. I have decided to learn French properly, and I'm starting evening classes next month.

You probably gathered if you got my postcard that Laurie came back, and this time he's going to stay. He says he'll marry me if he can get a divorce from his wife.

I know it's your busiest time, but please write if you have a minute. Even a postcard of the dreaded floral display! I miss you.
Love, Estella

She slept with Leo, Gemma thought. That's why the letter was so short. She was telling her sister, without actually telling her, and she wanted Shirley to say it was all right.

For the first time since she had begun reading the letters, she found herself wondering what Shirley's reply had been. She knew from her own experience as a correspondent that Shirley's letters were usually pretty standard one-pagers saying something jolly about the weather. She couldn't imagine how she would have reacted to Estella's confessions.

335

Feeling rather depressed, Gemma turned to the next letter. She noticed that although Estella usually seemed to write every month, this time there was a longer gap.

December 25th 1952
Dear Shirl,

I was so hoping that you would come up Christmas shopping like you did last year. I've been looking out for you at work. Sometimes I was so sure that this would be the day you came that I didn't go to the canteen for lunch but waited outside the doors in the cold for you. Anyway, I expect you've been busy.

I'm on my own this Christmas, Shirl. I didn't feel up to another Christmas in Jack and Georgina's freezing cold house, and the thought of kidney bean casserole again made me want to puke. Laurie's gone without me. I'm glad he did. It's given me a chance to write to you privately.

The thing is, Shirl, I think I may be pregnant. You know I've got that thing that Laurie gave me, well, I thought they were meant to last forever, but one of the girls at work told me that they weren't, and that you were meant to have them specially fitted for yourself by a doctor. She said I'd better have a close look at it, so I did, but when I held it up to the light there was this tiny hole, only like a pin prick in size. Do you think that would be enough?

I haven't come on since the end of September and you know you can normally set your watch by me. And now I feel sick the whole time. Maybe that's not a sign because it's only in the morning if you're pregnant, isn't it?

I was really frightened at first, but Laurie's had a bit of success with his exhibition and he's a lot happier these days. I don't know what he'll think. If my period still hasn't come, I'm going to tell him at New Year. Wish me luck, Shirl.

I was hoping that the reason you didn't come up to town at Christmas was that you've got good news in that department too . . . ?

I am thinking of you on Christmas Day and I'm raising my cup of tea to your health (tea's all I can keep down!).

Season's Greetings from Estella

February 1953
Dear Shirl,

It's official. I did a test at the doctor's and he said, 'Congratulations, Mrs Blair, you're going to have a baby, in July'! I hadn't really thought about it like there was a baby inside me, if you know what I mean. I walked home feeling very funny – like I should be terrified, but actually I felt really happy. Laurie wants me to see another doctor he knows, but I've told him that I couldn't do that. I think he'll come round. He's being very nice to me at the moment. I'd like to get married, but the trouble is his wife. It doesn't matter really because everyone thinks we're married, except some of the girls at work.

I think I felt it move today. It didn't feel like a baby, more like some butterflies in my tummy. It doesn't show yet, so it must still be quite small.

Please write with your news.

Love from Estella

March 1953
Dear Shirl,

Please come and see me. I don't know what I'm going to do. Laurie's left me for good. He said I was being very selfish wanting to have this baby at this time in his career. In the end I went to the doctor he suggested, but he was horrible and patronizing and I just couldn't go through with it. When I got back, Laurie had a fit. He said he couldn't be sure that it was his anyway. We said some things to each other that people should never say. He's gone now and I wouldn't have him back even if he begged.

The thing is everyone I know here is really Laurie's friend. Even Georgina said I should get rid of it, not because Laurie told me to, but for my sake as an independent woman, she says. I went to Leo because he's always been very understanding, but he just opened the till and pulled out a hundred pounds. I took the notes from him and tore them in two right in the middle of his bloody gallery. A bit of an expensive gesture that I'll

337

probably live to regret, but I felt a lot better after, I can tell you. I hate men, Shirl.

Please come as soon as you can because I want to ask you something face to face.

Your loving sister, Estella

And then there was a gap. Gemma looked at all the dates on the remaining letters, but there was nothing until the telegram six months later.

CHAPTER 28

They should have known better than to read letters from their mother together. Estella had come between them again. Just when she and Gemma had been beginning to get on so well.

Daisy wandered round the flat doing things. The pile of photocopies in the living room had become like a piece of difficult homework. She found herself creating diversions to put off the moment when she tackled it.

She kept going back to the last time they had read letters from Estella. Then, too, Gemma had waited for her.

She was sitting in the kitchen at Whitton House, staring into space, a row of mugs of tea the neighbours had made grown cold in front of her.

'Have a cup of tea!'

Everyone who visited the house said it, striding into the kitchen, trying to be useful, filling the heavy kettle on the range, not realizing how long it took to boil. Then standing, almost comically, shifting from foot to foot, wondering what to say for a half an hour.

Daisy was watching the undertakers carry the coffin down the stairs and out through the front door. They put it on a kind of collapsible metal trolley to wheel it through the front to the hearse. She remembered thinking what a silly kind of gadget it was, like something you might take on a camping holiday. She wanted to say, please carry her properly, but she didn't.

Then she stood and watched the hearse drive off down the lane and kept watching long after it had disappeared out of sight. She remembered thinking how wonderful the yellow roses smelt that climbed all over the front of the house.

Then she walked back into the kitchen. Gemma hadn't moved.

'She's gone,' Daisy said.

'I found these,' Gemma took two envelopes from the pocket of her dress. 'I'm meant to show them to the police, but I wanted us to read them first.' She slid the envelope with Daisy's name on it across the rough surface of the refectory table.

Daisy opened hers, read it and burst into tears. She pushed it across the table for Gemma to read too. 'What does yours say?' she asked, sniffing.

Gemma was still staring ahead of her, the piece of paper in her hand. Her skin had gone so white it was almost translucent and her eye sockets looked purple. She started shaking uncontrollably. Daisy leapt up and went to hold her, but Gemma threw her off with force, then she started howling, a horrible, primal sound. Daisy picked up Gemma's letter.

My dear Gemma,
This has nothing to do with you. Look after Daisy for me.
Much love, Estella

Too late, Daisy went to pick up her own letter, but Gemma's hand got to it first. And when she read it, the howling grew worse. Daisy was frightened. More frightened than she had been to see her mother dead. It sounded as if Gemma would never stop crying. Daisy thought she might be having a fit. She didn't know whether to call a doctor. She felt completely helpless.

'I know what you're thinking,' she kept telling her

340

sister, 'but it's not true. She did love you. And Bertie loved you so much. Much better than me. He really did.'

But nothing she said made any difference. Eventually Gemma got up and went to bed without saying a word. And Daisy sat up all night in the kitchen staring at the two letters, and wondering how her mother, whom she loved more than anyone in the world, could have been so cruel.

Daisy washed up the stack of cups in the kitchen and emptied the contents of the fridge into a grey dustbin liner. She preferred to remember Estella as she was in her prime, sweeping through the Uffizi gallery in a sea-green dress, talking Daisy through each painting just a little too loudly so that people shifted their gaze from Botticelli's *Graces* and stared at her.

The silly-sounding girl in the letters confused her. Her mother was beautiful, intelligent, above all, dignified. People were in awe of her. She had made a huge effort to expunge all the sordid traces of her youth, and Daisy thought they should respect that. It felt intrusive and wrong to read about her life in a dirty bedsit, using a second-hand diaphragm and still managing to get pregnant. How could she have been so stupid? Daisy didn't really want to know.

She vacuumed the living-room floor. Then she went out and bought all the Sunday papers, made herself a cup of coffee and sat down on the floor with the Review sections. From the kitchen came the drip-drip-dripping sound of the ice box slowly melting as the refrigerator defrosted.

There was an article comparing London life in the swinging Sixties to London life thirty years later. Was there no escape from nostalgia? It was illustrated with black and white photos of dolly birds in mini-skirts set against colour photos of the Safeways in the Kings

341

Road in the Nineties. Daisy decided she was sick of the Sixties, and sick of old bags turning up on television talking about zipless fucks and demonstrations in Paris. For all the talk of heightened consciousness and peace, what did anyone really achieve in that much celebrated decade?

She was fed up with people looking back and thinking the past was wonderful, and she was bored with people trying to find the reasons for things in their childhood. What good did it do? She wanted to live in the present and look towards something better in the future, not always be going backwards, like Gemma. If Daisy had her life again, she might do things differently, but she didn't and that was that.

It was a simple fact that Gemma didn't appear to understand. Estella was dead. Even if Gemma thought she could find out why she had been the person she was, what the hell difference did it make? The article began to blur in front of her eyes and Daisy flung the magazine aside in anger.

She decided it was time she tidied her desk. She opened a couple of bills that had arrived and wrote out cheques to cover them. She stacked the magazines neatly. She tore some old notes out of her ringbinder notebook and threw them in the wastepaper basket. The answerphone was full to capacity. Daisy had been meaning to listen to all the messages and write down the numbers she needed for some time. She pressed playback. Gemma's voice getting more and more cross with each message irritated her. Apart from that, most of the messages were for Oliver, including the one from Caroline she had so far failed to pass on. She supposed she ought to phone him at work and tell him. She supposed she ought to ask how he was getting on. Well, it was Sunday, so she couldn't. She wrote them down on a separate sheet.

The only other message for her was Cal Costelloe's

' grumpy question: 'If that is Daisy Rush's answer-phone, could she ring me?'

She thought of him in the film in his uniform. What was it about uniforms? Daisy smiled to herself and punched out the number he'd left. 'Can I speak to Cal Costelloe, please?' she asked.

'Who's looking for him?'

Daisy was rather taken aback by the gruffness of tone. If that was his PR, he should fire him.

'Daisy Rush.'

'I'll see if he's here,' said the voice, then she heard him shout, 'Cal, there's a girl on the phone for you. Are you in? Daisy something.'

And after a few seconds, Cal came to the phone, slightly breathless, as if he had been running. 'Daisy, how are you?'

'Fine,' said Daisy breezily, 'and you?'

'Fine,' he laughed.

'So, you called?' she asked. There was no response.

'I expect Patrick gave you my number,' she encouraged. If he was going to be cross with her, she might as well get it over with.

'He did.'

'So what's the problem?' Daisy finally asked.

Cal laughed again. 'I don't think there is a problem,' he replied lightly. 'I called to thank you for your article. I didn't know what to make of it, but I decided I should be flattered.'

Daisy remembered the paragraph about her fantasies before meeting Costelloe and felt herself blushing. 'Well, don't let it go to your head,' she said. 'Anyway, thank you for calling.'

'That was several weeks ago,' Cal said.

'I've been away on holiday. I only just got my messages,' Daisy explained, massaging the truth a little.

After a few moments' silence, she was about to say

343

goodbye, when he said, 'Look, we're about to have lunch here. Are you doing anything? Would you like to come over?'

'Well . . .' Daisy hesitated, she didn't really feel up to one of those parties. She had been to several 'informal' lunches or brunches given by film stars or people in the rock business. They were carefully designed to make journalists seem part of their circle so that they wouldn't feel able to write nasty things about them afterwards.

The food, however, she remembered, was usually delicious and American, like Eggs Benedict, or bagels with smoked salmon and cream cheese. There was usually Bloody Mary on tap.

It was the drip-drip-drip of her empty fridge that did it, and the thought of mopping up the pool of water from the ice box that was spreading across her kitchen floor. She wrote down the address, somewhat surprised by the unfashionable postcode.

The house was an unprepossessing semi in a cul-de-sac off Willesden Lane. The only thing that marked it out from its neighbours was a flashy-looking sports car parked in the road outside. The cab driver started moaning about not being able to turn round, so Daisy tipped him extravagantly, and wondered how it was that cab drivers always made her feel eternally grateful or guilty. She rang the bell.

A lanky boy of about twelve opened the door. 'Are you Daisy?' he asked. His voice was gruff because it was beginning to break.

'Yes.'

'Cal!' the boy shouted and turned away, leaving her standing on the doorstep.

Cal was wearing black jeans and a shirt even Daisy recognized as Manchester United's latest strip. 'You're very welcome,' he said, and held out his hand. Daisy shook it.

'You cut your hair,' he remarked softly as she squeezed past him into the narrow hallway, adding, 'It looks great.'

Daisy's hand went to her head. She felt rather exposed. If she had known she was visiting his parents' house, she wouldn't have chosen to wear her red crushed silk dress. Her eyes immediately took in the bits and pieces of Catholic kitsch on the walls, and she began to feel slightly sluttish, as she had once on holiday in Rome, when, wearing only a sleeveless T-shirt and shorts, she had been barred entry to St Peter's by a priest clad from head to foot in black.

Cal showed her through to the kitchen where his mother emerged from clouds of steam, manoeuvring a huge joint of meat from a baking tray to an oval serving plate. Pans of vegetables were boiling on the hob. A row of serving dishes stood ready to be filled. Daisy somehow knew that they had been set out especially for her.

'I'm pleased to meet you,' Cal's mother said, wiping a hand on her apron and smiling, revealing a row of perfect teeth, just like her son's.

'I'm very pleased to meet you,' Daisy replied. 'I thought it was going to be all media people,' she said with relief, adding quickly as she saw Mrs Costelloe's face fall, 'but this is so much nicer!'

There were five Costelloe children. Cal, the oldest, Desmond, the boy who had opened the door, twins Marie and Maeve, who were fifteen and very giggly, and his sister Nuala who had recently passed her driving test and for whom Cal had just bought the car outside. The car was obiously much admired by Nuala's fiancé, Joe, who was also sitting down for lunch, but it was causing Cal's mother grief.

'It'll be stolen within a week,' she said, after she had exhausted all the safety arguments.

'Find a garage,' Cal intervened. 'I'll pay for it.'

'Yes, that's the thing,' Daisy added, trying to be helpful. 'The main difficulty is parking. I never remember where I've left mine. I usually end up taking a cab.'

Cal looked at her and smiled.

'This is delicious, by the way,' Daisy said, heaping roast beef and gravy into her mouth. 'It's ages since I've had a proper Sunday lunch. In fact,' she continued cheerfully, 'I can't remember when I last ate a proper meal. Perhaps it was the octopus. Can't have been . . . I was in Greece,' she added, realizing that everyone was staring at her.

The twins had to put their hands in front of their mouths to stop themselves spraying food all over the tablecloth as they tried, unsuccessfully, to swallow their laughter.

'Do you live on your own, then?' Cal's father asked her.

Daisy hesitated, 'Well, yes, I suppose I do,' then flinched as Mr Costelloe suddenly shouted, 'If you can't behave, you can get down,' at the twins.

'You don't seem altogether sure about that.' He turned back to Daisy with a very winning smile. Daisy could see that he had once, not so long ago, been almost as sexy as his famous son.

'Well, the thing is, I've been living with someone for years, but we've separated recently, and I'm not really used to my new status yet,' Daisy explained.

'So that was the man on the answerphone?' Cal asked, as if it was a question that had been puzzling him.

That was the reason he had sounded so laconic on the phone, Daisy realized, telling herself to remember to record her own message as soon as she got back. She looked up and caught Cal exchanging glances with his father. They've been talking about me before, she thought.

Daisy could remember only one other occasion on which she was taken home to meet the parents. She was fourteen and the boy's name was Charlie Walton, the younger brother of one of Gemma's many beaux. Daisy had felt throughout the tea that she was being compared, unfavourably, with her older sister. It made her chatter too much. Charlie never asked her out again.

She had met Oliver's parents only once. On his father's seventieth birthday, Oliver had invited them both down to London. They had stayed at the Waldorf where they all met for a drink before going on to see *Don Giovanni* at Covent Garden. His father had spent most of the interval loudly comparing the performance to one he had seen Opera North do a few years before. Oliver, visibly struggling to contain his anger, had become morose and silent. His mother said very little until Daisy had found herself washing her hands beside her in the Ladies' when she had asked Daisy anxiously, 'Is Oliver happy with his life?'

'I think so,' Daisy had replied, thinking what an odd question it was, since it managed to be insulting to her and inappropriate for him at the same time. Happiness was almost too trivial an emotion to associate with Oliver. 'Well, as happy as he is able to be,' she continued. 'He's got such a gloomy side to him, hasn't he?' she added, lightly, attempting a shared intimacy to allow the mother space to talk.

She saw a flicker of recognition pass over his mother's freshly powdered face, then fade. 'Has he?' she asked, dispassionately, as if it were a character trait he must have developed since leaving home.

And Daisy had thought, well, you're either completely insensitive or a hypocrite, or both, and Oliver is right about you.

'Will you have some more crumble?' Mrs Costelloe asked.

'Yes, please,' said Daisy, and was rewarded with a smile by Desmond, who otherwise would have been the only person eating seconds of the pudding.

What fun it was to sit down to a meal with a family. Daisy had almost forgotten what it was like. Even though it was only a glimpse, she thought she could tell quite a lot about how the Costelloe family operated, just as anyone who had come to Whitton House for supper would have seen the dynamics of the Rush family.

Estella had been ostensibly in control, just as Mr Costelloe was here, but in fact the real power was wielded by the quiet one. Bertie didn't often demonstrate his authority, but when he did, you knew it, just as you would, she suspected, if Mrs Costelloe felt strongly about something. Generally, Daisy got on better with people who were up-front and loud, rather than retiring and manipulative.

Which parent did Cal take after, she wondered? He looked like his father, but he seemed more of an observer than a participant at the table. She could sense that he was getting restless, eager for the meal to be over.

Daisy scraped the last trace of custard from her bowl and put down her spoon.

'I'm glad to see a girl enjoying her food,' Cal's father said, glancing meaningfully at the twins who had only picked at their lunch and refused dessert. They looked at each other and raised their eyes to the ceiling. 'I'm very glad you could join us today, Daisy,' he continued, 'it's a special meal for us because it'll be a while before we're all together again.'

'Oh?'

'I'm off to America tomorrow,' Cal explained.

'Really?' Daisy said, trying to sound interested in a non-committal kind of way. 'How long for?'

'Not sure,' he said, scraping back his chair and standing up. 'Would you like to go for a walk?'

'What about the match?' Desmond asked him anxiously. 'It's nearly time.'

'I'll see it later,' Cal said.

'But Cal . . .' Desmond protested.

'He'll watch it later,' their father intervened and Desmond clammed up immediately.

'What match is that?' Daisy asked, as they walked along the street together.

'I sometimes wonder what planet you live on,' Cal said, 'it's Cup Final day.'

'Oh! Well, you must watch it,' Daisy protested, 'really. I'll watch it too, if you like . . .'

Cal smiled at her. 'Would you do that for me, Daisy Rush?' he asked, in a sing-song lilting Irish voice.

'Only because it's your last day in the country,' she replied, not wanting to appear too soft.

He chuckled. 'I'll see it later. But if they lose I'll know who to blame. By the way, this is off the record?'

'Heart-throb eats roast beef followed by rhubarb crumble?' Daisy laughed. 'Oh I don't know whether I could keep a scoop like that to myself . . .' Then seeing his face fall, she added, 'Of course it is . . .'

'It's just . . . why didn't you come to the screening I invited you to?' he suddenly asked, quite aggressively.

'Was that you? Oh, well, I was away . . .'

'And why didn't you return my call until today?'

'I forgot it was there. I thought you were going to give me a hard time about that interview . . . I don't know . . . Why are you interrogating me?'

'It's just that I've been thinking about you ever since we met . . .' he blurted out. 'When I didn't hear from you, I thought . . . and then today, you're here, and I don't have any time any more . . . I want to see you . . .'

'But you're going to Hollywood,' Daisy said,

confused by his outburst. It was so uncool, so young, so utterly un-filmstarry.

'Come with me!' he said to her, grabbing her hand.

It was the first physical contact she had had with him and it felt momentous. Daisy stared at the hand clasping hers. It was a nice dry hand attached to an attractive, masculine wrist. She knew she ought to say something, but she could think of nothing except that the time on his watch was just gone three.

'I was walking down the Kilburn High Road past McDonalds at five minutes past three on the FA Cup Final day, when we fell in love,' she imagined herself saying one day.

'Daisy?' he asked her, breaking the silence.

'This is silly,' Daisy said, 'you hardly know me, and I hardly know you. This sort of thing doesn't happen . . . not even in the movies,' she said, half-expecting him to disappear or shout 'Joke!'

She closed her eyes, took a deep breath, then opened them and he was still there, walking beside her, looking very boyish in his red soccer shirt with a number 7 on the back.

'How old are you?' Daisy asked him.

'Twenty-three,' he replied. 'Why?'

'Well, I'm far too old for you,' Daisy said, 'I'm twenty-eight.'

'I like older women,' he said, grinning mischievously.

She remembered photos of him with Eliza Beth.

'Well, I don't like toy boys,' she said cattily.

'You bitch,' he replied pleasantly.

'Five minutes into the relationship and we're having our first row,' Daisy quipped. 'I said it would never work.'

'So, we are having a relationship, then?' Cal pounced on the word.

'Well . . . no . . . this is ridiculous.'

Surreal. She was standing on a grotty inner-city thoroughfare with diesel exhausts blowing in her face, wearing a flimsy cocktail dress and being wooed by one of Britain's sexiest men.

'Why don't you buy your parents a nice house in a better area?' she asked him.

'I've bought them a place in Portugal. And they don't want to move. Their friends are here. OK? Any more questions?'

'Do you do this with every woman you meet?'

'No!' He looked hurt.

She had seen that expression the night before in the Screen on the Hill when he was refused a dance. How would she ever tell whether he meant something, or was just acting?

Daisy stopped outside a furniture store and looked in the window. There was nothing worth looking at, but it was easier to talk to his reflection in the plate glass than to face him. 'Cal, I really fancy you, and I don't know whether you're serious, but if you are, and this isn't some sort of practical joke, then I have to tell you that I don't want a relationship at the moment. I've just been in one for ten years and it didn't make me happy . . . and I'm sure it would be different with you . . . but at the moment I need a bit of space for myself and before I start sounding like something out of a Woody Allen movie . . .'

'Just a fuck would do then,' he interrupted, with a shrug of his shoulders.

Then she did turn and look at him straight on, and he held the cocky wide-boy expression just long enough to convince her, before holding up his hands to protect his face and shouting, 'That was a joke, Daisy,' as she chased him down the street.

After a couple of hundred yards, he let her catch him up and slap his arm, then he grabbed her hand and drew her to him and kissed her. Then she did know that he meant it, and she wondered, as she kissed him back with fervour, holding his beautiful face in her hands, why on earth she had been so uncharacteristically circumspect?

'We had our first snog outside Mr Cod,' she thought to herself as she opened her eyes and looked at the sign above Cal's head. It was the sort of thing you'd win a free CD for on a radio phone-in when the DJ was getting desperate – 'Ring and tell me the *least* romantic place *you've* had a magic moment . . .'

CHAPTER 29

Estella Smith and Bertie Rush
request the pleasure of your company
to celebrate their marriage
at Chelsea Register Office
on
24th December 1962

At the bottom of the card, Estella had written,

*Please come, Shirl. Vin's agreed to be a witness, and we'd like
you to be the other one. Here's £50 to get yourself a decent
outfit. Think of it as the money you leant me when I left home. E.*
P.S. For God's sake, don't wear a hat.

It was the last item in the shoe box. The end of the
story. Except that even this very brief note raised new
questions. Did Shirley go to the wedding? Who was
Vin? Was this really the first communication between
the sisters since Estella's letter saying that she wouldn't
be coming to their father's funeral?

Gemma put the card down, got up from the desk,
stretched and went to the sink to run herself a glass of
water. The sun was going in, but she had no idea what
time it was. She had been reading the letters all day,
some of them twice and three times. The long, long
letter Estella had sent after her baby was born had made
her cry.

It was the last full-length letter. After that, communication had become rather sporadic. From reading just one side of the correspondence, Gemma gathered that Shirley had given up writing back until 1958, when their father died.

It was during those five years that Estella must have changed. The terse, sarcastic note she had sent saying that, since he couldn't stand the sight of her when he was alive, she doubted whether her father would appreciate her presence at his funeral, was the voice of the Estella that Gemma had known. But now that she knew what her mother had been through, she understood it better and sympathized. She wished she had her back for just half an hour to tell her that. Not, she had to remind herself, that she had ever been able to be much comfort to Estella.

Infuriatingly, there were still so many gaps, so many questions Gemma was itching to ask. Did Estella ever see Laurie again? How did she meet Bertie? And who was Vin? Gemma knew she would have to pay Shirley another visit the next weekend.

Reluctantly, she replaced the top on the shoe box, took it upstairs, and hid it under the bed. She wanted it out of sight. If it sat in her living-room, she would keep going back to it, driving herself mad with wondering. Now she wanted company to distract her and take her out of the half-imaginary, half-remembered world she had inhabited all day. Her head felt full and confused, as if she had drunk too much red wine on a hot afternoon.

She wished that Ralph would come back now and suggest somewhere wonderful for dinner. She looked out into the mews, half-expecting to see him loping towards her, but there was nothing out there except shadows.

She picked up the phone and rang Jonathan. He wasn't in.

She tried Kathy's number. It rang for a long time, then, just as Gemma was about to give up, a man answered, 'Hello?'

'Roger?' Gemma asked, wanting it to be, but knowing immediately it wasn't.

'No, he's away. Can I take a message?' Oliver, on his best behaviour.

'Could you tell Kathy I called, it's Gemma,' she said.

'Gemma! We can't go on *not* meeting like this! Every time you call someone these days, you seem to get me by mistake! They've gone on holiday and left me all alone here. I'm bored, so talk to me . . .' he commanded, winningly, as if it was only yesterday that they had been sharing a house together.

A shiver of *déjà vu* trickled down Gemma's spine. She pictured his long languid body sinking back into Kathy's Habitat sofa and remembered him lying on the collapsed sofa in the front room at Boulter Street, demanding entertainment in much the same way. Then, she had felt inadequate, as if nothing she could possibly say would interest him. Now, she felt she must get off the phone before she said something disastrous.

'Tell me about your life these days,' Oliver persisted. 'How is the great world of literature?'

'I really can't talk now,' Gemma said quickly.

'But I thought you were ringing Kathy for a chat,' he replied, picking up her mistake instantly.

Still as sharp as ever, Gemma thought. No wonder he had become a lawyer. She would hate to be cross-examined by him. He had always been able to see through her. It was one of the reasons she had persuaded herself that he must, at some unconscious level at least, love her. There had been times when he seemed to be in possession of her soul.

'Well, not really,' she backtracked lamely. However could she have forgotten that Kathy was going away? 'I was just ringing to arrange to see her for a drink.'

'Well, come over and have a drink with me, why don't you?' Oliver said.

It was as if he had sensed a weakness, and was prepared to push to see how far she would go before cracking.

'I can't. I'm busy this evening.'

'Well, on which day are you not busy?' Oliver asked, throwing the initiative back to her, making it impossible to refuse without sounding rude or hysterical. 'Why don't we go to the American Bar at the Savoy? See if they can whip up a tolerable Manhattan. I'm sure you're an expert on Manhattans, aren't you?' She couldn't work out whether he was really encouraging her, or just teasing.

'Tuesday . . .' she said flustered.

She couldn't see any other way of getting off the phone. She told herself she would ring to cancel the next day, and, by then, he would have found some other person to toy with.

'Tuesday at six,' Oliver said, satisfied. 'I'll see you there. Do you want me to leave a message?'

'A message?' Gemma asked.

'For Kathy,' he said, as if he had caught her out again.

'Of course, well, yes, if that's OK . . .' Gemma said, her voice trailing off as she realized he had already replaced the receiver. She put down her phone and stared at it.

'Who are you meeting?' Ralph asked, and deposited a kiss on the back of her neck.

She hadn't heard him come in. He smelt of mown grass and beer and his face was red from the sun. She turned and kissed him back, closing her eyes, not wanting to catch his. 'Someone I used to share with at college.'

Now was not the time to tell him about Oliver. There

was nothing to tell anyway, she repeated inwardly. She was over all that.

'I'll just go shower, if I may,' Ralph said.

'Of course. Shall we go out to that Spanish place for dinner when you're through? I've been sitting here all day reading and I'm stir crazy and very hungry!'

He nodded. 'Great idea,' he said.

Life was so easy with Ralph, she thought. Ask him a direct question and he answered directly. She never felt that she had to manoeuvre round him, trying to second guess what he was wanting, as she had with other men. He knew that there was enough that was interesting in life without having to create problems. She liked his confidence, the fact that he knew who he was.

So why, she wondered, couldn't she tell him that she had just been speaking to a man who was as capricious as he was charismatic, who made her feel small and ignorant, but whose voice alone left her wobbly with excitement, and whose insistence on meeting her for a drink had made her imagine, once again, that he was her destiny?

'I think that Estella must have asked Shirley whether she would like to adopt the baby,' Gemma said.

Although she hadn't really wanted to go through it all again, Ralph had insisted that she relate the full story of her mother's letters to him, and she was glad he had, because talking out loud about it had crystallized some of the amorphous thoughts that had been buzzing in her head. It was as if she was sorting an untidy heap of papers into neat files.

'And Shirley obviously said she would, but then Estella changed her mind,' Gemma elaborated. 'There's this long letter, absolutely heart-wrenching, about how she didn't realize how much she would love him . . . it was a boy . . . and how she knows that if she

357

can't have him, then she just can't bear Shirley to have him . . . that it would be worse than not knowing where he was.' Ralph nodded, listening intently. 'And then she says she couldn't let him grow up in the small town she hated so much, under the same roof as her father . . .'

'She really hated that pretty little town, didn't she?' Ralph remarked.

Gemma sniffed and nodded. 'Then,' she continued, 'the saddest thing is that she says that she knows that she will lose the two things that are most important to her: her baby, and her sister's love, but she's doing it so that he will have a better life . . . and the letter ends something like . . . "This is the only selfless thing I've done in my life, Shirl, so please try to forgive me."'

Gemma wiped her eyes with the back of her hand.

Ralph offered her one of the little paper napkins from the box on the table. A gesture can make you love someone, she thought. He looks after me. He cares for me. He is a good man.

The waiter arrived with the tapas they had ordered. Ralph waited until he had deposited all the little plates on the table. He picked up an anchovy-stuffed olive and put it in his mouth and chewed, thoughtfully, as if digesting everything she had said. 'I suppose it was a big deal to Shirley because she couldn't have kids herself.'

'It must have been. Also, reading between the lines, I think that Shirley must have fought off a lot of opposition to the plan from somebody, probably their father. I don't know about Uncle Ken. But most of all, I think she desperately wanted a baby.'

'She took something from me that I wanted very much,' Shirley had said.

In those days, Gemma imagined, there wouldn't have been much help for infertile couples. No *in vitro* fertilization, no sophisticated hormone treatment, no surrogacy, no hope, except an unenforceable arrangement between two sisters.

Poor Shirley. And poor Estella. Perhaps it explained why she had been so very unmotherly to her next child. Perhaps she had been disappointed with a fair little girl after that beautiful dark-haired bouncing boy she described with so much love.

'I thought babies weren't supposed to have hair,' she had written, 'but he does, lots, just like me . . .'

'She saw herself in the child,' Ralph said. 'How devastating to have to give that up . . .'

'And then she lost the only support she had in Shirley . . .' Gemma faltered, overcome with guilt.

In her final request, Estella had asked her to look after Daisy, but she had ignored her. She had abandoned her, just as Shirley had abandoned Estella. It wasn't the same, she kept trying to reassure herself. Daisy had everything she wanted. Estella had had nothing and nobody, until Bertie came along to rescue her.

Gemma ate a forkful of tortilla. The food had gone cold, and her appetite had disappeared.

'Did you call your sister?' Ralph asked her, uncannily tapping into her thoughts.

'Not yet,' Gemma said, looking at her watch. It was late, but not too late for Daisy.

'Call her now. I'll get the check,' Ralph said.

Gemma hurried gratefully from the restaurant.

'I think that I'll take a day off tomorrow and go to see Shirley,' Gemma said to him later as she towel-dried her hair.

Daisy had not been in. She couldn't say what she wanted to say to an answerphone. Especially not one which still had a message recorded by Oliver.

'Good idea. Do you want me to come with you?' Ralph asked. He was sitting up in her bed, watching her.

'No thanks. I mean, thanks but no thanks. I think it's going to be difficult enough to get Shirley to talk about all this. She might be more nervous with a stranger around . . . I don't mean . . .'

'You don't have to explain,' he said kindly. 'I don't know what other men have done to you, Gemma, but you don't have to be so defensive with me . . . I understand why you wouldn't want me there, and I'm not hurt . . . OK?'

'Yes,' she said, relieved.

'Come here,' he said, pulling back the sheet to let her into bed. She snuggled up to his chest. He smelt nice and soapy from his shower.

'Why is it that you always wash your hair when you're tense?' he asked her, smoothing away damp strands from her forehead.

'Do I?'

'You do.'

'Maybe it's because Estella once poured tinned fruit all over it when she was cross with me?'

'She did what?'

'Well, I was on fire . . .' Gemma said.

Ralph laughed loudly. 'She surely was a character, wasn't she?'

'Yes.' Gemma felt tears welling up again. She began to sob.

'There, there,' Ralph said, stroking her arm.

She took it as a signal that he wanted to make love. She began to stroke him back, sniffing away the tears. She felt grateful to him for being so nice to her.

'Hey!' he said, as she touched his thigh. He drew her gently away from him. 'We don't have to do that, you know. Every time I touch you doesn't mean that I want to fuck you . . .'

'You don't?' she looked at him.

'Well, of course I do, but not when you're exhausted. You've had a tough day, Gemma.'

She relaxed in his arms. It was lovely to be held and cherished.

'It's a long process,' Ralph said to her.

'What is?' she asked, sleepily.

'Getting you to trust me.'

She smiled and he kissed her on the nose. 'Do you trust me?' she asked him, but she was asleep before he answered, 'Of course I do.'

CHAPTER 30

'At last I've found someone to make an honest woman of me, Shirl.'

The flat south-coast accent had almost disappeared, but the hug was as warm and enthusiastic as ever. She held on for a long time, until Shirley started to feel embarrassed and pushed her gently away.

Estella had been waiting for her at the end of the platform. When she saw her standing there, Shirley thought how kind it was of her to take the time to meet her on her wedding morning when she surely had better things to do. After spending most of the war years there, it wasn't as if she would be lost in London.

Later, on the train home, when she recalled the expression of undisguised relief that flickered over her sister's face when she caught sight of her, she realized that Estella had been there to check her appearance. The thought made her smile. Stell was cutting her off at the pass! The relaxed hour they had spent together in a coffee bar drinking strong fresh coffee from glass cups and saucers could so easily have been a frantic search for suitable clothes, had Shirley been wearing the wrong things.

She was pleased that the plain dark-green shift and jacket, and the black and green paisley silk scarf she had bought for the occasion had come up to her sister's rigorous standards. She had chosen the colours knowing Stell would approve of them. The dress had hung on its padded hanger on the door of their wardrobe until Ken said, 'Why d'you have to buy that gloomy old thing. It's a wedding, i'n't it, not a funeral?'

He just couldn't understand it. If it had been up to him the fivers Stell had sent would have gone back with a note telling her where she could stuff her bloody wedding invitation. But Shirley had been adamant.

'It does you no good to bear a grudge all your life,' she told him, 'and you mustn't mind her sending me money. Stell was never shy of hurting people's feelings, but she doesn't mean any harm . . .'

'Well, you wouldn't catch me going,' he retorted.

And Shirley had stopped short of telling him that was just as well because he conspicuously wasn't invited.

Privately, Shirley was rather pleased with the way she looked in the dress. It slimmed her down. She had tried it on several times in front of the wardrobe mirror in the bedroom, straining her head to see the back view, smoothing the fine wool gaberdine over her pelvic bones and experimenting with different ways of tying the scarf. The fact that Ken didn't approve almost made her like it more.

She hadn't thought twice about the invitation. She had known from the moment she had opened it that she would go. Ten years of unresolved anger and sadness just floated away. Of course she must be her sister's witness. Who else was there to give her away?

She liked Bertie the moment she set eyes on him, when she and Stell walked into the register office. They were a bit late and you could tell he'd been wondering whether she would turn up. It was as transparent as that. He was a bit older than she had expected. But you forgot about that when he talked to you because he was a real charmer and made you feel that there was no-one else in the world he would rather be speaking to. As a matter of fact, she thought he wouldn't have minded a bit what she had been wearing. He probably wouldn't have even noticed.

'I must be the luckiest man in the world,' he told Shirley after the ceremony, and he really looked as if he meant it.

In the coffee bar on the King's Road that morning, Estella had explained how they met. She had started going to evening classes in art and he was her teacher. 'Don't know what it is about me and art teachers,' she remarked drily, seeing her sister's look of horror. 'No, honestly, Shirl, he's nothing like Laurie . . .'

One evening they happened to be walking to the tube together, and he asked if she would like a coffee. It became a bit of a habit. Soon it was two coffees, then a meal. Just talking, Stella insisted, nothing but talking. She had never met anyone like him. He was so interesting, so *simpatico*. Shirley hadn't known what that meant, so Stella explained.

Then, one evening, he was saying goodbye to her at the tube when he reached forward and put his hand under her chin, as if he were about to judge a piece of sculpture. He looked at her with such tenderness, Stell said, she thought he was about to cry. He told her quietly and seriously he had fallen in love with her, but that he could not leave his wife and child because, he said, they had committed no crime other than to love him.

After that, Estella told her sister, she had decided it would be best to stop going to class. Shirley had raised her eyebrows at that bit. It sounded a bit restrained for Stella, but she swore it was the truth. They hadn't seen each other for two months, she protested, and she assumed she would never see him again. Until one evening, at closing time, he came into the restaurant where she was manageress, presented her with an armful of roses and declared, much to the amusement of Vincenzo, that he would never forgive himself if he lost her.

That weekend he drove her out to the country for a picnic and parked near a beautiful country house with an overgrown garden. After they had eaten their sandwiches, he asked her whether she would like a closer look at the house. Thankful she had worn jeans rather than a frock, she climbed over the fence behind him and followed him through the brambles stealthily, keeping her head down so as not to be seen from the house. There was an unmown tennis court and a swimming pool covered in green slime. Estella whispered how shocking it was that the owners kept the place in such a state. He had chuckled. They approached the house, ducking through the under-growth, like two army cadets on an assault course. There was a greenhouse built on to the back, but the plants inside were dried out and brown. Bertie pushed open the door. It creaked, and Estella jumped.

'D'you think it's deserted?' she asked, nervously, half expecting an irate owner to come out at any minute and shoo them away like naughty children.

'Let's see,' Bertie said, bravely.

In the kitchen there was a huge refectory table and a dripping stone sink. They stood there, watching the dust motes dance in the sunlight.

Then Bertie had said, 'Do you think you could be happy here?'

She hadn't known he was rich until then, Estella told her sister, several times. Teachers weren't, were they? He always dressed so shabbily, and his jackets had leather patches on the elbows. But she was to discover that he only taught evening classes because he liked the company. Being an illustrator was too solitary a life for him.

Would Estella, he asked, taking her hand in his, be prepared to share his life and fill this lovely house with colour and life?

Shirley realized that she had been staring at the morning paper without reading a word. Estella had been happy there, for more than twenty years, she thought. She had made the house her own, with her own taste and furnishings. She had become quite the lady of the manor, and it suited her. Until Bertie died. Then she had been so overcome with grief that she couldn't go on. That's what Shirley had always told herself anyway. It was the only logical explanation.

Unless you knew Stella. Because if you knew her, you knew it couldn't be that simple. Stella was a survivor. Distraught at the loss of the man she loved who had given her so much? Of course she was. But suicidal?

Shirley poured herself a cup of tea. It had gone cold, but she drank it anyway. Then she washed up her breakfast things. The flat looked clean and tidy. She wondered whether there was time to give it a quick going-over with the vacuum cleaner. She needed something to occupy herself. Her palms were sweaty, and she didn't think it was because of the heat.

She had expected to hear from Gemma sooner. She had been prepared for a visit at the weekend, then nothing happened, and she had begun to wonder whether something was wrong. She knew her niece would have questions. Gemma was thorough. She always had been. So why was she taking so long?

Then, she had called, first thing in the morning and said she was taking the day off work, and suddenly it seemed too soon, and Shirley felt panicked all over again.

She decided to go and lie on the bed. It was cool in the bedroom with the curtains still drawn. The front of the doll's house was closed. The novelty of it had soon worn off, and she thought what an old fool she had been to buy it. It was a pretty ornament, and now that Gemma had found herself a nice man, well, maybe one day there would be a great niece to give it to. Shirley closed her eyes and tried to relax.

During the first long winter of the war, when they were cooped up in the room above the shop, Stella used to make her play the wishing game.

Stella's dreams were always more ambitious than Shirley's. While Shirley's imagination could only extend to wishing for a bicycle, Stella had wanted a car with a driver.

'I want to wave from the back seat like the little princesses,' she said, after seeing a newsreel of the Royal Family visiting the East End.

Shirley had coveted a pale-blue velvet dress she had seen in the town's department store; Stella had yearned for the sort of wardrobe you walk into, with rows of clothes on rails, all neatly sorted and stuffed at the shoulders with tissue paper, and pairs of leather shoes with matching handbags in soft cotton covers to keep them clean.

Shirley dozed, letting the images flutter around in her head.

Stella had achieved a real dream house with roses growing round the door. She had married a rich man. Stella used to count the stones on her plate when they had eaten rice pudding and prunes for tea. Tinker, tailor, soldier, sailor, rich man. Sometimes Shirley suspected that Stella counted the fruit as she spooned them onto her plate, but it never occurred to her to resent her sister's wealth and freedom. Stella had always been special.

Shirley visited Whitton House a couple of times after the wedding. It *was* lovely there. When Gemma was born, she went up for a week to help out. But she knew, without Stella ever mentioning anything, that she didn't really feel comfortable when Shirley was there.

Stella had put herself in a different world with her lah-di-dah accent and manners. They had a different way of doing things, little things, like laying the table the right way. The sharp intake of breath when Shirley forgot, followed by the rapid rearrangement of spoon and knife, spoke louder than any words of criticism.

Shirley was acutely aware that she didn't have the right conversation for the friends who were always dropping in – colleagues of Bertie's, and the fashionable set Stella had cultivated in the very à la mode restaurant she had run, artists and writers and bohemian types who nevertheless seemed to have lots of money. They bought their clothes in the King's Road and talked a lot about nuclear disarmament. It didn't escape her notice that Stella never introduced her as her sister. Once, when she inadvertently made a reference to the chip shop, she saw Stella wince with embarrassment. She never understood why she had to do so much pretending, especially as they all talked so much about a Labour government and the end of the class system. But that was just her way.

Shirley went back to the coast and voted Conservative as usual, and was pleased that her sister seemed to have found contentment at last. Occasionally Stella would ring, late at night, and talk to her. Sometimes, if she closed her eyes and cupped the receiver, it was just like the old times, when they used to share a bedroom and chatter to each other in the dark. When Stella sent her daughter down each year, Shirley got a version of what life was like at Whitton House. Gemma became the innocent messenger between their two worlds.

The sharp buzz of the doorbell woke Shirley up. She sat up slowly, collected herself, and went to greet her favourite niece.

*   *   *

'What I don't understand,' Gemma said, taking another biscuit from the tin, 'is why you decided it was time to let us learn all this about our mother.'

The questions had been easy until this one. There had been some surprises, like Gemma's interest in Vincenzo, the suave Italian restaurateur who had picked Estella out from behind the counter at Lyons and made her waitress, and eventually manageress, at his smart London restaurant, La Piazza, or Estella's, as it had been colloquially known among the *cognoscenti*. Shirley had never really known what their relationship was. She had observed that there were tears in his eyes when Stella and Bertie exchanged vows, but she had put it down to his being foreign.

Most of it Gemma had clearly worked out. Shirley had no idea what had happened to her side of the correspondence. Estella had probably thrown it all away. She had lived in so many different addresses between Laurie and Bertie. Anyway, she didn't think that her letters would have added much. Stella had a knack of writing a letter as if she was talking to you. Shirley had always found it difficult to say something different about her life each time. As far as she remembered, all the notes she sent went something like 'weather's been nice, business not bad for the time of year . . .'

'Shirley?' Gemma said, snapping her back from her memories. 'Are you all right?'

'Well,' she began, 'there's one thing you haven't asked that I expected you to . . .' Gemma frowned and waited for her to continue. 'You haven't asked me what happened to Estella's baby boy . . .'

'I thought he was adopted?' Gemma said.

'Well, yes, he was, but that's not the end of the story, is it? Wouldn't you like to know what became of your brother after that?'

369

Brother. It hadn't occurred to Gemma to think of him as a brother. She thought of him as a little baby. Not even as a man, as he must be now. She did a quick calculation. A man of over forty. She had another older brother. And he must now be more or less exactly the same age as Jonathan. How weird! No wonder Estella had hated having Jonathan around so much.

'Do you know what became of him, then?' she asked, fascinated. 'Surely, in those days people were just adopted and that was that. It's only recently that the child's had a right to know about his birth mother, isn't it?'

'Yes, quite recently, I think,' Shirley said, 'but I think the law applies to all ages.'

'What are you saying, exactly, Auntie?' Gemma asked. Her heart had started to beat faster, with a mixture of fear and excitement.

'Stell had him adopted. She never told me until after. You know that?'

'Yes, I know that,' Gemma said, as patiently as she could.

She wanted her aunt to get on with the facts. She seemed to keep backtracking. Gemma couldn't tell whether it was deliberate repetition, or old age making her forget what she'd just said.

'Yes, well, that's all in the past . . . I never knew who had adopted him, I didn't ask. I never talked to Stell about it again, but I don't think that she knew either,' Shirley rambled on. 'They always tried to get the kids a better home, you know, a Christian home, and he was a beautiful baby by all accounts . . .' Shirley's eyes filled with tears. 'Thanks,' she said as Gemma handed her a tissue.

'Please, Auntie, go on,' Gemma pleaded.

Shirley took a deep breath. 'A couple of months ago, I got a letter from social services saying that my adopted son wanted to meet me . . .' She looked up. Gemma's mouth had fallen open.

'They'd used our maiden name . . . that was on his birth certificate, I suppose. I never knew whether she put down the father's name,' Shirley said, in danger of losing the drift again. 'The letter was meant for Stell . . . I tore it up.'

'Why didn't you tell me?' Gemma interrupted.

'Hold your horses . . .' Shirley was clearly going as fast as she could.

Gemma could see it was hard for her. She told herself to keep calm, but it was becoming increasingly difficult to be patient.

'Well, this was what I thought,' Shirley continued. 'If they don't know she's passed away, they must be a long way off . . .' – she paused – '. . . but then, you see, after a few weeks another letter came, except this time they'd done their homework, tracked me down, and they were asking me for information. So I wrote to them. I told them Stella's dead now and it's all best forgotten . . .'

'But . . .'

'Hang on . . . they don't give up, you see . . . so I had a think about it. Consulted my conscience, if you like. The thing is, Gemma, I had promised Stell, you see, but then I thought, well, maybe it's not up to me anyway. The boy's got two sisters. It's up to you to decide whether you want to meet him . . . but I wanted you to know about Stell first,' she added, 'so that you didn't think badly of her, you see . . .'

'But of course I wouldn't . . .' Gemma began to protest, then stopped.

A couple of weeks before, she remembered, she had hardly been able to speak Estella's name for fury. Now that she felt she knew her better, she was sad that their mother hadn't been able to trust them all with the truth. There had been so many evasions in her life. The difficulty with lies was that they required a scaffolding of other lies to hold them up. The truth would have been so much simpler.

'Did my father know about the baby?' Gemma asked.

'I don't think so. No, I'm sure he didn't.'

In her head Shirley could hear Estella's voice the morning of her wedding, 'Promise you won't tell, Shirl, promise!'

And Estella's voice, years later, the night she died, 'Promise, Shirl, you will never tell anyone . . .'

'Go to bed, Stell, we'll talk in the morning,' she had replied inadequately.

'Promise me . . .'

It was the last thing she heard her say.

Now she had broken that promise she was almost expecting something momentous to happen: a thunderbolt to strike her down, a heart attack, perhaps. But nothing happened. The carriage clock the Shop-keepers' Guild had given them on their twenty-fifth wedding anniversary ticked softly. It was the only sound in the perfectly still room.

Eventually, Gemma said, 'Well, I know I would like to meet my brother, and I'm sure Daisy would too, but I'll have to ask her . . .' Shirley looked at her, picking up on her hesitation straightaway. 'We've had a bit of a falling out,' Gemma admitted, 'I think I've been a bit silly really . . .'

When she thought about what Daisy had done to annoy her so much, it seemed so trivial. She had read a couple of letters a little sooner than Gemma would have liked her to. On the scale of things, that hardly amounted to much of a sin. She felt ashamed of herself.

'Things get out of proportion in families,' Shirley said, understanding, 'but you're lucky to have a sister, Gemma. It's the best relationship of all. Oh, they can annoy you all right. They can drive you mad. And they can hurt you, worse than anyone else. But if I could have anyone I've loved back, I'd choose Stell straightaway. I shouldn't say that, should I? Poor old Ken. But, I'm telling you, Gemma, there's no love like it.'

CHAPTER 31

It was so hot that there was a haze hanging over London like a fine grey cobweb. Smog, Daisy thought, sitting down on a park bench, is what you get in Los Angeles. In the sky above the city she counted four planes, with even spaces between them, glinting in the sun.

Daisy wondered whether he was on one of them, then realized that they were stacking up to land, not taking off. By now he would be somewhere over the Atlantic, sipping warm white wine from a plastic cup and picking over his little tray of food, trying to match each soggy item with what it said on the menu card. Wrong again, she thought, and switched him to first class, where he was drinking champagne from a crystal flute, asking the smiling hostess who fancied him to put a pillow under his head, kicking off his shoes, stretching out his toes, marvelling at the space between the seats.

She had never travelled first class, but she had seen the adverts. It seemed an awful lot of money for a bit of extra leg room and a free sponge bag with a trial-sized cologne.

She imagined him opening his leather-bound menu and considering his choices. She wondered if, at altitude, smoked salmon tasted the same as caviar, the way the chicken always tasted the same as the beef. She envisaged him opening the courtesy copy of the *International Herald Tribune*, failing to recognize any news story, feigning interest for a few minutes so that the businessman in the next seat wouldn't think him a total lightweight, before folding it up and shutting his eyes to doze.

Daisy closed her eyes and held her face up to the sun. Was he thinking of her now, up there, as she was thinking of him? Or had he given in to sleep the way her body wanted to, but her brain wouldn't allow? And if he was thinking of her, were the thoughts just in his head, or were they all over his body, like hers seemed to be? Did he wriggle in his seat involuntarily when he remembered the night before? Did a silly giveaway smile keep appearing on his face? Did he already miss her with a strange kind of emptiness he had never felt before?

Daisy took herself back to how it had been with Oliver at the beginning. Then, making love was about being enveloped, possessed, triggered to sublime sensation by his power and his passion. At the end of their relationship, it had felt like being invaded.

With Cal, it was about exploring, sharing, doing wonderful things to each other, and talking, laughing, even. She could not remember once laughing while having sex with Oliver.

Cal's body was beautiful, and yet so very manageable. She had felt at ease with it immediately. Daisy felt that smile creeping onto her face again. His skin was smooth, honey-coloured and firm. She had never been to bed with someone so young, and, God, it made a difference, she thought, naughtily, letting out a chuckle, then looking round quickly and guiltily to see that nobody had heard.

The Heath was virtually deserted. At lunchtime, it would be packed with office workers with sandwiches walking about on the mossy mown grass in their bare feet. But at this time on a Monday morning, there was nobody about, except a couple of old men with dogs,

375

and a nanny pushing a twin buggy. It was a good place to think.

It was only one night, Daisy kept telling herself. Not even a whole night. He had left by midnight to go home and pack. She stood at the door in her towelling robe urging him not to tell his parents in case they thought her a slut.

'Of course I won't,' he said, impatiently, as if she were wasting the little time they had.

'Please come with me . . .' he asked again.

He must have known she wouldn't. So was he just saying it because it was a nice thing to say, like she had said 'I love you' when she climaxed? Or did he mean it? How could he even know whether he meant it? How could she know if she did? How did you know whether love at first sight was really love until years later when you were still together. Even then, she thought, ruefully, love could become just a habit that was painful to kick.

Daisy frowned. If only it weren't quite so far away, L.A.

She had never been to the States. Oliver had once suggested driving a Buick from the east coast to the west, but somehow they had never got round to it, and anything less wouldn't do. Daisy had always fancied the idea of going to New Orleans for Mardi Gras, but when Shrove Tuesday arrived each year and Oliver made pancakes, she realized that they had forgotten to book it once again. New York had been out of bounds because of Gemma. She had never fancied Florida for one of their late-booking sun breaks because she imagined it seething with alligators and geriatrics. She had never even considered California.

What on earth would she do there, she asked herself. No, it was ridiculous to give it a second thought.

Los Angeles was flat and sprawling. It wasn't the sort of place where you turned a corner in the middle of the city and found yourself in a stretch of countryside like the Heath. Daisy looked at the panoramic view. She had London at her feet. In the heat it seemed to shimmer, like a mirage.

Los Angeles had the movies, but London had art, comedy, concerts, plays. Daisy tried to remember the last time she had been to the theatre. Reading her mother's letters and remembering how much Estella relished her trips to the city had made Daisy feel rather guilty about the lack of culture in her life. She told herself she must take more advantage of the city.

What would Estella have thought of Cal, she wondered suddenly. 'Cal? Is that short for callow youth?' she could almost hear her mother saying.

'Actually, he's not . . . anyway, just because you always went for older men doesn't mean I have to,' Daisy argued internally, then stopped herself, shocked by the resentment she suddenly felt towards Estella.

The letters had made her feel betrayed. Her mother had lied to them all. She had pretended to have such a close relationship with her younger daughter, but all she was doing, Daisy thought unkindly, was trying to live her life again through her. The letters had fundamentally altered the way Daisy remembered her adolescence: all the whispered thoughts Estella had encouraged her to share, all the gifts and holidays and indulgences had been attempts to make up for her own privations and mistakes. When Daisy had expressed a casual desire to lose her virginity, most mothers would have issued warnings and threats. Estella booked her an appointment at the Family Planning Clinic and provided a mature and accomplished lover. At the time it had made Daisy feel very special. Now, she felt manipulated.

Daisy stared at the view, fighting back the desire to cry. She wanted to get up and stamp her feet and scream. Why had Gemma unearthed those bloody letters? Why was everyone around her so determined to turn her world upside down?

And where had Gemma disappeared to? Daisy had rung her at work but was told she was not in. So she had rung her at home and got the answerphone. She had been going to say sorry, even though she didn't see why she should, but she was in beneficent mood and somebody had to go first. Now the moment had passed. She felt cross with Gemma for not being there. Once again, she had been deserted.

Two tears rolled down Daisy's face. First Estella, then Gemma, then Oliver, then Gemma again, then Cal. In the end everyone deserted her, she thought, becoming more and more sorry for herself. She began to sob.

'Got a fag, love?' A voice interrupted her welter of self-pity. It was the bag lady. Her bag lady. The woman she had danced with in the rain.

'No, I don't smoke, remember?' Daisy said, wiping her eyes with the back of her hand and sniffing. She hadn't heard her approaching. The woman looked at her curiously. She doesn't recognize me, Daisy thought, irrationally disappointed.

'We danced together', she said, 'in the rain, you tap-danced with Mae West in *Diamond Lil* . . .' For some reason, it had become hugely significant that she remembered. The woman's look changed to suspicion. She beetled away, frightened. Daisy got up from the bench and ran after her. 'It's OK,' she panted, 'look, it doesn't matter. Here, buy yourself some . . .' She held out some change.

Some people made choices on the toss of a coin, Daisy thought, peering into the window of the estate agent. So, what was so different about deciding to change your life because a bag lady didn't remember dancing with you? Suddenly it had all seemed so straightforward.

She saw the woman hurrying away with all her possessions stuffed into three plastic carrier bags, and she thought with the clarity of a vision, 'I am homeless too. I don't belong anywhere.'

There was nothing to tie her to London now. No roots, no real friends, no Oliver. She had been excited about having Gemma around again, but all she had managed to do was drive her away, she thought despondently.

From the similar properties in the window, it looked as if she could live easily on the rent she could get for her flat. She pushed open the estate agent's door. Or she could sell it, but that would take a little time, and the hassle of dealing with solicitors and surveyors was the last thing she wanted when she had decided to cut loose.

Now she had the opportunity to really do something with her life, Daisy thought, excited at the prospects. She could travel, to India, maybe, or Africa. She might even find herself writing about something worthwhile, or doing something valuable. Suddenly she felt over-whelmed by a kind of missionary zeal. She pictured herself in long khaki shorts, swatting away flies as she doled out cornmeal porridge in an African village.

First of all, though, she would need a little time to prepare her world itinerary, a little space to take stock of her life. And where better than a Spanish-style villa with a pool, somewhere hot, like Los Angeles?

CHAPTER 32

One drink, Gemma thought. She would just have one drink, then she would leave. What harm could there be in that?

She had called to tell Ralph that she had forgotten to cancel a drinks' appointment and would be a little late. He was having some friends around for dinner. She felt a bit guilty about leaving him to do all the preparation, but he was such a capable cook she didn't really think he would miss her help. Anyway, she would be there before they sat down to eat.

'No problem,' Ralph had assured her, 'just come along when you're through.'

He hadn't asked who she was meeting. If he had, she would have told him. It wasn't as if it were a secret.

She had tried a number of times to ring Oliver to cancel, but by the time she had got through the busy switchboard, he had already left the office. She could have stood him up, she supposed, as she walked down Charing Cross Road, but that seemed unnecessarily rude. After all, she thought, he had never done anything to hurt her. Not recently, anyway.

She was going to be early. Gemma dawdled in front of a bookshop, pretending to look beyond her reflection to the display of summer reading in the window. She was wearing a red linen shift under a short-sleeved black linen jacket. She tried to remember what she had been wearing the last time she had seen him. Usually when she thought about him, she pictured him lounging in the front room at Boulter Street. He didn't fit in with her memories of Whitton House, but that was in fact where she had seen him last. She must have been wearing black then. She had worn nothing but black jeans and T-shirts for months after Bertie's death.

It was Boy who had got her back into colours. They had been window shopping in SoHo one Sunday after brunch. 'All the colours of Kenzo, but half the price,' he had commented knowledgeably as they stopped outside the vibrant pink exterior of Betsy Johnson. The wire mannequin in the window was wearing a rara dress in clinging cotton jersey printed with over-sized pink cabbage roses.

'You would look good in that,' he pointed.

'It's like curtain material,' protested Gemma.

'Better than your widow's weeds,' he replied. 'Try it on, and if you like it, I'll buy it for you.'

She liked it. She twirled in front of the mirror at the back of the shop, the skirt fanning out in a circle. It was something she never would have chosen for herself. It made her feel different, like clothes from the dressing-up box.

After that, she always went clothes shopping with Boy. He had taken her education in fashion very seriously, and once Gemma had acquired a taste for designer clothes and shoes, she became an eager disciple.

'You were a bit of a sartorial Eliza Doolittle, when I first met you,' he had once remarked, putting on what he thought was a Cockney accent, 'but now I seem to have created an Imelda Marcos.'

Gemma smoothed her dress over her thighs, wishing that someone would invent a linen that didn't crease, then she noticed that her sheer black tights had a snag just above the hemline. There wasn't enough time to run up to Covent Garden to buy a new pair. The outfit which this morning had looked so smart and fresh, was rapidly beginning to look tired and tatty.

In the Ladies' Room of the Savoy, she rubbed a bar of soap on the ladder to stop it running. It was what they used to use at school. Either that or nail-varnish, she remembered. You could always tell whose tights had run because they reeked of that unmistakable pear-drop smell. If she sat carefully, she thought, he won't see it. She slicked her lips with lipstick the exact shade of her dress and blotted it. Then she grinned at herself automatically, baring her teeth, checking for scarlet flecks. It would have to do.

It was ridiculously vain to let one little blemish in her appearance so disturb her peace of mind, she told herself, as she walked up the staircase to the American Bar, trying to breathe evenly. One last check in the mirrored wall, then she stepped towards the bar. It was only a distance of twenty feet or so, but she felt as exposed as a model on a catwalk.

He wasn't there. She ordered a vodka tonic, sipped it, then turned around on the bar stool and surveyed the room as nonchalantly as she could. A middle-aged man with curly grey hair smiled at her as her eyes flicked past him. She froze. It hadn't occurred to her that she might not recognize Oliver. Surely he couldn't have changed that much? She let her gaze creep surreptitiously back to the man and was relieved to see that he had gone back to his *Financial Times*. A couple of women were chattering loudly at one table and emptying the plate of home-made potato crisps as if it were their first food of the day. A man in full evening dress, who looked as if he had recently combed black boot polish through his hair, appeared at the piano and started to play 'New York, New York'.

She turned back to the bar. The bartender offered her a canapé from a huge silver platter. She took a pumpernickel finger with two clear orange beads of salmon roe glistening on top of a smear of cream cheese and was about to put it in her mouth when his voice said, 'Gemma?' so close behind her she could feel his breath on her earlobe.

She swirled round on her high bar seat, her knees almost colliding with his crotch.

He stepped back, and that look, that distinctive flash of surprise, fury and amusement that was the quintessence of Oliver, appeared on his face for just a second. All the times she had tried to understand what it was about this man that had given him such a hold on her and there it was, instantly. That irreverent look, that electrifying mix of intelligence and humour and sex.

'Hi,' she said, feeling immediately like the naïve student he had first encountered.

'Well,' he said, and stepped back one pace, 'well, Gemma, you have grown up!'

'And you look just the same . . . except for . . .' she paused just enough to see him frown, 'the suit,' she added, given a little confidence by the way he was looking at her. She could see that she pleased him, and she felt that all the work and money she and Boy had put into her appearance had been just for this moment.

'Two Manhattans over here,' Oliver waved at the bartender. 'Is that OK?' he asked her.

'Of course,' she said, draining her vodka tonic, not wanting to break the rhythm by quibbling about a drink.

Just one, she told herself. Just one drink *with him*.

'Let's get a table before it starts filling up,' Oliver said.

'Is this a regular watering hole of yours?' she asked, picking up her handbag, following him and wondering why she had used such a pecular phrase. It must be his lawyer's suit, she decided. Her only knowledge of

English lawyers was from watching reruns of *Rumpole of the Bailey* on Masterpiece Theatre and that was the sort of thing they said.

'I've been here once or twice,' Oliver said, sitting down, 'so, cheers Gemma!' He raised his glass and sipped the cocktail. 'I can't get over how beautiful you've become . . .'

She could feel herself blushing.

'I don't know how I managed to share a house with you for a whole term and not notice,' he continued.

'A year, it was a year.'

'I'm sorry?'

'Three terms,' Gemma said, feeling slightly pedantic, 'we shared a house for three terms, a year.'

'Oh yes,' he responded with a dry laugh, 'even more astonishing then!'

She waited for him to continue, but he was checking out the room as she had done a few minutes earlier. Finally, his gaze returned and his tiger-eye irises settled on hers. He had a quizzical look, as if he was waiting for her to speak.

'So, you became a solicitor,' Gemma fumbled to open a proper conversation.

'Does that surprise you?'

No, it was just something to say, she wanted to reply. Instead she said, 'I thought you would become a barrister.'

'I'm surprised you know the difference,' he said, 'most people haven't the faintest idea.'

'Well, I don't really,' she had to admit.

He looked at her impatiently, then visibly softened, 'I suppose I was more interested in the real work that goes on in preparing a defence, not just the peformance on the day,' he began, adopting a noble tone, 'and I have no interest in prosecuting on behalf of a system that's riddled with corruption.' He glanced at her to see her reaction. She nodded dutifully. 'Technically, as a barrister you're not allowed to refuse a brief. Of course they all do,' he went on.

'So what sort of people do you defend?' she asked, surprised that he sounded so pompous.

'Murderers, rapists, drug dealers . . .'

'You mean alleged murderers, rapists . . .' she interrupted.

He gave her a look that made her feel about ten years old. 'It's not up to me to decide on guilt or innocence,' he said.

'So would you defend someone if you knew they were a rapist?'

'I wouldn't be allowed to defend someone who had told me they were guilty . . .'

'No, that's not what I meant . . .'

'I know what you meant,' he said. 'I get asked that question by every woman with half a brain I meet.' He must have noticed her look of mortification. 'Let's say that I don't allow myself the luxury of thinking about what my clients might have done. My attitude to all the people I defend is there but for the grace of God go I . . .'

'But you're not a criminal!' she exclaimed.

'What a middle-class girl you are!' he replied. 'Who knows what either of us would have been if we'd been brought up by a single mother who had to become a prostitute to pay the gas bill,' he said.

It was a typically extreme example, but there was no point in denying it. She had temporarily forgotten that Oliver couldn't bear to lose an argument. He had an almost oriental fear of losing face. That hadn't changed, but he had never been such a bullshitter, she thought, or perhaps he had, and she just hadn't been able to detect it.

Their glasses stood empty on the table. Gemma wondered why on earth she had attempted to tackle Oliver on the morality of his profession. She had put him in a combative mood, made herself look stupid, and soured the atmosphere between them, all in one go. She glanced at her watch. She couldn't bring herself to part with him on this note, not after ten years. It would be such an anti-climax.

'Another?' Oliver asked her pleasantly, picking up her glass.

'Well, yes, why not?' she smiled at him politely.

'I hear that you publish raunchy fiction,' he said, as the waiter deposited refills in front of them.

'Well, yes, I suppose so.' She certainly didn't want to get into the tired old argument most people wanted to have about literary versus commercial fiction.

'Good for you,' he said simply, then he looked at her as if he were making an appraisal. 'I seem to remember you were always a bit of a goer beneath that innocent exterior.'

She blushed. So he remembered.

After Daisy had taken him from her, she had felt unable to speak to Oliver. She had fled to Whitton House the same afternoon, running home only to find her father dying. Then events had taken over, making the whole experience of Oxford and their charmed life together seem like a distant dream.

Between her father's funeral and her mother's death, when Oliver and Daisy were staying at the house, she had managed to avoid being in the same room with them. Once, in the passage upstairs, she saw him coming out of Daisy's room and walking towards her. The corridor seemed suddenly very narrow, but she squeezed against the wall and looked beyond him as he walked past with a slightly mystified expression on his face. Now, she couldn't understand why she had not challenged him.

'I don't know if you look like a publisher,' he was saying.

'What do I look like then?' she couldn't resist asking,

the alcohol beginning to make her slightly flirtatious.

'Hmm.' He looked at her again, his eyes running down her body deliberately, like expert fingers.

She felt naked.

'You look more like someone famous, a film star, perhaps.'

'Oh, don't tell me, Grace Kelly in *To Catch a Thief*,' she said wearily.

'Yes . . . you've been told that before?'

'I'm afraid so,' she said. 'I hate that description. I always think Grace Kelly looks so kind of chaste and goody-goody . . .'

'A snow-capped volcano,' Oliver responded, leaning towards her, 'that's what Hitchcock said.'

'Did he?' she said coyly, as if it was the first time she had heard it. And then the alcohol added, 'So do I look as if I have liquid fire inside me?'

'Liquid fire,' said Oliver, with a smile, 'what a lovely thought. Another drink?'

'Yes, please, but something soft,' Gemma said.

'Shall we get a bottle of champagne?'

It was a rhetorical question. Before she'd had a chance to decline, he had waved the waiter over and ordered it.

At least she knew where she was with champagne, Gemma reasoned. She had no idea what the ingredients of a Manhattan were, but two of them had made her feel very hot and light-headed. She excused herself and went to the Ladies.

Her face felt like a beetroot, but in the gilt-framed mirror it looked as pale as usual. The only sign that she had been drinking, she thought, was that her eyes looked deeper, hollow almost, and slightly watery. She applied some more lipstick and checked her watch. It wasn't yet eight o'clock.

One glass of champagne, she thought, taking a deep breath, and then I shall make my excuses and leave.

'I understand that your husband died?' Oliver said as she sat down.

Gemma thought that it was strange how they both seemed to have decided to avoid mentioning Daisy. It would have been more normal for him to say Daisy told me that your husband died. She wondered why he hadn't. Then she realized that she hadn't replied.

'Yes. He was gay,' she said, 'I mean, I didn't mean . . . I just meant that he wasn't really my husband in the usual sense – although I did love him,' she added, appalled by the words that were tumbling out of her mouth. No more alcohol, she told herself. 'I'd better be going,' she said, picking up her handbag and putting it on her lap as if to protect herself.

'Oh, you can't leave me to finish this on my own,' Oliver replied, holding up the half-full bottle of champagne. 'I'm feeling pissed already . . .'

'Are you?' she giggled, somehow relieved by his admission. 'So am I, actually, and I'm meant to be going out to dinner . . .' It was the alcohol that had qualified the sentence. 'I mean . . .' she began to retract, but Oliver was too quick for her.

'Oh, I thought we had the whole evening ahead of us,' he said, looking exaggeratedly desolate. 'We've barely even said hello,' he teased.

'Hello,' Gemma said, huskily, beginning to enjoy the game. 'There we are, I've said it.'

'Oh, but that's not how you say it properly,' Oliver replied, with a look of mock reprimand on his face. Then he leaned towards her, very slowly brushing her cheek with his lips, and whispered, 'Hello,' softly into her hear.

It was as if he had kissed her with sherbet. She was acutely aware of the tingling patch of soft skin his lips had touched.

She stared at her lap. The run in her tights had started to creep like a white caterpillar over her knee.

He was looking at her. She knew that he was. If she looked back, she felt she would be committing herself in some way. Her heart was beating in her head, but her brain felt suddenly lucid, as she fingered the clasp of her handbag, deciding.

The pianist was playing 'These Foolish Things': 'Oh, how the ghost of you clings . . .' he crooned.

The whole world seemed to have gone into slow motion.

What was going to happen had always been inevitable.

She lifted her eyes to meet Oliver's and he understood.

He put his arm round her shoulders and drew her towards him.

Then he kissed her, and it felt so intensely private that when she finally opened her eyes, she was almost surprised to find herself still sitting in a noisy, smoky bar in the centre of a busy city.

She could taste the champagne, smell his body, feel the five o'clock stubble on his chin. When he withdrew his lips they were red and for a horrible moment she thought he had drawn her blood.

She picked up a paper drinks coaster and dabbed at the scarlet lipstick on his mouth.

He caught her hand and kissed her palm. She quivered with the intimacy of it.

Then he said, 'Let's go.'

Her tights and knickers came off in the taxi. It was still light outside. She sat staring straight ahead, imagining that if she didn't look involved, the cab driver, glancing into his mirror, would not realize what was going on. It was deliciously illicit, pretending that nothing was happening, while Oliver fingered her under her dress.

As soon as they were inside the house they fell upon one another like wild animals, ravenously kissing, biting, collapsing to the floor in the hall and rolling around amongst the Wellington boots.

Then he pulled her to her feet and led her upstairs to Kathy and Roger's bed.

That was when the fantasy started to become reality. She protested weakly. It didn't feel right. She hung back in the doorway.

'They're away, stupid,' he said, stepping out of his trousers.

'I know that,' she replied.

'Come here,' he said, opening his arms to her.

She sat down on the bed, too drunk to find other words to explain her objection.

He looked almost comical lying there in his white shirt, his erection making a tent of the shirt tails. The sight of him sobered her up enough to ask him to wear a condom. He complied, grudgingly, taking one from his pocket as casually as if he were shaking a cigarette from a packet. She was confused, not knowing whether to feel flattered or offended that he had come to their date prepared. She looked away as he put it on. Suddenly she wasn't sure that she wanted this. Then he was standing in front of her, his erect penis level with her eyes. She thought, why are condoms such a horrible pink colour?

And then he threw her back on the bed, hoisted up her red dress and entered her with an urgency that felt brutal rather than passionate.

She felt as if she were drowning in the reality of him inside her, suffocating with his weight on top of her. Then he came, letting out an extended growl. It was such a feral noise, she couldn't believe he wasn't putting it on. She made the mistake of laughing and all the heady sweat of anticipation and sex disappeared instantly and completely. The sheets felt cold.

He looked down at her with that look of his, but it

wasn't a sexy look anymore. He withdrew and rolled over beside her.

She waited, patiently, not quite daring to say anything. Surely that wasn't it? That was just the desperate fuck they had both been waiting for all this time. Now they would make love.

She turned over on to her front and started to unbutton his shirt. He continued to stare at the ceiling.

She opened the shirt and began to caress his chest. He tolerated it without reaction for several minutes, then he pushed her away.

'What's the matter with you?' was the last thing she remembered him saying, before the wave of nausea overwhelmed her and she just managed to turn away from him in time to throw up into the painted water jug on Kathy's bedside table.

Gemma was in Whitton House. She could hear her mother crying downstairs. She wanted to go and comfort her, but there was a noose round her neck holding her back.

'I've ruined all my children's lives! I've ruined all my children's lives,' Estella was sobbing.

'No!' Gemma screamed.

She woke up shaking with fear. Birdsong. It was only birdsong. And there was no rope, just her dress rucked up around her neck. She sat up and peered around the gloomy room. It looked familiar, but she knew she shouldn't be there. Her mouth tasted sour. Above her head, three elephants drifted about in the half light. On the other side of the room, she could just see the doll's house.

She had fled to Zoe's room and fallen asleep there, she realized, throwing back the Jungle Book duvet cover and discovering she was naked, except for the dress round her neck. As she struggled to tug it over her head the events of the evening before began to drift back in gruesome snatches.

Gemma shivered with belated embarrassment. She looked around the room for something to cover herself with, but there was nothing apart from a nine-year-old's dressing-gown, with woolly lambs appliquéd to the patch pocket, hanging on the back of the door.

She wrapped Baloo the Bear around her shoulders, crept into the bathroom and peered into the mirror. She looked terrible. She applied some toothpaste to her index finger and cleaned her teeth as best she could. Then she rinsed her mouth with water and drank a mouthful or two. As her head started to clear, the catalogue of guilt began to swamp her.

She had had sex in her best friend's bed and fallen into a drunken coma in her godchild's room. She had lied to her boyfriend.

She had rung Ralph from the lobby of the Savoy saying that she had developed a migraine. All the time she was speaking, Oliver had been behind her, kissing her neck, pushing himself into her buttocks, and she was trying to keep a straight face, trying to sound authentically headachey. Ralph wasn't stupid. How could she have done that? She tried to block out the images, but they wouldn't go away.

The irony of it was almost laughable. As well as giving herself a throbbing headache, she had chosen to swap the best relationship she had ever had for a night with the love of her life. But instead of a fantasy fuck, she'd been not very well and truly screwed.

Sadder than that, she thought, staring at herself in the mirror, forcing herself to look into her own eyes and admit it, was the realization that it had been just like that before. For ten years, their first session in the kitchen at Boulter Street had taken on iconic status. Perhaps it had been seeing 9½ *Weeks* soon afterwards, she thought wryly, that had made her mistake the discomfort of the draining board for eroticism, and premature ejaculation for sexual ecstasy.

But there was something much worse. Gemma tried to tell herself that the alcohol had made her imagine things, that somehow her feelings of guilt had become entangled in her dreams, but she couldn't leave the house without being sure.

Oliver was sprawled across the large pine double bed. He still had his socks on. In the cold, grey light of dawn he looked middle-aged and a little paunchy around the waist. She looked at him and was disgusted with herself. This man whom she had worshipped, this embodiment of mystique, was snoring loudly.

Gemma approached the bed gingerly. His arms were still in the sleeves of his shirt, but his chest was bared just as she had left it. He snuffled and heaved his body away as if he sensed her looking, but he didn't wake up. She stepped a little closer, her hands shielding her eyes as if the frightening bit of a late night movie were about to appear. She peered through the gaps in her fingers, then pressed her hands hard to her eyelids.

No. She told herself, it cannot be.

She let her hands drop to her side, took a deep breath and looked again calmly.

It wasn't her imagination. There was a purple birthmark the shape of a sickle just below Oliver's left pectoral.

'Oh my God,' Gemma whispered to herself, throwing back her head in anguish, 'what have we done?'

CHAPTER 33

July 1953
Dear Shirl,

Having a baby is a beautiful thing. Not the actual having it, that's pain you wouldn't wish on your worst enemy, but afterwards when you're holding him on your chest, feeling him tuck up his little legs like a frog and nestle there, trusting you completely, that's the most wonderful feeling.

I knew that it would change my life, but I didn't know how. I just thought it would be something else to cope with. I didn't bank on this overwhelming sense of responsibility for this tiny person. He is a person, Shirl. He's not just half me and half Laurie, he's himself. I never knew babies had hair, but he has, lots of dark curls, just like me. The nurses say that he'll probably lose that, but I know he won't. He has blue eyes. The nurses say that all babies have blue eyes. When he cries, I tell them that he has his father's temper, and they look at me disapprovingly! He is himself. I could never imagine what my baby was like when he was inside me, and now he seems so much an individual I can't seem to connect him with the thing that was in my tummy, turning somersaults and kicking.

In the middle of the night I creep along the corridor to the nursery, pick him up and bring him back to bed with me. They don't like you doing that, but there's a nice midwife who turns a blind eye, because I've only got him for such a short time. When he's lying there next to me, smelling me, rooting around for my breast like a soft little animal, and feeling all secure when he finds it, I look down at him and I just know that he

*will be sweet-natured and clever. I talk to him, Shirl! I tell
him to grow up into a good man who will be kind to women. I
tell him that I love him. Do you think I'm going daft, Shirl?
They say that some women do after having a baby. I don't
care.*

*I tell him that he's a lucky boy because he's going to have a
family he knows who love him, and a family he doesn't know
at all, who live a long way away, but who love him too, and
who will think about him every day.*

*That's why I'm writing to you, Shirl. You see, I'm having
him adopted properly. I'm sorry, Shirl, specially after
everything I've put you through.*

*Don't get me wrong, I think you would be a lovely mum. It's
just that now I know that I would be too. I never thought I'd
feel that. I know that if I gave him to you, I'd always look at
him and think, that's my baby. And if I ever got myself out of
the hole that I'm in, I would want him back. It's not fair to
treat him like a library book on loan for a few months, or years,
is it?*

*Then there's Dad. I know how hard it was for you to
persuade him to have the baby under his roof. I've tried to tell
myself that he's not such a bad old thing, but, truth is, Shirl, I
hate him, and I've always hated him, and I don't want my
baby to grow up with such an unforgiving old sod for a
grandad. I know Dad. He wouldn't be able to look at my son
and not think he was my bastard, and he'd make your life hell,
too.*

*I don't want my son to grow up smelling of fish and chips like
we always did. I don't want him looking out to sea on a rainy
day and dreaming of a better life. I want him to live that life.
Do you see? It's one thing I can give him, Shirl. It's the only
thing I can do for him. I have to do my best, Shirl, do you
understand that?*

*They're taking him tomorrow, Shirl. I thought it would be
easier if you didn't see him. I'm going to give him his last bath
now. I have to memorize every inch of his perfect little body.
Each ear, each little finger, each tiny toe, that button nose,*

those dimpled knees, that purple crescent moon just above his heart.

I know that I'm losing the two most important things in my life – my baby and my sister's love – but try to forgive me, Shirl. It's the only truly selfless thing I've ever done.

Your sister, Stella

Gemma was kneeling beside her bed. The shoe box was upside down and Estella's letters were lying where she had scattered them on the white duvet cover, like pieces of patchwork from a half-sewn quilt. A tear dropped on the sheet of lilac writing paper she was holding, and the ink that had dried forty years ago began to run. She blotted the letter with the corner of a pillowcase.

What now? The emotions were too overwhelming. She must deal with the practicalities. But she was shaking.

Eventually she heaved herself to her feet, took off her crumpled red dress, and threw it into the bin in the bathroom, knowing she would never wear it again. Then she stepped under the shower. The fierce blast of hot water cauterized her hangover and scrubbed up her appearance, giving her face a livid blush of broken veins, but she still felt dirty inside. She put on a black Fortuny-pleated ankle-length skirt and a fitted white cotton shirt with short sleeves. 'Do you think you're a bloody nun, or something?' Daisy had shouted at her last time. Gemma looked in the mirror and managed to raise a weak smile at her shriven appearance.

She picked up her briefcase. It was still too early to ring in and tell her secretary that she would be late. She didn't think she could justify another day off on urgent family business, but she had no idea what was going to happen, or how long it would take. On her way out, she caught sight of the answerphone. It was flashing. She deliberated for a second or two, then pressed Play.

The first message was from Ralph just checking to see that she had got home OK. She could hear the murmur of his dinner party in the background. He sounded concerned, but not unduly so. Her phone call had obviously convinced him. That made her feel worse.

The second message was from Daisy. 'Gemma,' she said, rather formally, 'please ring me because I have something rather important to tell you.'

The third and fourth messages were from Ralph. 'Just wondering how you are?' and, touchingly, 'Sorry, if you're lying in a darkened room with a headache, the last thing you want to hear is the phone ringing. Just to say goodnight. Hope you feel better in the morning. I love you.'

Gemma fled, letting the door slam behind her.

Daisy heaved two very full bin-liners down the staircase to the communal hall, then she opened the front door. Gemma was standing there about to press her bell. The two sisters stared at each other disbelievingly for a couple of seconds, then Gemma said, 'I'm so sorry for everything I've done to you,' and crumpled in a heap around Daisy's shoulders.

'That's OK.' Daisy hugged her back.

Gemma held on sobbing for a few minutes, then she suddenly stopped, wiped her eyes with the back of her hand, and said, 'What on earth are you doing up at this time in the morning?'

And they both giggled.

'I've been up all night sorting,' Daisy said. 'I've got rather more stuff than I thought . . .'

All the clothes that wouldn't fit in one large suitcase had gone to the Hampstead Oxfam shop the previous afternoon. She had wanted to give her thick red winter coat to her bag lady, but realized it wasn't practical to drive round all afternoon in the hope of finding her.

Decisions had to be made about all the other stuff she had accumulated over the years. Some decisions were easy. The huge pile of newspapers stacked in the corner of the second bedroom waiting to be read went straight to the recycling bin down the road. Other possessions proved less easy to discard. She had spent a long time agonizing about what to do with the photocopies of Estella's letters, the photograph album and the carved wooden box which contained her memories of her mother. Finally, she had shoved them all into a plastic Waitrose bag, hoping that inspiration about their fate would arrive before she found herself boarding the plane with it as hand luggage.

'Let me just put this stuff by the bins,' Daisy said, 'then I'll make us a cup of coffee.'

Gemma watched her sister bump the grey plastic bags down the steps. 'Are you spring cleaning?' she asked doubtfully.

'No, I'm leaving, actually,' Daisy said, 'come in . . .'

Gemma hesitated. She didn't feel comfortable in Daisy's flat. The taste of Oliver was too pervasive, his presence seemed to lurk in every corner. 'You don't fancy going for a walk, do you?' she suggested, thinking it might be easier to say what she had to say in the open air.

'Why?' Daisy asked, beginning to think how odd it was for Gemma to turn up at such an hour, and wondering why she wasn't a little more curious about where she was going. She seemed preoccupied. 'All right then,' she agreed, seeing Gemma's anxious look.

She checked her hip pocket for keys, then slammed the front door of the building. They walked side by side towards the Heath.

'It's cold at this time in the morning, isn't it?' Daisy said, her teeth chattering.

'Do you want to go back for a jacket?'

'No, I'll be all right.' Daisy wondered who would be the first to say something that wasn't utterly banal.

Sweet-chestnut trees with giant raspberry blossoms lined the path up the hill. The air was damp with dew and felt as fresh as the green of the young leaves. As the sun's rays began to break through the chill of dawn, an earthy smell of mown grass rose from the turf. A lone jogger smiled at the two sisters as he puffed past them. It was a beautiful morning.

Finally, as they reached the top and stopped walking to look at the view, Gemma broke the silence. 'Did you read all the letters?' she asked, staring into the distance towards Canary Wharf.

'Oh, not that again,' Daisy replied, exasperated. 'I thought we just agreed to move on from that, back there.'

'No, I didn't mean . . . I just meant, did you? It doesn't matter whether it was after or before I did, that's not what I'm asking . . .'

'Well, yes, I had a look,' Daisy said, 'but, to be honest, it made me feel a bit funny. And then, well other events took over . . .'

'Which one?'

Gemma was still fixated on the letters. Daisy sighed, 'Not one in particular,' she replied, slightly irritably, 'just reading all of them, it felt like eavesdropping on someone else's conversation, knowing I shouldn't . . . didn't you feel that?'

'Not really,' said Gemma, surprised.

How different they were, she thought, given that they came from identical sources of genes. Although she had always felt close to her, she had never really known what was going on in Daisy's head. She found it easier to imagine what was going on in Kathy's, or Meryl's. Daisy always seemed to have her own oblique take on things.

'What about this one,' Gemma extracted the lilac page from her handbag. It fluttered in the breeze.

Daisy ran her eyes over it. 'Very sad,' she said.

'Is that all you thought?' Gemma persisted.

'Oh, for heaven's sake, Gem, I've got a plane to catch this afternoon,' Daisy exclaimed. 'I don't have time for this.'

'You really don't get it, do you?' Gemma asked quietly.

'I'm starving,' Daisy said, starting to run straight down the hill, galloping through the grass like a child. 'Do you think anywhere's open for breakfast?' she called back.

Gemma followed her. 'Daisy, stop!' she said, panting behind her, brandishing the letter. 'Read the penultimate paragraph!'

Daisy sighed, took the piece of paper, read it, then handed it back. 'Well?' she asked.

'It's Oliver,' Gemma shouted at her, exasperated. She hadn't wanted it to come out like that. 'Oliver is our brother.'

'Are you all right?' Daisy asked, frowning at her with concern.

'Yes, well, not really, but are you?' Gemma said, amazed at Daisy's calm demeanour.

'Of course I am, but, Gem, what are you getting at? You've lost me, I'm afraid.'

Was she refusing to understand because the consequence of understanding was so awful? Gemma tried to explain patiently. 'Oliver is adopted, right? You told me that the other day. He is looking for his mother, right? He was born in 1953, yes?'

'But so were thousands of children,' Daisy replied.

'But how many with a purple birthmark like a new moon on their chest?' Gemma asked quietly.

She looked at the ground. Her black glacé kid shoes were covered in damp grass cuttings. When she finally dared raise her eyes and look at her sister, Daisy's face was pink in an effort to stifle laughter. 'Gem, don't be so silly,' she burst out, 'that's not a birthmark, it's a burn from a drinks coaster!'

'What? How do you know?' Gemma asked doubtfully.

'Well, you do learn things about people when you live with them for ten years . . .' said Daisy, starting to walk on.

'Hold on, are you one hundred per cent certain?' Gemma pressed.

'Of course I'm certain,' Daisy replied, musing. 'How peculiar that you should remember his scar . . .'

Then, catching the guilty look on Gemma's face, she realized. 'Except you didn't remember from all that time ago, did you?'

'I saw him last night,' Gemma confessed.

There was no point in trying to cover up. It didn't matter anymore! She stood smiling inanely at Daisy, not knowing whether to shriek with joy, or sink into the ground with humiliation.

'God, you didn't waste much time, did you?' said Daisy crossly.

'It wasn't like that . . .' Gemma faltered.

Maybe it was like that. She hadn't thought about what Daisy might think, or perhaps she had, and that was one of the unacknowledged reasons she had felt so guilty afterwards.

'Come on,' Daisy said, 'let's have something to eat.'

She pushed open the door of the café and they were enshrouded by a warm damp fug of frying bacon and coffee.

Daisy ordered sausages, eggs, beans and four rounds of toast with butter.

She felt furious with Oliver. She had rung him the day before to tell him she was leaving. She felt she owed him that, and she wanted to know what to do with the things they had bought together. It had been an exhausting conversation. Somehow she didn't want him to know where she was going, but he had pressed her until she gave in and told him, then he mocked, and she became angry. Then his tone had changed abruptly and he had pleaded, almost pathetically, to come back. He needed her, he said. She had felt sorry for him and horribly guilty. And all the time, she thought, he had known that he would be fucking her sister later that day.

'I'm sorry,' Gemma said, slightly frightened by the look on her sister's face. 'Just tea, please,' she said to the man behind the counter.

'Oh, for heaven's sake, have something to bloody eat,' Daisy exploded. 'Just forget your bloody figure for half an hour and stop making me feel such a pig.'

'All right, I'll have a fried egg,' Gemma obeyed meekly, 'with chips,' she added quickly.

They sat down at a Formica table. Daisy peered shortsightedly at the headlines of the next table's newspaper. Gemma stared at the framed print of Van Gogh's chair on the wall as if it were a work of art she had not seen before.

'I am sorry. I don't know if I knew what I was doing, but I am sorry . . .' Gemma said, eventually.

'Oh, it's all right,' Daisy said, wearily. 'I don't suppose I've really got any right to mind, but I do, somehow.'

Gemma was playing idly with the plastic tomato of ketchup that sat fatly next to the salt and pepper. A blob squirted into the air and landed on her white Kelly bag. She rubbed at it furiously with a paper serviette but it left a brownish pink stain on the leather.

Daisy couldn't stop herself laughing. It seemed so symbolic. She had been about to ask, bitchily, how it had been with Oliver. Now, she almost felt she didn't need to. Gemma looked worse than she had ever seen her. Her eyes were slightly bloodshot, her skin was blotchy, the cold white shirt highlighted all the imperfections that had erupted after a night on the tiles. And now that white Kelly bag which Daisy had detested from the moment she first set eyes on it, because its very existence somehow managed to epitomize her sister's righteousness and make her feel a failure, was bloodied with ketchup.

'Well, at least neither of us has committed incest,' she said jovially. 'Actually, Oliver told me about meeting his birth mother only yesterday. I'm surprised he didn't mention it,' she added a little wickedly.

She wasn't in fact surprised at all. It was almost as ignominious a tale as the history of Oliver's scar. It would be treacherous to tell Gemma, she thought, because she was sure Oliver would put some ridiculous gloss on it for public consumption. Well, it would serve him right.

'Apparently his mother had an affair with the gas man and he was the result,' she announced. 'Her husband would only have her back if she had the baby adopted. Apparently there was no mistaking the resemblance . . .'

Daisy had secretly found it rather an amusing story, although the day before she had felt a little sorry for Oliver. It seemed such a prosaic background for him to spring from. She was sure that he had hoped at least to be the illegitimate son of an earl and a serving girl. Perhaps it wasn't such a good idea after all to find out where you came from. 'Oh, lighten up, Gem,' she said, noticing her sister wasn't laughing.

The man behind the counter shouted out their order. Gemma stood up to go and collect it. As she turned towards the back of the café, Daisy noticed that she was on the verge of crying. Gemma put Daisy's breakfast down in front of her. 'How you can think of eating all that!' she said.

'I've got a big day in front of me,' Daisy replied, tucking in.

Gemma pushed a chip into the yolk of her fried egg, then put down her fork. 'Yes?' she said, distractedly. 'So what have you got on?'

'I'm moving out of my flat and going to live abroad,' Daisy said.

'Oh really?' responded Gemma, and Daisy knew that she hadn't been listening.

Daisy demolished a sausage in two bites.

'Did Estella know that Oliver was adopted?' Gemma suddenly asked.

Daisy crunched a piece of toast. 'How should I know?' she said, with her mouth full. 'Why on earth does it matter?'

Gemma's mind was cranking through frames of memory like a hand-operated projector. Black curly hair, a purple birthmark . . . the only thing that didn't fit were the blue eyes, but the midwives at the nursing home for unmarried mothers had said that all babies had blue eyes. Which meant that eye colour must change . . .

'If I could make a mistake about Oliver's scar, then so could she,' Gemma said, her voice beginning to tremble, 'and she saw his chest, you told me, she embraced him, the day before you left . . .' She had found the image of her mother and Oliver locked together in the stifling heat of the greenhouse unsettling from the moment Daisy had mentioned it.

Now Daisy's face had suddenly become serious too, as each tiny piece of information began to assemble, like a difficult jigsaw, into a terrifying montage.

'I've ruined all my children's lives,' Gemma said, 'that's what Estella told Shirley that night, the night before . . .'

'Stop!' Daisy shouted.

Two workmen who had just pushed open the door of the café looked behind them guiltily, then stepped out of the way as Daisy rushed towards the door with Gemma following her.

Daisy was running up the street. She ran as fast as she could. She could hear her footsteps on the pavement and she could feel her lungs burning with the sudden burst of exercise, but she couldn't see where she was going because right in front of her eyes, the image she was trying so hard to escape would not go away. Estella dead, lying on her bed. She had killed herself because her sins had visited themselves upon her. Her son was fucking her daughter.

'My darling daughter, I hope you will never know why . . .'

'No!' Daisy screamed.

It was all a mistake. Estella had killed herself for nothing.

'You stupid woman,' Daisy screamed, 'you stupid, stupid, stupid . . .'

Suddenly she was in the middle of the road that ran down the side of the Heath and a black cab had screeched to a halt and just missed her. The driver yelled out of the window, 'Why don't you look where you're going?'

'Why don't you go to hell?' she screamed at him.

Then Gemma was there, and Daisy was thumping her with both fists, and Gemma was ducking the blows, trying to grab her hands and hold her down like a hysterical toddler.

'It's not fair, not fair, not fair . . .' Daisy was crying, gasping for breath.

'I know.' Gemma managed to get both arms round her and hold her as tight as she could. 'I know, darling, I know.'

They stood locked together in grief, sobbing into each other's neck.

A traffic jam began to build up just behind them. Above her sister's gasping cries, a cacophony of car horns shrieked in Gemma's ears.

'Let's get out of the road,' Gemma said quietly, raising her head from Daisy's shoulder.

'Why are you always so practical?' Daisy asked between sobs.

'I'm not.'

'You are when you're with me,' Daisy said, taking the tissue that Gemma had fished out of her bag and blowing her nose loudly.

'Well, I'm your big sister, aren't I? I've got to look after you.'

'I suppose so,' Daisy said, resting her head again on Gemma's shoulder. It felt nice there.

'Come on,' Gemma said, after a long time, 'let's go home.'

'What about the bill?' Daisy asked as they started walking slowly back.

'I paid it when we gave our order,' replied Gemma.

'What a bloody waste,' said Daisy, and Gemma wasn't sure whether she was referring to their breakfast or their mother's life.

Daisy couldn't believe that there would ever be a time when she would think about it without a great tidal wave of guilt engulfing her. She had never before been able to imagine her mother's thoughts as she took the pills, but now she knew, and she didn't think it would be possible to live with that knowledge.

Gemma kept telling her it wasn't her fault. Estella had been grieving, she insisted, trying to rationalize the unthinkable. She was in a state of shock after Bertie's death. She only needed one little thing to tip her over the edge. And when she saw Oliver, who did actually look rather like her, and had that scar . . .

'Oliver behaves rather like her too, actually,' Daisy chipped in. 'Estella was always trying to pretend that she came from somewhere better than she did. Oliver is the same, except that he tries to pretend he comes from somewhere much more interesting than his uptight middle-class mother and father. I suppose that's the difference between the generations. Estella thought it was cool to be posh and Oliver thinks it's cool to be working class . . .'

She smiled weakly at her own observation. Gemma smiled back, encouraging her to be positive, and said, 'Estella had depths that we knew nothing about.'

'She was a bloody liar, you mean.'

'But Daisy . . .'

'But Daisy, nothing. Think about it Gemma. If she did think that Oliver was our brother, how could she have left me to go off with him?'

'Well, maybe she didn't think it, and we've got this all wrong,' Gemma said, wishing badly that she had kept her analysis to herself.

Daisy looked at her sister lovingly. She knew that she was trying to make things better. How she now envied Gemma that last note Estella had left. It was bad for Gemma, but not so bad. Gemma had been absolved.

'This has nothing to do with you.'

Whereas it had everything to do with Daisy. How could she survive with that knowledge? Of course she would survive, Daisy thought. She would have to struggle on. If she knew one thing now it was that she would never kill herself, however painful her life was, because dying only made it harder for those who loved you. It didn't solve anything.

Perhaps one day she would be able to think about Estella's last act and the guilt would lap around her ankles rather than knocking her off her feet. There had been a time, she remembered, but couldn't quite believe now, when she had not been able to think about her mother without missing her so much that it hurt. Human beings had an enormous capacity for adapting.

'Are you sure that you're doing the right thing?' Gemma made another attempt to change the subject. She had just finished cleaning the kitchen floor. She

407

squeezed out the mop in the bucket and leaned on the handle.

They had been working solidly since they arrived back at the flat and Daisy had informed her that she only had five hours before her flight. Gemma had been brilliant at helping her clear up. In a funny kind of way, Daisy thought, she had never enjoyed cleaning a house so much. The vacuuming and cleaning had given them something to occupy their hands, which seemed to make talking easier. They had talked as they hadn't done for many years.

'Yesterday I thought so, absolutely,' Daisy said, filling the kettle with water, 'but today, I just don't know what to think.'

'Stay for a while. I'm sure that you shouldn't be making any big life decisions in your present state of mind.'

'The tenants are moving in tomorrow . . .' Daisy said.

'Come and live in my little house . . .' offered Gemma.

'No, I do think I need some time on my own,' Daisy said, sitting down with a cup of coffee.

'What about meeting our real brother?' Gemma asked, joining her on the sofa and putting a sisterly arm around her. 'We've got to meet our brother. He's been in touch with Shirley . . .'

'You meet him,' Daisy said, holding her hand. 'I wouldn't know what to say right now . . . you know, if he asked about our mother . . .'

'We needn't tell him what we think happened,' Gemma said gently.

'But I wouldn't want to lie,' responded Daisy, 'that's where all this started.'

'Yes,' Gemma agreed, 'but we don't know for sure that we're right.'

'Don't we?' Daisy asked.

*   *   *

'Why Los Angeles?' Gemma asked later, when Daisy had quietened again. 'It's so far away and you don't know a soul there.'

'Well . . . actually . . .' Daisy began to tell her all about Cal. '. . . I'm sick of being odd,' she finished, 'I've always had an odd family and a difficult lover . . . now I want a bit of normalcy, as I believe they say in the States, and an ordinary man . . .'

That made Gemma laugh out loud. 'Daisy Rush,' she said, 'you're the only person I know who would think that flying out to stay with a major Hollywood heart-throb was ordinary!'

Daisy looked slightly annoyed then started laughing too. 'What about you, Gem?' she asked.

So Gemma told her all about Ralph. 'It was perfect,' she said, resignedly, 'but I had to let my obsession with you-know-who ruin it, and now . . .' and then she surprised herself and her sister by bursting into tears.

'Last call for BA flight . . . to Los Angeles.'

'Well, that's it, then,' Daisy hugged Gemma once more.

'Good luck,' Gemma said, trying not to cry. She wanted Daisy's last sight of her to be happy. There had been too much sadness.

'Good luck to you too,' Daisy said. 'Thanks for coming to the airport. It will be all right with your American. I just know it will . . .'

'Hurry,' Gemma told her.

Daisy turned and ran towards the sign saying Passengers Only. Then she stopped, holding her passport between her teeth, and ran back to Gemma. 'Look after this for me,' she said, handing over the plastic Waitrose bag that contained all her memories of Estella.

EPILOGUE

Gemma gazed at the bunch of deep velvety-red roses that had arrived that morning. She would have to find some more vases. Every Monday there was another delivery of flowers, more beautiful than the last. The pink and purple stocks from the week before were still fresh, their summer perfume evoking walled Elizabethan gardens in her cool, air-conditioned office.

She was trying to write a letter to Daisy, but she couldn't decide which news to tell her first:

Relations between Kathy and Roger had improved dramatically since their holiday. The last time she had seen her, Kathy was tanned and smiling. A change of air had been just what they had both needed, she told Gemma confidently, looking very much as if she did not want to be reminded about her husband's infidelity. So Gemma had changed the subject and asked about their houseguest.

'Oliver? He's moved in with his outdoor clerk, thank God,' Kathy had replied, adding in a confidential tone, 'Honestly, Gem, he seemed to be screwing anything that moved. I didn't want to tell you at the time, but he even made a pass at me. "Kathy," he says, ever so charmingly, "I cannot understand how I knew you all that time at Oxford and never realized how beautiful you were . . ." What's the matter, Gem, what have I said?'

Estella's son was called Stephen. He was a doctor. He had Estella's eyes, with very dark lashes which looked peculiar because he was almost completely bald. Gemma had arranged to meet him for tea at Browns Hotel. She recognized him as soon as she stepped through the revolving door. He was sitting stiffly in a chintz armchair, watching anxiously for her arrival. He couldn't hide his surprise when she introduced herself, and asked her several questions before remembering his manners, standing up and guiding her through to the tea room.

Their encounter was as she imagined meeting someone from a dating agency might be. She wanted so much to like him, but she found almost immediately that she did not. For the next hour or so they chatted with strained enthusiasm, both knowing somehow that whatever polite resolutions they made to keep in touch, they would not meet again.

His reasons for tracing his mother seemed to have more to do with his interest in genetically-inherited health problems than in finding his roots. When Gemma informed him that Estella had committed suicide, he asked whether it was because of grief at the loss of her husband, or whether there was a history of depression in the family. She told him she thought the former was more likely.

No, Gemma thought, all of that can wait until I have time for a long, chatty phone call.

She tore open the package she had just received from the printer, extracted one card, and scrawled a few lines at the bottom of it.

Daisy heard the bleep of the fax machine from her sun lounger by the pool. She jumped up. Gemma often sent something through at this time of day, just before she left work. A cutting from a newspaper, a cartoon from *Private Eye*, sometimes a short note, and once, just three kisses and her name, in case Daisy was missing home.

'You don't have to answer it like a phone, the fax will still be there later,' Cal murmured.

'I know, but I like to see it come through,' Daisy replied, tying a brightly coloured sarong over her breasts and sliding her feet into flipflops with plastic flowers on.

'Come here first.' He took off his sunglasses. She went over and sat beside him. 'Even though you're a lot older than me,' he said, kissing her nose, 'you behave like a child.'

'Too right,' Daisy said, and, in one swift movement, upended his lounger into the pool.

The fax read:

GEMMA AND RALPH
INVITE YOU TO CELEBRATE THEIR MARRIAGE
AT CHELSEA REGISTER OFFICE
ON AUGUST 22ND, 1995

Below that Gemma had written –

Yes, I have told him everything.
Will you be my witness?

THE END

MARSH LIGHT
by Kate Hatfield

Helena and Irene Webton could not be more different. Thirty-year-old Helena is a successful restorer of antique furniture; she is also watchful, damaged, and so private that even her lover has to be kept at a distance. Irene, her stepmother, is flamboyant, feisty, fat, and fed up with her role as the well-behaved wife of a High Court judge. Her first play is about to go into rehearsal, and she is determined to build a career in the theatre before it's too late.

They both adore Irene's son, Ivo, whose gilded good looks and cleverness ease his path through life. But not everyone shares their devotion, and there are those who believe something much more sinister lies behind his mask of charm and brilliance. When one of them tries to persuade Helena that Ivo could be involved in crime, she is faced with a horrible dilemma. Should she ignore the evidence, confront him – or involve the police and risk disaster for them all?

Marsh Light is a wholly engrossing novel about loyalty, trust and betrayal that further establishes Kate Hatfield as a remarkable storyteller and a sensitive chronicler of family relationships.

0 552 14486 X

JUST LIKE A WOMAN
by Jill Gascoine

The Francken marriage appeared – from the outside – to be a stable and happy one. Daisy had arrived in Idaho thirty years before as a G.I. bride with two-year-old Marjorie (the reason for the hasty wedding) clinging to her hand. Several years and two more children on, she had realised that she just had to make the best of it – though she hadn't reckoned on having to live with her vicious and sharp-tongued mother-in-law who made it plain Daisy was a mistake, nor on Bob's casual infidelities. She survived – by completely submerging her own desires and wishes to the rest of the family. In the Francken household, Daisy came last.

Then, at fifty-one, Daisy discovered she was pregnant again. Facing the confusion and anger of the family she decided, for the first time in her life, to do what *she wanted* – go full term if she could and keep the child. Her decision proved the catalyst that blew the family apart, disclosing one revelation after another about the lives they had led for so many years.

Help, when it came, was from a surprising and unexpected source, from a younger, caring man she had scarcely noticed before. And as her family disintegrated around her, a new phase began to open in Daisy's life.

0 552 14442 8

BLONDE WITH ATTITUDE
by Virginia Blackburn

More at home with hangovers than takeovers? With a client more concerned with bedsheets than spreadsheets? It's not too much to handle when you're a blonde with attitude.

Emily, with a stressful job in a firm of City PR consultants, was finding her life out of control. Waking up once again in a strange bed, with little recollection of the night before, arriving late at work with laddered tights and roots in need of retouching, inadequately briefed for an important meeting with a new client – who turns out to be an all-too-dreadful reminder of the night before – her chosen career looks, to say the least, precarious. Her immaculate secretary Camilla is only too anxious to expose Emily's shortcomings to her boss, while her friends are all undergoing such acute personal crises that Emily requires frequent absences from work to sort out their problems in various City wine bars. Her gorgeous ex-boyfriend Jack seems more interested in blonde bimbos. And attempting to get her life back in control by escaping to her solitary flat proves difficult when Nigel, her track-suited social worker neighbour, is determined to forge a closer and more meaningful bond.

How Emily escapes from the toils of the City and learns to become a real human being again is told in this entrancing and witty story.

0 552 14514 9

A SELECTED LIST OF FINE NOVELS AVAILABLE FROM CORGI BOOKS

☐ 13992 0	**LIGHT ME THE MOON**	*Angela Arney*	£4.99
☐ 14514 9	**BLONDE WITH ATTITUDE**	*Virginia Blackburn*	£5.99
☐ 13895 9	**THE MAN WHO MADE HUSBANDS JEALOUS**	*Jilly Cooper*	£6.99
☐ 12887 2	**SHAKE DOWN THE STARS**	*Frances Donnelly*	£5.99
☐ 13830 4	**THE MASTER STROKE**	*Elizabeth Gage*	£4.99
☐ 14442 8	**JUST LIKE A WOMAN**	*Jill Gascoine*	£5.99
☐ 14382 0	**THE TREACHERY OF TIME**	*Anna Gilbert*	£4.99
☐ 14537 8	**APPLE BLOSSOM TIME**	*Kathryn Haig*	£5.99
☐ 14407 X	**THE STEPS OF THE SUN**	*Caroline Harvey*	£5.99
☐ 14486 X	**MARSH LIGHT**	*Kate Hatfield*	£6.99
☐ 14285 9	**ANGELS ALONE**	*Kate Hatfield*	£5.99
☐ 14220 4	**CAPEL BELLS**	*Joan Hessayon*	£4.99
☐ 14207 7	**DADDY'S GIRL**	*Janet Inglis*	£5.99
☐ 14390 1	**THE SPLENDOUR FALLS**	*Susanna Kearsley*	£4.99
☐ 14397 9	**THE BLACK BOOK**	*Sara Keays*	£5.99
☐ 14045 7	**THE SUGAR PAVILION**	*Rosalind Laker*	£5.99
☐ 14331 6	**THE SECRET YEARS**	*Judith Lennox*	£4.99
☐ 14332 4	**THE WINTER HOUSE**	*Judith Lennox*	£5.99
☐ 14002 3	**FOOL'S CURTAIN**	*Claire Lorrimer*	£4.99
☐ 13737 5	**EMERALD**	*Elisabeth Luard*	£5.99
☐ 13910 6	**BLUEBIRDS**	*Margaret Mayhew*	£5.99
☐ 10375 6	**CSARDAS**	*Diane Pearson*	£5.99
☐ 14123 2	**THE LONDONERS**	*Margaret Pemberton*	£4.99
☐ 14298 0	**THE LADY OF KYNACHAN**	*James Irvine Robertson*	£5.99
☐ 14466 5	**TOUCHED BY ANGELS**	*Susan Sallis*	£5.99
☐ 14296 4	**THE LAND OF NIGHTINGALES**	*Sally Stewart*	£4.99